*The Carlton Brothers – three gorgeous men,
each about to discover the riches that
money cannot buy…*

Millionaires'
Destinies

Three super stories from one of
our favourite authors!

G000320408

Millionaires' Destinies

SHERRYL WOODS

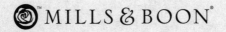

All the characters in this book have no existence outside the imagination of
the author, and have no relation whatsoever to anyone bearing the same name
or names. They are not even distantly inspired by any individual known or
unknown to the author, and all the incidents are pure invention.

First published in Great Britain 2010
Harlequin Mills & Boon Limited,
Eton House, 18-24 Paradise Road, Richmond, Surrey TW9 1SR

MILLIONAIRES' DESTINIES
© by Harlequin Enterprises II B.V./S.à.r.l 2010

Isn't It Rich?, *Priceless* and *Treasured* were first published in Great Britain by
Harlequin Mills & Boon Limited in separate, single volumes.

Isn't It Rich? © Sherryl Woods 2004
Priceless © Sherryl Woods 2005
Treasured © Sherryl Woods 2004

ISBN: 978 0 263 88045 8

05-0910

Printed and bound in Spain
by Litografia Rosés S.A., Barcelona

ISN'T IT RICH?

BY
SHERRYL WOODS

Sherryl Woods has written more than seventy-five novels. She also operates her own bookstore, Potomac Sunrise, in Colonial Beach, Virginia. If you can't visit Sherryl at her store, then be sure to drop her a note at PO Box 490326, Key Biscayne, FL 33149, USA or check out her website at www.sherrylwoods.com.

Chapter One

Richard Carlton made three business calls on his cell phone, scowled impatiently at the antique clock on the wall of his favorite Old Town Alexandria seafood restaurant, made two more calls, then frowned at the Rolex watch on his wrist.

Five more minutes and he was history. He was only here as a favor to his Aunt Destiny. He'd promised to give some supposedly brilliant marketing whiz kid a chance at the consultant's contract for the family corporation's public relations campaign despite her lack of experience working with a major worldwide conglomerate.

He was also looking for a consultant who could help him launch his first political campaign. His intention had been to hire someone more seasoned than this woman Destiny was recommending, but his aunt was very persuasive when she put her mind to something.

"Just meet with her. Have a nice lunch. Give her a chance to sell *you* on her talent. After all," Aunt Destiny had said with a suspicious gleam in her eye, "nobody on earth is a tougher sell than you, right?"

Richard had given his aunt a wry look. "You flatter me."

She'd patted his cheek as if he were twelve again and she was trying to call attention gently to one of his flaws. "Not really, darling."

Destiny Carlton was the bane of his existence. He doubted if there was another aunt like her in the universe. When he was barely twelve, she'd breezed into his life twenty-four hours after his parents' small plane had crashed in the fog-shrouded Blue Ridge Mountains.

His father's older sister, Destiny had lived a nomad's life, cavorting with princes in European capitals, gambling in Monaco, skiing in Swiss Alpine resorts, then settling into a farmhouse in Provence where she'd begun painting more seriously, eventually selling her works in a small gallery on Paris's Left Bank. She was exotic and eccentric and more fun than anyone Richard or his younger brothers had ever met. She'd been just what three terrified little boys had needed.

A selfish woman would have scooped them up and taken them back to France, then resumed her own life, but not Destiny. She had plunged into unexpected motherhood with the same passionate enthusiasm and style with which she embraced life. She'd turned their previously well-ordered lives into a chaos of adventures in the process, but there had never been a doubt in their minds that she loved them. They, in turn, adored her, even when she was at her most maddening, as she had been lately, ever since she'd gotten some bee in her bonnet about the three of them needing to settle down. To her despair, he, Mack and Ben had been incredibly resistant to her urgings.

Over the years, despite Destiny's strong influence, Richard had clung tenaciously to the more somber lessons of his father. Work hard and succeed. Give back to the community. Be somebody. The adages had been drilled into him practically from infancy. Even at twelve, he'd felt the weight of responsibility for the generations-old Carlton Industries sitting squarely on his thin shoulders. Though an outsider had held the temporary reins upon his father's death, there was no question that the company would eventually be Richard's to run. A place would have been found for his brothers as well, if either of them had wanted it. But neither had shown the slightest interest, not back then and not now.

Back then, while his brothers had gone home after school to play their games, Richard had taken the family obligation to heart. Every weekday he'd gone to the historic old brick building that housed the corporate offices.

Destiny had tried her best to interest him in reading novels of all kinds, from the classics to science fiction and fantasy, but he'd preferred to scour the company books, studying the neatly aligned columns of figures that told the story of decades of profit and loss. The order and logic of it soothed him in a way he had been helpless to explain to her or to anyone. Even now, he had a better understanding of business than he did of people.

When he was twenty-three and had his M.B.A. from the prestigious Wharton School of Business, Richard slipped into the company presidency without raising so much as an eyebrow among the employees or among the worldwide CEOs with whom Carlton Industries did business. Most assumed he'd been all but running it behind the scenes since his father's death, anyway. Even as a kid, he'd displayed amazing confidence in his own decision-making.

Now, at thirty-two, he had the company on the track his father would have expected, expanding bit by bit with a strategic merger here, a hostile acquisition there. He was still young, successful and one of the city's most eligible bachelors. Unfortunately, his relationships tended to be brief once the women in his life realized they were always likely to take a back seat to the pressing—and often far more interesting—needs of the family company. The last woman he'd dated had told him he was a cold, dispassionate son of a bitch. He hadn't argued. In fact, he was pretty sure she had it just about right. Business never let him down. People did. He stuck to what he could trust.

Since he'd been so unsuccessful at romance, he'd turned his attention elsewhere in recent months. He'd been considering a run for office, perhaps the Alexandria City Council for starters. His father had expected all of his sons to climb to positions of power, not just in the corporate world, but in their community and the nation. Helping to shape Richard's image and get his name into print as a precursor to this was just part of what his new marketing consultant would be handling.

His timetable—okay, his father's oft-expressed timetable—for this was right on track, too. His father had espoused the need for short-term and long-term strategic planning. Richard had doubled the number of years his father had planned ahead for. He liked knowing where he should be—where he *would* be— ten, twenty, even thirty years down the road.

For someone whose precise schedule was so detailed, wasting precious minutes out of his jam-packed day waiting for a woman who was now twenty minutes late pretty much drove him crazy. Out of time and out of patience, Richard snapped his fingers. The maître d' appeared instantly.

"Yes, Mr. Carlton?"

"Could you put my coffee on my account, please, Donald? My guest hasn't arrived, and I have another appointment to get to back at my office."

"No charge for the coffee, sir. Would you like the chef to box up a salad?"

"No, thanks."

"Shall I get your coat, then?"

"Didn't wear one."

"Then at least let me call a taxi for you. It's started to snow quite heavily. The sidewalks and streets are treacherous. Perhaps that's why your guest is late."

Richard wasn't interested in finding excuses for the no-show, just in getting back to work. "If the weather's that bad, I can walk back sooner than you can get a taxi here. Thanks, anyway, Donald. And if Ms. Hart ever shows up, please tell her…" His voice trailed off. He decided the message he'd like to have relayed was better left unsaid. It was bound to come back to haunt him with his aunt, who was one of Donald's favorite customers. Though he considered his duty to Destiny's young friend done, his aunt might not see it the same way. "Just tell her I had to go."

"Yes, sir."

He opened the front door of the restaurant, stepped outside onto the slick sidewalk and ran straight into a battering ram. If he hadn't had a firm grip on the door, he'd have been on the ground. Instead, the woman who'd hit him headfirst in the midsection, stared up at him with huge, panicked brown eyes fringed with long, dark lashes just as her feet skidded out from under her.

Richard caught her inches from the icy ground and steadied her. Even though she was bundled up for the weather, she felt delicate. A faint frisson of something that felt like protectiveness hit him. It was something he'd previously experienced only with his younger brothers and his aunt. Most of the women in his life were so strong and capable, he'd never felt the least bit inclined to protect them from anything.

The woman closed her eyes, then opened them again and winced as she surveyed his face. "Please don't tell me you're Richard Carlton," she said, then sighed before he could respond. "But of course you are. You look exactly like the picture your aunt showed me.

"That's the way my day has gone," she rattled on. "First I get a cab driver who couldn't find his way to the corner without a map, then we get stuck behind a trash truck and then the snow starts coming down worse than a blizzard in the Rockies." She gazed at him hopefully, brushing at a stray strand of hair that was teasing at her still pink cheek. "I don't suppose you'd like to go back in, sit down and let me make a more dignified entrance?"

Richard bit back a sigh of his own. "Melanie Hart, I presume."

She gazed at him, her expression thoughtful. "I could pretend to be somebody else, and we could forget all about this unfortunate incident. I could call your office later, apologize profusely for missing you, make another appointment and start over in a very businesslike way."

"You're actually considering lying to me?"

"It would be a waste of time, wouldn't it?" she said with apparent regret. "I've already given myself away. I knew this whole lunch thing was a mistake. I make a much better impression in a conference room. I think it's the setting. People tend to take you more seriously if you can use an overhead projector and all sorts of charts and graphs. Anyway, I told Destiny that, but she insisted lunch would be better. She says you're less cranky on a full stomach."

"How lovely of her to share that," Richard said, vowing to have yet another wasted talk with his aunt about discussing him with anyone and everyone. If he did decide to run for office, her loose tongue would doom his chances before he got started.

"I don't suppose your stomach's full now?" Melanie Hart asked hopefully.

"No."

"Then you're bound to be cranky, so I'll just slip on inside and try to figure out how I managed to mess up the most important job interview of my entire life."

"If you decide you want an outside opinion, give me a call," Richard said.

He considered brushing right on past this walking disaster, but she looked so genuinely forlorn he couldn't seem to bring himself to do it. Besides, Destiny had said she was very good at what she did, and Destiny was seldom wrong about personnel matters. She was a good judge of people, at least when she didn't let emotion cloud her judgment. Richard very much feared this was one of those instances when her heart might have overruled her head. Still...

He tucked a hand under Melanie Hart's elbow and steered her inside. "Thirty minutes," he said tersely as Donald beamed at them and led them back to the table Richard had vacated just moments earlier. It had a fresh tablecloth, fresh place settings and a lit candle. He was almost certain that candle hadn't been there before. He had a suspicious feeling Donald had been expecting him back all along and had hoped a little atmosphere would improve his sour mood. No doubt the maître d' and his aunt were in cahoots. He'd probably called Destiny with a report five seconds after Richard had walked out.

When Donald had brought a fresh pot of coffee, Richard glanced at his watch. "Twenty-four minutes, Ms. Hart. Make 'em count."

Melanie reached for her attaché case and promptly knocked over her water glass...straight into his lap.

Richard leaped up as the icy water soaked through his pants. The day was just getting better and better.

"Oh, my God, I am so sorry," Melanie said, on her feet, napkin in hand, poised to sop up the water.

Richard considered letting her do it, just to see how she reacted once she realized exactly where she was touching him, but apparently she caught on to the problem. She handed the napkin to him.

"Sorry," she said again while he spent several minutes trying to dry himself off. "I swear to you

that I am not normally such a klutz.'' At his doubtful
look, she added, ''Really, I'm not.''

''If you say so.''

''If you want to leave, I will totally understand. If
you tell me never to darken your door, I'll understand
that, too.'' Her chin came up and she looked straight
into his eyes. ''But you'll be making a terrible mistake.''

She was a bold one, no question about that. Richard
paused in his futile attempt to dry his trousers. ''How
so?''

''I'm exactly what you need, Mr. Carlton. I know
how to get attention.''

''Yes, I can see that,'' he said wryly. ''There's un-
forgettable and then there's disastrous. I'm hoping for
something a little more positive.''

''I can do that,'' she insisted. ''I have the contacts.
I'm clever and innovative. I know exactly how to sell
my clients to the media. In fact, I have a preliminary
plan right here for your campaign and for Carlton
Industries.''

When she started to reach for her attaché case
again, Richard grabbed the remaining water glass on
the table and moved it a safe distance away, then sat
back down while she scattered a flurry of papers in
every direction. When she was finally done, he said,
''I appreciate your enthusiasm, Ms. Hart, I really do,
but this isn't going to work.'' To avoid hurting her
feelings, he tried to temper his dismissal. ''I need
someone a little more seasoned.''

He refrained from adding that he wanted someone
less ditzy, someone a little less inclined to remind him
with every breath that she was a female and that he
was a male who hadn't had sex for several months

now. He did not need an employee who stirred up all these contradictory reactions in him. In this day and age that was a lawsuit waiting to happen.

His response to Melanie Hart bemused him. He'd gone from annoyance to anger to attraction in the space of—he glanced at his watch—less than twenty-five minutes. Relieved that her allotted time was nearly over, he tapped his Rolex. "Time's about up, Ms. Hart. Nice to meet you. I wish you luck and best success."

She gave him that forlorn, doe-eyed look that made his stomach clench and his pulse gallop erratically.

"You're kissing me off, aren't you?" she said.

It was an unfortunate turn of phrase. Richard suddenly couldn't stop looking at her mouth, which was soft and full and very, very kissable. He obviously needed to find the time to start dating again, if he was going to react this way to a woman as wildly inappropriate as Melanie Hart.

"I wouldn't put it that way," he said finally. "I'm just saying it's a bad match. If you're as talented as my aunt says, you'll be snapped up by another company in no time at all."

"I already have other clients, Mr. Carlton. In fact, my business is thriving," she said stiffly. "I wanted to work for you and for Carlton Industries because I think I have something to offer you that your in-house staff cannot."

"Which is?"

"A fresh perspective that would drag your corporate and personal image out of the Dark Ages." She stood up. "Perhaps I was wrong. Perhaps your current stuffy image has it exactly right."

As Richard stared, she whirled around and marched

out of the restaurant with her head held high, her back straight and the tiniest, most provocative sway of her narrow hips he'd seen in a long time.

Damn, what was happening to him? The infernal woman had just mowed him down, soaked him with water and told him off, and he still couldn't take his eyes off of her. Of course, the real problem was that she wanted to work for him…and for some totally insane and inexplicable reason, he wanted her in his bed.

"And then I soaked him with water," Melanie related to Destiny Carlton a few hours later over drinks at what had once been the Carlton family home. Now Destiny apparently lived there alone. "I'll be lucky if he doesn't catch pneumonia and sue me. I think I can pretty much count on getting a polite rejection letter in tomorrow's mail just to take away any lingering doubts I might have that he absolutely, positively hated me. Heck, he'll probably send it over by courier tonight to make sure I don't come waltzing into his office tomorrow and burn the building down."

Destiny laughed, oddly delighted by this report. "Oh, darling, it couldn't have gone better. Richard is much too pompous. He takes himself too seriously. You're just the breath of fresh air he needs."

"I really don't think he saw the humor in the situation," Melanie said with genuine regret.

She'd liked Richard. Okay, he was a little bit rigid and standoffish, but she could improve on that. She could coach him on smiling more frequently. She'd had one glimpse of his killer smile and it had made her knees weak. If he smiled more and frowned less, he could win over every female voter in Alexandria, no matter where he stood on the issues. She really thought she could do great things for Carlton Industries and for its CEO. It was a challenge she'd been looking forward to. Now she'd never have the chance. And while her company wasn't exactly thriving, the way she'd told him it was, a coup like this would have assured its future.

"I'll talk to him. I'm sure I can smooth things over," Destiny said.

"Please, no," Melanie insisted. "You've done enough. You got me the interview in the first place. I'm the one who blew it. Maybe I can think of some way to salvage things."

"I'm sure you can," Destiny said with an encouraging smile. "You're very clever at such things. I knew that the moment we met."

"We met when I dented your rear fender," Melanie reminded her.

"But it only took a few minutes for you to convince me it was time for a new car, anyway. You had me on the dealer's lot and behind the wheel of my snappy little red convertible within the hour, and I'm no pushover," Destiny asserted.

Melanie laughed. "Who are you kidding? You were dying to buy a new car. I just gave you a reason and steered you to a client I knew would give you a great deal."

"But don't you see? That's exactly what marketing is all about—convincing people to go ahead and get something they've wanted but haven't thought they needed. Now you merely have to convince my nephew that he—or, rather, Carlton Industries—can't live without you."

An alarm suddenly went off in Melanie's head at

Destiny's slip of the tongue. She studied the older woman warily, but there was nothing in her friend's eyes to suggest duplicity. Still, she had to ask. "Destiny, you're not matchmaking, are you?"

"Me? Matchmaking for Richard? Heavens no. I wouldn't waste the energy. He would never take my advice when it comes to matters of the heart."

She made the protest sound very convincing, but Melanie didn't quite buy it. Destiny Carlton was a kind, smart, fascinating woman, but she clearly had a sneaky streak. She also adored her nephews. Melanie had picked up on that the first time they'd met. Destiny had gone on and on about their attributes and how she despaired of ever seeing them settle down. Who knew what she might do to get them married off?

"I'm not in the market for a husband," Melanie told her firmly. "You know that, don't you?"

"But you are in the market for a challenging job, right? That hasn't changed?"

"No, that hasn't changed."

"Well, then," Destiny said cheerily. "Let's put our heads together and come up with a plan. Nobody knows Richard's weak spots better than I do."

"He has weaknesses?" Melanie asked skeptically. He'd struck her as tough, competent and more than a little arrogant. If there was a chink in his armor, she hadn't spotted it, and she was well trained to spot flaws that the media might exploit and see that they were corrected or hidden from view.

Destiny beamed at her. "He's a man, isn't he? All men can be won over if the tactics are right. Have I told you about the duke?"

"The one who chased you all over Europe?"

"No, dear, that was a prince. This man—the duke—was the love of my life," she confided, her expression nostalgic. Then she shook her head. "Well, that's in the past. Best not to go there. Let's concentrate on Richard. There's a little cottage on the river about eighty miles from here. It's very peaceful. I think I can get him down there this weekend."

Melanie eyed her friend warily. She wasn't sure she liked the sound of this. The last time she'd trusted Destiny's instincts over her own, look what had happened.

"And?" she asked cautiously.

"Then you show up with some of his favorite gourmet food—I'll help you plan the menu—and your marketing plan. He won't be able to resist."

There were so many things wrong with that scheme, Melanie didn't know where to begin. If doing a presentation in a restaurant was awkward and unprofessional, then chasing the man to some out-of-the-way cottage was downright ludicrous and rife with the potential for disaster.

"If he goes there to relax, won't he be furious if I intrude?" she asked, trying to curb Destiny's enthusiasm for the idea.

Destiny waved off her concern. "He doesn't go there to relax. He goes there to get more work done. He says it's less noisy than his place here."

"Then I'll still be an unwelcome interruption," Melanie protested.

"Not if we get the menu exactly right," Destiny said. "The way to a man's heart, et cetera. I have a few bottles of his favorite wine right here. You can take those along, too."

Melanie wasn't convinced. "It seems a little risky.

No, it seems a *lot* risky. I am not one of his favorite people right now.''

Her comment fell on deaf ears. ''Anything worth having is worth a little risk,'' Destiny said blithely. ''What can he do? Slam the door in your face? I've raised him better than that.''

That didn't sound so awful. Melanie weighed the prospect of facing Richard's annoyance once again against the possibility of getting a dream contract for her new company. Landing Carlton Industries would be a coup. Helping to shape Richard Carlton's first run for political office would be an even bigger one, especially if he won. In this politics-happy region where candidates from every state in the country abounded, she'd soon be able to name her own price.

Making her decision, she gave Destiny a weak smile. ''Okay, then. What am I serving?''

Chapter Two

Three large hampers of food arrived at Melanie's small home in Alexandria's Delray neighborhood not far from historic Old Town at two o'clock on Friday, along with a heavy vellum envelope addressed in Destiny's elaborate script. Melanie regarded it all with grim resignation. This was really going to happen. She was really going to invade Richard Carlton's privacy and try to convince him that he needed her—professionally, at any rate.

As soon as the uniformed chauffeur bowed and left, Melanie's assistant and best friend slipped out of the office that had been created from what was meant to be the master bedroom in the 1940s-era house, peeked into the wicker baskets crowding the foyer, then turned to her.

"Wow, Mel, is someone trying to seduce you?" Becky asked, clearly intrigued by the excess.

"Hardly," Melanie said. "In fact, I'm pretty sure the hope is that I'll seduce Richard Carlton."

Becky gave her a hard, disbelieving look. "I thought that meeting went really, really badly."

"It did. But his aunt seems to think I can salvage it, if I just ply him with food and alcohol in a secluded little cottage by the sea."

Becky, who had solid business instincts under her romantic facade, didn't seem impressed by the theory. "And how exactly are you supposed to coax him into going there with you?"

"Destiny is taking care of that." Melanie slit open the envelope, read the message, glanced at the two sheets of typed instructions included, then sighed.

"What's that?" Becky asked, eyeing the papers with suspicion.

"My marching orders," Melanie said wryly. "She even thought to include cooking instructions. She must know about my tendency to burn water."

Becky chuckled, caught Melanie's sour look and immediately sobered. "Since you've apparently bought into this idiotic scheme, then I think it was very thoughtful of her."

"I'm sure she was just thinking of her nephew's health."

"Tell me again why she's so determined to help you land this contract," Becky prompted.

"I wish I could say that I'd impressed the hell out of her with my professional credentials, but that's not it. She thinks Richard is stuffy and I'm a breath of fresh air," Melanie explained. At least that had been the reason Destiny had expressed for going to all this trouble.

"In other words, she has an ulterior motive,"

Becky concluded, leaping to her own conclusion. "The whole seduction thing."

"Don't say that," Melanie pleaded, not liking that Becky had almost instantly confirmed her own suspicions. "Don't even think it. This is business, not personal."

"Yeah, right."

"It is, at least for me. If I get this contract, I will no longer have to lie awake nights worrying about whether I can pay your salary."

"Then by all means, get down to this cottage and start cooking," Becky said, snapping the lids on the hampers closed. "By the way, if that pie doesn't win him over, then the man's not human. It smells heavenly. I had a candle once that smelled exactly like that, like warm cherry pie just out of the oven. Every time I lit it, I ate. I gained ten pounds before the darn thing finally burned out."

Melanie chuckled. From the day they'd met in college, Becky had claimed that everything up to and including high humidity caused her to gain weight. She was constantly bemoaning the ten pounds she supposedly needed to lose. The extra weight hadn't hurt her social life. She had the kind of lush curves that caused men to fall all over themselves whenever she walked into a room.

"Come on, Mel, have a heart and get this stuff out of here," she begged now. "I'll hold down the fort for the rest of the day."

Melanie knew she couldn't very well back out now. She'd agreed to this crazy scheme. She had to follow through with it, and she might as well get on the road and get it over with. Reluctantly she gathered up her coat, her purse and her business plan for Carlton Industries.

"You're going to have to help me haul this food out to the car," she said. "I think Destiny went a little overboard and packed enough for the weekend, not just dinner."

"Maybe she has high hopes for just how well dinner is going to go," Becky suggested, struggling to balance two heavy wicker baskets as she followed Melanie to her car.

"Or maybe she's counting on a blizzard," Melanie replied grimly. It would be just her luck to get herself snowed in with a man who'd all but said he never wanted to lay eyes on her again. "Have you seen a weather report?"

"Haven't needed to," Becky said, gesturing toward the western sky, which was a dull gray, the usual precursor to snow.

Melanie groaned. "Okay, then, if it does snow and I'm not back on Monday, promise me you'll come and dig me out. Buy a damn snowplow if you have to."

"Maybe I'll just wait to hear you confirm that on Monday," Becky said with a sly grin. "Could be you won't want to be rescued."

"Promise me," Melanie said, gritting her teeth. "Or I swear I will fire you, even if I get this contract and we're rolling in money."

"Fine. Fine," Becky soothed, still fighting a grin. "I'll come rescue you if you're not back by Monday." The smile broke free. "Or at least I'll tell the cops where to start looking for the body."

Melanie winced. "Don't joke about that. It could go that badly."

Becky's expression sobered at once. "Mel, you're really worried about this, are you?"

"Not that he'll kill me, no," Melanie said honestly. "But it's entirely likely that he'll toss me right back out into the snow and I'll die of humiliation."

"Nobody dies of humiliation, at least not in the public relations business. We're the masters of spin. Remember that. It's what we do best."

"I'm sure knowing that will warm me right up when I'm sitting in a snowbank freezing my butt off," Melanie said.

Becky laughed. "Just keep your cell phone handy so you can call nine-one-one. I hear the paramedics really get off on trying to save people from frostbite in that particular region."

So much for sympathy and support from the woman who was not only her assistant but her closest friend. Melanie started her car and skidded down her icy driveway till she hit the cleared pavement of the road. She did not look back, because she was pretty certain that traitorous Becky was probably laughing her head off.

Richard wasn't at all sure how he'd let his aunt convince him to spend the weekend at the cottage, especially since he'd been down here for a couple of hours and there was still no sign of Destiny. Nor had she phoned. He was beginning to worry. Not that a woman who'd traipsed all over the globe on her own couldn't handle anything that came up, but she was his aunt. Ever since his parents had died, he'd worried obsessively about everyone who was left in his life. He'd barely been able to watch Mack play professional football because a part of him had been terrified that his younger brother would have his neck snapped by some overly aggressive defensive player. As it turned out, it had been a far less deadly knee injury that had ended Mack's career on the field. Richard had been the only one in the family relieved to have Mack safely ensconced in the team's administrative office as a part owner these days.

When Richard finally heard footsteps on the front porch, he threw open the door. "It's about time," he groused to cover his irrational concern. Then he got a good look at the bundled-up woman outside. "You!"

"Hello again," Melanie said cheerfully. "Surprise!"

Richard felt his stomach ricochet wildly, and not in a good way. "What was Destiny thinking?" he murmured, half to himself. She was behind this. She had to be.

As for Melanie, she was obviously a lot tougher than he'd realized. The blasted woman didn't seem to be the least bit put off by his lack of welcome. She beamed and brushed right past him into the small foyer, peering around at the living room with undisguised curiosity.

"I'm fairly sure Destiny's only thought was that you'd probably be starving by now," she said, giving a totally unnecessary reply to his rhetorical question. "She asked me to tell you she was sorry about the change in plans. Something came up."

"Yeah, I'll bet," he muttered. Then the scent of warm cherry pie wafted toward him. "What's in the basket?"

"Give me a few minutes to unpack it all and I'll

show you. By the way, there are two more baskets in the car. If you'll get those, I'll deal with this one.''

"You could just make your delivery and head back to Alexandria," Richard said, still holding out hope that he could cut this encounter short.

"On an empty stomach? I don't think so. I've spent the last two hours smelling this cherry pie—I'm not leaving till I've had some. There are a couple of steaks in one of the baskets and potatoes for baking, butter *and* sour cream—which is a little excessive, if you ask me—plus a huge Caesar salad. There are also a couple of excellent bottles of French wine. I'm told it's your favorite, though personally I think the California cabernets are just as good and far less expensive.''

Destiny at her sneakiest, Richard concluded with a sigh. She'd sent all of his favorite foods, despite her alleged concern about his cholesterol. He picked up the basket and closed the door, then stepped aside to permit Melanie to come all the way into the cottage. "Come on in."

"Said the spider to the fly," Melanie said, injecting an ominous note into her voice as she brushed right past him and headed with unerring accuracy right toward the kitchen. Destiny had probably given her a complete floor plan. He couldn't help wondering if his aunt had also provided a key, in case he tried to lock her protégé out.

He gave Melanie a wry look. "Where we're concerned, I think you've got that backward. I'm the intended victim here."

"Whatever," she said, clearly unconcerned. She met his gaze, her eyes a dark, liquid brown. "Those other baskets," she prodded.

"What?" Richard blinked, then grasped her meaning. "Oh, sure. I'll get 'em now." He fled the kitchen and the disconcerting woman who seemed to be taking it over. Maybe a blast of frigid air would clear his head and help him to come up with some way to get her out of there.

Unfortunately, by the time he started back inside, nothing short of hauling Melanie bodily back to her car and turning on the engine had come to him. Since that was pretty much out of the question, he was doomed. A big fat snowflake splatted on his forehead as if to confirm his decision. He looked up, and several more snowflakes hit him in the face.

"Great, just great," he muttered. The minute—no, the second—he spotted Destiny again, he was going to wring her neck.

Inside he plunked the baskets down on the round oak table where he, Destiny and his brothers had shared many a meal and played many a game of Monopoly or gin rummy. He grabbed the slim local phone book from the counter and began almost desperately leafing through the pages. There was an inn nearby. If Melanie left now, right this instant, she could be snuggled up in front of *its* fire in minutes.

"Who are you calling?" she asked as she unpacked the food.

"The inn."

"Why?"

"It's snowing. You're going to need a place to stay."

Her determinedly cheerful expression finally faded. "It's snowing," she echoed.

"Hard," he added grimly.

She sighed and sank down at the table. "Do you

think it's possible that your aunt controls the weather, too?"

She asked it so plaintively that Richard couldn't help the chuckle that sneaked up the back of his throat. "I've wondered that myself at times," he admitted. "She has a lot of powers, but I'm fairly certain that's not one of them."

He gave his guest an encouraging look. "It'll be okay. The inn is lovely. It's not a bad place to be stranded."

As he spoke, he dialed the number. It rang and rang, before an answering machine finally came on and announced that the inn was closed until after the first of the year. He heard the message with a sinking heart. There was a small motel nearby, but it was no place he'd send his worst enemy, much less Melanie Hart, not if he ever expected to look his aunt in the face again. Of course, he planned to strangle her, so her opinion was likely to be short-lived.

"What?" Melanie asked as he slowly hung up.

"The inn's closed till after January first."

She stood up at once and reached for her coat. "Then I'll leave now. I'm sure I can get back up to town before the roads get too bad."

"And have me worrying for hours about whether you've skidded into a ditch? I don't think so," he said, reaching the only decision he could live with. "You'll stay here. There are lots of rooms."

"I don't want to be an inconvenience," she told him. "There are bound to be some other places I can get a room, if the roads get too bad once I start back."

"No," he said flatly, carefully avoiding her gaze so she wouldn't see just how disturbed he was by the prospect of being stranded here with her for an hour, much less a day or two.

"I feel awful about this," she said with what sounded like genuine regret. "I knew it was a bad idea, but you know how your aunt is. She gets something into her head, and everyone else just gets swept along."

"Tell me about it."

"As soon as we eat, I'll go to my room and you won't have to spend another second worrying about me," she assured him. "I'll be quiet as a mouse. You won't even know I'm here."

"Wouldn't that pretty much defeat the purpose of this visit?" he asked.

"Purpose?"

"To talk me into reconsidering hiring you," he said. "We both know Destiny didn't send you down here just to deliver dinner. Her driver could have done that."

"Caught," Melanie conceded, looking only marginally chagrined.

"Well, then, now's your chance. Start talking," he told her as he opened a bottle of wine to let it breathe.

"Not till we've eaten," she insisted. "I want every advantage I can get." She looked over the ingredients for their dinner, now spread out on the table. "Of course, if you want dinner to be edible, you might want to pitch in."

"You can't cook?"

"Let's just say that a peanut butter and jelly sandwich and microwaved oatmeal are my specialties."

Richard shook his head. "Move over," he said, nudging her aside with his hip, then almost immediately regretting the slight contact with her soft curves.

"And stay out of my way," he added for good measure.

She didn't seem to take offense. In fact, she looked downright relieved. "Can I set the table? Pour the wine?"

"Sure," he agreed. "The dishes and wineglasses are in the cabinet right up there."

He glanced over as she reached for them and found himself staring at an inch of pale skin as her sweater rode up from the waistband of her slacks. She had a very trim waist. He wanted very badly to skim a finger across that tiny bit of exposed flesh to see if it was as soft and satiny as it looked. He wasn't used to being turned on by so little. She had to be some kind of wizard to make him want her without half-trying. Only because he didn't want to let on how hot and bothered he was did he resist the desire to snag the bottom of her sweater and tug it securely back into place. He could just imagine her reaction to that. She'd know right then and there that she had the upper hand. Who knew how she'd use that little piece of information.

"Have you had this place a long time?" she asked when she finally had all the dishes in her arms. As she turned and set the precariously balanced load on the table, her sweater slid back into place, thank God.

"Since we were kids," he told her as he scrubbed the potatoes. "Destiny missed the water and the country when she came back from living in France, so we piled into the car one weekend and went exploring. She spotted this house and fell in love with it."

"I can understand why. The view of the Potomac is incredible. It must be wonderful to sit on the front porch in the summer and watch the boats on the water and listen to the waves.''

''I suppose it is,'' he said, distracted by the dreamy note in her voice.

Melanie gave him a knowing look. ''How long has it been since you've done that?''

''Years,'' he admitted. ''Usually when I come down here, I bring a pile of paperwork and never set foot outside. I come because it's peaceful and quiet and I know no one will interrupt me.'' He regarded her with a wry expression. ''Not usually, anyway.''

Melanie nodded as if she'd expected the response. ''I'd read that you were a workaholic.''

''Just proves the media gets it right once in a while.''

''Haven't you ever heard that all work and no play makes one dull?''

He shrugged. ''I never really cared.''

She studied him curiously. ''What kind of image do you see yourself projecting as a candidate?''

Richard paused as he was about to put the potatoes into the oven. He hadn't yet given the matter much thought. He should have. Instead, he'd based his decision to run for office on the expected progression of his life carefully planned out by his father, probably while Richard was still in diapers.

''I want people to know I'm honest,'' he began, considering his reply thoughtfully. ''I want them to believe that I'll work hard and that I'll care about their problems, about the issues that matter to them.''

''That's good,'' she said. ''But did you go to public school?''

''No.''

"Have you ever had to struggle for money, been out of work?"

"No."

"Ever been denied a place to live because of the color of your skin?"

He flushed slightly. "No."

"Do you have good medical insurance?"

"Of course. So do my employees."

"Ever had to go without a prescription because you couldn't afford it?"

"No." He saw where she was going, and it grated on his nerves.

"Then what makes you think they'll believe you can relate to their problems?" she asked.

"Look, I can't help that I've led a life of privilege, but I can care about people who haven't. I can be innovative about ways to solve their problems. I know a lot about business. Some of those principles can be applied to government as well," he said, barely able to disguise his irritation. "Look, I don't get this. If you think I'm such a lousy candidate, why do you want to work for me?"

She grinned. "So I can show you how to be a *good* candidate, maybe even a great one."

He shook his head at her audacity. "Confident, aren't you?"

"No more so than you are. You believe in *your*self. I believe in *my*self. That could be the beginning of a great team."

"Or a disaster waiting to happen," he said, not convinced. "Two egos butting heads at every turn."

"Maybe, but if we remember that we both have the same goal, I'm pretty sure that will get us through any rough patches."

Richard considered her theory as he heated the fancy grill that was part of the restaurant-caliber stove he'd had installed once he'd taken up gourmet cooking to relax. He tossed on the steaks. "How do you want it?" he asked.

Melanie stared at him, looking puzzled. "Want what?"

He grinned. "Your steak."

"Well-done," she said at once.

"I should have guessed."

"I suppose you eat yours raw," she muttered.

"Rare," he corrected.

"Same thing. It's all very macho."

"I suppose you think I should give up beef or something to appease the vegetarian voters."

"Don't be ridiculous. There must be a zillion very popular steak houses in the Washington area. There's your constituency."

"I like to think I can relate to people who prefer lobster, too."

She laughed and shook her head. "My work is so cut out for me."

"You don't have the job," he reminded her.

She stepped up beside him and snagged a slice of red pepper from the pan of vegetables he was sautéing. Then she grinned. "I will," she said with total confidence.

Richard got that same odd sensation in the pit of his stomach, the one he used to get right before a roller coaster crested the top of the tracks and pitched down in a mad burst of speed. He looked at Melanie as she licked a trace of olive oil from the tip of her finger and felt that same mix of excitement and fear.

He hadn't been in waters this deep and dangerous in years. Maybe never.

Damn Destiny. She'd known exactly what she was doing by pushing this woman into his life, and it didn't have a bloody thing to do with getting him elected to office or polishing the image of Carlton Industries around the globe. Melanie was to be the key player in Destiny's latest skirmish to marry him off.

Well, he didn't have to take the bait. He could keep his hormones under control and his hands to himself. No problem. At least, as long as Melanie stopped looking at him with those big, vulnerable brown eyes. Those eyes made him want to give her whatever she wanted, made him want to take whatever he wanted.

Yep, those eyes were trouble. Too bad she wasn't one of those sophisticated women who wore sunglasses night and day as part of their fashion statement. Then he might have a shot at sticking to his resolve.

As it was, he was probably doomed.

Chapter Three

Though he'd stopped scowling after his second glass of wine, Richard didn't seem as if he was being won over, Melanie concluded reluctantly. He was being civil, not friendly. And he definitely wasn't leaving her much of an opening to start pitching her PR plan. Drastic measures were called for. Destiny had seemed certain that food was the answer, so Melanie had added a touch of her own to the meal.

"I stopped and picked up ice cream for the pie," she told him, hoping she'd guessed right that a man who loved cherry pie would prefer it à la mode.

He actually smiled for the first time—a totally unguarded reaction, for once. Just as Melanie had remembered, the effect was devastating. The smile made his blue eyes sparkle and emphasized that there really were laugh lines at the corners. It also eased the tension in his square jaw.

"Acting against Destiny's warnings, no doubt," he said. "She probably has the cardiologist on standby as it is."

Melanie grinned back at him. "I have his name and number in my purse," she joked, then added more truthfully, "along with cooking instructions and directions to this place. Destiny left very little to chance."

He seemed uncertain whether to take her seriously. "Not that I would put it past her, but she didn't actually give you the name of a doctor, did she?"

Melanie laughed. "Okay, no, but she does seem to be concerned that your particular nutritional habits combined with your workaholic tendencies will land you in an early grave. Do you ever relax?"

"Sure," he said at once. "I'm here, aren't I?"

Melanie gestured toward the computer that he'd been glancing at longingly ever since her arrival. "Unless you're on there doing your Christmas shopping, I don't think this qualifies."

He regarded her with a vaguely puzzled expression. "When is Christmas?"

"Less than three weeks."

He nodded, then reached for the pocket computer he'd tossed on the counter earlier, and made a note.

"Reminding your secretary to get your shopping done?" she asked him.

He looked only slightly chagrined at having been caught. "Winifred's better at it than I am," he said, not sounding the least bit defensive. "She has more time, too. I give her a few extra hours off to do *her* shopping, along with mine."

Melanie nodded. "A successful man always knows how to delegate. Do you give her a budget? Sugges-

tions? Does she tell you what's in the packages, so
you're not as surprised as the recipients on Christmas
morning? I've always wondered how that worked.''

He took the question seriously. ''Most of the time
she puts little sticky labels on the wrapped boxes so
I can add my own gift card. She seems to think my
handwriting ought to be on there.'' His eyes glinted
with sudden amusement. ''Occasionally, though, she
likes to go for the shock value, especially with my
brothers. Last year I gave my brother Mack—''

''The former Washington football hero,'' Melanie
recalled.

''Exactly, and one of the city's most sought after
bachelors.'' He grinned. ''My secretary bought him a
rather large, shapely, inflatable female. I'm pretty sure
Destiny had a hand in that one. She'd been trying to
convince Mack that he doesn't have to make it his
personal mission to date every woman in the entire
Washington metropolitan area. She seemed to think
he might be better able to commit to a woman with
no expectations.''

''Your family has a very odd sense of humor, if
you don't mind me saying so.''

''You don't know the half of it.''

''Did it work?''

''Not so's I've noticed,'' he admitted. ''Mack is
still happily playing the field.''

''I see. And my job would be to see to it that no
one else discovers these little family quirks?'' Melanie asked, daring to broach the subject that had
brought her to this cozy, out-of-the-way cottage. ''If
I get the job, that is.''

''I thought we'd pretty much settled that question
last time we met,'' Richard said.

Melanie shook her head. "I didn't like the outcome. I'm here to change it."

"Darn. I thought maybe you were here to seduce me," he said, almost making his expressed disappointment sound sincere.

Melanie gave him a hard look. That was a line of conversation that needed to be cut short in a hurry. She hadn't liked the seduction angle when she'd guessed it was part of Destiny's plan. She liked it even less coming from Richard. Okay, maybe she was marginally intrigued, but it was a bad idea any way she looked at it.

"Not in a million years," she said emphatically.

He seemed startled by her vehemence. "Why is that?"

"Been there, done that."

His gaze narrowed. "Meaning?"

She opted for total honesty so he'd understand just how opposed she was. "I made the serious mistake of sleeping with my last boss. I thought I was madly in love with him and vice versa. When the affair ended, so did my job. Now I work for myself. I won't make the same mistake a second time, not with a boss, not with a client."

"Good rule of thumb," he agreed. "But I'm not your boss *or* your client."

"I want this consulting contract more than I want you," she declared, proud of herself for managing to make the claim without even a hint of a quaver in her voice. Deep down inside, she knew the balance of that equation could change if she let it.

He chuckled. "At least you're admitting to the attraction."

Melanie silently cursed the slip. "Doesn't matter,"

she insisted. "It's not powerful enough to make me lose my focus."

"Now there's the way to win a man's heart."

Realizing that her attempt to make a point might have bruised his ego, she quickly added, "Not that you're not attractive and rich and an incredible catch for some woman."

"Nice save."

"I'm quick on my feet in tense situations. It'll serve me well as I'm fending off the media when you decide to run for office."

"I thought the whole idea was to captivate the media, not to fend them off."

"Well, of course it is," she said irritably. The man had a way of twisting her words to suit himself. She leveled a look into his eyes to prove she could hold her own, no matter what the level of intimidation. "But there are bound to be things you don't want to talk about, skeletons in the closet, that sort of thing."

His expression turned grim. "I don't have skeletons in my closet."

"No trail of brokenhearted women who'll feel the need to tell all when the stakes are high?"

"No," he said tersely.

She studied him with a narrowed gaze. "Men?"

He laughed. "Hardly, unless you consider the accountant I fired for trying to steal from the company to be a potential problem."

"Good to know. Then you should be a dream client."

His gaze met hers and he shook his head. "I don't think so, Melanie."

"But I have a plan," she said, reaching for her

proposal. It was a darned good one, too. She'd slaved over it for days.

His gaze never left her face. "So do I."

Her pulse kicked up a notch. "We're not on the same track, are we?"

"Not so far," he agreed, his expression sober, his eyes filled with unexpected heat.

To Melanie's sincere regret, somewhere deep inside, she wasn't nearly as upset by that as she should have been. Even so, she was holding out for what *she* wanted...the very lucrative contract. Sleeping with Richard to get it simply wasn't in the cards.

"Then I suppose I should help you clean up," she said as if the rest of it didn't matter. "Then I'll get out of your hair so you can go back to work. Good thing I'm never without a good book to read."

"No room for negotiation?" he inquired.

"None," she said flatly.

"Fine," he said, giving up what had been little more than a fainthearted battle to begin with. "Never mind cleaning up. I'll take care of it. You can take the guest room at the top of the stairs on the left. The bathroom's next door."

It rankled that he thought he could dismiss her so easily. "You cooked," she said with determination. "I'll clean up."

She met his gaze, challenging him to argue. He didn't. He merely shrugged. "Suit yourself." He turned his back and headed to his computer. Within seconds, he appeared to be thoroughly engrossed in a screen of what appeared to her to be incomprehensible columns of figures.

Obviously the man didn't like to lose, didn't like the fact that she'd thwarted his plan to turn this weekend into a romantic encounter. Never m... ...that the encounter was one he hadn't really wanted. ...He was obviously more than willing to take advantage ...circumstances since the opportunity had presente... self. Of course, he was just as willing to forget about it, which meant he'd only been toying with her, playing a game he'd been prepared to lose.

Ignoring Richard, Melanie managed to get the dishes, pots and pans into the dishwasher with a minimum of banging, despite her desire to make as much racket as possible. She still held out a slim hope that in the clear light of day, Richard would recognize that he had behaved badly and would at least consider her proposal on its merits. Destiny believed her nephew was a man of integrity, and Melanie very much wanted to believe her friend was right.

"Good night," she muttered as she stalked past him on her way upstairs.

He mumbled a response, as if he were totally distracted, but she knew better. She could feel his gaze following her as she left the room and climbed the stairs.

Inside the guest room, which had charming chintz wallpaper above old-fashioned white beadboard especially suited to a beach cottage, Melanie sank onto the queen-size bed with its antique iron headboard and tried to figure out how the evening had gone so dreadfully awry. It wasn't as if she'd never been propositioned before. It happened all the time. It wasn't as if Richard had pushed after she'd said no. In fact, he'd taken her at her word and remained reasonably good-humored about the firm rejection.

And wasn't that the real problem? Had she wanted him to ride roughshod over her objections? Had she wanted him to sweep her into his arms, kiss her until she melted and then carry her up to this very romantic bed? She'd never been one to lie to herself, and the truth was that a part of her had wanted exactly that. Thankfully, sanity had prevailed—his apparently more so than hers. Her principles remained intact, as much a credit to his restraint as to her stern words. She would be able to face him in the morning with head held high.

She picked up a down pillow and pummeled it. Fat lot of comfort those principles were going to be during the rest of this long, cold night.

Richard was up at dawn after a restless night. He felt oddly disgruntled, as if he'd done something wrong, something he ought to apologize for, but damned if he knew what that was. He'd made his desire for Melanie clear. She'd said no. He'd accepted that. The exchange should have ended the evening with no hard feelings.

Instead, she'd stalked off as if he'd offended her. Damned if he would ever understand women. He thought he'd given her what she wanted, a night alone in her own bed.

Of course, what she really wanted was that consulting job, and he wasn't prepared to offer her that. She'd drive him crazy in days, maybe even hours.

He was drinking his first cup of his special-blend coffee, when he heard her tentative footsteps coming downstairs. Uncertain what to expect, he tightened his grip on his cup and watched the doorway with a grim expression.

Instead of the dour, accusing woman he was expecting, in walked Little Mary Sunshine, all smiles and bright eyes.

"Good morning," she said cheerfully. "Isn't the snow gorgeous? I've never been at the beach after a snowstorm before. It really is like a winter wonderland out there, don't you think?"

"I suppose," he said cautiously.

"Haven't you even looked outside?"

"Of course I have." The truth was, he'd been too dismayed by the sight of the impassable roads to take much joy in the picturesque landscape.

As if she'd read his mind, she laughed. "You're panicked because there's no chance of me getting out of here this morning, aren't you?"

"I'm sure you have things you'd rather be doing," he said defensively. "Places you'd rather be."

"Not really," she said cheerfully.

Richard stared at her. Only after he'd studied her closely did he detect the faint wariness in her eyes. She was putting on a show for him, and it was a pretty decent one. It had almost had him fooled.

"Want some breakfast?" he asked.

"Cereal will do."

"I was thinking of making French toast with maple syrup. That's what Destiny always makes when we're here. She considered it a vacation treat."

Her eyes lit up, and this time her enthusiasm seemed genuine. "And you can make French toast?"

He laughed at the hint of amazement in her voice. "It's not that hard."

He moved past her, gathered a few eggs, butter and milk from the refrigerator.

"I'll set the table," she said, heading toward the dishwasher.

"I've already put the dishes away," he told her.

"How long have you been up?"

"Hours."

She gave him a knowing look. "Couldn't sleep?"

"I'm always an early riser."

"Not me. I like sleeping in. Being up at dawn is unnatural."

"Not once you've seen a sunrise over the river," he said. "Grab a couple of plates and a bowl, then come over here."

She set the dishes on the table, then regarded him warily. "Why over there?"

"I'm going to teach you how to make this. You might as well go away from this weekend with one new skill."

She backed off as if he'd suggested teaching her alligator-wrestling. "I don't think so. You probably only have a dozen eggs here. I can ruin more than that without half-trying."

Richard refused to back down. "Over here, or I'll think you're scared of being close to me." He met her gaze. "Maybe even tempted to take me up on that proposition I made last night."

"That was a bad idea," she reminded him.

"Yeah, I got that."

"But I'm not scared of you."

He bit back a grin. "If you say so." He held out an egg. "Break this into the bowl. Try not to get any shell in there."

She smashed it with so much enthusiasm, he suspected she was pretending it was his skull. Egg and shell dribbled into the bowl. He dumped the mess into the sink and handed her another egg. "Try again."

"Wouldn't it be easier if you just went ahead and did it?"

"Easier, but you wouldn't learn anything."

"It's not your job to be my cooking instructor."

"It is if I ever expect you to prepare a meal for me."

Her hand stilled over the bowl. "I thought we'd settled that. There's not going to be anything personal between us."

"That would be the smart plan," he agreed, not entirely sure why he was so determined to pursue this. He was always, always smart. He skirted around mistakes at all costs, especially when they were staring him right in the face in a way that made them totally avoidable.

"It's the only plan," she insisted.

"Not really." He placed a hand over hers and guided it gently to the side of the bowl, then cracked the egg. It fell neatly into the bowl without so much as a sliver of shell. Melanie stared at it in obvious surprise.

"Now do that without my help," he instructed.

She broke another egg and then a third one, looking more incredulous each time she succeeded. "Well, I'll be darned." She gazed up at him. "Now what?"

"Now we add a little milk, a touch of vanilla, and whip it till it's frothy."

Clearly more confident, she reached for the milk and added a too-generous splash. She was a little too stingy with the vanilla, but he refrained from comment and handed her the whisk. She stared at it as if it were a foreign object. Richard bit back another smile. "You use it to whip the eggs."

"Why not a beater?"

"This is easier." He nudged her aside with his hip and took the whisk. "Like this."

She watched him closely, a little furrow of concentration knitting her brow. He couldn't help wondering if she was this intense about everything she did. Best not to go there.

"Now you do it," he said, handing the whisk back.

She tackled the task with more enthusiasm than finesse, but she got the job done with only a minimal amount of splashing. There was enough egg left in the bowl for at least a couple of pieces of French toast.

Hiding his amusement, Richard put some butter in a pan, then handed her the bread. "Dip it in the eggs till both sides are coated, then put it in the pan once the butter's melted. I'll get the syrup."

He turned away for no more than a few seconds, but that was long enough for her to manage to splatter her hand with the now-sizzling butter. He heard her curse and turned back to find her with tears in her eyes.

"Let me see," he commanded.

"It's nothing," she protested. "Just a little burn. I told you I'm hopeless in the kitchen."

"Not hopeless, just inexperienced. Sit down. I'll get some ointment for your hand."

"The French toast will be ruined," she argued.

"Then we'll make more." He took the pan off the burner, grabbed the first-aid kit, then pulled a chair up beside hers. "Let me see."

She held out her right hand, which already had a blister the size of a dime. He took her hand in his, trying not to notice how soft it was and how it seemed to fit so perfectly in his own. He put a little of the salve on the blister, but couldn't bring himself to release her hand. Instead, he waited until her head came up and her gaze met his.

"I'm sorry about last night," he apologized. "I never meant to make you uncomfortable. I don't even know why I said those things. I just wanted to push your buttons, I guess."

Temper immediately flashed in her eyes. "It was some kind of game? You didn't really want to sleep with me? I knew it. What kind of man are you?"

Uh-oh. That had definitely come out all wrong. "No," he said at once. "That's not it. Dammit, somehow whenever I'm with you, my words get all tangled up."

"I seem to have the same difficulty," she admitted with obvious reluctance.

He wanted to be sure she understood. "I do want you, but I also respect what you were saying about not getting involved with a client or even a prospective client. Besides, it's not as if we know each other well enough for me to haul you off to bed. That's not a step two people should take on impulse."

"No," she agreed softly.

He risked another look into her eyes. The temper had faded, replaced by heat of another kind entirely. She lifted her uninjured hand and touched his cheek.

"Impulses are a risky thing," she said.

"Melanie." His voice sounded choked.

"Yes, Richard."

"It's still a bad idea. You were right about that."

"I know," she said, but her hand continued to rest against his cheek.

"I still want to kiss you," he murmured honestly, aware that he was testing the waters, waiting for a response. When she didn't protest or back away, the last of his resolve vanished. "Ah, hell," he whispered, reaching for her.

She tasted of mint-flavored toothpaste and coffee. It wasn't a combination he would normally have found the slightest bit seductive, but right this second it struck him as heavenly. He wanted more.

Her lips were as soft and clever as he'd dreamed about during the long, lonely night. Her tongue was downright wicked.

But even as his senses whirled and his blood heated, his conscience wouldn't stay silent. A nagging voice kept asking him what the hell he thought he was doing. Seducing the sexiest woman to cross his path in months did not strike him as an adequate answer. It certainly wouldn't hold up to a grilling by his aunt, who was this woman's friend. Destiny might have a plan for the two of them, but he was relatively confident this wasn't it.

Eventually he let the voice in his head win, releasing Melanie reluctantly and sitting back on his chair, his hands clenched together as if he didn't quite trust them to do what his head told them to do.

"Sorry," he murmured.

"I kissed you back," she said honestly.

He grinned at her determined attempt to be fair. It was not an attitude he especially deserved, and they both knew it. "True enough," he said anyway, because he liked putting some heat into her eyes.

"You don't have to gloat," she grumbled.

He held up his hands. "Not gloating," he swore solemnly.

She regarded him with an intense, unsmiling expression. "Richard, just so you know, nothing's changed. I still won't sleep with you and I still want that contract.''

Richard didn't doubt either claim. He just wasn't sure he could live with them. Worse, he didn't know why the devil that was, which meant mistakes could start piling up before he figured it out if he didn't watch himself around her every single second. The trouble with that plan was that he much preferred simply watching her.

Chapter Four

Still feeling shaky from Richard's unexpected and thoroughly devastating kiss, Melanie retreated to the living room immediately after breakfast. She grabbed a legal pad and pen and settled in front of the warm fire, determined to get some work done for some of her more appreciative clients. She had plenty of challenges on her plate. She didn't need a stubborn man who wasn't interested in listening to her advice.

Despite her best efforts to concentrate, though, her mind wandered back to that kiss. No matter how hard she tried to steer her thoughts to something productive, she kept coming back to the way Richard's mouth had felt on hers, the way he'd managed to make her blood sing without half-trying. She found herself doodling little hearts like some schoolgirl with a crush. This was bad, really bad. Annoyed with herself, she impatiently flipped the page, cursing when it tore.

"Having trouble concentrating?"

She jumped at the sound of his voice, then scowled at the teasing note in it. "No."

He laughed. "I won't call you on that. However, since I can't seem to concentrate, either, I was going to suggest that we go for a walk and grab some lunch in town."

"We just had breakfast."

Richard gestured toward his watch. "Four hours ago," he noted. "You really have been drifting off, haven't you? What were you daydreaming about?" He gave her an amused, knowing look, then added, "Or were you fine-tuning your PR plan for me in case I decide to relent and let you present it?"

He reached for her legal pad with a motion so quick and sneaky, he managed to get it away from her. When he saw the hearts she'd drawn, he grinned.

Melanie wondered if it was possible to die of embarrassment. If so, now would be the perfect time for the floor of this place to open and swallow her up.

"Actually I was thinking about this really sexy television reporter I met last week," she lied boldly, thankful that she hadn't scribbled any initials on the page to give herself away and confirm the obvious conclusion he'd leaped to. That would have been totally humiliating. At least now he could only guess where her mind had been drifting. He couldn't prove a thing.

Richard took the bait, regarding her with curiosity. "Which reporter?"

"What difference does it make?"

"Just wondering about your taste in men," he claimed.

She didn't buy that for a second. Her taste in men was the last thing on his mind. He was just trying to trip her up. She named the most eligible bachelor on any of the news teams in town. He was an insipid bore, but maybe Richard wouldn't know that.

Unfortunately, he lifted a brow at her response. "Really? Everyone tells me he's pretty, but not too bright."

There was no mistaking the derisiveness in his voice. That "pretty" label sealed it.

Melanie refused to be daunted by his attitude. "Maybe I'm not interested in holding a conversation with him," she suggested.

Richard merely laughed. "You're going to have to do better than that, sweetheart. One rule of thumb when you're lying, you have to make it believable."

"I'm not surprised you know that," she muttered.

He ignored the gibe. "Come on, kiddo. On your feet. The exercise will clear your head, maybe get all those hot thoughts of your young stud muffin out of your brain."

Melanie sighed. He was right about one thing—she really did need a blast of cold air. Maybe then she'd stop making an idiot out of herself. It was not the best way to get Richard to take her work seriously.

Richard couldn't recall the last time he'd gone for a walk in the snow just for the sheer fun of it. Of course, in this case it was also a way to get out of the house and away from those wayward thoughts he was having about the impossible woman staying with him. The fact that she'd tried to sell him a bill of goods about that insipid reporter suggested she was aware that the temptation was getting too hot to handle, too.

Outside, though, the air was crisp and cold off the river. The sky, now that the storm had ended, was a brilliant blue. The sun made the drifts of white snow glisten as if the ground had been scattered with diamonds. He was glad he'd thought to put on his sunglasses. Of course, the almost childlike excitement shining in Melanie's eyes was just as blinding, and the glasses couldn't protect him from that.

When they'd left the house, she'd been totally guarded, most likely because of his teasing. Now all of that seemed to be forgotten. Every two feet, she paused to point out some Christmas-card-perfect scene.

"Look," she said in a hushed voice, grabbing his sleeve. "A cardinal."

Richard followed the direction of her gaze and found the cardinal, its red feathers a brilliant splash of color against the snow, a holly tree as its backdrop. Its less colorful mate was sitting on a tree branch, almost hidden by the dark green leaves and red berries. The birds were common, but Melanie made it seem as if this were something totally special and incredible. Her enthusiasm was contagious.

Melanie sighed. "I wish I had my camera."

"We can pick up one of that throwaway kind at the store," he suggested.

She looked at him as if he'd had a divine inspiration. "Now?" she asked with so much eagerness that he laughed.

"You are so easy to please," he teased. "A cheap camera and you're a pushover."

"I've decided to go with the flow today," she informed him.

Now there was a notion he could get behind. "Oh, really?"

She frowned at him in mock despair. "Not that flow," she scolded.

He shrugged. "Just a thought."

She gave him an odd look. "It's not as if you really want to seduce me," she said with surprising certainty. "So why do you say things like that?"

"What makes you think I don't want to seduce you?" In truth, the idea had been growing in appeal by leaps and bounds.

"You've admitted as much," she reminded him. "Not that I think you'd turn me down if I agreed to take you up on it, but you're really flirting to annoy me."

Richard wondered about that. He seemed to be taking the idea more and more seriously by the minute. Melanie wasn't his type, but there was something about her, something refreshingly honest and open and enthusiastic. He couldn't recall the last time he'd encountered that particular combination, much less been drawn to it. Maybe Destiny was right about that much, at least. Maybe he was ready for a change in his life, a spark of excitement and a few heady thrills. It would beat the mundane existence he'd been telling himself he was perfectly contented with.

He glanced at Melanie, noting the expectant look on her face as she awaited a reply to her challenge. "Maybe I am trying to annoy you," he agreed. "Then again, perhaps I'm just trying to prepare you for the moment when I make my first totally irresistible move."

She blinked at that, but then a smile broke across her face. "I don't think so," she said with complete confidence.

Vaguely disgruntled by her conviction, he asked, "Why not?"

"Because you don't play games. You take life far too seriously to be bothered with them."

His gaze narrowed. "Destiny's theory again?"

"No, my own personal observation," Melanie assured him. "I'm a good judge of people. That makes me an excellent public relations person, because I know how to make the public see what I see."

Richard was more curious than he'd expected to be about her perceptions. "What would you make them see about me? Not that I'm stuffy, I hope."

"No, I'd emphasize that you do take responsibility seriously, that you've worked hard at Carlton Industries and would work just as hard for your constituents. Those are good, solid recommendations for a candidate."

"I thought you didn't think I'd be a viable candidate because I hadn't walked in the shoes of those who've struggled," he reminded her.

She shrugged. "Maybe you convinced me otherwise."

"Or maybe you want this contract so badly, you're willing to say whatever it takes to get it," he said with an edge of cynicism.

She stopped in her tracks and scowled at him. "If you believe that, then you don't know me very well," she said, sounding genuinely miffed. "I don't work for anyone I don't believe in."

"You don't know me well enough to believe in me," he countered.

"Actually, I think I do. After your aunt suggested we meet, I did a lot of research before I agreed. I talked to people. I read everything in print. I wanted to be sure that Destiny wasn't being totally biased about your capabilities or your honesty and integrity. She wasn't. You're a good man, Richard. The consensus on that is unanimous." She gave him a considering look. "Whether you have what it takes to win an election is something else entirely."

Richard bristled at the suggestion that he wasn't up to the challenge of running for office or winning. "What is it you think I might be lacking?"

"An open mind," she said at once.

He started to argue, then saw exactly the trap she'd laid for him. "Because I made up my mind about hiring you before we'd even met," he guessed.

"That's one reason," she agreed. "And because now that we have met, you can't divorce my professional capabilities from the fact that I'm a woman who rattles you."

"You don't rattle me," he claimed, doubting whether he sounded the least bit convincing.

She regarded him with amusement. "There's the first real lie I've heard cross your lips."

"That you know of," he said, not denying that he'd lied in that instance. She did rattle him, no question about it. He'd just hoped to convince her otherwise. The woman saw too darn much. He didn't like it that she could get into his head. He prided himself on keeping most people off guard and at a distance. That kind of safety suited his comfort level.

"The first lie," she insisted.

Richard sighed. "Okay, say you're right about that.

Say I'm addicted to telling the truth *and* that you rattle me, so what?''

"Now we're getting somewhere," she said more cheerfully.

He stared at her in confusion. "Where?"

"You're very close to admitting that you've been mule-headed and stubborn and that you will read my business proposal when we get back to the cottage."

He regarded her incredulously. "You got that out of my admission?"

She grinned. "Brilliant, aren't I?"

He laughed despite himself. "Not necessarily brilliant, but sneaky. You're a lot like my aunt, in fact."

"I'll take that as a compliment."

He sighed. "To be honest, I'm not sure you should."

Melanie was feeling confident and in control when they sat down to lunch at a small café in the center of town. She was finally making progress. Maybe coming all the way down here hadn't been such a harebrained idea, after all. If she'd done this well before the man had even eaten, just think what she could accomplish once a crab-cake sandwich, some coleslaw and homemade apple cobbler with ice cream had improved his mood.

He gave her an odd look as she ordered the hearty lunch, then chuckled. "Trying to ply me with food, so I'll be in a more receptive frame of mind?"

"It did occur to me," she said. "Of course, you don't have to have what I'm having. And lunch is on me, by the way. I'm wooing a prospective client."

"I'm buying," he contradicted for the waitress's benefit. "As for the meal, I have to have what you're having if I expect to have the energy to keep up with you.'' He gave the amused waitress a conspiratorial wink. "Same thing for me, along with the strongest coffee you have.''

The older woman grinned. "Honey, we don't serve it any other way.''

"Too bad you're not running for office here,'' Melanie said when the woman had gone to place their order. "You'd have her vote locked up.''

Richard sighed. "It's not supposed to be about charisma.''

"It's not supposed to be, but it is, at least in part,'' she argued. "A dull man with a good message *can* get elected—it's just harder. You have both. Why not capitalize on it, instead of pretending that one thing doesn't matter?''

"In other words, I'm not going to get out of kissing babies and shaking hands,'' he said.

"Few politicians get elected without doing both,'' she said. "People want to see that the man they're electing is real, that he's human. They like to look him in the eye and gauge for themselves whether he's honest. They like to know that his handshake's firm.''

Funny thing about that, Richard thought, falling silent. More than once he'd been accused of not being human—by competitors faced with his hard, cold stare during negotiations, by women who'd hoped for more from their relationship. He'd come to accept that there was something missing inside him, some connection he'd lost when his parents had died. Once, he'd despaired of ever getting that piece of himself back, but now, looking at Melanie, feeling her vitality and warmth touching him, he had a feeling he might be able to get it if only he reached out.

Then he immediately shook off the fanciful notion.

Melanie was here for one reason and one reason only, to strike a deal with him. Not to heal him. Like so many others, she simply wanted something from him. He didn't dare lose sight of that, despite the fact that he'd managed to veer her away from her mission on more than one occasion since her arrival.

Her fingers skimmed lightly across the back of his hand, startling him.

"Hey," she said softly, her expression puzzled, "where'd you go?"

"Back to reality," he said grimly.

Before she could ask the question that was so obviously on the tip of her tongue, their lunches came. Richard had never been so relieved by the sight of food in his life. He bit into his crab-cake sandwich with enthusiasm, but noted that it was some time before Melanie finally picked hers up, as if she couldn't quite get past his sudden shift of mood and all the questions it raised.

Once she'd tasted the crab-cake, though, her attention was totally focused on the sandwich. "Terrific crab, don't you think?"

He nodded. "Even out of season and frozen, it's delicious. Better than any I've had at some of the finest seafood places in Washington."

"Wonder what that spice is?" she mused, taking another taste. "It gives it a little kick."

"Given your avowed inability to cook, what difference does it make?"

"For something this good, I could learn," she insisted. "I'm not totally hopeless."

"Why bother, when you can just come here?"

"It's not like I get down this way all the time," she said. "In fact, I've never been to this part of Virginia before."

"Now that you know about the crab cakes, I'll bet you'll be back," he said. "Who knows, maybe I'll even invite you."

"I could probably starve before that happens," she said. "Maybe they'd ship them up to me. Even I could be trusted to cook them, if they're already prepared." Her expression turned wistful. "It would be so nice not to eat every meal out, at least if I want anything edible. Nuking a frozen dinner doesn't do it for me, except in an emergency."

Richard could relate to that. He ate far too many of his own meals at his desk or in restaurants, except on those occasions when Destiny commanded his presence at her table. She was an excellent cook, when she took the time to do it, and it had spoiled him for anything less than the best. The conversation around her table was also lively and challenging, even when it was a simple family meal with his two brothers. They didn't get together for those meals nearly often enough anymore. He needed to change that.

Funny how he recalled the laughter more than the actual food on the table. It had been good, but it was being with the three of them that he missed the most. He hadn't realized how lonely his life had become until just this moment. Not that he didn't see Destiny or talk to her almost daily and his brothers almost that often, but it wasn't the same as it had been when they'd all lived under one roof.

Sighing heavily, he gazed at Melanie. "Tell me about your family," he coaxed.

She stared at him as if he'd asked her to reveal her deepest secrets. "My family?"

"Yes. Big? Small? Where are they?"

"I have two older sisters, both married, both totally unambitious and disgustingly content with their husbands and kids. They still live in Ohio, within a few miles of our folks. They all pester me about my solitary lifestyle. They don't get it.''

''Were you close?''

She smiled. ''As close as three girls can be when they're fighting over the same dress to wear to a dance.''

''Do you envy them? What they have now?''

''At times,'' she admitted, her expression thoughtful. ''I love what I do and I am ambitious, but that doesn't mean I don't wish I had someone to share it with.''

Her thoughts so closely mirrored what Richard had been thinking only moments before, it made him sigh again. ''I know what you mean,'' he admitted with rare candor.

Melanie regarded him with surprise. ''You do?''

''Sure. What's the thrill of conquering the world, if there's no one to tell, no one who'll get excited about it?''

''Exactly,'' she said at once. ''It doesn't mean we're dissatisfied with what we have or that we're ungrateful, just that we recognize that there can be more. That's a good thing, don't you think?''

''Self-awareness is always good, or so they say.''

''So, if you know there's something lacking in your life, why haven't you married any of those women with whom you've been involved?'' she asked.

Richard shuddered. ''Because I couldn't imagine bringing a single one of them into a place like this for a crab cake and homemade apple cobbler.''

Melanie's expression softened. ''Really?''

''Yes,'' he said. ''But don't let it go to your head.''

''Of course not,'' she said at once.

"And it doesn't mean I'll think about hiring you," he added for good measure.

"I know that," she agreed, but she looked a little smug.

"It just means that you remind me a lot of Destiny," he explained, trying to sort through his feelings even as he attempted to explain them to her. "You're outspoken and unpredictable and…" He faltered.

"Open to new ideas?" she suggested.

Richard laughed. "Don't push it."

"But people who are open to new ideas aren't—"

"Stuffy," he supplied before she could say it. "I know. I get it."

She studied him intently. "Do you really?"

"Yes," he assured her.

"Then maybe we should go back to the cottage," she suggested.

"So I can read your proposal?"

"That, too, but I was also thinking of getting totally wild and letting you kiss me again."

Richard stared at her, bemused by the outrageous suggestion. "Why would you do that?"

"Because I have an open mind."

"Which means seduction could be back on the table?" he asked, wanting to be sure he got it exactly right before he made a damn fool out of himself. He hadn't wanted a woman as badly as he wanted Melanie Hart in so long, he wasn't sure he could trust his own instincts.

"You never know," she said with a shrug.

"I think you need to be clearer than that," he said, as he tossed a handful of bills on the table to pay for lunch, then grabbed his coat.

"What fun is life, if everything has to be spelled out ahead of time?"

He frowned at her. "It may be more fun, but my way averts disaster."

She accepted his help with her coat, then faced him, her expression totally serious. "Okay, then, here it is. Not that I'm crazy about it, but right now, this minute, I want you to kiss me again. I am still opposed to anything more happening between us, because it could get messy, especially if I wind up working for you."

"I see," he said.

"However," she added, then grinned, "I might be open to persuasion."

His pulse kicked up at the tiny opening.

"Maybe not today," she added pointedly. "Maybe not tomorrow. But the future could hold all sorts of surprises."

Despite the fact that she'd pretty much told him he was going to go to bed frustrated tonight and possibly for many nights to come, Richard couldn't seem to help whistling as they walked outside into the cold air.

Melanie frowned at him. "You seem awfully chipper for a man who's just been told he's not going to have sex."

He laughed. "Is that what you said?"

"I certainly thought it was."

"Not what I heard," he said. "I heard that there would be no sex *tonight,* but that tomorrow—as a very famous fictional Southern belle once said—most definitely is another day." He took her hand and kissed it. "I'm a very patient man. Was that in that research of yours?"

She regarded him with a vaguely shaken expression. "I thought I was very thorough, but I must have missed that."

"Keep it in mind. It could be important," he told her, then scooped up some snow and pelted her with it. Best to cool them both down for the moment, he thought.

Eyes wide, she stared at him in shock for fully a minute before her eyes filled with that fire he'd come to crave.

"You are so dead," she said, bending down to make a soft snowball of her own.

"I doubt that," Richard said, not even bothering to run.

"You don't think I'll throw this at you?"

"Oh, I think you'll throw it," he said, then grinned. "I just think you'll miss."

Even as he started moving, she hauled off and managed to hit him lightly on one cheek.

"Bad move, darlin'," he said, coming back for her, even as she frantically scooped up more and more snow and threw it with dead-on accuracy. He had her off her feet and on her backside in a deep drift of snow before she realized what he intended.

Sputtering with indignation, she stared up at him and then started laughing. Only when he was laughing right along with her did she snag his ankle, give him a jerk and land him on his butt right beside her.

Richard didn't waste time protesting her sneakiness. The snow was cold as the dickens. Only one way he could think of to counteract that. He rolled over and caught her, then captured her mouth under his. He'd hoped for a little heat, but he got a full-fledged blaze. Apparently she didn't hold a grudge.

Of course, if she also stuck to her resolve about keeping sex out of the equation, at least for tonight, it was going to be a very long time till morning.

Chapter Five

Okay, maybe it was freezing cold out, but that was no reason for her to be playing with fire, Melanie thought, as she gazed into Richard's turbulent eyes. They were filled with the kind of stormy emotions she hadn't expected at all, not from a man reputed to have no heart.

She'd been counting on that reputation for being distant when she'd agreed to see him the very first time. She'd known from looking at his pictures that he'd appeal to her physically. She'd known from listening to Destiny that his tragic early years would pluck at her heartstrings. But she was not normally drawn to arrogance or to men who were emotionally shut down. She'd figured those two traits would keep her safe.

After their first meeting, when those traits had been evident in spades, she'd been comforted. Now this...

Forget his heart, she commanded. Where was her head? Had her brain cells frozen on the walk back to the cottage? Is that why she'd been tossing out taunting comments about kisses and sex and then rolling around in the snow with Richard? Those were definitely not in her business plan.

Before she made a mistake they would both regret, she leaped up and brushed herself off, then faced him as if nothing the least bit provocative had been going on, not in the restaurant, not now. "You surprise me," she said lightly. "I would never have imagined you loosening up enough to play around in the snow like some kid."

He rose, looking too blasted dignified, his expression completely sober. "Yes, well, I imagine despite all that research of yours, I still have a few surprises left."

Melanie sighed at the return of his straitlaced demeanor. She was beginning to think it was nothing more than self-protective armor, and that made her weak-kneed all over again. "Richard, I'm sorry, but what just went on here?"

He shrugged. "I suppose, for a couple of minutes, both of us lost track of why we're together."

"In other words, we were behaving like a male and female who are attracted to each other, rather than prospective business associates," she said. "I'm sorry."

"Not your fault. I'm the one who's sorry for crossing a line."

"But I invited you to cross it."

He scowled at her. "Quit being so damned reasonable," he muttered. "There's no way this weekend could have anything other than a bad ending."

Melanie felt worse than ever. For a few minutes Richard had forgotten himself, pushed aside his responsibilities and found his long-lost inner child. He'd revealed his human side. Then she'd gone and ruined that by getting too uptight and serious. Of course, if she apologized one more time, he was liable to blow sky-high. He seemed to be operating on a very short fuse. It would have been a good time to get out of town, but unfortunately the local roads had yet to be cleared.

She held out her hand, determined to get them back on a safer footing. "Truce?"

He gave her a mocking look. "I hadn't realized we were at war."

"But we're heading in that direction," she said. "And it *is* my fault. I sent out all sorts of mixed messages."

He gazed into her eyes, his expression forbidding. "Maybe it would be smarter to stay at odds," he suggested. "We don't seem to be able to handle anything else without getting offtrack."

It was true, though Melanie couldn't imagine why that was. Forget all the issues about working with him, he was far too intense—okay, far too stuffy—to be attractive to her, beyond his obvious physical appeal. And yet he *was* attractive, no question about that. Otherwise she wouldn't have come so darn close to throwing herself at him without one second's consideration of her deeply held principles about mixing business and pleasure.

She imagined that he found the whole attraction thing to be just as confusing. She was nothing at all like the rich, sophisticated, edgy women with whom he was normally seen around town. She'd seen him

in black tie often enough on the society pages to recognize the glamorous type of woman he preferred.

Given that, there was only one thing to do. If they
both accepted the notion of anything personal between them being insane, then perhaps the next few
hours wouldn't be too awful. In fact, perhaps by
morning they'd be able to laugh about everything,
shake hands and say goodbye with no lingering regrets. She'd write off any chance of landing this PR
consulting contract and cut her losses. Anything else
would be complete lunacy.

Even as she was coming to that conclusion, Richard reached into his jacket and pulled out a key.
"Why don't you go on back to the house?" he suggested, offering it to her.

"Where are you going?" she asked as she accepted
the key and tucked it into her own jacket pocket.

"For a walk," he said. "I'll pick up one of those
cameras for you."

Melanie opened her mouth to offer to come with
him, but he'd already turned on his heel and taken
off. Clearly he was eager to escape her company. This
was what she'd wanted not five seconds ago, but now
she was having second thoughts.

She heaved a sigh as she watched him go, shoulders hunched against the wind that had kicked up off
the river. He looked so alone. How was it possible
that a man as rich, brilliant and sexy as Richard Carlton could be so completely alone?

She had answers to all sorts of questions about him
stored away in her research files, but not to that one.
Naturally that meant it was the one she found most
intriguing, the one that opened a tiny little place in
her heart to him.

And that, she concluded with complete candor, was the one that could prove to be her undoing.

Richard knew it was ridiculous to feel cranky and completely out of sorts because a woman had changed her mind—and the rules—on him. It happened all the time, and he'd never given two figs about it before. Women were unpredictable creatures, that was all. It wasn't personal. He'd watched Destiny dispatch so many perfectly respectable suitors over the years, he'd come to accept the behavior as normal.

But he'd taken Melanie's sudden change of heart damn personally, which meant that on some totally unexpected level she'd gotten to him. How the devil had that happened?

He wrestled with that unanswerable question all the way to the fast-mart, where he picked up a disposable camera, then had a sudden inspiration to buy a just-released video and some popcorn for that evening. If they were going to be stuck here together for another night, entertainment that didn't require conversation seemed like a fine idea.

As he trudged back toward the cottage through the deep snow, he tried to recapture some of his earlier delight in the quiet, snow-shrouded landscape, but it wouldn't come. Without Melanie, it was a bit as if that cardinal had flown away, taking all of the color with it.

He groaned at the thought. He did not want Melanie Hart adding color to his life. He didn't want to start waxing poetic about her influence on him or his surroundings. He wanted to go back to that serene time earlier in the week before he'd ever met the annoying woman. Then the prospect of several uninterrupted hours in front of his computer or with his mountain of paperwork would have been the bright spot on his weekend agenda.

Unfortunately, recapturing that serenity was all but impossible when Melanie was going to be underfoot the second he crossed the threshold at the cottage. And she would be underfoot. She seemed to be the kind who liked to talk things out, make perfect sense of them, instead of accepting that they'd nearly made a dreadful mistake and moving on. He'd seen that let's-talk-about-this look in her eyes right before he'd turned on his heel and left her a few blocks from the cottage. He hoped to hell she was over it by now.

He was half-frozen by the time he reached the cottage. He was grateful for the blazing fire she'd started, but as he waited for Melanie to appear, to start pestering him with comments or analysis or, God forbid, yet another apology, he grew increasingly perplexed by her absence. Had she taken off, even though the local roads were still all but impassable? Come to think of it, had he paid any attention to whether her car was still in the driveway? He couldn't remember noticing.

Panicked that she might have done something so completely impulsive and dangerous because of him, he bounded upstairs and very nearly broke down the guest-room door with his pounding. He heard her sleepily mumbled "What?" just as he threw open the door.

Undisguised relief flooded through him at the sight of her in the bed, the comforter pulled up to her chin, her hair rumpled, her eyes dazed.

"Is something wrong?" she asked in that same husky, half-asleep tone.

The comforter drooped, revealing one bare shoulder and a tantalizing hint of breast. Heart pounding, Richard began backing away. "No, really. Sorry."

"Richard?"

Even half-asleep, she was constitutionally incapable of letting anything go, he concluded grimly. He was going to have to explain himself, or at least come up with something plausible that wouldn't give away how frantic he'd been when he'd imagined her risking her neck on the icy roads.

"Um, the front door was open," he said, improvising quickly. "I thought someone might have broken in. I just wanted to be sure you were okay."

Her gaze narrowed. "The front door was open?"

"Just a crack," he said, guessing that she was about to worry that piece of information to death.

"But I closed it. I know I did. I didn't lock it, because I wasn't sure if you had another key with you and I wasn't sure if I'd hear you if I fell asleep and you knocked, but I'm sure it was securely shut."

"No big deal," he said. "As long as you're okay. Go back to sleep. Sorry I disturbed you."

She smiled and stretched, allowing another tiny slip of the comforter. She seemed to be oblivious to the sexy picture she presented.

"I'm awake now. I might as well get up."

Because she seemed about to do exactly that without regard for her lack of attire—or what his vivid imagination believed to be her lack of attire—Richard bolted. He wasn't sure his heart could take the image of a totally unclad Melanie being burned in his mind forever.

He was downstairs, in the kitchen, making another pot of very strong coffee, when she finally appeared, her face scrubbed clean, her hair tidied. He'd liked it better all tousled, but it was evident she was trying to reclaim her professional—totally untouchable—decorum. He could have told her that not even the most modest power suit of all time could accomplish that. She was an innately sexy woman, the kind who conjured up forbidden images, at least for him.

"Coffee?" he offered.

"No, thanks. Too much caffeine and I'll never sleep tonight."

Richard was pretty sure he wasn't going to sleep anyway, so a little caffeine wasn't going to matter. "I bought a video for us to watch later," he said, gesturing to the table.

She picked it up, studied it, then grinned. "You bought a romantic comedy?"

"I heard it was good," he muttered defensively. "I thought all women liked that kind of sappy stuff."

"We do. I'm just surprised you took my feelings into account."

"My aunt raised me to be a thoughtful host."

"Even when you're an unwilling one?" she asked skeptically.

"Even then," he insisted. "Maybe it's most important of all then. And Destiny obviously knew that I'd mastered that lesson when she sent you charging down here. Otherwise, she wouldn't have risked it."

Melanie met his gaze and opened her mouth. Richard cut her off. "I don't want to hear another apology. We both know you're here because of my aunt. If anyone's to blame for the awkwardness of the situation, it's Destiny."

"She was just trying to help both of us out," Melanie replied. "You can hardly blame her for caring about you and for trying to do me a favor."

"Yes, I can," he said grimly. "When it takes the form of meddling, I most certainly can. If this was only about that contract, she'd have planted you in my office on Monday morning, not in this cottage on a Friday night, armed with my favorite wine and food."

Melanie grimaced. "Maybe we shouldn't go there. We don't seem to see eye-to-eye on your aunt's motivation. In fact, maybe I should go in the living room and sit in front of the fire and get some work done, and you can stay in here and do the same."

Richard bit back a grin. "Retreating to neutral corners, as it were."

"Exactly."

"Maybe that's not such a bad idea," he said as he gazed directly into her eyes. He thought he detected a faint hint of longing there. Best not to give himself the chance to discover if he was right.

She stood there, looking undecided, then finally sighed. "See you later, then."

"Yeah, see you later." When she was almost out of sight, he called after her. "Melanie?"

She hesitated but didn't turn back to face him. "Yes?"

"Anything in particular you'd like for dinner?"

She turned then, her expression perplexed. "There are choices?"

"Sure. Why would you think otherwise?"

"Destiny made it seem as if..."

"As if I would be starving if you didn't show up down here," Richard guessed. He grinned. "Told you what she was up to."

Melanie nodded. "Damn but she's good," she said, sounding more admiring than annoyed.

"It's something we should both keep in mind, don't you think?" he responded.

"Oh, yes," she said, squaring her shoulders. "I will definitely keep that in mind. As for dinner, surprise me."

As if I could, Richard thought, but he nodded. Maybe when it came to dinner, he could come up with something totally unexpected. Lord knew, though, that the woman seemed able to read his mind when it came to anything else.

Melanie grabbed her cell phone and marched outside, oblivious to the cold. She punched in Destiny Carlton's number, then waited for a connection. When it came, the signal was faint, but she could hear Destiny's cheerful voice.

"You are one very sneaky woman," Melanie accused, though without too much rancor.

"Melanie, darling. How are you? Are you stranded down there with Richard?" There was an unmistakably optimistic note in her voice.

"I'm sure you knew I would be," Melanie grumbled.

"Not knew, *hoped*," Destiny corrected. "Is it going well? Has he agreed to hire you yet?"

"No."

"Oh," Destiny said, clearly disappointed. "Maybe I should have a talk with him. Where is he?"

"In the kitchen working, and I am not letting you talk to him," Melanie said. "I think you've done quite enough meddling for one weekend."

"Has something gone wrong?" Destiny asked worriedly. "You two haven't had words, have you?"

"Not the way you mean. What we *have* done is compare notes. Now I'm even more suspicious of your motives than I was the other day. In fact, I'm convinced that your intentions were not entirely aboveboard and honorable."

"That's a fine thing to say when I've only been trying to help you out," Destiny said with indignation.

"Nice try," Melanie retorted, not buying the huffy act for an instant. "And I'm sure that getting me this contract is at least a small part of what you're after, but you want more out of this weekend, don't you?"

"I have no idea what you're suggesting," the older woman claimed blithely. "Whoops, there's my other line. I'm expecting an important call from Richard's brother Mack. Have a lovely time down there, darling, and give Richard a kiss for me. Don't you two dare leave until the roads are cleared. I don't want to be worried sick that you're skidding into a snowdrift."

She was gone before Melanie could respond. Give the man a kiss for her, Melanie thought irritably. Right. That was exactly what Destiny was after, and the more kissing the better. She punched in Destiny's number again, but this time the connection wouldn't go through at all. Melanie sighed, jammed the cell phone back in her pocket and went inside.

Richard walked into the living room just then and regarded her quizzically. "What on earth were you doing outside without a coat?"

"Calling your aunt."

His lips twitched. "And?"

"She denies that this was a setup for anything other than getting a business deal worked out."

"What did you expect, that she'd admit to it?"

"Yes, I expected her to be honest."

"I'm sure she was. In fact, I imagine if you went over every word that came out of her mouth, you wouldn't find a single thing that wasn't accurate and truthful."

Melanie considered the conversation she'd just had with the maddening woman and concluded Richard was right. Destiny had skirted carefully around any outright lies, while admitting nothing. "She should be the one going into politics," she muttered.

"Heaven help us if she chose to," Richard said. "She doesn't suffer fools gladly, and the political arena is crawling with idiots. Destiny's completely nonpartisan when it comes to calling it as she sees it. After a few weeks, no political party would have her."

"Just think how refreshing it would be to listen to her, though," Melanie speculated.

"Refreshing is not the word I would have chosen," Richard replied. "But, then, I've been listening to her most of my life and have seen what she's like once she gets a bee in her bonnet. She's relentless."

"And you think that's what we are, a bee in her bonnet?"

"I'd stake my life on it."

"Well, too bad," Melanie said forcefully. "She's just going to have to lose this one. You and I have agreed on that."

She looked up to find Richard staring at her, that disconcerting heat once again blazing in his eyes.

"Have we really?" he asked softly.

Her pulse leaped. "Yes, of course, we have," she said, trying hard to sound irrefutably emphatic.

"Then Destiny will just have to accept it," he said, with what sounded like a vague note of regret in his voice.

Melanie swallowed hard, trying not to choke on her own regrets. "Suddenly I'm starving," she said. "Must be all that fresh air and exercise."

Richard finally tore his gaze away. "I'll start dinner then. Would you like a glass of wine? There's another bottle of cabernet."

"Sure," she said eagerly. One glass would calm her nerves. And one was her limit. Two would weaken her resolve, and it was already nearly in tatters.

She followed Richard into the kitchen. "Do you think we'll be able to get away from here in the morning?"

"The main roads will definitely be clear, and I imagine even that insubstantial little car of yours will be able to get out to the highway."

He sounded almost as eager to put an end to this weekend as she was. If he mattered to her in a personal way, his words would have hurt her feelings. As it was, there was just a tiny little nip to her ego. Or so she told herself.

"Stay here while I cook," he suggested, his fingers lingering against hers as he handed her the glass of wine.

"Not a good idea," she said.

"Why?"

"You know the answer to that. We seem to lose our heads when we're in the same room for too long."

"And that's such a bad thing?"

"Richard!"

He shrugged. "I just thought it would be nice to have some company." He grinned. "I'll give you a knife, and you can cut the vegetables. If I get out of line, you can defend yourself."

Melanie laughed, despite all the warning bells going off in her head. She pulled out a chair and sat down at the kitchen table, taking a long swallow of wine. Then she met his gaze.

He looked surprisingly relieved.

"Thank you," he said.

"Whatever," she replied, then grinned. "But I want a very big knife."

"Now there's a sentence guaranteed to strike terror in a man's heart," he said, laughing even as he handed her a deadly looking butcher knife, then added a more suitable paring knife for the vegetables.

They managed to get through the dinner preparations without bloodshed and without a single sly innuendo or seductive comment. Part of Melanie was relieved by that. Another part of her felt as if she'd lost something important.

It was because of that part that she set her glass aside at the end of the meal and stood up. "I'll say good-night now," she told him.

"You don't want to see the movie?"

"I've seen it," she fibbed, because she couldn't risk letting her defenses down for one more second.

"Why didn't you say something earlier? I could have gone out and gotten another movie."

"Maybe you should watch this one," she told him. "The hero winds up with the girl."

She felt his gaze on her as she left the room and

knew he had gotten the message that he needed a few pointers if *he* was ever going to do the same. She wasn't sure why it seemed to matter so much to her that he understand that, but it was. And that was more troubling than anything else that had gone on all weekend long.

Chapter Six

Richard had stayed up till midnight watching the romantic comedy he'd bought. He'd heard the unspoken message in Melanie's parting shot the night before. The suggestion that he had no idea what women wanted, that he couldn't keep one, had rankled.

If he wanted a woman in his life, he'd have one. He'd achieved every other goal he'd set for himself. He didn't doubt for a second that he could have a wife if he wanted one. He'd simply chosen to remain single. Period.

He'd been tempted to follow Melanie upstairs and tell her that, but had managed to stop himself from making that mistake. A discussion with Melanie—in her bedroom no less—could not lead to anything but trouble.

Still, he had watched the movie. He hadn't much enjoyed watching the hero twist himself inside out trying to figure out how to win the heroine's heart. If that was what Melanie—or any other woman—wanted from a man, she was fresh out of luck with him.

After watching the end of the video, he'd gone to bed in a foul mood. And he was still feeling cranky and out of sorts when Melanie breezed downstairs in the morning looking fresh as a daisy. Obviously she hadn't lain awake all night grappling with any aspect of their relationship. Or, more precisely, their nonre-lationship.

"You look chipper," he said in a way that even he could hear made "chipper" into a less-than-positive thing.

"Feeling great," she concurred, ignoring his testy tone. "Is that bacon I smell?"

"Yes, and I have batter for waffles, if you want one," he offered.

"Heaven," she said as she poured herself a cup of coffee. "Did you sleep well?"

"Like a baby," he lied.

She gave him a doubtful look but didn't question his claim. "I noticed that the road in front of the house has been plowed. I'm sure you'll be relieved to have me out from underfoot and have this place back to yourself," she said. "I'll take off as soon as I've had something to eat."

Instead of cheering him up, her announcement made him want to dawdle. Because that was so completely ridiculous, he immediately poured batter onto the steaming waffle iron and snapped the lid closed. He took the plateful of bacon he'd microwaved earlier out of the oven where he'd been keeping it warm, then slammed it down on the table with more force than necessary. Melanie gave him another questioning look but remained silent.

"Juice?" he asked. "There's orange." He peered into the refrigerator as if there were some uncertainty, then added, "And cranberry."

"Orange juice would be good," she said, watching him closely. Apparently she could no longer contain her curiosity, because she added with concern, "Richard, are you upset about something?"

"Absolutely not," he said sharply, in a tone guaranteed to contradict his words.

Melanie retreated into wounded silence, which was what he'd been hoping for—wasn't it? Instead, he felt like he'd kicked a friendly puppy.

"Sorry," he muttered. "Obviously I got out of bed on the wrong side this morning."

She shrugged. "Just proves you're human."

"Stop that! Stop letting me off the hook," he snapped, annoyed with her, with himself, with the universe.

She stared at him. "Okay, what's really going on here? Have I missed something? Did you want me to take off right away? Have I tested your patience long enough?"

Richard sighed. "No. It's not you. It's me. To be honest, I don't know what I want. Blame my lousy mood on stress, not enough sleep, whatever."

"You said you slept like a baby."

Naturally she'd been paying close attention to his stupid lie and just had to call him on it. He should have expected that. Frowning, he admitted, "I lied."

"Why?"

"Because you came in here all cheerful and bright eyed and I didn't want you to think I'd lost even a second's sleep last night.'' He kept his gaze firmly fixed on the waffle iron when he made the admission.

''Are we having some sort of competition?'' she asked, sounding genuinely perplexed.

''My entire life has been about competition,'' he muttered, as he snagged the golden waffle, put it on a plate and placed it in front of her.

''With whom? Your brothers?''

He shook his head. ''With myself. I set goals, mostly based on my father's expectations, then I battle with myself to attain them.'' He gave her a wry look. ''So far I'm right on track.''

''But are you happy?'' she asked quietly.

''Of course,'' he said quickly, possibly too quickly.

Melanie kept her steady gaze on him and waited.

''Mostly,'' he amended finally. He'd been completely happy until he'd watched that ridiculous movie and started questioning the lack of a woman in his life.

''What do you win in these competitions of yours?''

''Respect,'' he said immediately.

''You mean self-respect.''

Richard shook his head. ''No, just respect.''

She regarded him quizzically. ''Your father's?'' she asked, her voice incredulous. ''Is that it, Richard? Are you still trying to earn your father's respect?''

As she said it, he heard how ridiculous that sounded. His father had been dead for twenty years. ''That would be impossible,'' he said, shaken by the sudden awareness of what he'd been doing for far too long. He'd been living his life to please a man who could no longer be satisfied—or dissatisfied—with his accomplishments. And overnight he'd been examining his entire life based on a movie premise…and on one offhand comment from a woman who barely knew him.

"Yes," Melanie told him. "It would be. Self-respect is far more important, don't you think?"

This was more self-analysis than Richard could cope with on an empty stomach. "Enough of this," he said brusquely. "How's your waffle?"

Her gaze held his, challenged him, but then she finally let it drop to the forkful of waffle she was holding. "Perfect," she said. "You could always open a restaurant, if you get tired of running a multinational conglomerate."

"We have restaurants," he noted as he sat down with his own plate and poured maple syrup over the waffle.

She chuckled. "I doubt you've seen the inside of the kitchen in any of them."

Richard shrugged. "They have fine chefs and great managers. They don't need me in there. All I care about is the bottom line of that division."

"Adding up all those numbers is what gives you pleasure?" she prodded.

"Of course. It's what I do best. Numbers are logical."

"And that's important to you, isn't it? You need everything in your life to be logical."

He frowned at her. "You say that as if it's a crime."

"Not a crime," she said lightly. "Just not much fun."

How many times had he listened to exactly the same lecture from Destiny? It hadn't bothered him half as much when his aunt had tried to get through to him. "I have fun," he insisted.

"When?"

"All the time."

"Are you talking about all those charity balls you attend?"

He nodded. "Sure."

"Then why do you always look so miserable in the pictures they take for the papers?"

"Miserable?" he repeated, astonished. "I'm always smiling."

Melanie shook her head. "Not with your eyes," she told him. "That's where the truth is, you know, in the eyes."

Richard's gaze automatically sought out her eyes and saw compassion and warmth and even a hint of yearning. She was right. The truth was in the eyes. He wondered if she had any idea what message was shining in hers.

All he knew for certain was that the message scared him to death, because it so closely mirrored what he was trying so damn hard to hide.

"How did your weekend go?" Destiny inquired innocently on Monday morning when she put in one of her rare appearances in Richard's office.

He'd been expecting her today, though. He was ready for her, or at least he thought he was. "The house is still standing, if that's what you're asking. I came away without any broken bones."

"And Melanie?"

"I didn't strangle her." He gave his aunt a hard look. "What are you up to, Destiny? I know what you told Melanie, but I'm not buying the innocent act. I want the truth.''

"I'm trying to find you a good marketing person," his aunt claimed. "Did you even look at her proposal?''

He had. He'd studied it in the wee hours of Sunday morning when he'd been unable to sleep for thinking about the movie…and about Melanie's presence in the guest room. She was an annoying little chatterbox, but she'd been growing on him. The entire weekend he'd been able to think of only one way to shut her up. Since she'd ruled that out, she'd wisely scampered off to bed alone and he'd stayed up nursing the last of the wine while he watched that ridiculous comedy with its feel-good happy ending. When was real life ever like that?

Suddenly aware that Destiny was regarding him with an amused expression, he tried to focus on their conversation. "She has some interesting ideas," he conceded.

"Then hire her.''

"She's ditzy," he said, falling back on his original impression because recent impressions were far too complicated. "She'd drive me crazy in a week. Maybe less.'' He knew that for a fact, because she'd driven him crazy in just two days. She'd upended his need for logic and made him crave all sorts of things he'd never expected to need. She'd tapped into emotions he'd spent a lifetime avoiding.

"What's wrong with that?" Destiny asked, her eyes filled with knowing laughter.

Richard cringed. It was almost as if Destiny had been an eyewitness to the way Melanie had rattled him and thoroughly approved of it. Maybe she was merely psychic. Whatever, if she got it into her head that her scheme was working, she'd never let up.

Before he could list all the things wrong with any kind of relationship with Melanie—business or otherwise—she said, "You need someone around to drive you crazy. Everyone else in your life bows to your every whim."

"You don't," he pointed out.

"Yes, but I'm your aunt. I might get on your nerves, but you cut me a lot of slack."

"I'll cut you a lot less now that you've sent Melanie into my life," he vowed.

She laughed, clearly unintimidated. "If you don't hire her, you'll regret it."

In Richard's opinion, if he didn't sleep with her, he'd regret that more, but he wasn't about to share that insight with his aunt. Especially since it was probably exactly what she'd had in mind in the first place when she arranged all of this.

He really needed to get on the phone with Mack and Ben and warn his brothers that their aunt was dedicating herself to playing matchmaker these days. If she tired of her lack of success with him, they were definitely next in line. He owed them the heads-up. Then, again, it might be more fun to let her take them by surprise, the way she'd sneaked up on him.

"Why don't you meddle in Mack's life?" he suggested hopefully. "Or Ben's?"

Destiny's eyes sparkled with merriment. "What makes you think I haven't?" she inquired blithely, then turned and sailed out of his office, leaving him speechless and not one bit closer to being off the hook.

* * *

Melanie stared glumly at the Carlton Industries folder on her desk. It had been such a wonderful opportunity for her, but the odds of Richard ever changing his mind and hiring her were so astronomical, she might as well run the folder through the shredder.

She was genuinely considering doing just that when Becky came in with two cups of latte and cranberry scones from the café down the street. She held them just out of Melanie's reach.

"If I give you these, will you tell me everything that went on between you and Richard Carlton this weekend?" she asked.

"No," Melanie said, snatching the coffee out of her friend's hand. She could live without the scone if she had to. Caffeine was another story.

"Testy, aren't you? It must not have gone very well."

"That depends on your definition of success," Melanie replied, taking her first sip of the heavenly latte. "He didn't toss me out in the snow."

"Interesting," Becky said with a thoughtful expression. "Then you were stranded there all weekend?"

"Yes."

"And with all that time on your hands, you couldn't convince him to hire you?"

"I never even convinced him to read the proposal," she admitted grimly. "I was just about to shred my copy and write the whole thing off as a loss."

Becky stared at her in shock. "What kind of defeatist attitude is that? You never give up."

"I do when the odds of winning are impossible."

Becky's gaze narrowed. "Did he seduce you?"

Melanie scowled at her. "No."

"Did he at least try?"

Melanie thought back over the weekend and the dance they'd played. Richard had tossed out a proposition, she'd dodged it, he'd parried, then she'd taken a turn muddying the waters. "It was a bit confusing," she said finally.

"Then he did try," Becky concluded. "And you what?"

"I said no, of course."

"And then?"

"What makes you think that wasn't the end of it?"

Becky gave her a knowing look. "It was a long weekend."

"Okay, then I threw myself at him."

"Interesting."

"No, stupid. I corrected the mistake almost immediately."

"Almost?"

"Soon enough," Melanie said. "I didn't sleep with him. In fact, I only kissed him once. No big deal."

"Oh, right. The sexiest, richest man in all of Alexandria, maybe in the entire Washington metropolitan region, kisses you, and it's no big deal."

Melanie sighed. "Okay, the kiss *was* a big deal, but that's as far as it went and it won't be happening again. He couldn't get me out of there fast enough yesterday morning."

"Probably because he was tempted," Becky concluded. "Men do that, you know. They act all weird and crazy when they're losing control."

Melanie heard something in Becky's voice, a faint catch, that hinted she was no longer talking about the weekend Melanie had just shared with a prospective client. "Something happen with you and Jason?" Jason was the love of Becky's life, or so she'd persuaded herself. He was the fourth one this year, but even Melanie was almost convinced he was a keeper.

Becky's eyes immediately clouded up. "We broke up. More precisely, he broke up with me."

That was new. Usually Becky was the one running for cover. Melanie tried to muster the appropriate amount of sympathy, which was getting harder and harder to do. It was somewhat easier with Jason, because she'd genuinely liked him. She'd even thought Becky had gotten it right for once. "Oh, sweetie, I'm so sorry. I know you thought he was the one."

"He is the one," Becky said fiercely. "He's just being stubborn and scared and stupid."

"It's really hard to argue with stubborn, scared and stupid," Melanie pointed out. "You should know. You've done it often enough yourself."

"But if it's what you want, you have to fight for it, right?"

"I suppose."

Becky gave her a challenging look. "Okay, then. I will if you will."

"Meaning?" Melanie asked cautiously.

"I'll keep fighting for what I have—what I want— with Jason, if you'll keep fighting for Richard."

"This isn't about Richard and me. What's going on with us isn't personal," Melanie replied irritably. "It's about the Carlton Industries contract."

Becky gave her a sympathetic look. "Oh, sweetie, it might have started that way, but it's taken on a whole new twist. I can see it in your eyes, hear it in your voice. The sooner you wake up and accept that, the better off you'll be."

"It's about the contract," Melanie insisted stubbornly.

"Fine. Whatever gets you to pick up the phone and call the man," Becky said.

"I will not call him. The ball's in his court."

"Not if you packed up all the balls and brought them with you when you left his house," Becky said, then sighed heavily. "Okay, never mind. I recognize that tone. I'll stop pushing. Just promise me you won't shred the file."

Melanie stared at the file she'd been fingering throughout the conversation as if it were some sort of talisman that linked her to Richard. "Fine. I won't destroy the file." She stared hard at Becky. "And you won't call Jason."

"But—"

"No, buts," Melanie said firmly. "Let the man grovel for once. You know he will."

"Eventually," Becky agreed confidently. Her cheerful mood returned. "Before I land him, the man is going to have groveling down to a fine art."

"Now there's a goal." Melanie regarded Becky wistfully. "I wonder if Richard knows the first thing about groveling?" She thought of how goal oriented he claimed to be and sighed. "Doubtful," she concluded.

"Maybe he's trainable," Becky suggested.

Destiny had had a certain amount of luck teaching him manners, but she'd started at a relatively early age. Melanie had a hunch she was catching Richard far too late to change his ingrained habits.

Too bad, too, because more than once over the weekend, she thought he'd displayed amazing possibilities…and not one of them had anything at all to do with his candidacy for City Council.

She was still pondering that when the phone rang. Becky picked it up.

"Hart Consulting," she said cheerfully, then listened, her expression going from surprised to dismayed so quickly that Melanie's heart was thudding when Becky finally handed over the receiver.

Becky punched the hold button before Melanie could speak. "Prepare yourself. It's that columnist from the morning paper. He's asking about you and Richard."

"About the consulting?" Melanie asked hopefully.

Becky shook her head. "About the weekend you spent together. He seems to have details."

Oh, hell. This was a publicist's worst nightmare, even when she wasn't personally involved. Worse, it was too late to duck the call. Melanie sucked in a deep breath and prepared for some fancy tap dancing. She had to find out how much the reporter knew, or thought he knew.

"This is Melanie Hart," she said briskly.

"Pete Forsythe, Ms. Hart. How are you? We met at the heart association gala last month."

"Of course, I remember you, Mr. Forsythe. What can I do for you?"

"I'm looking for confirmation on something I heard this morning from an extremely reliable source."

"Oh?"

"It involves you and Carlton Industries CEO and chairman Richard Carlton."

"Really? I can't imagine where you'd hear anything linking the two of us in any way. I barely know Mr. Carlton.''

"But you do know him," he persisted.

"We've met.''

"Is there any truth to the rumor that the two of you are involved? That you spent this weekend with him at a family cottage at the beach?''

Melanie's laugh sounded forced, even to her. "Don't be ridiculous. As I said, I barely know the man. Sorry, Mr. Forsythe. I can't help you.'' She hung up before he could press her into saying something she'd regret, something that would send Richard into a blind rage.

"Is he going to print an item anyway?'' Becky asked.

"More than likely.''

"Are you going to warn Richard?''

Melanie considered it and decided it wouldn't help anything. She hadn't given anything away. Richard might be angry enough to call Pete Forsythe and protest the man's intrusion into his privacy, which would only add fuel to the fire. Better to let Forsythe think that there was no fire, that the rumor was off the mark. Maybe then, if he had even the tiniest shred of integrity, he'd have second thoughts about printing it.

"No," she told Becky. "Maybe without my confirmation, Forsythe will conclude that there's nothing to the gossip and drop it.''

Becky promptly shook her head. "I think you're being blindly optimistic. This is too juicy. I'd certainly want to know if a powerful man like Carlton, who's thinking of running for office, was holed up in a cozy little getaway with a major PR consultant. That's hot stuff in this town. With what he has now, he can spin it a lot of different ways. An intimate rendezvous? A campaign strategy session that confirms Richard's intention to run for Council? Either way, it's news.''

Melanie couldn't deny that. She could only pray that Pete Forsythe was the kind of reporter who'd want confirmation from at least one of the participants before printing anything, before deciding on what angle to pursue. He hadn't gotten any sort of confirmation from her, and she doubted he'd risk going straight to Richard. Carlton Industries spent a lot of money in advertising, and Richard was a powerful man in the business community. Would Forsythe or his paper risk offending him for a titillating tidbit in tomorrow's paper? The story could still die, she told herself staunchly. Really.

Sure, she thought grimly, and pigs could fly.

Chapter Seven

"Why was one of Alexandria's most eligible bachelors huddling in a secret hideaway with a marketing expert last weekend?" Pete Forsythe's insider column in the Washington paper asked a few days later. "Could it be that Carlton Industries CEO Richard Carlton is finally getting ready for that long-rumored plunge into politics? Or was this *rendezvous* personal? He's not talking and neither is the woman, but we've confirmed that he was tucked away during last weekend's snowstorm with Melanie Hart, an up-and-coming star on the local marketing and public relations scene."

Richard tossed the newspaper in the trash where it belonged and buzzed his secretary. "Winifred, get Melanie Hart over here now!"

"Yes, sir."

Melanie must have been lurking in the lobby, because she was in his office in less than ten minutes. She looked good, too. Great, in fact, as if she'd prepared for just the right look to get him to pay more attention to her than this situation she'd created by blabbing their business all over town. If she was still trying to convince him to hire her, she'd gone about it all wrong. He was fit to be tied.

"I had a feeling I'd be hearing from you. I was already on my way over here," she told him, studying him worriedly. "I saw the paper this morning. How furious are you?"

"On a scale of one to ten, I'd say twelve thousand," he retorted. "I do not intend to play out my campaign intentions or my personal life in some damned gossip column. You ought to know that."

She stared at him a minute, apparently absorbing his barely disguised accusation, then said icily, "I do. I know it, not because I have a clue what goes on in that impossibly hard head of yours, but because it's a bad strategy. It diminishes you as a candidate to have people perceive that you're sneaking around with a woman for any reason whatsoever."

Richard was taken aback by her blunt response. What made her think she could get away with being some sort of victim? He scowled right back at her. "Then what the hell were you thinking?" There it was. He'd said it. Now let her dance around and try to avoid the obvious. Only the two of them knew about the weekend, and he'd never spoken to Forsythe.

"Me?" she said, radiating indignation. "I had nothing to do with this. This isn't exactly great for my reputation, either."

His frown deepened, but for an instant his fury wavered. She'd made the denial sound almost believable. His temper cooled marginally as he struggled to give her the benefit of the doubt. What she'd said made sense. He regarded her intently, wanting desperately to believe she hadn't betrayed him. "Then you're swearing to me that you did not plant that item?"

She gave him another one of those withering looks intended to make him feel like slime.

"Absolutely not," she swore.

Richard knew then that he owed her an apology, but he couldn't quite bring himself to utter it, not without asking a few more questions. "Did you speak to Forsythe?"

Her expression faltered at that. "Yes, but—"

Richard seized on the admission, not even waiting for her explanation. "Why the hell would you even take his call? I didn't. He never got past my secretary. No good can ever come from talking to a gossip columnist. You're a professional. You should know that."

"What I know is that sometimes a *reporter* can be an ally, if you know when to talk and what to say," she retorted. "Besides, I was already committed to taking the call before I knew why he was calling. As soon as I realized what he was after, I thought it would be wise to find out exactly what he'd heard. Once he started asking questions about you and me being at the cottage, I danced around the answers and hung up."

Richard sighed. She was making too damned much sense to be flat-out lying. "Then you never confirmed the story?"

She scowled at him. "Do I look that stupid?"

"Then who the hell was so reliable that Forsythe would print the story without confirmation from one of us? Someone in your office?"

"No. Becky would never do something like that."

"Not even in some misguided attempt to do you a favor?"

"Never."

"Who else knew you were down there?" he demanded, then stared at her stricken face as understanding dawned on both of them. He said it first. "Destiny, of course."

Even though she'd clearly been leaning in the same direction, Melanie looked genuinely shocked that he would accuse his aunt of betraying them. "Surely, she wouldn't do such a thing?"

Richard's laugh was forced. "Oh, yes, she would, especially if she thought planting that story in the paper would accomplish her goal."

"Do you know what her goal is? Because frankly, I'm a little confused."

"No, you're not. You've already confronted her about it. She wants us together," he said grimly. If he hadn't known it before, he did now. This was the act of a very determined matchmaker.

"You mean me working for you," Melanie replied, still trying for a positive spin.

"No, *together* together," he said impatiently. "A couple."

Melanie turned pale, and for the first time since entering his office, she sank onto a chair. "Are you sure?"

"Oh, yes. I know my aunt and she's all but admitted as much, though if she'd been half as good at skirting the truth with Forsythe as she was with me, we wouldn't be in this mess. That tells me she very deliberately spilled the beans.''

"This is crazy," Melanie said. "She can't just manipulate us into doing what she wants. We're two reasonable adults who are perfectly capable of making our own decisions, and we've decided that we're completely unsuited." She met his gaze. "Haven't we?"

"That was the way we left it this weekend," Richard agreed.

"Then all we need to do is tell her that."

"I did."

"And?"

He dragged the paper out of the trash and waved it in her direction. "This was her response. She's obviously not giving up."

"She's your aunt. Do something."

Richard gave her a rueful look. He'd never been any good at thwarting Destiny when she was on a mission. It was smarter to give in than to wait to be mowed down. Maybe Melanie would have a better tactic.

"Any suggestions?" he asked.

He waited as her expression turned thoughtful, then forlorn.

"None," she said finally. "You? You know her better than I do. Surely you can think of something to get her off this tangent."

Short of strangling her, there weren't a lot of viable options, even fewer he could live with. It struck Richard that they were simply going to have to play this out. He felt only minimally guilty that he didn't feel nearly as bad about that as he probably should. Still, he managed a resigned air as he said grimly, "Then we have absolutely no choice. We give her what she wants."

Melanie stared. "Huh?"

He grinned. "I thought you were quicker to catch on to things."

"Not this," she admitted. "This seems a little out there, like a publicity stunt that's doomed to failure."

"It'll work. Trust me," Richard said, injecting a note of certainty into his voice.

"Let me be sure I have this straight," Melanie said, as if she were grappling with a Nobel Prize caliber physics theory. "You're suggesting that you and I pretend to be together to get Destiny to back off?"

Watching the flash of heat in Melanie's eyes, Richard began to warm to the idea. The part of himself he'd been struggling to ignore all weekend long was ecstatic about this new strategy, despite its obvious risks. In fact, he had no intention of looking too closely at the risks.

"That is exactly what I mean," he said, trying not to sound too eager.

Melanie looked doubtful, not disgusted. He took that as a good sign.

"Won't she be hard to convince?" she asked.

Richard considered his aunt's insightful nature. "Very hard," he agreed. In this case, that might work to his advantage. It would buy him some time to see if these odd feelings of his when he was around Melanie really meant anything. Since he'd never experienced anything quite like them before, he couldn't be sure.

"Then where are we going to draw the line?"

Richard studied the woman seated on the edge of her chair, bright patches of color in her otherwise pale cheeks. "We might have to be a little flexible on that."

Melanie shook her head. "I don't think so," she said adamantly. "Couldn't you just hire me, the way she asked you to? Wouldn't that satisfy her?"

"Sweetheart, I think it's fairly clear by now that that was just a smoke screen. Heaven knows why, but she won't be happy till we've walked down the aisle."

Horror registered on Melanie's face. "I am not marrying you."

"No kidding," he said, more than ready to agree with her on that. Not even he was prepared to carry this charade to that extreme, but a few weeks of getting close to Melanie and giving Destiny what she so clearly wanted held a certain undeniable appeal. "I think we can draw the line there. No marriage."

"No sleeping together, either," she added, giving him a hard stare. "I want to be clear about that, too."

"We might have to negotiate on that one," he said, feeling a whole lot better about things. Maybe he could turn this into a win-win situation instead of a disaster, after all. "So, Ms. Hart, you're hired."

She blinked in confusion. "As your new marketing person?"

"No. As my fiancée-to-be. No pay, but there will be a lot of perks."

"You want me to market myself to your aunt as your fiancée?" she asked, her expression incredulous.

"Fiancée-to-be," he corrected. "For starters."

"Whatever," Melanie said dismissively. "Isn't that a huge leap? She can't possibly think we're engaged or even about to be engaged. We've just barely met, and she knows that first meeting did not go well at all.''

''Ah, but last weekend,'' Richard said, affecting a tone of pure rapture.

''Oh, stuff a sock in it,'' Melanie said irritably. ''She won't buy an engagement this quickly. She's too smart for that. She might think I'm dumb enough to fall for you in ten seconds flat, but she's bound to know that you're not the type to fall in love at first sight. Heck, you've probably already told her that I'm not your type.''

He flushed at that. ''Doesn't matter. Destiny is a romantic at heart,'' Richard said. He'd never noticed that about his aunt before, but her meddling was giving him whole new insights into her personality quirks. ''She wants us together. If we go out a few times, let her catch us kissing from time to time, then say we're engaged in a week or two, trust me, she won't look any deeper.''

''This is crazy,'' Melanie said again. ''There has to be some other way besides lying to your aunt.''

He gazed into her eyes. ''Let me be clear about something. This isn't just about my aunt, Melanie. After Forsythe's column, we have to convince the entire world that you and I fell madly, passionately in love and can't bear to be apart.'' He gave her a wry look. ''It was the last thing either of us expected, of course.''

''Of course,'' Melanie said with a decidedly sarcastic edge to her voice.

He picked up his pen and made a note to start arranging some family get-togethers, then glanced at Melanie, who looked as if she might be about to explode. ''We're all set, then, right?''

She stared at him incredulously. "No, we are not all set. I hate this."

"I'm not crazy about it myself, but I can't see any other solution. We have to make it real. People will forgive a prospective candidate a lot if there's love involved. They're not so forgiving of sleazy affairs."

She was shaking her head. "I don't think so."

"Do you have a better plan to extricate us from this?"

She regarded him with an undeniable hint of desperation in her eyes, then sighed. "No."

He took pity on her. "I'll let you stage a bang-up scene when you dump me," he offered, fairly sure that a chance to humiliate him would appeal to her baser instincts. It might make her feel better about letting him back her into this corner, which, frankly, was more fun than he'd had in ages. Maybe he did owe Destiny, after all.

As he'd predicted, Melanie looked intrigued by the prospect of getting even. "In public?" she bargained.

"Won't be any fun if it's not in public," he agreed, willing to endure the humiliation if it gave him a few weeks to woo Melanie into his bed. That was his short-term—his *only*—goal. He had to remember that. Getting even with Destiny, getting public perception back on his side, those were purely a bonus. Happily-ever-after was out of the question. He didn't believe in it. Or, perhaps more accurately, he didn't trust himself to want it.

"How long do we carry out the charade before I get to dump you?" Melanie inquired.

Richard gave the question the serious consideration it deserved. Melanie had a right to know how much of a commitment she was making. "For as long as it takes to get Destiny off our backs and make it believable for everybody else.''

"A month?" she asked hopefully.

"She'll never buy it."

"Two?"

"How about six and we'll see where we stand?" He gazed deeper into her eyes. "There's no one in your life who'll object, is there?"

"Sadly, no," she said. "Believe me, I'd love to have an excuse to get out of this." She gave him a knowing look. "But you knew that, didn't you?"

"I was reasonably confident that you wouldn't have traipsed after me to that cottage if there had been an important man in your life."

Her gaze narrowed. "I came down there on business. Even if there was a man in my life, he wouldn't have the right to object to me taking a business trip."

"He wouldn't have left you down there, snowbound with me, though, would he? Not if he had an ounce of sense. He'd have been there to rescue you by dawn on Saturday."

"Nothing happened that needed to be explained or forgiven," she retorted, eyes flashing.

Richard gave her an innocent look. "Really? Here I thought that was when we fell in love."

Melanie groaned. "Do you have any idea how much I hate this?" she asked again.

"You've mentioned that," he admitted. "But you're going to go along with it, aren't you?"

For a minute it almost looked as if she might balk, but then she finally nodded.

At her acquiescence—albeit reluctant—Richard felt the oddest sensation in his chest. It felt a whole lot like relief. Or maybe elation. He couldn't be sure. It wasn't a sensation he'd ever experienced before. That was happening a lot lately.

Melanie's head was spinning. She had just agreed to pose as Richard's almost-fiancée for the foreseeable future. There was no question in her mind that this was going to be a role she could handle by making an occasional appearance by his side in public. He was going to insist that she give it her all to make it believable, at least to one person. Unfortunately for both of them, there was also little doubt that Destiny was going to be a hard sell.

So why try? Melanie asked herself that repeatedly on the drive back to her office. Why had she agreed to this? Because she'd felt guilty over that stupid item in the morning paper? That hadn't been her doing. Because she had some insane idea that this was the only way to get Destiny to leave them alone? Richard might be convinced of that, but she wasn't. Not entirely, anyway. So, what was the real reason?

Because some teeny-tiny, totally insane part of her wanted it to be true. Even as the thought crept in, she was shouting no-no-no to herself as emphatically as she possibly could. The noise was so loud in her head, she barely heard the cell phone when it rang. Relieved to have an excuse to turn off her own chaotic thoughts, she punched the button on the dash that put the call on speaker.

"Yes," she barked.

"Show time," Richard said.

"What?"

"We're having dinner with Destiny tonight."

"How did that happen? I just left you ten minutes

ago. Word couldn't have gotten back to her that quickly.''

"I called," he told her without the least hint of regret. "Preemptive strike.''

"Are you crazy? I haven't even gotten used to the idea. I'll bungle this.''

"Just follow my lead. I'll pick you up at seven. Wear something glamorous. Destiny likes to dress for dinner.''

He hung up before Melanie could get a vehement objection to cross her lips. What was he thinking? Maybe he figured it was like swimming—better to toss her into the deep end to test her mettle than to wishy-wash around in the kiddie pool for weeks.

If she was going to do this, she needed help. She punched speed dial for her office.

"Becky, I need you to meet me at Chez Deux in ten minutes.''

"Why?''

"I'll explain when I see you. Dig a charge card out of the office safe.''

"Which one?''

"The one with the biggest credit line," she said grimly.

Under other circumstances, Melanie loved to shop. Not that she was ever extravagant, not with a comparatively new business to run, but she loved clothes. Chez Deux with its line of secondhand designer clothes suited her budget and her desire to dress for success. Normally, however, she was picking suits off the rack, not evening wear. If she forgot the reason for this shopping expedition, it could still be fun.

She found a parking space a block away, then

trudged carefully over the cobblestone sidewalks to avoid the occasional patch of leftover ice.

"Hey, Jasmin," she greeted the owner when she got to the classy little shop, which accepted consignments from many of Washington's best-dressed women.

"Ms. Hart, how nice to see you," Jasmin Trudeau said. "We have some lovely new suits in your size."

"Not today. Today I'm looking for something a little fancier, for a formal dinner party."

The petite woman's eyes lit up. "Then the rumors are true, *n'est-ce pas?* I saw the story in this morning's paper."

Melanie wanted to deny it, but Jasmin was one of the city's biggest sources of socialite gossip. If Melanie declared the story entirely untrue, it would be all over town by evening, pretty much defeating this charade she and Richard were embarking on.

"I am having dinner with Mr. Carlton tonight," she admitted, leaving it at that.

"Then you must look your very best. I have just the thing," Jasmin said. "It came in only yesterday. I have not even put it on the rack yet. One moment and I will get it for you."

Becky arrived just then, looking harried and curious. "What on earth is going on?"

"I'm buying a dress," Melanie said.

"I got that much. What kind of dress and why?"

"A fancy, expensive dress. I need the fortification."

Becky stared at her blankly. "Huh?"

"Let me get this over with, and I'll take you out for a long leisurely lunch, so you can tell me I haven't completely lost my mind."

Becky hid her disappointment and silenced her questions as Jasmin reappeared with a strapless dress in bronze satin.

"This dress was made for you," Jasmin said. "Do not look at the price. If it looks as fabulous on you as I think it will, you will not care what it costs."

Melanie was already itching to slip the rich fabric over her head. She took it gingerly and headed for a dressing room. In seconds she had stripped off her clothes and slipped the dress on. Only when she had it zipped up did she risk a look in the mirror. "Oh, my," she whispered. She felt like Cinderella after she was outfitted for the ball, not quite like herself...or maybe more like herself than she'd ever been before.

"Hey, stop hiding in there and get out here," Becky commanded. "Jasmin and I are dying of curiosity."

Melanie stepped out of the dressing room. Both women's eyes widened.

"You look *fabulous*," Becky said.

"Mr. Carlton will not be able to resist you," Jasmin added, as if that were a bonus.

Before Becky could ask what the heck the other woman meant by that, Melanie said quickly, "I'll take the dress." Jasmin had been right. She didn't care what it cost. Whatever it was, it was a small price to pay to walk into Destiny's house tonight feeling confident as she and Richard launched this charade. And she could always have it cleaned and bring it right back here on consignment to recoup some of the cost, though something told her she would never give it up.

Once she'd added an outrageously expensive jeweled purse, she signed the credit-card slip without giving it a second glance. Maybe if her accountant turned a blind eye, she could figure out some way to turn this into a business expense.

When the transaction was completed, she took her purchases to her car. Becky trailed along behind, muttering a barrage of questions that Melanie determinedly ignored. Only when her packages were stowed away and they were seated in a nearby restaurant with coffee on the table and salads on the way did she finally look her friend in the eye.

"You have to promise that you will never breathe one single word of what I am about to tell you," she told Becky. "Not one word. Not to your own mother. Not even to a lawyer, a priest or anyone else sworn to uphold your confidentiality."

Becky solemnly crossed her heart. "My God, Melanie, what have you done? You didn't kill Pete Forsythe, did you?"

"No, though in retrospect, that might have made more sense than this."

"Then you saw Richard?"

"Oh, yeah."

"And he was furious?"

"About as furious as I anticipated when I told you I was going over there this morning to try to head off an explosion."

"Did you figure out who leaked the story?"

"He's convinced it was Destiny."

"His own aunt?" Becky said incredulously.

Melanie nodded. "It gets worse. He's also convinced she won't be happy until he and I really are involved, so he's decided we need to pretend that we are."

Becky blinked hard, then her expression slowly

changed to comprehension. "That explains the dress."

"Yep. We're having dinner with Destiny tonight."

"You actually went along with this?" Becky asked, sounding incredulous. "You're going to lie to a woman who befriended you?"

"A woman who befriended me with ulterior motives," Melanie corrected. "It's a fine point, but an important one."

"Oh, brother."

Melanie met Becky's gaze. "Am I crazy?"

"Probably."

"Is there any way this can not go horribly wrong?"

"Not that I can see," Becky said, sounding surprisingly cheerful.

"Why are you suddenly finding this so amusing?" Melanie demanded.

"Because you are both so obviously delusional."

"Why do you say that?"

"Richard thinks he's doing this to get even with his aunt, am I right?"

"Yes."

"And you're doing it out of some misguided sense of guilt, correct?"

Melanie nodded.

"Ha!"

Melanie frowned at her. "What is that supposed to mean?"

"You're both doing it because you want it to be true. He wants to be involved with you. You want to be involved with him. Neither of you is willing to be honest about it." Becky took a little bow. "You're welcome."

Melanie gave her a sour look. "I didn't thank you."

"You should have," Becky told her. "It's the most honest thing that's been said at this table since we sat down."

Melanie opened her mouth to deny it, then snapped her mouth shut again. There had been enough lies and half-truths and deceptions floating around today.

"This really is going to be a disaster, isn't it?" she said eventually.

Becky nodded without hesitation. "That would be my assessment, yes." She gave Melanie a sympathetic look. "You could still fix it."

"How?"

"Make it real."

"No. Neither of us wants that."

Becky rolled her eyes.

"Okay, Richard doesn't want that and I'm almost certain I don't, either. We hardly know each other, but I do know he's a man who's not in touch with his feelings, he's still a potential client and he's stodgy. Those are all things that make him bad for me."

"You're hopeless," Becky said. "At least I'm in touch with my feelings." She grinned. "Jason is groveling, by the way. It's lovely."

"Good for Jason." She gave Becky a defeated look. "How am I going to fix this?"

"You're obviously not, at least not the mature, intelligent way, since you won't acknowledge the truth. That means you have to go with the flow."

"I'm lousy at going with the flow," Melanie reminded her.

Becky grinned. "I know. That's what's going to make this so much fun to watch."

Chapter Eight

Richard rarely questioned his decisions once he'd made them. Having second thoughts was the mark of a man who didn't know his own mind, and he prided himself on his clarity of thought. Or he had until today.

Now that the dust had settled over that ridiculous rumor in the morning paper, he realized that talk would have died down in a day or two with no real harm done. That was how he should have handled it, simply let it go away of its own accord. Instead, he'd turned it into this big charade that was going to turn his life inside out for weeks, maybe even months to come.

He'd gotten caught up in the heat of the moment. He'd wanted to pay Destiny back for her meddling. He'd wanted to go on spending time with Melanie without having her underfoot professionally. That was both unfair and insulting. He was surprised she'd gone along with it. She should have told him to take a hike. He couldn't help wondering why she hadn't. Maybe she was suffering from the same momentary lunacy that was affecting him.

Now he'd gone and compounded his mistake by deciding to drag a perfectly nice woman into his aunt's web of intrigue, when he should have been doing everything in his power to keep the two of them as far apart as humanly possible. His head pounded just thinking about what dinner was going to be like.

Hoping for backup, he picked up the phone and called his brother Mack.

"Well, well, if it isn't the newly proclaimed Romeo of the family," Mack taunted when he heard Richard's voice.

"Go to hell."

Mack laughed. Mack was used to having his name bandied all over town, linked with a different socialite each time. Richard was not.

"As soon as you're through enjoying this, I have a favor to ask," Richard announced grimly.

"Anything," Mack said, instantly sober. "You know that. Should I go over to the paper and put the fear of God into Pete Forsythe? I've been dying to have a legitimate excuse for a long time now. Unfortunately, most of what he reports about me is true. The man's a menace to the privacy of all bachelors."

"Not worth getting your knuckles roughed up," Richard said.

"I wasn't planning to resort to brute force, despite my reputation from the football field," Mack said, sounding wounded that Richard thought so little of him. "I can be intimidating in other ways."

Richard chuckled despite his lousy mood. "Believe me, I am aware of that. Actually, though, I was hoping you'd back me up at Destiny's tonight. Intimidate her a little."

"Oh, no," Mack said. "She is obviously on one of her matchmaking tears. When she gets this way, I prefer flying under her radar."

"Believe me, she's going to be too busy focusing on me tonight to worry about you," Richard told him. "I'm taking Melanie Hart to dinner."

Mack whistled. "Oh, brother, you are living dangerously, aren't you? Or is something really going on between you and this woman?"

"There is nothing going on," Richard assured him. "But I want Destiny to think otherwise."

"Why the hell would you want that?"

"I'm hoping Destiny will back off if she's convinced I'm doing exactly what she wanted," Richard explained. "And if you tell another living, breathing soul I said that, I'll make sure that Destiny tries to hook you up with the most avaricious, impossible female in this entire region. Believe me, I know some of the worst. I'll give her a list of candidates guaranteed to make your life miserable."

"Speaking of intimidation," Mack said quietly, "you're not bad at it yourself."

"Thank you. Will you be there?"

"How could I possibly refuse such a gracious invitation to dine with my family?" Mack said with a sarcastic bite to his voice. "Are you calling Ben?"

"No, I think you'll do for now."

"But baby brother might enjoy this," Mack objected. "He's never seen you on the ropes before.

We've always thought you were invincible, afraid of nothing."

"Very amusing. Besides, Ben doesn't enjoy anything that means he has to leave his farm in Middleburg and stop brooding for an entire evening. On top of that, he's too honest for conspiracies."

"And I'm not?" Mack inquired with a touch of indignation.

"Not even close. You thrive on them. That's why you're so good at using sneaky, clever tactics to lure the best, most unavailable football talent to your team," Richard said. "Seven-thirty, okay?"

"Despite the number of times you've insulted me in this conversation, I'll be there," Mack promised. "Hope I can keep a straight face."

"Consider the alternative," Richard told him grimly.

After he'd hung up, he kept staring at the phone. He loved his brother. He knew Mack would go to the mat for him or for Ben, but an actor? No way. It was entirely possible he'd just made his second-worst mistake of the day. Apparently he was on a real roll.

Melanie had anticipated a barrage of last-minute instructions from Richard on the drive to his aunt's. Instead, beyond an approving once-over and a friendly-enough greeting when he'd picked her up, he'd remained stoically silent. It was getting on her nerves.

"Don't you think maybe we should go over our plan?" she asked finally.

He glanced at her then, the line of his jaw hard. "You think I actually have a plan?"

"I was hoping for one, yes. You have a reputation

for being very organized, for leaving nothing to chance.''

His laugh sounded forced. ''So I do. Apparently it's my day for doing the unexpected.''

''So there really is no plan,'' she surmised, feeling suddenly queasy. She could wing it with a mob of reporters, but this? This was definitely not a situation in which she should be flying by the seat of her pants. Surely, Richard should understand that. She cleared her throat. ''Um, don't you think maybe we should stop for a second and get a few things straight?''

This time when he glanced her way, his gaze lingered. ''You really are nervous, aren't you?''

''Well, duh! What do you think? I am about to face a woman I like and respect and pretend that I'm falling for her favorite nephew. I anticipate a lot of questions. Don't you?''

''I'm not her favorite. Destiny doesn't have favorites. She's always been very clear about that.'' He grinned. ''Mack and I both know it's Ben. He has her artistic talent, if not her quixotic nature. Mack loves sports, which she doesn't get at all, and she thinks I'm stuffy.''

''Okay, whatever,'' Melanie retorted, not sounding remotely sympathetic. ''The point is that we're lying to her and we don't have our stories straight.''

''Mack will be there. He'll be a good buffer. He's quite a talker. We may not have to say much.''

She stared at him in shock. ''Oh, goody. I get to lie to your brother, too.''

''No, he gets that this is a sham.''

Her stomach dropped. ''And that's better? You expect him to lie, too?''

''No, I expect him to take some of the heat off of

us. Mack has a way of stirring Destiny up. You'll see. It's actually rather fascinating to watch.''

"Why on earth would your brother agree to be a party to this?" When Richard didn't answer, she reached her own conclusion. "You bribed him, didn't you? Or threatened him?''

He frowned at that. "Only in a brotherly kind of way," he insisted as if that made it so much better. "I told him if he didn't help, I could see to it that Destiny turned her misguided attentions on him.''

"And?" She knew there was more. There had to be.

"I might have hinted that I could influence the choice she made and that the woman might not be to Mack's liking.''

Melanie regarded him with dismay. "Do you hate your brother that much?''

"Of course not," he said, staring at her as if she were crazy.

"Then why would you even suggest such a thing, given how thrilled you are to be in this particular mess?''

"Misery loves company," he suggested glibly.

Melanie merely buried her face in her hands and prayed for a quick end to the entire evening.

Melanie didn't seem happy, which made two of them, Richard concluded as he pulled into the three-car garage at what had once been his home. The brick town house in Old Town Alexandria combined two old homes into one gracious enough for entertaining and big enough for the large family his parents had anticipated. It had black shutters and brass trim and an occasional tendril of ivy that had escaped the gardener's attention climbing up the pink brick.

In recent years Destiny had remained there as first he, then Mack and then Ben had moved into homes of their own. For the first time he considered that maybe his aunt was doing all this matchmaking craziness because she was lonely. Too bad he couldn't fix *her* up. Maybe that would end this madness.

Unfortunately, even the thought of trying to turn the tables and hook Destiny up with some man made him smile. His aunt would not be amused. Her personal life was not a topic he or his brothers approached without serious trepidation. She always cut them off before they could complete their first query. He would have thought that a woman so tight-lipped about her own intimate secrets would be more careful about sticking her nose into his.

As he got out of the car, he took a second look at the flashy red convertible she'd bought recently and shook his head. It was entirely possible she was going through some sort of midlife crisis, though come to think of it the convertible suited her personality a whole lot better than the minivans she'd driven when they were boys.

"Your aunt loves that car," Melanie noted. "I was with her when she bought it."

He regarded her with surprise. "You were?" Then he recalled the rest of the story. "You were the woman who ran into her car that day and totaled it? That's how the two of you met?"

Melanie winced. "I thought you knew."

He shook his head. "This just gets better and better. I thought she'd met you on some committee or other. I figured she'd seen you doing PR and recommended you because of that. Instead, she met you in a traffic accident." He rubbed his now-throbbing temples. "It all makes perfect sense."

Melanie blinked. "It does?"

"Sure. She really has gone 'round the bend. Instead of going in there and trying to convince her we're involved, I ought to be trying to convince her to see a shrink."

Melanie glowered at him. "Do you know how insulting that is? To both of us, in fact."

He heard the anger in her voice and knew this whole evening was within a nanosecond of blowing up in his face. He forced a smile. "Sorry. My head hurts."

"It should. Given the size of your ego, I'm shocked it hasn't exploded."

He grinned. "Nice one. Are we even yet?"

"Not by a long shot," she said, sweeping past him. "Let's get this over with."

"By all means," he said as he shut the garage door behind them, then led her toward the front entrance. The door was open and light was spilling out onto the street. "Mack must have beat us here."

Sure enough, his brother was in the foyer and his aunt was chiding him for not wearing an overcoat.

"Destiny, I parked less than ten yards away from the front door," Mack said, defending himself as if he were twelve, rather than a grown man. "It's not that cold out. Besides, I have all this muscle."

"Between your ears, mainly," Destiny said, cuffing him gently. "I really thought I raised you with more sense."

"You did," Mack said, kissing her. "You made me the man I am today, no question about it." He grinned at Richard over her head. "Look who's here. Big brother and his new girl."

Destiny whirled around, a smile spreading across her face. She rushed forward and embraced Melanie with genuine affection. "Darling, I'm delighted you're here. Don't mind Mack. Too many sacks on the football field knocked out most of his manners."

"I had fewer sacks than any quarterback in the National Football League," he countered. "I'm very quick on my feet."

"You were," Richard agreed. "Unfortunately it only took one sack to wipe out your knee and destroy your career." He pulled Melanie forward. "Melanie Hart, this is Mighty Mack Carlton, ex-football hero who is still reliving his glory days on the field every chance he gets, especially if it'll help him score with some female."

"A fine way to talk about your brother," Destiny scolded, linking her arm through Melanie's. "Pay no attention to either one of them. They're barbarians. I'd disown them, if it weren't too late."

Mack grinned at her. "Destiny, there's still time to change your will. You can leave all your money to your cats. Sad, lonely spinsters do that all the time."

Destiny scowled. "I'm neither sad nor lonely, and I don't own any cats."

"Then get some," Mack advised. "You're going to need the company when you run all of us off."

Destiny turned to Melanie. "See what I have to put up with? Consider this fair warning. If you continue going out with my nephew, you'll find that we're a tough crowd to love."

Richard wondered if that was an out he could use.

While he was pondering the possibilities, Mack jumped in.

"Listen to her," Mack advised Melanie. "Get out while you can."

Melanie glanced toward Richard, her expression hopeful. She clearly wanted him to give her some signal whether this was indeed the moment she should cut and run for the nearest exit.

Richard winked at her. "Have a drink instead. It'll make the rest of the evening more bearable."

Between Mack's teasing and Destiny's quick retorts, Richard and Melanie remained safely off the hot seat at least through the appetizers. But when Destiny led the way into the dining room and seated Melanie right next to her and him at the opposite end of the long table, Richard knew the gloves were about to come off. There was nothing he could do to protect Melanie now. He hoped she really was quick on her feet with diplomatic evasions.

"Darling," Destiny said to Melanie over the soup, "have I told you how delighted I am that Richard invited you to join us this evening?"

Melanie managed a weak smile. "Thank you."

"The two of you have so much in common," Destiny continued in the same slick tone she might use if she were about to sell her a used car.

"We do?" Melanie said skeptically.

"Of course you do. Or perhaps I should say that your talents and interests are complementary. You have exactly what Richard needs to fulfill his destiny."

Richard choked on a sip of water. He hadn't expected his aunt to go quite this far. It was beginning to look as if she wanted to seal this deal tonight. He wouldn't be surprised to see her whip out an engagement ring.

"I'm sure Melanie appreciates the intended compliment, but I think you're embarrassing her," Richard said, giving Melanie a bolstering smile. "Mack, why don't you tell us about the team's chances in the play-offs?"

Destiny cut Mack off before he could utter the first word. "There will be no talk of football over dinner," she said firmly.

Mack rolled his eyes. "You say that as if it involves talk of blood and gore."

Richard sat back happily, his mission accomplished. He knew from past experience that Mack and Destiny could spend hours debating whether football was a real sport or simply some macho excuse for a bunch of men to pummel each other senseless. Only the mention of boxing set her off more.

To his shock, Destiny waved off the comment. "I will not be drawn into this discussion tonight." She frowned at Richard. "Don't think I don't see what you're up to."

"Me?" Richard asked innocently. "What did I do?"

"You're trying to keep me from asking Melanie too many personal questions. You seem to have forgotten that I knew her before you did."

"Believe me, I have not forgotten that," Richard said grimly. "Not for an instant."

"Did she tell you about her sisters?"

"Yes."

"You know that she graduated from college magna cum laude?"

"I did not," Richard admitted. "Are you planning to trot out her résumé over the fish course?"

Destiny gave him a look that might have terrified him a few years back. Now he knew there was no real anger behind it. It was simply an intimidating tactic she'd found handy. He grinned at her. "Just thought I'd ask."

"Well, excuse me for trying to get it through your thick skull that she's very talented," Destiny said. "Talk to him, Mack. Tell him he's cutting off his nose to spite his face by trying to defy me."

Mack bit back a grin. "I think he heard you, Destiny."

Richard gave his aunt a bland look. "So if I were to hire Melanie right here, right now, you'd be happy?"

"That's all I ever wanted," Destiny said, her face the picture of innocence.

Richard shrugged, then turned to Melanie, who was listening to the exchange with an increasingly bemused expression. "You're hired."

She stared at him. "Really?"

"Really," he confirmed, then glanced at his aunt. "Satisfied?"

"I think you've made a very wise decision," she said happily. "That means the two of you will be working very closely together. Melanie, dear, would you like to move in here?"

Melanie choked on a sip of water. "Excuse me?"

"I thought it might be more convenient," Destiny said blithely.

"I have my own place."

"Not even two miles from here," Richard said, amused by his aunt's blatant attempt to maintain complete control over her protégé. "The only thing more convenient would be for her to move in with me."

Destiny's expression immediately brightened. "Perhaps until the election—"

"Absolutely not," Melanie said before Richard could gather his wits after the audacious suggestion. "I really don't need that much access to my clients, believe me. Sometimes a little distance is best for all concerned."

"Oh, I can't imagine that's true," Destiny said. "The more you know, the better prepared you'll be to represent Richard."

Melanie forced an insincere smile. "Something tells me I'm going to have plenty of inside information."

Destiny made no attempt to hide her disappointment. "Well, if you think that's best, dear. After all you are the expert. I'll certainly help all I can. Mack?"

Mack nodded, fighting a grin. "Believe me, I'll be Johnny-on-the-spot, whenever Melanie needs anything."

Richard didn't like the gleam in his brother's eye when he spoke. He gave him a warning scowl. "I think maybe it'll be best if Melanie and I work out my marketing strategy on our own with no outside interference. Too many cooks have a way of muddying the waters."

"I think they spoil the broth," Mack corrected, laughing. "But it's your call, big brother. If you want to keep Melanie all to yourself, I'm sure Destiny and I will respect your wishes, won't we, Destiny?"

Destiny could not be put off so easily. "If I have

suggestions from time to time, I'm sure Richard and Melanie will welcome them.''

"As if we could stop them," Richard muttered.

"Of course we'll welcome them," Melanie said, sounding more cheerful than she had at any time since their arrival. "I think this is going to turn out to be a match made in heaven."

Richard winced as his aunt beamed.

"I couldn't have said it better myself," Destiny said.

Mack choked back a laugh, then focused on his salmon. Richard looked around the table at the people who were apparently determined to drive him insane and sighed. This evening had not gone according to his roughly conceived plan. Not even close.

"I thought it went really well," Melanie said as they were driving home.

Richard's grim demeanor suggested he didn't agree.

"Okay, you may as well say it," she said. "You hate this, don't you?"

"Hate it?" he echoed. "I went in there with the upper hand. I came out like a man on the ropes."

"At least we're not engaged," Melanie said, determined to see the positives. "We're not even faking an engagement."

"Not yet," Richard said. "If you think that issue's off the table, you really are naive."

"Not off the table," she said defensively. "But we bought ourselves some time. Once Destiny gets all caught up in your campaign—"

"I do not want my aunt in the middle of my campaign," he said fiercely.

"Why on earth not? She's savvy. She knows people."

"She's sneaky, and I don't like the people she knows."

Melanie stared at him. "Don't you know the same people?"

"Yes, which is why I want no part of them," he said flatly. "Weren't you the one who kept stressing that I need to broaden my constituency?"

"Yes, but you also need money to run an effective campaign."

"I have money."

She stared at him incredulously. "You're going to spend your own money?"

"I have it," he repeated. "And that way I won't be beholden to a single special interest. That ought to make you happy."

"It makes me delirious," she said. "But are you sure it's wise? This is the time to start putting together the kind of powerful backing you'll need down the road."

"For?"

"A run for governor, for the Senate, whatever. I imagine this is just the start of your political aspirations. You can't finance all those campaigns out of your own pocket."

"Who knows, maybe after this I'll hate being a politician so much, I'll never run for anything again. We'll just have to wait and see," he said. "In the meantime, I don't want money from a bunch of people who'll think it's going to buy them access or favors."

Melanie was stunned, but it gave her an incredible angle to pursue once Richard had officially announced his intention to run. The public would eat it up.

"Let's get back to Destiny," he said. "Watch her, Melanie."

"Please, she's just trying to be helpful."

"There's helpful and then there's Destiny's version of help. I've seen her decline to chair a dozen different fund-raisers, but guess who makes all the critical decisions?"

"Your aunt," Melanie surmised, easily able to conceive of Destiny not staying behind the scenes.

"It won't be any different with my campaign."

"Let her make all the suggestions she wants to. We don't have to use a single one. We just have to listen," Melanie reminded him.

"No one will break our kneecaps if we don't," he agreed. "But there are other forms of coercion." He glanced over at her. "Want me to tell you what her first suggestion is going to be?"

Melanie was willing to play along. "Sure."

"She's going to ask you if you don't think I'd be a much stronger candidate if I were married," he said. "It's known as planting the seed. Destiny does love to dabble in her garden. She views me as one more plant she has to successfully nurture."

"But I don't think you have to be married to be successful, not that being a family man couldn't add another element to your image," Melanie said.

Richard gave her a triumphant look. "There you go. You just gave her the precise opening she'd need."

Melanie stared at him blankly. "I did?"

"Sure. I'm a good candidate now, but put a wife by my side and I'd be even better. Guess who the wife's supposed to be? You're here. You're handy. And we obviously get along well, don't you agree?" he asked mockingly.

Melanie hated the fact that he was actually making sense. She could see Destiny happily traipsing down this path. Her high spirits were sinking fast. "Like it or not, we're going to wind up engaged, aren't we?"

Richard nodded, his expression grim. "It's only a matter of time."

Melanie sank back against the rich leather of the seat and swallowed a sigh. She'd just landed the job of a lifetime, and it came with so many strings she was going to wind up hog-tied.

Chapter Nine

Richard tried to concentrate on the fax from his European division chairman explaining why profits were down and an intended acquisition had fallen through. Nothing in the report made a bit of sense, but maybe that was because Melanie's image kept swimming in front of him, making the words hard to read. The woman was driving him crazy, and she hadn't even been on his payroll for twenty-four hours yet.

Not that the fault was entirely hers. He was the one who'd been manipulated into making her a part of his everyday world. He'd been expecting her to turn up at the crack of dawn, but so far there had been no sign of her. Maybe—if the gods who protected fools were feeling very kindly—she'd decided against accepting the job coordinating his campaign PR. Maybe she possessed more sense than he did.

"You look a little wiped out, my friend," Mack

said, making a rare appearance in Richard's office at what was for Mack the ungodly hour of seven in the morning.

Richard stared at his brother. "What brings you by? I thought you preferred not to set foot in here out of fear that I might lock you into an office and put you to work for the family company."

"I think we established what a bad idea that would be a long time ago. I know football. I don't give a rat's behind about making widgets, or running restaurants or whatever else all those mysterious divisions do. I was lousy at Monopoly, if you remember. I kept selling my hotels and the land they sat on dirt cheap."

Richard gave his brother a wry look. "Frankly, I don't remember you ever sitting still long enough to play board games."

"There were a few rainy days when Destiny wouldn't let me outside to play football," Mack said. "You always whipped my butt, which did not bode well for my future at Carlton Industries. I may not be the business whiz you are, but even I could read the handwriting on that wall."

Richard regarded him with surprise. "You steered clear of the company because I beat you at Monopoly?"

"No, I steered clear because you love it and I don't, the same way Destiny left it behind for our father. This business ought to be run by someone who lives and breathes it. You do. Ben and I don't. Simple as that."

"Okay, if you're not here to stake a belated claim on a corner office, why are you here?"

"To do a postmortem on last night, of course," Mack said with a broad grin. "How are things going for you and your new campaign advisor? I'll bet that was a twist you never expected when you set up that dinner at Destiny's last night."

"I am not up for that conversation at this hour of the morning," Richard said, unwilling to admit how deftly he'd been maneuvered into making that decision. "I'll see Melanie later, establish some ground rules and we'll be okay."

"Will that be before or after you ask her out on another fake date?" Mack wondered aloud. "Or has the grand charade been scrapped?"

Richard's gaze narrowed. "Did Destiny put you up to coming in here this morning just to harangue me?"

"Nope. I'm here on my own," Mack insisted. "I haven't had this much entertainment in weeks, not since some of the guys and I stopped watching *The Young and the Restless* during lunch in my office. Your plot's better, by the way. I can hardly wait to see how it turns out."

Richard groaned. "Keep it up, Mack. You're walking on thin ice."

Mack grinned, evidently undaunted by Richard's increasingly sour mood. "I liked her," he said. "In case you're interested."

"What's not to like?" Richard conceded. "Melanie's attractive, bright. And she has a good sense of humor. She must if she's willing to put up with all this craziness."

"Plus she's kind to old ladies," Mack said with a straight face.

Richard chuckled in spite of himself. "I'd like to be around when you suggest to Destiny that she's old."

Mack winced. "A slip of the tongue, I assure you. Destiny is ageless."

"She is, isn't she?" Richard said with some regret. "Otherwise I could pretend that this is all about senility and ignore her."

"I think we can agree that our aunt is crazy like a fox." Mack's expression sobered. "Maybe you should pay attention to her, Richard. Seems to me you could do a whole lot worse than having Melanie in your life in whatever capacity turns out to fit best."

"Have you forgotten? She *is* in my life," Richard said, barely containing a sigh. "I'm having them clear out a little office right down the hall so she'll have a base right here in the building. With any luck, she'll never use it."

"Not what I meant, and you know it."

"Give it up, Mack. I have enough to contend with having Destiny sneaking around behind my back meddling. Don't you get any ideas."

"Hey, bro, I'm right out in the open." Mack's expression turned serious. "Listen to me. I think you're making a mistake if you don't give the woman a chance instead of playing games just to pacify Destiny. Go out on a real date with Melanie. Get to know her. Let your defenses down for once in your stodgy life."

"Now I'm stodgy?"

"You've always been stodgy. It's the natural by-product of deciding you had to be mature and responsible at the age of twelve, after Dad and Mom died. Thank God, Ben and I had you. Otherwise, we might have matured before our times as well."

"Whatever," Richard said, tired of the discussion. It was hitting uncomfortably close to the truth. Even

with Destiny on the scene back then, he'd felt like he
had to take charge, manage things to keep them from
spinning any further out of control. One minute he'd
been a normal kid, the next he'd been twelve-going-
on-thirty.

"Of course," Mack said a little too casually, "if
you're really not interested in anything personal with
Melanie, I might be."

That damn vein in Richard's head started throbbing
again. He wondered if it was a precursor to the stroke
he was likely to have before all of this insanity ended.
"Stay away from her," he said tightly. "No matter
what I do or don't do, you stay the hell away from
her."

Mack stood up, looking exceptionally pleased with
himself. "Thought so," he gloated.

Richard glowered at him. "What does that mean?"

"You're the one with the agile mind," Mack said.
"Think about it."

He sauntered out of the office whistling, leaving
Richard to wrestle with the riddle his brother had left
behind. Not that the answer was all that difficult to
unravel. He just didn't want to see it.

Melanie passed Mack in the hallway as she was
heading for Richard's office. He greeted her with a
knowing grin she couldn't quite interpret.

"Good morning," she said cautiously. "Have you
seen Richard?"

"In his office," Mack said. "You might want to
give him a couple of minutes before you go in there."

"Is he in a meeting?"

"Nope, just wrestling with his inner demons,"
Mack said, a note of satisfaction in his voice.

"What just happened in there, or dare I ask?" she asked, wondering if Mack took as much pleasure in stirring up Richard as he did in rattling Destiny.

"You won't hear it from me," Mack said. "Brotherly loyalty and all that." His expression sobered. "But, Melanie, try to remember something—Richard is one of the good guys."

"I know that."

"Don't lose sight of it, no matter what happens, no matter how crazy things get around here, no matter what shenanigans Destiny is up to," he said urgently. "Richard presents this secure facade to the world, but he needs someone in his life who can see past his rock-solid wall of defenses."

"I'm helping him with his campaign," Melanie pointed out. "I'm not here for any other reason, despite what he may have told you."

Mack grinned. "The charade thing. Yeah, I know about that. Funny thing about charades. If you really throw yourself into one, the line between truth and fantasy starts to blur."

"Not for me," Melanie said confidently.

"Lucky you." He regarded her seriously. "Or maybe not."

Before she could ask what he meant by that, he was gone, whistling that chipper tune again. Apparently Mack was going to prove to be as annoyingly enigmatic as the rest of the Carltons.

Sighing, she continued on to Richard's office, rapped on the door, then stuck her head inside. "Okay to come in? Your secretary's not in yet."

Richard gave her a sour look. "She's not in because I'm not usually bombarded by visitors at this hour."

Melanie refused to be daunted by his mood. "I ran into Mack in the hall. Did you two have words?"

"Mack and I never have words," Richard said. "He never sticks around long enough to have words. He breezes in, stirs things up and takes off."

So that was it. She'd suspected as much. "He seemed to be in a very good mood."

"Of course he was. This was one of his better hit-and-run missions."

"What did he want?"

Richard's gaze narrowed. "Did you come over here at this hour to discuss my brother?"

"No, I came to get started on your marketing plans. All the rest is what's known in the civilized world as conversation, idle chitchat, small talk, whatever."

"I don't have time for chitchat." He gestured at the papers on his desk. "I've got a major division that's underperforming. I need to figure out why."

He could be telling the truth or it could be an excuse. Melanie couldn't tell from his bland expression. "Then I'll get out of your hair," she said easily. "When can we talk? I want to establish a plan, a budget, that kind of thing. If you have a campaign manager, I need to meet with him. He—or she—can take a lot of this strategy stuff off your shoulders."

Richard closed his eyes and rubbed his temples.

"Headache?" Melanie asked sympathetically. "Little wonder, given everything you have on your plate. How about some tea? If you have a kitchen around here somewhere, I can make it before I head back to my office."

"You're not here to make me tea, dammit!"

She stared at him until he sighed.

"Sorry. I shouldn't have snapped."

"True enough," she said, determined not to make more out of his lousy mood than necessary to make her point that she wouldn't accept it. "Is that a yes or a no on the tea?"

He gestured to a door across the room. "There's a kitchen setup in the conference room. There should be some tea in there. If you don't mind making it, I'd love some."

"Lemon, sugar, anything?"

"Nothing."

She went into the conference room, which was paneled and elegantly furnished. A lavish arrangement of fresh flowers sat in the center of the rosewood conference table. Anyone walking into the room would know that this was a top-flight company, run by people with taste and refinement. She wondered if that was Destiny's doing or Richard's.

The kitchenette had a two-burner stainless-steel stove, a matching stainless-steel refrigerator, a cupboard filled with fine china and crystal and a drawer filled with sterling silver place settings, everything necessary for entertaining well-heeled board members.

Melanie filled a teakettle with water and put it on to boil, then searched for the tea. She found a wooden tea chest with a dozen different blends, chose a packet of Earl Grey and then put it and a porcelain cup onto a small tray. When the water was ready she filled a matching porcelain teapot, added it to the tray and returned to Richard's office.

Without saying a word, she poured water over the tea bag, then backed away. "I'll wait to hear from your secretary about scheduling that meeting."

As she started past Richard, he snagged her hand. "I really am sorry. My head's throbbing, I'm in a lousy mood, but that's no excuse for biting your head off."

She smiled at him. "As long as you see that, there might be hope for you yet."

"Even I'm not too old to learn a thing or two," he said. "As long as you're here, why don't you stay and we can talk over some of your ideas? I don't have a meeting scheduled until eight-thirty."

"What about that pile of paperwork?"

"It can wait. I'm not thinking clearly enough to deal with it anyway."

Melanie nodded and sat down. "Okay, then, here are the things we need to nail down. How much time do you want me to spend on your marketing plan? Do you want an initial strategy that can be turned over to staff, or do you want me to stay on to coordinate it? Originally we talked about some consulting on Carlton Industries marketing, as well. Is that priority or is the campaign? I don't need answers right this second, but you do need to think about all this. I don't want to run up a bill, unless we've agreed on every aspect."

"I appreciate that," Richard said, regarding her with a vaguely surprised expression.

"What?"

"I didn't expect you to be so…" He faltered.

"Organized?" she suggested mildly. "Could be that first impression I made. I really am good at what I do. Destiny wasn't wrong about that."

"I'm beginning to see that." He reached for a stack of folders on the corner of his desk and passed them to her. "These are résumés for prospective campaign managers. Look 'em over and give me some input." He scanned his day planner. "We'll meet again at three. I'll be able to give you fifteen minutes, so be on time and keep it short. I've set up an office for you down the hall. You can use it when you're here. If you need anything that isn't there, tell Winifred, my secretary. She'll see that you have it. We'll deal with all the other issues once the campaign manager has been hired. He should be in on that meeting."

"Agreed," she said at once. "I'll see you at three, then."

She was almost out the door, when he called her back. "Yes?" she said.

"Do you have plans for dinner tonight?"

"Richard—"

He cut her off before she could voice the protest. "This is business. I have to attend a fund-raiser at eight. Destiny's co-chair. There will be a lot of people there you should get to know." He grinned. "And it will make Destiny happy to see you with me."

"Then the charade's still on?" she asked, not entirely sure how she felt about that. The dancing of her pulse suggested she was happier than she should be.

"Of course," he said. "We agreed to keep it up until she backs off."

Melanie was struck by a worrisome thought. "Have you considered what might happen if she discovers this was all a game being played out for her benefit?"

"Believe me, letting her find out is not an option," Richard said grimly. "That's why we can't let down our guard for a second. She'll be expecting me to bring you tonight."

At this rate, Melanie concluded that she was going to go broke buying an appropriate wardrobe for black-tie events. "What time?" she asked, resigned.

"I'll pick you up at seven-thirty."

Melanie nodded. "If there are more formal events like this where I'm going to be expected to show up on your arm, I'll need more notice. I don't have a fairy godmother who can magically make me look presentable."

His lips twitched. "Fair enough," he said. "But don't say that around Destiny. I have a hunch she'd be thrilled to be cast in the fairy-godmother role. Dressing three boys did not allow her to utilize her creative flair for fashion. No matter how ingenious the designer, a tux is still basically a tux."

Melanie laughed. "Yes, I imagine that could prove frustrating to a woman like Destiny." She tapped the folders in her arms. "I'd better get busy with these."

Richard nodded. "See you at three, then."

"Right."

Melanie backed out of his office and closed the door behind her, then leaned against it. There had been at least three occasions in there when she'd wanted to dive across that massive desk of his and kiss him till his expression brightened. That would have been about as smart as nose-diving off the top of the Washington Monument.

Now she was expected to spend yet another evening with Richard, pretending to be something more than a freelance marketing consultant, and at the end of the evening she was expected to go home—alone—and keep the man out of her dreams. If this kept up, she was going to have to talk to him about hazardous-duty pay. She could not see one single way that this was going to have anything other than a very unhappy ending.

Melanie sifted through the pile of résumés, making notes on those she felt to be the strongest candidates for running Richard's campaign. She also jotted on sticky notes and put them on each folder for those she considered wrong for the job. She wasn't sure how much Richard intended to rely on her opinion or whether this was some sort of test he'd devised to see if they were on the same wavelength, but she intended to give him a thoughtful, intelligent response on each applicant.

One or two were so inexperienced they were laughable, but most fell into the middle range, with adequate experience, bright ideas and ambition. There were three whose applications stood out. She put those folders on top, then rubbed her knotted shoulders. She'd been sitting too long. She'd skipped lunch, because she was so determined to do this assignment thoroughly and intelligently. She wanted badly to prove to Richard that he hadn't made a mistake in hiring her as a consultant, even if his motives for doing so had nothing at all to do with her qualifications for the job.

Becky poked her head into Melanie's office. "Safe to come in?" she asked.

"Sure."

Becky came in and sat down. "Tell me again why you're going through all those résumés."

"Richard asked for my input."

"So you immediately dropped everything to handle that?"

"I didn't drop everything," Melanie said defensively. "I rescheduled a couple of appointments. No big deal. It happens all the time."

"Something tells me it's going to be happening a lot more often now," Becky said.

"If it does, it's only because Richard will be paying us big bucks."

"To dance to his tune," Becky said. "I don't like it. Neither will all the people who've been paying us regularly for months or even years. They may be little fish, but they're *our* little fish."

"I'm not going to neglect them," Melanie vowed, then studied Becky's skeptical expression. "What's really going on, Becky? I thought you understood how important it was for us to nab this account."

"I don't like to see you jumping through hoops for this man. You're too good for that."

"It's not for some man," Melanie said. "It's for a client."

"Then the whole charade for his aunt's benefit is off?"

"Not exactly," she admitted.

"Figured as much," Becky said grimly. "And you don't see how risky that is? You're not the least bit attracted to him? This isn't at all personal?"

Melanie bit back the quick and easy lie that had formed. "Okay, maybe it is a little bit personal," she admitted. "A part of me does want to impress the daylights out of him. But it's not going to get out of hand."

Becky rolled her eyes. "It's been one day, sweetie, and in my humble opinion, it is already veering wildly out of control."

"Wildly?" Melanie scoffed. "I canceled a couple

of appointments and spent a few hours reading these files. Come on, Becky, that's not unreasonable when we take on a new client.''

''If you say so.''

''I do.'' Before she could say more, her private line rang. Melanie picked it up. ''Hello.''

''Ms. Hart?'' an unfamiliar female voice asked.

''Yes.''

''This is Winifred, Mr. Carlton's secretary. He asked me to tell you that he has to cancel the three-o'clock meeting, but he'll still pick you up at seven-thirty this evening.''

''I see,'' Melanie said, avoiding Becky's gaze. ''Thanks for calling.''

When she hung up, Becky gave her a knowing look. ''Meeting's off?''

Melanie nodded, feeling exactly like the idiot Becky so clearly thought she was.

''I notice you didn't jot down another time. Did he reschedule?''

''No. Maybe he intends to go over it tonight.''

''Tonight?''

Melanie winced at Becky's incredulous tone. ''I guess I forgot to mention the fund-raiser we're going to.''

Her friend merely shook her head. ''Yes, I'm sure he'll want you to share all your notes with him, while he's shaking hands with all the movers and shakers who'll be there.''

''We'll have time on the drive over,'' Melanie said with waning confidence. ''Or after.''

Becky gave her a pointed look. ''Mel, how far are you prepared to go to keep this stupid account?''

Melanie was stunned by her friend's implication. "What are you suggesting?"

"I'm suggesting that you're about to walk a very fine line here and, frankly, given that sparkle you get in your eye whenever Richard's name is mentioned, I'm not sure you won't tumble headfirst across it."

"That's an awful thing to say," Melanie said, genuinely hurt that Becky's opinion of her was so low.

"It's an awful thing to think," Becky said. "You're my dearest friend and I love you to pieces, but I'm absolutely terrified that you're about to do something you'll regret."

"Are you worried for me or for the business?" Melanie asked cynically.

"You, of course," Becky said without hesitation. "Though I have to think that your professional reputation could suffer, too, if people perceive that you're literally in bed with one of your major accounts."

"I am not sleeping with Richard," Melanie retorted.

"Yet," Becky said, not backing down.

"I've made it clear that I won't sleep with him," she insisted.

Becky sighed. "We're in a funny business, Mel. We spend a whole lot of time helping people to create a public perception. We're best at it when perception and reality are the same. We're both too honest to do a very good job of spinning the truth."

"In other words, if people suspect I'm sleeping with Richard, it won't matter if I'm not," Melanie said, defeated by what was obvious even to her.

"Bingo."

"How the hell did I get myself mixed up in this

mess?'' she asked a little plaintively, even though she knew the answer all too well. She'd caved to Destiny's sneakiness and Richard's insistence.

"That one's easy," Becky told her. "You wanted to do a favor for a friend." She grinned. "How were you supposed to know you'd fall head over heels in lust at first sight?"

"I'm not in love with Richard," Melanie said emphatically.

Becky's grin spread. "I said *l-u-s-t*," she corrected. "But I find it very interesting that that's not what you heard." She stood up. "My work here is done. I'm going home."

"It's not even three o'clock."

"I know, but you need time to yourself to get all gussied up for tonight."

"Maybe I should wear sackcloth," Melanie said.

"I doubt it would help. Something tells me Richard's too smitten to notice."

"It's a charade, dammit!" Melanie shouted, but Becky was already gone. Melanie heard her chuckling as Becky closed the front door behind her.

She scowled at the pile of résumés she'd wasted most of the day studying. It would serve Richard right if she told him to hire some inexperienced, incompetent idiot, but she wouldn't. She'd make him take her seriously yet. After all, Becky was right about one thing—when their farce of a relationship ended, she needed to make sure that her professional reputation emerged unscathed.

Chapter Ten

Richard knew he'd made a tactical mistake canceling that meeting with Melanie the instant he saw her face. There was no welcome in her expression, no hint of a sparkle in her eyes. She was cool, polite and about as distant as any stranger he'd ever met. If he didn't fix this fast, it was going to be a long evening.

Fortunately, he'd anticipated something like this and made a couple of quick adjustments to the evening's schedule. One wouldn't come into play until later, but for now he pulled an extravagant bouquet from behind his back. "I thought you might like these," he said, watching her closely for some sign that the gesture was making inroads.

"They're beautiful," she said softly, burying her face in the fragrant assortment of lilies and roses. "Let me put them in water." She fled the room without a backward glance.

Satisfied that at least she hadn't tossed the flowers right back in his face, Richard took the time to look around her living room, which he'd barely glimpsed on his earlier visit. He supposed it was done in that style they called shabby chic, an assortment of old and new pieces assembled with a certain flair for color. It was not something he would ever have chosen for his own decor, but it was surprisingly inviting. If this evening hadn't been so important to Destiny, he'd have been content to stay right here, even with Melanie's gaze shooting daggers at him.

He glanced around when she came back with the flowers in a large crystal vase. She set it in the middle of the low, glass-topped coffee table, then regarded him with another cool glance.

"We should be going," she said stiffly.

The formality grated. Richard couldn't seem to stop himself from reaching for her. "Not until I've gotten this out of the way," he murmured right before he kissed her.

She resisted for half a heartbeat, then sighed against his lips. When he finally released her, she stared at him with more heat in her eyes.

"You don't play fair," she accused.

"Only as a last resort," he said. "I couldn't think of another way to cut through all that ice."

"You could have said you were sorry about canceling that meeting after I spent the entire day preparing for it," she said. "It made me wonder if you really cared about my input after all. This deal of ours is only going to work if you take me seriously. Otherwise, I want out now."

He'd guessed that would be her interpretation. "Of course I do, or I wouldn't have asked for it," he reassured her. "If we're going to work together, you need to understand that my schedule changes all the time. It's a fact of life. I have to respond to emergencies, react to last-second opportunities. I had two hours to get an offer on the table for a company I've been after for years. We really had to scramble once we found out there was a chance the management might look favorably on an offer from us in order to stave off a hostile bid from someone else. I was in with the attorneys right up until the deadline at five o'clock."

Melanie looked somewhat satisfied with the explanation. "Okay, I overreacted, probably because I saw this as my first big chance to impress you. Plus, you seemed to take it for granted that I'd drop everything to get ready for that meeting, and you didn't even bother to have your secretary reschedule."

"Because I was going to see you tonight myself. I was hoping the flowers would get me off the hook," he said.

"Admittedly, they were a nice touch," she told him, a smile finally teasing at her lips. "But a few sincere words would have been better." She gazed into his eyes. "Then, again, I imagine you're not used to apologizing to anyone for your actions, are you?"

"I do when it's necessary," he said, disconcerted by her too-accurate assessment. He wasn't used to anyone questioning his actions. What was it Destiny had said, that too many people bowed to his every whim? Taking another person's feelings into consideration was going to be a new—and most likely humbling—experience, at least if tonight was any example.

"Which you deem to be the case how often?" Melanie inquired tartly. "Once a year? Less?"

"Less," he admitted with a shrug. "I am sorry for canceling the meeting. My schedule was too tight in the first place, even without that unexpected opportunity to bid on the company I want. I should never have scheduled another meeting, but I knew how anxious you were to get started and I wanted you to see that I intend to listen to your advice."

For the first time since his arrival, her expression brightened. "You do?"

Richard laughed. "Don't let it go to your head. I said I'd listen, not that I'd act on it."

She grinned. "That's a start. I thought you were just dismissing me today because you figured whatever I had to say wasn't important."

"Honestly, Melanie, I do want to hear your impressions. You can tell me in the car."

"How far away is this fund-raiser?"

"Ten minutes."

She nodded. "I'll talk fast. There are only a few people worth talking about anyway."

When they walked outside, she stopped and stared at the limo waiting by the curb. "Very fancy."

"I find it useful when I hope to get some work done." He met her gaze as he ushered her into the luxurious car. "Or when I want to devote all of my attention to the person I'm with."

"Oh, boy," she murmured. "How am I supposed to concentrate after you say something sweet like that?"

"We could just put aside all these pesky business things till later and go back to kissing," he suggested slyly. He was fairly certain he'd never get enough of kissing her.

When he started to lean toward her, she held him back. "I don't think so. You didn't hire me for my kissing prowess."

He laughed. "You sure about that? We do have two deals, you know."

She gave him a look filled with confusion. "Believe me, that has not slipped my mind for a single second. Something tells me it's going to be keeping me awake at night."

Richard bit back another laugh. "Trust me, sweetheart, I've had the same thought." He regarded her hopefully. "If we're going to be awake anyway, we could spend the night doing something interesting."

She gave him a look clearly meant to freeze his libido in its tracks.

"I don't think so," she said icily.

Richard might have taken her at her word if there hadn't been the tiniest flicker of pure fire in her eyes. He was counting on that flame to defrost all that ice eventually. He just prayed he could manage to control himself till then. Exercising his restraint was getting to be more difficult with every second he spent with her.

Melanie was startled when the first person they ran into as they entered the hotel ballroom was Mack. He seemed to be on the lookout for them, because he instantly latched on to Richard's arm and pulled them right back into the bustling corridor, where a half-dozen registration tables had been set up so people could pick up their table assignments.

"Brace yourselves," he said grimly. "Pete Forsythe is here, looking like a cat who was let free in the aviary. One glimpse of you two and he'll have the lead for tomorrow morning's column.''

"Won't that be fun?" Melanie muttered, then brightened. "We could use this, you know."

Richard and Mack both stared at her.

"How?" Richard asked.

"He wants a juicy tidbit. Let's give him one. Let's end the speculation right here and now and tell him that you are definitely considering a run for Alexandria City Council and that you've hired me to advise you."

Richard was already shaking his head. "I'm not ready to announce that yet, not without a campaign manager in place, and we're at least a couple of weeks away from that. The earliest I intend to announce is mid-January."

"You're not announcing it," Melanie explained patiently. "You're only conceding what everyone already knows, that you're *thinking* about running. Then you acknowledge our business relationship and, *poof,* we get rid of the speculation about a romance. The truth will be so boring, he might not even print it."

Mack laughed. "Very clever. Listen to her, Richard. I know this guy. He thrives on scandal and innuendo. This will sound way too tame for his readers."

Richard finally nodded. "Okay, then, let's go feed him this dull little tidbit and pray that Destiny hasn't seen fit to give him an entirely different scoop."

"Such as?" Melanie asked, not entirely sure she wanted to know the answer.

"News of our imminent engagement," Richard said.

"She's seen us together once," Melanie pointed out.

"But she has an active imagination," Mack said. "And she does love to embroider the truth when it suits her purposes. If she has a chance to prod along this budding romance, she'll grab it. Unfortunately, Richard has a point, too."

"We could duck out right now, before Forsythe sees us," Richard suggested.

"No way," Melanie said, refusing to be daunted by Richard and Mack's dire predictions. "That's exactly the wrong thing to do. If Forsythe hears we were here or has caught even a glimpse of us, he'll go wild wondering why we disappeared during the hors d'oeuvres. He'll probably run right into the lobby to check the guest register to see if we slipped away upstairs."

"Our names won't be there," Richard reminded her, then grinned. "Unless…"

"Forget that," she said succinctly as Mack tried to smother a laugh. "Besides, it won't matter what he finds. He'll just conclude you bribed the desk clerk. Tomorrow morning we'll be reading all about how we disappeared to be alone together. I still think my original plan is best. We have to march in there as if we have absolutely nothing to hide, which we don't. Beyond that, it's a very crowded room. It's possible we can meet and greet, make our presence felt and get out without ever crossing paths with Forsythe. He can pick up the word about why we're here together from other sources."

Mack nodded his agreement. "I'm with Melanie,

bro. I'll go in first and run interference,'' he suggested with a look of pure anticipation.

Richard frowned at him. "I thought you always hid behind those huge offensive linesmen."

"Very funny," Mack retorted. "Either way, I'm more experienced at this sort of thing than you are."

"Running interference or avoiding Pete Forsythe's speculation?" Richard asked.

"Both," Mack said succinctly.

"By the way, where's your date?" Richard asked.

"I came alone," Mack said. "Less fodder for Destiny. Besides, I didn't want to steal your limelight." He grinned. "You know, in case you decided tonight was the night to make your big announcement."

Richard gave him a dire look. "You are going to be such dead meat when Destiny sets her sights on your love life. I'm going to help her in every way I can."

Melanie grinned at the brotherly byplay. "Richard, I'm not so sure it's wise to antagonize the man who's going to throw himself between us and Pete Forsythe."

Richard held up his hands. "Okay, okay. Do your thing, little brother. Get us to Destiny unscathed."

Mack proved to be remarkably adept at maneuvering through the crowd. Apparently all that experience eluding tackles was paying off, Melanie concluded as they made their way toward the head table where Destiny was holding court with several distinguished-looking gentlemen. To Melanie's astonishment, she realized that two of them were senators and one was a top aide to the president. She suddenly felt as if she'd fallen down the rabbit hole and landed at the

Mad Hatter's tea party. She was definitely out of her usual element in such lofty company.

Destiny welcomed them with a beaming smile, then performed the introductions with a graciousness that made Melanie sound as if she owned a top-flight firm on New York's Madison Avenue. The men regarded her with an automatic respect she wasn't used to garnering after an introduction. She was used to having to prove herself and her right to work in such exalted circles. Heck, she still hadn't proved herself to Richard.

"Richard, you fox," Senator Furhman said. "Leave it to you to find someone who's beautiful, smart and talented, while the rest of us are stuck getting advice from balding old fogies."

Melanie waited to hear what Richard would say to that. It would tell her a lot about his diplomacy and tact, to say nothing of hinting at his opinion of her professional skills. Not that he had much to go on yet.

He met the senator's gaze. "I'd recommend you hire her yourself," he said, then grinned. "But not until I'm in office."

"Then you are definitely running for Council in Alexandria?" the presidential aide asked.

"Definitely considering it," Richard admitted as he and Melanie had just agreed.

Listening to him, she decided he was going to be a quick study, which would make her job much easier.

"Why not for Congress?" Senator Furhman asked. "Waste of time, a man of your caliber starting at the bottom like that."

"Public service at any level is never a waste of time," Richard said, an edge in his voice.

"Well, of course not," all three men were quick to say.

Melanie grinned at the smooth way Richard had put them in their place without overtly offending them or suggesting that their own ambitions were in any way suspect. He was going to be a good candidate, no question about it. No one would rattle him.

"Gentlemen, if you'll excuse us, Melanie and I have things to discuss tonight." He leaned down and gave his aunt a kiss. "Sorry. We can't stay."

Melanie and Mack both gave him a startled look. Richard merely gave them an enigmatic smile.

"You ready, sweetheart?" he asked her.

The seemingly deliberate use of the endearment caught Melanie off guard. It was impossible to tell if it had been meant for Destiny's benefit or for that of her friends or maybe even for Pete Forsythe's ears.

"Darling," Richard prodded when she remained silent. "Ready?"

Melanie nodded numbly. "Sure."

Not until they were outside in the cold night air waiting for the limo to reappear did she face him and demand, "What was that about?"

"You mean the hasty exit?"

"That and the hint that we had more fascinating ways to spend the evening? I thought we'd decided that was a bad message to be putting out there."

"You thought so. I don't. Besides, this message was specifically for my aunt. We've agreed to that," he said.

Melanie wasn't appeased. "You said it in front of

witnesses, who are even now probably seeking out Forsythe to spill what they heard.''

"I'm tired of worrying about him."

"You have to worry about him," Melanie said impatiently. "You have to use the media to get *your* message across, not feed their appetite for intrigue. I thought you'd promised to listen to my advice."

"I did, which is why we got out of there, so I can listen to what you have to say and hear myself think." He opened the door of the limo for her. "I'm starved. Why don't we pick up something and take it back to your place?"

Melanie frowned at the suggestion. "You're not getting any crazy ideas of a personal nature, are you?"

He laughed. "Several of them, to be honest, but I'll settle for going over those résumés."

She shook her head. "You really know how to show a girl a good time."

"Before you get too huffy, wait till you see what I have in mind for takeout," he said. "I guarantee you'll like it better than the rubber chicken on the menu back there."

"If you say so," she said, still not entirely convinced that he wasn't up to no good.

He settled Melanie in the limo, then went up front to have a private word with the driver. When he came back, he said, "He'll drop us off, then bring back dinner."

Melanie knew she ought to be ecstatic that they were no longer under Destiny's watchful eye and were far from Pete Forsythe's speculative gaze. She ought to be even happier that they were actually going to talk business.

Instead, all she could think about was how dangerous it was going to be for her to be alone with Richard with no one around to stop her if either one of them lost control of their apparently madcap hormones.

"You're going to want to change out of that dress before dinner," Richard said the minute they walked into Melanie's living room.

She gave him a suspicious look. "Oh?"

He grinned. "I'm not telling you to slip into something more comfortable," he chided. "Though if that's what you want to do, I won't object. I have a particular fondness for women in satin and lace."

"Don't get your hopes up," she retorted. "I'm thinking a sweat suit."

To her surprise, he grinned. "Make it an old one."

"Why?"

"That dinner I ordered doesn't exactly mix with high fashion. Of course, if you want to live dangerously…" His voice trailed off.

Melanie stared at him. She couldn't quite get a fix on this oddly playful mood of his. "What on earth did you order?" she asked suspiciously.

"It's a surprise. I think you'll be very happy."

"You don't know enough about my taste in food to be able to make that claim," she retorted.

"Sure, I do."

"How?"

"You have your resources. I have mine. Unless you intend to be totally stubborn, go change. I'll fix us a drink. Do you have any red wine?"

She actually had several bottles of the wine she knew he preferred. She was not proud of the fact that she'd gone out and bought them, hoping for an occasion like this.

"There's a wine rack in the kitchen," she told him. "The selection's hardly as extensive as what you must have, but there's bound to be something there that will do."

Relieved to have him occupied, she fled to her room to change. She abandoned the baggy sweat suit idea—she did have some pride, after all—and settled for a comfortable pair of slim-fitting jeans and a becoming russet sweater.

She was on her way back to the living room, when the doorbell rang. The chauffeur stood on the stoop with two huge insulated bags designed to keep carryout food hot. Melanie stared at the familiar logo on the bags, mouth gaping.

"You ordered barbecue?" she asked as Richard came up behind her and took the bags. "From Ohio?"

"Your assistant said you go into raptures every time you talk about it," he said. "I figured I owed you something after canceling that meeting. I wanted to make you smile." He studied her intently. "You're not smiling yet."

"Give me a minute," she said, still wrestling with the appearance of food from an Ohio restaurant on her doorstep as if it were being delivered around the corner. "When on earth did you talk to Becky?"

"About twenty minutes before I had my secretary call and cancel the meeting. Once I spoke with Becky, I wanted to be sure I could pull this off before I had Winifred call you. I knew you'd be disappointed in me, and I wanted to make up for that."

"Oh, my God," she whispered. No wonder Becky

had been so worried earlier. She'd already spoken to Richard and knew he was planning this extravagant surprise. Becky also knew how Melanie was likely to react to a man who did something this totally unexpected and extraordinary.

Richard studied her with a narrowed gaze. "You're still not smiling. You do like this barbecue, right?"

"It's amazing," she said. "It's one of the things I miss most about home."

"That's what Becky said."

"But for you to go to all this trouble," she said, still stunned. "It must have cost a fortune to have this flown in."

"That's what corporate jets are for. Next time, we'll fly over and eat there. You can see your family."

Feeling totally dazed, Melanie turned around and walked past him. Until this instant she hadn't comprehended what it meant to be a man like Richard Carlton, a man who could do something this outrageous on a whim. She'd been frightened by her growing feelings for him before. Now she was terrified. It would be way too easy to be seduced by grand gestures like this and forget all about the dangers of getting seriously involved with the man making them.

She sat down at the kitchen table, picked up her glass of wine and took a careful sip to steady her nerves. Richard put the bags on the table, sat down opposite her and regarded her worriedly.

"Are you upset about this? I thought I was doing something nice."

Melanie met his gaze and finally allowed herself a small smile. "You did. In fact, no one has ever done anything so incredibly sweet and nice and over-the-top for me before.''

"Okay, I'll confess I'm new to this. Is that a bad thing?'' he asked.

"It could be,'' she admitted, her smile fading.

"Why?''

"It's wildly seductive,'' she said before she could censor herself.

"Oh, really?'' he said, clearly intrigued. "How seductive?''

She gave him a scolding look. "Don't even go there. I meant that I don't know what to do with it.''

He regarded her blankly. "Eat it. In fact, if the aroma coming out of these bags is anything to go by, that is definitely what we should do with it.''

"I meant I don't know how to handle a gesture like this,'' she said impatiently. "It's too much.''

"It's dinner.''

"From *Ohio!* From my favorite restaurant, where I used to go with all my friends when we wanted to celebrate a special occasion.''

"Would you have been happier if I'd brought in Chinese from down the block?''

"Not happier,'' she admitted. "But that would have made sense.''

He reached for her hand, then pressed a kiss against her knuckles. "That would have been safe, that's what you really mean, isn't it? It would have been ordinary, acceptable, not scary.''

She nodded slowly, trying not to notice that he was still holding her hand, that he was still sending shivers down her spine just with that touch.

"Why are you so desperate to feel safe around me?''

"Because we're playing a game, Richard," she said a little desperately. "That's what we agreed to."

"And barbecue from Ohio changes the rules?"

"Pretty much," she said, afraid she was sounding both ungrateful and ridiculous.

"Want me to throw it out?" he asked, picking up the bags.

Reacting purely to the needy growling in her stomach that came with each whiff of the familiar food, she grabbed the bags away from him. "Don't you dare. I don't pretend to know why you really did this, but I want that barbecue."

He grinned. "Shall I get the napkins?"

"Get lots of them, because this is not food that can be eaten neatly," she said, opening the bags to find enough baby-back ribs, coleslaw, potato salad and corn bread to feed a half-dozen people. She looked at Richard incredulously. "Were you expecting company?"

"I figured if it was that good, you'd want leftovers." He grinned. "Besides, Becky made me promise there would be some for her in return for her not telling you what I was up to."

Melanie shook her head. "If she can bamboozle you to make a deal like that, maybe I should send her out to negotiate our contracts from now on."

"I think you do okay on your own," he told her.

"Thank you." She looked him over. "If you expect to have a prayer of staying clean, lose the tie, roll up your sleeves and tuck a napkin in your collar."

He grinned and did as she'd instructed. He immediately looked more casual, more relaxed...more seductive. Lord, give me strength, she prayed. "And thank you for this food," she added aloud.

Richard gave her a questioning look.

"Just saying a little blessing before dinner," she said.

Judging from the amusement flickering in his eyes, she had a hunch he knew that was only a small part of what she'd been praying for.

"Melanie?"

"Hmm?" she murmured distractedly as she took her first bite of the tender, perfectly seasoned pork. She had to stop herself from moaning with pleasure.

"Look at me," Richard commanded.

She met his gaze and nearly shuddered at the heat she saw there. "What?"

"Fair warning. I usually do safe and I usually do ordinary, but you seem to inspire me to go beyond that."

She swallowed hard and nodded. "Yes, I think I get that now." Heaven help her.

Chapter Eleven

Richard was not the least bit surprised to find Destiny waiting for him when he arrived at his office the next morning. He'd known that her curiosity would get the better of her. It was not every night that he slipped out of a major social event attended by business and political leaders to be with a woman. He'd calculated the effect before he'd done it. That one move alone was going to convince his aunt he was serious about Melanie.

Unfortunately, the fact that it had started as a game to get Destiny to back off was beginning to get a little fuzzy in his head. At some point last night, things had turned serious, at least for him. Until he understood why that was, he was going to be doing a delicate balancing act between convincing Destiny the romance was real and assuring Melanie that it was not. Damn, but subterfuge was complicated. That's why he'd spent his life avoiding it, in business and in his personal life.

"Did you and Melanie enjoy your evening?" Destiny asked without preamble. The glint of anticipation in her eyes suggested she was hoping for some very juicy details.

"Very much," he said neutrally.

"Did you do anything special?"

Richard gave her a sharp look. "You know about dinner, don't you?"

His aunt grinned. "That you flew it in from her favorite teen hangout in Ohio? Yes, I did hear about that. I must commend you, Richard. It was a nice touch, something I might have dreamed up had you asked for my input."

"Is everybody in my company on your payroll, too?"

"If you're asking if they all spy for me, the answer is no. I just make it my business to stay well-informed where my nephews are concerned. It's amazing how cooperative some people are willing to be when you're pleasant to them."

He heard the implied criticism, but he was in no mood for it. "You need to get your own life and stay out of mine."

She shrugged. "Maybe one of these days, when I'm satisfied that you, Mack and Ben are happy."

"We'd be a lot happier without you poking around in our personal lives."

"Really?" she asked doubtfully. "You'd never have met Melanie if not for me. Can you honestly say you were happier before she came along?"

"I was at peace," he said, trying to recall what that had felt like. Probably lonely, if he were to be totally honest about it. Melanie hadn't been around all that long, but he was already having difficulty imagining his life without her.

"Darling, that's not the same thing at all," Destiny said. "In fact, it seems to me you had a little too much peace in your life."

"I was content with that," he said, even though he knew he was not only lying but wasting his breath.

"Well, Melanie's in your life now," Destiny said breezily. "I hope you won't do anything foolish to ruin it."

"I doubt you'll give me a chance," he muttered.

She chuckled. "Not if I can help it. Christmas is coming, you know. Will Melanie be joining us next week?"

"You mean for the traditional Carlton excess?"

She frowned at the edge in his voice. "I love the holidays. Sue me. And despite your sour mood this morning, you usually do, as well."

She was right, though Richard had no intention of giving her the satisfaction of admitting it. "I assume if I don't invite Melanie myself, you'll do it behind my back," he grumbled, even though he'd already planned to include Melanie in their Christmas Eve and Christmas Day celebrations. Let Destiny believe he was making a huge concession just for her benefit.

"I'm hoping that it won't be necessary for me to go behind your back," she said mildly. "Remember dinner's at eight on Christmas Eve. Then I expect you all back for brunch at eleven on Christmas Day. We'll open our gifts then. Be sure to get something special for Melanie. Do it yourself. Don't leave it to Winifred."

"I think I can remember the schedule," he said,

ignoring the barb about assigning his shopping to his secretary. "We've been doing the same thing for twenty years."

"Tradition is important. Someday you'll appreciate that."

Richard supposed that was possible. He'd never given it much thought before. For a moment his imagination took flight and he pictured years of family traditions created with Melanie for their family. As soon as the thought crept in, he stamped it out. He was getting carried away. If he wasn't careful, this whole charade thing was going to get out of hand. Maybe that's what Melanie had been trying to tell him last night, that it was *already* out of hand. If so, he was very much afraid she'd gotten it exactly right.

"Richard's on line one," Becky announced with surprisingly good cheer when Melanie walked into her house after a meeting with a client she'd been putting off ever since Richard's business had taken over most of the minutes of her day.

Becky held out the phone. "You want to take it here?" she asked, her expression hopeful.

Melanie shook her head. "I'll get it in a sec," she said, wanting to figuratively catch her breath before speaking to the man who'd literally taken it away the night before with his wildly impulsive gesture.

"Once you two have talked, you can tell me all about dinner last night," Becky added. "I can't wait to hear every little detail. I've asked, but Richard doesn't seem inclined to spill the beans on whether he got lucky."

"Good God, please tell me you didn't ask him that," Melanie said.

"Not in those exact words," Becky said, grinning.

At last, some evidence of discretion and good sense, Melanie thought. Avoiding Becky's probing questions was also a rather powerful incentive for keeping Richard on hold indefinitely. She did not want to engage in a postmortem with a woman who knew her as well as Becky did. Becky would see straight through any attempts to deny that she was falling for Richard.

"I think I'll take the call in my office," Melanie said, walking into the room and firmly closing the door behind her.

She heard Becky's indignant gasp as the door clicked shut.

When Melanie felt reasonably composed, she picked up the receiver. "Good morning," she said briskly, determined to keep things cool and professional this morning, the exact opposite of the way they'd been the night before. "Sorry to keep you waiting. I'm just back from a meeting."

"No problem. How are you?"

"Doing great. You?"

"Fine," he said, sounding amused. "Is Becky standing over your shoulder listening to every word? She seems awfully curious about last night."

"I think that's to be expected under the circumstances, since you saw fit to take her into your confidence."

"You have a point," he conceded. "I won't make that mistake again. You didn't say, though. Is she there?"

"No, as a matter of fact, I shut the door to my office. I don't think she can hear me, though I imagine her ear's pressed against the door," she said a bit more loudly.

The comment was greeted by an indignant huff from the outer office.

"Now, then what can I do for you?" she asked Richard.

"We need to talk about Christmas," he said. "It's next week."

Melanie bit back a smile. "So I've heard. I'm surprised you remember. Winifred must have made a note on your calendar."

"Actually Destiny was here this morning," he said.

"So that explains your sudden recollection of the holiday," she teased. "Family prompting. Did she ask you to pass it on to all the other workaholics you know?"

"No, but she is expecting you to join us for Christmas Eve dinner and brunch on Christmas Day," he said. "I promised to invite you."

Melanie was completely caught off guard. Spend the holiday with his family? She wasn't sure she could pull that off. It seemed way too…intimate. "Isn't that carrying things a bit too far?"

"Not if we expect to convince Destiny we have a real relationship. You're not going home to visit your family, are you?"

"No, but—"

"Then there's no reason you can't join us. I'll give my aunt credit for one thing—she does do the holidays up right. You'll have a good time and, goodness knows, you'll get plenty to eat."

"It's not being entertained or fed that I'm worried about."

"Then what is it?"

"It's a lie, Richard. On Christmas," she added, as if that were somehow worse than all the other lying going on.

"I see your point."

"Do you really?"

"Believe it or not, I'm not in the habit of lying to people myself," he said. "These are extraordinary times."

"Not that extraordinary," she insisted. "How can we keep this up? I'm getting more uncomfortable all the time."

She waited through a long silence.

"Maybe we need to speed up the timetable a bit," he suggested finally.

Melanie wasn't reassured by his cautious tone. "Meaning?"

"Let me give this some more thought," he said. "Just promise you'll be there."

"I don't suppose these will be huge gatherings where I can get lost in the crowd," she asked, hopeful.

"Afraid not. The bashes come between Christmas and New Year's. These two occasions are just for family."

"Oh, God," Melanie murmured. "Richard, are you really sure about this?"

"I don't see an alternative," he told her, not sounding nearly as dismayed as he should have. "It would be highly unusual if you weren't there. In fact, it would be tantamount to an admission that we're not serious."

"You aren't beginning to enjoy this predicament we're in, are you?" she asked suspiciously.

"It's a necessary evil," he claimed, though he didn't sound very sincere. "Trust me."

"Trust you?" she echoed doubtfully.

"I haven't been wrong about Destiny so far, have I? She's behaving totally predictably."

"I suppose."

"Relax, Melanie, this won't be so bad. You know Destiny and Mack. The only person you haven't met is Ben, and he'll probably study you appreciatively with his artist's eye and never say two words."

"Are you telling me there's a member of the Carlton clan who isn't glib?"

Richard fell silent for so long, Melanie was afraid she'd said something dreadfully wrong. "Richard?"

"Ben used to be as chatty as the rest of us," he said slowly. "He's had a tough time the last couple of years."

"What happened?"

"He doesn't discuss it, so we don't, either. I'm sorry I can't prepare you any better than that. If it'll ease your mind any, you should know that he's the handsomest one of us all."

"Quiet, rich and gorgeous. I could be in love," Melanie joked.

"Don't get any ideas," Richard said. "You're wildly in love with me, remember?"

"Oh, right," she said. "Sometimes I lose track of the details in our arrangement."

"Very amusing," he said without the faintest hint of humor in his voice. "I guess Christmas would be a good time to put a spin on this you won't be able to forget."

Something in his tone alerted her that he was dead serious. "Richard, what is that supposed to mean?"

"Christmas is coming," he said. "It's not the time to ask a lot of questions."

Her heart took a sudden stutter-step. "Richard, don't you dare do anything foolish."

"Of course not. I'm stodgy, remember?"

He hung up abruptly before she could remind him that there had been nothing stodgy about his grand gesture the night before, nor about any of the kisses they'd shared. She had a sudden sinking sensation that he was about to top himself. The thought scared her to death.

Melanie was wearing a simply cut emerald velvet suit she'd found at Chez Deux when Richard picked her up on Christmas Eve. She looked amazing. She also looked a little as if she were being carted off to the guillotine. He regretted that he was the cause of that.

"There's no reason to look so terrified," he reassured her. "It's just dinner."

She gave him a skeptical look. "How many courses?"

"I have no idea. I never counted. What does that have to do with anything?"

"Just dinner is meat, potatoes, vegetables and maybe a pumpkin pie for dessert. Is that what we're likely to have tonight?"

He grinned. "Doubtful. Okay, I see your point." She'd been making quite a lot of good ones lately.

"Do you really? Something tells me that this meal is also going to be accompanied by a lot of expectant stares," she told him.

"Could be."

"And that doesn't scare you?"

"This is my family. They don't scare me," he insisted.

"Not even Destiny?"

He laughed. "Oh, well, if we're talking about Destiny specifically, she has put the fear of God into me from time to time."

"Especially lately, I imagine."

"Actually I've been warming to her mission," he said mildly, just as he pulled his car into the garage.

Melanie stared at him, obviously convinced she couldn't possibly have heard him correctly. He took some satisfaction in having caught her off guard.

"What did you just say?" she demanded.

He pretended not to hear her as he exited the car and went around to hold her door. She didn't budge.

"I asked you a question," she said, frowning up at him.

"We'll discuss it later," he promised. "We don't want to keep everyone waiting."

"Something tells me it would be smarter if we did," she grumbled, but she did get out of the car.

Inside, they found the rest of the family already gathered. Even Ben had put on a tux for the occasion, but he still wore his usual dour expression. Richard worried about the fact that Ben still hadn't snapped out of his dark, brooding mood, but Destiny insisted that people recovered from tragedy at their own pace.

At least Ben made an effort to smile when Destiny introduced him to Melanie.

"I've heard a lot about you," Ben said.

Melanie glanced at Richard, then back at Ben. "Really?"

"Actually, it's my aunt who's been singing your praises. Mack is entirely too absorbed with his own women to mention that Richard is involved with someone, and Richard only calls to see if I've remembered to come out of my studio long enough to eat.''

Melanie grinned. ''I've heard you're a talented artist. I'd love to see your work.''

To Richard's astonishment, Ben nodded.

''Come out to the farm sometime,'' he told her. ''I'm sure Destiny will bring you.''

''If anyone brings her, it'll be me,'' Richard grumbled, oddly disconcerted by the fact that Ben seemed to have taken an instant liking to Melanie. He studied his brother, trying to pinpoint whether his overall outlook had changed or whether this was purely a reaction to Melanie. He couldn't tell. He hadn't expected both of his brothers to be thoroughly besotted by her within minutes. Good thing he'd made his own plans to stake his claim.

''I thought you didn't let strangers poke around in your studio,'' Richard said.

Ben smiled with more animation than Richard had seen in months.

''But Melanie's not a stranger, is she? From what I gather she's practically family,'' he said in a tone that sounded almost like the Ben of old, full of life and mischief.

Destiny had filled him in, all right, Richard thought grimly. Or Mack. Either way, Ben seemed to be enjoying it, and that counted for a lot these days.

Melanie linked her arm through Ben's. ''Don't believe everything you hear,'' she confided. ''Some people are more confident than they should be. Now, would you mind pouring me a glass of wine, since your brother hasn't seen fit to do it yet?''

"It would be my pleasure," Ben said, crossing the room with her.

Richard stared after them in amazement. Even Mack looked astonished.

"Stop gaping," Destiny scolded. "Richard, you of all people should know what an amazing woman Melanie is."

"I had no idea she was a miracle worker," he mumbled, his gaze still following her as she chatted with his brother. Seeing her work her magic on Ben reassured him that his plan for tomorrow's family gathering was a wise one. It was time to raise the stakes. He simply wasn't sure anymore whether it had anything at all to do with Destiny.

Melanie felt like the worst sort of fraud. She was beginning to hate this stupid agreement she'd made with Richard to deceive Destiny into thinking they were getting serious about each other. Half a dozen times the night before, she'd been tempted to spill the truth and let the chips fall where they may, but she hadn't been able to bring herself to utter the words. She had a feeling her reticence was just the tiniest bit self-serving. She liked Richard. She liked his family. And some part of her that was doomed to heartbreak didn't want the charade to end.

She suspected that Richard knew that, too, and was using it to keep her in the game. He was sneaky like that, not in a mean way, but to protect his own interests. Whatever those interests were. She was no longer sure about that, not after some of the hints he'd been dropping lately. And not after he'd kissed her for so long the night before, church bells had been chiming the end of midnight services when he'd stopped. At least, she hoped those were the bells she'd heard ringing. Otherwise, she was in more trouble than she'd imagined.

"I should not be doing this," she told herself even as she showered and began dressing to return to Destiny's for Christmas brunch. "Nothing good can come from it." She stared at her reflection in the steamy bathroom mirror and nodded agreement, then sighed. "But I'm going anyway." Her tone was more resigned than defiant.

Once she was dressed, she made calls to her family to wish them a happy holiday.

"We miss you," her mother said. "When are you coming home?"

"Soon, I hope," Melanie promised, feeling instantly homesick.

"Stop pestering the girl," her father said. "She's busy. She'll come when she can."

"Thanks, Dad. I love you guys."

"What are you doing today?" her mother asked.

Now there was a quagmire if ever she'd seen one, Melanie thought. "Having brunch with friends," she said neutrally.

"Anyone we know?" her mother wanted to know.

"No."

"You're pestering again, Adele."

Her mother chuckled. "How am I supposed to find out anything, if I don't ask? Melanie never volunteers anything. She's exactly like you."

"Then that should tell you that poking and prodding won't get you what you want to know," her dad countered. "You ever have any luck with that with me?"

"Now that you mention it, no," her mother said. "Okay, I'll give up for now, since it's Christmas."

"Probably the best gift you've ever given the girl," Melanie's father teased.

"Oh, Dad, it is not," Melanie said, laughing at the familiar bickering. "Be nice, or she'll cut you off without any pumpkin pie."

"Never happen," he said. "She knows I've got her present hidden away where she'll never find it and she's not getting it till I've had my pie."

"You two are a riot," Melanie said. "How do you do it?"

"Do what?" her mother asked, sounding puzzled.

"Stay married for all these years and have so much fun with each other," Melanie elaborated.

"Why, we love each other, of course," her mother said.

"Indeed we do," her father agreed. "And she's never stopped laughing at my jokes. Laughter may be the most important thing there is in a relationship, aside from love."

"And trust," her mother said. "Don't forget that." She hesitated. "I don't suppose you're asking because there's somebody special in your life?"

Melanie sighed.

"There she goes again," her father said at once. "Say goodbye, Adele."

"It was worth a try," her mother grumbled. "Merry Christmas, darling!"

"Merry Christmas," Melanie said, slowly hanging up the phone, her eyes suddenly stinging with tears. Now she was deceiving her parents, too, at least by omission.

She was still swiping at the tears when she went to

answer the door. Richard took one look at her and pulled her into his arms without comment. She clung to him and let the tears flow.

When she finally stopped crying, she backed away, avoiding his gaze. "I'm sorry."

"Homesick?" he guessed.

That was only part of it, but she nodded, surprised by his understanding. "I just got off the phone with my folks."

He studied her face, then brushed away one last stray tear. "I could have you in Ohio in an hour."

She stared at him, astonished. "You would do that?"

"If it would put a smile back on your face."

Once more she was reminded of what it was like to know someone who could make such an offer so casually. "You will never know how much it means to me that you would do that, but I'm okay. I'll get home soon."

"You sure?"

"Yes," she said, feeling a hundred-percent better knowing that she could have gone home if it was what she'd truly wanted. It made the waiting easier. "Let me check my makeup and get my presents, then I'll be ready to go. I'm dying to see what you got your family for Christmas." She grinned. "I'll bet you're dying to see them open their gifts, too."

"I'll have you know that I went shopping," he called after her as she went into the bathroom.

Melanie laughed. "But did you actually buy anything?"

"Yes," he insisted. "You'll see. I promise you, you'll be impressed. I even did my own gift wrapping."

"I can hardly wait to see it," she said as she finished touching up the mess her tears had made of her makeup.

On her way back to the living room, she picked up her own token gifts for the Carltons and grabbed her coat.

"Did I mention that you look lovely?" Richard asked as he helped her on with her coat.

"No, but maybe that's because I was bawling my eyes out when you came in."

"You looked lovely even then," he assured her.

Feeling suddenly lighthearted, she patted his cheek. "Just for that, I hope Santa is very good to you."

His gaze caught hers and lingered until she felt heat rise in her cheeks.

"Something tells me it's going to be the best Christmas ever," he said quietly.

Melanie had that exact same feeling.

Brunch was yet another gourmet meal, evidently prepared by Destiny herself. She'd given the cook the holiday off.

"Why should she be working on Christmas, when there's nothing I enjoy more than cooking for my family?" Destiny explained.

"Well, it's all wonderful," Melanie told her honestly. "I'm impressed."

"It's nothing, really," Destiny said, but she looked pleased, probably because she wasn't used to getting a lot of compliments from the nephews who took her cooking skills for granted.

"Can we stop talking about the food and get to the good stuff?" Mack pleaded, sounding as if he were at least twenty years younger.

Destiny gave him an indulgent smile. "What are you hoping to find under the tree, Mack? They were fresh out of bachelorettes where I shopped."

"How about the keys to a new Jaguar?" he asked hopefully.

"Dream on, little brother," Richard said. "You'll be lucky if you get ashes and switches this year. We all know how badly you've misbehaved."

"I could find you a dozen women who are grateful for that," Mack retorted.

Destiny laughed. "Oh, I managed to do a little better than ashes and switches." She smiled at Melanie. "Even at this age, they're little better than greedy hooligans on Christmas morning. I don't know how I failed them."

"You didn't fail us," Richard assured her. "You taught us the joy of giving…" He paused, then added with a grin, "And receiving."

When Melanie spotted the mound of gifts under the tree, she knew he hadn't been kidding. To her amusement, the three men began tossing the boxes around until there was a little pile beside everyone there, including her. She added her own gifts to their piles, then watched as they tore through paper with an eagerness she would never in a million years have expected from this sophisticated family.

When Richard realized she hadn't opened the first gift, he nudged her. "Hey, you need to get started." He plucked a small box from the pile beside her. "How about this one?"

Melanie took note of the inept wrapping job and concluded it was from him. Something about the size of the box made her decidedly nervous. She made a great show of shaking it, then slowly removing the paper as the others watched and waited expectantly.

When she saw the velvet jeweler's box, her heart skipped, then lurched into a frantic beat. "You didn't," she whispered, her gaze on Richard.

"Open it," he commanded gently. "Please."

Inside, she found a diamond the size of a small boulder. Melanie stared at it in shock.

Ever since their phone conversation a week earlier and the hints he'd subsequently dropped, she had been expecting Richard to do something to catch her completely off guard, but she'd never anticipated anything like this.

She gulped, then looked into all those happy, expectant faces. She couldn't do this. She just couldn't.

Before she could think about it, she dropped the ring, jumped up and ran from the room.

Richard found her outside, taking great gulps of icy air. "Are you okay?" he asked worriedly.

"No, I'm not okay," she replied, her voice shaky. "What were you thinking?"

"That this would be the perfect time to convince Destiny that we're serious."

"You should have warned me."

He sighed. "In retrospect, I should have." He studied her intently. "You really weren't expecting an engagement ring? Not even after all the hints I dropped?"

She shook her head.

"Think you can put this on and go back in there and fake being deliriously happy?" he asked, holding out the ring.

Melanie backed away, hands clasped behind her back. "Even if I were willing to agree to a phony engagement, which I'm not certain I am, I can't wear that.''

"Of course you can."

"What if I lose it? What if it gets stolen?" she asked.

Richard shrugged. "It's insured. Besides, we need a ring like this for the engagement to be convincing."

Melanie regarded him with dismay. "You never struck me as the type to go for ostentatious jewelry."

"I don't. Destiny does."

"Are you sure about that? She strikes me as a very classy woman."

"She is, but a ring like this will definitely get her attention."

She lifted her gaze to his. "Richard, I'm not sure how much more of this I can take," she said honestly.

"I know. Just think of the satisfaction you'll feel when you get to throw this back in my face. I'll probably end up with a black eye or a bloody nose."

Vaguely cheered by that prospect, she nodded slowly. "Okay, then. I'll wear the ring." She let him put the monstrosity on, then hefted her hand in the air and studied it. "It's a good thing this is just a game."

"Isn't it, though?"

But even as he said it, Melanie thought there was an odd expression of regret in Richard's eyes. It made her see something in Richard she'd never expected to see...vulnerability. It reminded her of something Mack had said to her back at the beginning of this farce, that Richard needed someone who could see past his defenses. Now that she had, she realized that was even more dangerous than anything that had happened between them up until now.

Chapter Twelve

Richard stared at Destiny and Melanie huddled together in a corner and concluded that his aunt had bought the phony engagement hook, line and sinker. He was surprised by how guilty that made him feel. He forced himself to examine why that was, but the answer was fairly obvious. He'd never before gone to such elaborate lengths to get even with Destiny for meddling. Usually he just took her interference as a fact of life, something she did out of love—annoying but essentially harmless. He had no idea why he'd felt compelled to go to such an extreme this time. He had a feeling it had a lot to do with his conflicted feelings for Melanie herself.

"Guilty conscience?" Mack inquired, regarding him with amusement.

"I don't want to talk about it," Richard said, not

in the mood to share his soul-searching, even with his brother.

Mack shrugged. "Fine with me, though if you were to ask, I could probably help you sort through all these pesky emotions you're feeling about now."

"When did you turn sensitive?"

"Scoff if you like, but I have more experience in this area than you do, big brother. I have shaded the truth on more than one occasion to evade Destiny's scheming. I'm not especially proud of it, but sometimes I've found it to be a necessity."

"No question about it," Richard said. "I'm just not sure that's a plus."

Mack gave him a knowing look. "You actually believe Destiny is buying all this, don't you?"

Richard was stunned by the suggestion that Destiny wasn't being taken in. "Of course. Just look at her. She's practically gloating at having won so easily."

"Ha!"

Richard frowned at his brother. "What the hell are you suggesting?"

"That our beloved aunt still has the upper hand, that she knows exactly what you're up to and that she is playing along till you dig yourself in so deep you'll never get out. Trust me, this engagement will be real before all is said and done. Destiny will see to it. She's a pro, my friend, and you are a rank amateur when it comes to this kind of scheming."

"You can't be serious," Richard said, even though it made a convoluted kind of sense. Destiny was sneaky enough to do something like that, to give him and Melanie enough rope to hang themselves or, more precisely, to tie themselves together permanently.

"Have you figured out a way to extricate yourself

from this once things get out of hand?'' Mack inquired.

Richard nodded, his gaze now riveted on the two
women across the room. What the devil were they
talking about? For all he knew the two of them were
in cahoots, plotting against him. Maybe Melanie had
been in on the scheme from the beginning, Destiny's
scheme that is, not his. Good God, he couldn't even
keep the schemes straight anymore. Mack was right.
He needed a well-formulated escape plan. Fortunately
he'd considered that.

''Of course I have a plan,'' he told Mack. ''You
know I never go into anything unless I have an exit
strategy.''

Mack rolled his eyes. ''This isn't a business deal.''

''Yes, it is,'' Richard said, then felt ridiculous.
''Okay, in a way, it is. Melanie and I have an agreement.''

''In writing?''

''Of course not.''

''So if she changes her mind and decides she likes
being engaged to you, that she wants to be married
to you, you're prepared for that? Or do you have lawyers on standby ready to break this verbal contract
the two of you have?''

''Yes,'' Richard said, then decided that wasn't an
admission he was prepared to deal with. ''I mean no.
No lawyers. Mack, you're making my head hurt. This
is a straightforward arrangement. Melanie and I give
Destiny what she wants, proof that we're together—''

''It's an illusion,'' Mach reminded him.

Richard scowled and kept talking. ''Then we break
up. I mope around for a while until Destiny finds
some other poor woman to try to foist off on me.''

He grinned at Mack. "Or until she decides you're the better candidate for serious romance."

Mack shuddered. "Bite your tongue."

Richard warmed to that scenario. "Yes, indeed. I think that's the way it'll go. She'll be furious that I've messed this up, decide I'm totally hopeless, then give up on me. She'll turn to you, then Ben. Given Ben's current attitude toward the opposite sex, I'll be a doddering old man before she gets back to me again."

"You are so delusional," Mack said. "Even Ben sees Destiny's scheming more clearly than you do and he's oblivious to most of her flaws. He was still laughing his head off when he left here."

That caught Richard's attention. "Ben's gone? When did he leave?"

"Ten, fifteen minutes ago. He slipped out as soon as Destiny's attention was otherwise engaged." He laughed uproariously at his own pun.

Richard was not nearly as amused. He was also worried about his brother. "Why didn't you try to stop him from leaving?"

"Have you ever tried to stop Ben from doing whatever he's set his mind on?" Mack asked. "He's the most stubborn of all of us, and that's saying something. Lighten up. He came today and he actually let down his guard for a while with Melanie."

Richard wasn't comforted by the positive spin. "I hate that he's exiled himself to that isolated farm of his."

Mack sighed. "He needs time, Richard. What happened with Graciela nearly destroyed him."

Richard frowned. "It wasn't his fault."

"He blames himself anyway."

"He needs to listen to reason," Richard said impatiently. "You've told him that. I've told him that. I'm sure Destiny has repeated it ad nauseam. Maybe I should have another talk with him."

"No," Mack said with surprising vehemence. "Destiny's right about this one. Ben needs to heal at his own pace. He doesn't have your thick skin or my cavalier attitude toward life. One day he'll wake up and put the entire tragedy into perspective, but it won't happen until he's ready. If we push him, he'll just dig his heels in deeper. Next thing we know, he'll put a lock on the front gate out there and refuse to let any of us in."

Richard knew Mack was right, but his heart still ached for Ben. Graciela Lofton hadn't been worth all this pain and anguish. No woman was, he thought until he caught a glimpse of Melanie laughing at something Destiny had said. He found himself sighing.

Maybe one woman was worth it, he conceded. Melanie was smarter than he'd initially given her credit for being, sexier than hell and a good sport. It was an admirable combination, one he hadn't run into often.

So why the hell was he so dead set on pushing her out of his life just to make some elaborate point with Destiny?

For a few hours Melanie allowed herself to get caught up in the fantasy. She couldn't seem to tear her gaze away from the disgustingly ostentatious ring that Richard had slipped on her finger. A part of her actually felt this awful kind of letdown that it was only there temporarily.

Not that she wanted this particular ring, not that she even wanted to be engaged to Richard for real, she told herself staunchly, but it would be nice to have that kind of permanent connection to somebody. To know that he'd be there for her in a crisis, to fall asleep in his arms, to make love to. When was the last time she'd had that? During her ill-fated affair with yet another boss and the closeness then had been as much of an illusion as her supposed engagement to Richard was. She sighed heavily, drawing Richard's attention.

"Are you okay?" Richard asked, glancing at her quickly as he drove toward her place.

"Just tired," she said. "Trying to keep all the threads of our story straight wore me out."

He nodded, his jaw tight. "I can relate to that."

"How? You spent most of the afternoon huddled with Mack. He knows we're lying. I was with Destiny, who had a million and one questions about our plans."

"What did you tell her?"

"That you caught me completely off guard today, that we have no plans."

"Sounds reasonable. What was so tricky about that?"

She gave him a withering look. "Are you kidding? Ever heard about nature abhorring a vacuum? Well, Destiny has nothing on nature. She now has lists of her lists."

"Lists?" Richard echoed, his expression dire. "Oh, God."

She grinned despite her own trepidations. "I see you're familiar with her list-making skills. Frankly, I was in awe, and I consider myself to be a halfway decent organizer."

"What sort of lists was she making?" Richard asked warily.

"Guest lists, caterers, florists, photographers, bridal salons, gift registries. I believe there is also a short list of preferable wedding dates to be checked first thing in the morning with your church. I lost track after that one." She gave him a plaintive look. "She wants to book the church. Isn't it some kind of sin to book a church for a wedding you know will never take place?"

Richard forced a grim laugh. "Probably not a sin, but definitely a complication we could live without. You haven't met our minister. He would not be amused."

"Oh, and did I mention Destiny has also drafted the engagement announcement for your approval, though I wouldn't count on her waiting? She seems a bit eager to get it into print."

"Maybe Mack is right," Richard muttered under his breath, his gloomy expression deepening.

"What?"

"Mack," he said. "He thinks she's on to us and is now determined to push us beyond the brink so there will be no turning back."

"It wouldn't surprise me," Melanie said glumly. She regarded him hopefully. "When can we break up?"

Richard didn't respond. He merely pulled the car to a stop at the side of the road and set the brake.

"Richard? Did you hear me?"

"I heard you."

"Well?"

"Give me a minute. I need to think about it."

Melanie wasn't about to give him a minute. She

wanted a solution and she wanted it now. "This plan is backfiring on us, isn't it?"

"Could be."

"Then fix it, dammit."

He gave her an enigmatic look. "Any suggestions?"

"Tell her the truth," Melanie said impatiently. "How's that for a novel idea?"

"I'm not even sure I know what the truth is anymore," he admitted, his expression oddly wistful.

"I'll tell you what the truth is. We are not engaged!" she said, her voice rising.

"You're wearing my ring," he reminded her mildly.

"It's fake."

"I can assure you it's not."

She scowled at him. "I mean it doesn't mean anything. The engagement is a fraud, a hoax, a stupid game."

"It definitely started that way," Richard agreed.

Something in his tone stopped her from continuing her own ranting. "Richard?"

He lifted his gaze to hers, his eyes troubled. Then, before she could guess his intention, he leaned across and touched his lips to hers, softly, tenderly. Heat flared as if he'd touched a match to kindling.

They sat by the side of the road, the motor idling, oblivious to the passing traffic, caught up in a kiss that shook Melanie to her very core. She wanted to cling to him, to keep his mouth against hers forever, to taste him, to let that heat build and build until there wasn't a thought left in her head, until she was only feeling these intense, wicked sensations that he stirred in her.

She hadn't bargained for this, had told herself a million times not to get involved, not to let down her guard for even an instant. All good resolutions. All wasted. She was involved. She was in love.

She was doomed.

Even knowing that—heaven help her—she couldn't seem to stop kissing him. Richard was the one who finally backed away, looking as shattered as she felt. A small, annoying smile tugged at his lips.

"What?" she grumbled.

"That kiss felt damn real to me," he said.

"It can't be," she protested, still trying to cling to some tiny shred of sanity.

"Who says?"

"I do. We agreed—"

He shrugged, still looking vaguely amused. "Things change."

"But they haven't changed," she insisted vehemently. "I won't let them change. I can't."

He blinked at her fierce tone. "Why?"

"I work for you, dammit. I told you I will not be put in that position again."

He nodded slowly, his expression suddenly shuttered. "So you did."

His easy acceptance of that should have filled her with relief. It didn't.

"Please take me home," she requested quietly.

"No problem."

Trying to put some professional distance between them, she asked, "Are we going to meet with the finalists for your campaign manager's job this week?"

He shook his head. "I'm having Winifred postpone that."

She gave him a sharp look. "Why?"

"Let's just say I'm reexamining my priorities."

She stared at him blankly. "What does that mean?"

"I'll let you know when I figure it out."

Melanie was still pondering Richard's enigmatic remark when Destiny called first thing in the morning a few days after Christmas.

"Richard tells me he's given you the day off," she said cheerily.

"I have other clients," Melanie reminded her.

"No one works during the holidays."

Melanie couldn't deny that. Her phone had been silent for several days now. Even Becky was off at the holiday sales, a ritual she engaged in with the fervor of a true shopaholic.

"I was hoping to catch up on a few things while the office is quiet," Melanie claimed. What she did not want to do was spend time trying to come up with more believable fibs to feed to Destiny. She felt crummy enough about the growing pile of lies as it was.

"Whatever you're doing can wait," Destiny said. "I have other plans." Her tone suggested Melanie was expected to fall in with them without question.

"What?" Melanie asked suspiciously, visions of all those lists still haunting her.

"Just a little preliminary scouting expedition," Destiny said cheerfully. "It'll be fun."

"You want to go shopping today? I'd rather eat dirt."

"We'll start with lunch and champagne. That should get you into the proper spirit," Destiny said, undaunted by Melanie's lack of enthusiasm. "I'll pick you up in an hour. Wear comfortable shoes."

She hung up before Melanie could come up with one single protest that Destiny would buy.

Even though she dreaded the entire outing, Melanie quickly got swept along on Destiny's tide of excitement. She tried reminding herself that her enjoyment of Destiny's exuberance was what had gotten her into this predicament with Richard in the first place, but that didn't seem to work as well as she'd hoped. The woman's high spirits were contagious.

Before Melanie knew it, she was caught up in the whole shopping thing. She told herself it wouldn't hurt, just this once, to try on a few wedding gowns in some of the most exclusive shops around. Who knew when she might have another chance to indulge in such a fantasy? As long as she didn't sign a single credit-card slip or exit a shop with a package, what was the harm?

Her delusion lasted for about the space of a heartbeat. Within no time the shopping excursion began spinning wildly out of her control. Destiny on a mission was a force to be reckoned with. She knew the owners of every elegant boutique in Old Town Alexandria, Georgetown, and in the fanciest malls in the region. She was an indefatigable shopper.

She also knew her own mind and had little patience for salesclerks who wasted time showing them anything less than the best. Despite the brakes Melanie tried valiantly to put on, Destiny merely waved off her objections and headed for the next store. Short of planting her heels and making the woman drag her along behind, Melanie was at a loss. Her vow not to use her credit card for a single purchase was never once tested. Destiny wielded hers with the skill of a woman for whom money held no meaning beyond its purchasing power.

"I can't let you do this," Melanie uttered more times than she could count. She was wasting her breath. The packages kept piling up. The only conceivable thing that might slow Destiny down would be running out of trunk space, Melanie thought hopefully as she tried to cram one more package into the already jammed trunk.

"Looks like that's it for the day," she said a bit too enthusiastically. "We're out of room."

"Nonsense. We'll just have everything else sent," Destiny said, turning to march off to the next store on her exhaustive list.

"You can't be serious," Melanie said. "I'm wiped out."

"Really?" Destiny regarded her with surprise. "I'm just getting my second wind, but if you're tired, I'll take you home." She beamed. "I can't tell you when I've had such a wonderful time. What time should we get started tomorrow? Another day or two like this one and we'll have made real inroads."

"In what? Bolstering the national economy?"

Destiny laughed. "That, too. Is ten o'clock good for you?"

Melanie ran through a frantic litany of excuses. Alone, none of them seemed to do the trick, but combined they finally bought her the next day off.

"The day after then," Destiny said adamantly, obviously not inclined to be put off a second time. "I'll pick you up at nine. We'll start with florists and caterers, then do a bit more shopping."

Melanie felt her stomach start to churn. "I can't let you do all this. It's wrong."

"I'm enjoying every minute of it."

She was, too. Melanie could see it in her eyes and that made her feel even guiltier. Panicked that the frenzy would only get worse, the second Destiny had gone, she got into her own car and drove to Richard's office. He was bound to be there. She hauled along a few packages—the veritable tip of the iceberg—to help her make her point.

Richard glanced up when she came charging in under a full head of steam. His gaze narrowed. "I wasn't expecting to see you today."

"Yes, well, the day is full of surprises. I wasn't expecting this, either." She dumped the packages on his desk. It made the piles on Christmas morning seem a little sparse. "Look what she's done," she moaned.

"Destiny?" he guessed as if there might be some other crazed shopper in the family.

"Who else?" she snapped. "She picked out china and silver, bought my veil—it's hand-tatted French lace, by the way—and started on my trousseau. She would not take no for an answer. She said I have a position to live up to as your fiancée. She wouldn't let me pay for a thing, not that I could afford to pay for one sterling-silver place setting, much less the twelve she ordered. We have to stop this, Richard. It's getting out of hand. No, it's beyond that. It's completely crazy. Destiny had the time of her life and I feel like the lowest slug on the planet."

Even as she ranted, he reached into a bag and pulled out a silky negligee. His eyes immediately filled with heat.

"Yes, I can see that," he murmured.

It was said in a placating tone she found totally annoying. Nor did he look nearly as distressed as Melanie had anticipated. "Richard, are you hearing what I'm saying? This has to stop. She's spending a fortune on a wedding that is not going to take place. She's out of control. This whole mess is out of control."

"I hear you." He held up the negligee, that hot gleam still in his eyes. "This doesn't have to go to waste, though, does it?"

She stared at him. "What?"

His gaze caught hers. "It would be a shame to let this go to waste, don't you think?"

Her pulse raced. "Are you crazy?" she asked, her voice a little too breathless. Surely he wasn't suggesting...

"Come away with me," he said, "Please."

"I don't think—"

He smiled. "There you go. Don't think. I've spent the whole day doing enough thinking for both of us. Just say yes, Melanie. We'll go down to the cottage for a few days."

"So we can figure out how to handle this?" she said, still trying to maintain the illusion that that gleam in his eyes did not mean what she thought it meant—okay, what she *wanted* it to mean.

His smile spread. "That's one reason."

She regarded him suspiciously. "What's the other one?"

"So I can see you wearing this," he said quietly, letting the filmy material run through his fingers. He met her gaze again. "And take it off of you."

Oh, God, she thought, her heart hammering.

"Well?"

In her head, she heard herself saying no. It was loud, clear and decisive. She repeated it just to be sure.

Then she looked into Richard's expectant gaze.

"Yes," she whispered.

Apparently she wasn't satisfied that her life hadn't descended into total heartbreak yet. She was determined to career wildly straight into disaster.

Chapter Thirteen

Though Richard had spent the entire day trying to figure out the best way to handle things with Melanie and Destiny, he hadn't come to any satisfactory conclusions by the time Melanie had come bursting into his office twenty minutes earlier. Leaning back in his chair, listening to Melanie's outpouring of dismay over their duplicity, watching the color rise in her cheeks, hearing the passion in her voice had convinced him of one thing. He wasn't going to let her go the way he'd originally intended.

To the contrary, in fact. He was going to do his best to figure out some way to keep her in his life. After all the scheming, he realized he might have a teensy bit of trouble getting her to trust him, but he'd overcome tougher obstacles in his life.

He might still be more than a little miffed over his aunt's meddling, but Destiny had gotten it right. Melanie was exactly what he'd needed. He should have known Destiny wouldn't make a mistake with his happiness on the line. No one on earth knew him better, flaws and all. She'd found a woman capable of balancing his natural stodginess, a woman who could make him feel alive, a woman whose passion would make him lose his head and his heart...if only he dared to risk them.

As he'd listened to Melanie, he'd realized that for him all bets were off. Unfortunately, he'd made a commitment to her that she could end their phony relationship. He'd realized that he had one chance— if he was lucky—to convince her that ending things wasn't what she wanted, either.

For a man not normally inclined to risk rejection, he'd taken a huge chance by inviting her down to the cottage. Letting her know that he had more than talking on his mind had been an even bigger risk, but he couldn't deceive her about his intentions. He might take all the well-intentioned lies to Destiny reasonably lightly, but he would not lie to Melanie. They had enough hurdles to get over without adding that.

Looking across his desk at her now, heat in her cheeks, her eyes bright, he knew he would do whatever was necessary to persuade her to stay with him forever. Never before had he allowed anyone to begin to matter so much. The power of his feelings for her very nearly overwhelmed him.

"Are you sure about this?" he asked. "Do you really want to go to the cottage with me?"

She nodded.

"You know I'm asking you there to do more than talk."

A smile played on her lips as she gestured toward

that breathtaking concoction of deep blue silk and lace. "You made that clear."

"Your employment as a consultant to my campaign has nothing at all to do with this," he said to make sure she understood that. "Your work here is secure, no matter what happens between us personally. I'll put that in writing if you like."

"No need," she said. "I quit."

Richard blinked, certain he couldn't possibly have heard her correctly. "What?"

"I said I quit," she repeated more confidently. "I don't need your business."

Now there was a wrinkle he hadn't anticipated. He'd counted on that tie keeping her around, even if he messed up something this week. It had been his sketchily formed backup plan.

"But I want you to go on working for me," he said, surprised to find that he meant every word of it and not just because it had been his fall-back plan for contact with her. Damn, if it wasn't one more thing he owed Destiny for. He regarded Melanie intently. "You're too good to lose. I read your notes on the prospective campaign managers. They were sharp and insightful. You got a far better fix on their qualifications than I did by looking at the exact same material."

Satisfaction glowed in her eyes. "Then I'll be happy to bill you for that, but I still quit."

"Why?"

"It will just muddy the waters. I don't know where this trip to the cottage will lead, but I do know that I don't want to be worrying about whether I'll have a job when things end between us. And, frankly, it would be far too painful for me to be around you, when things do go badly.''

When, not *if.* She'd said it twice. Richard heard her certainty that the relationship would end and wondered what it would take to convince her otherwise.

In the meantime, he had to find some way to keep her from quitting. He needed all his ties with her to be strong. To his astonishment, he'd gotten used to having her underfoot. He didn't want to lose any aspect of that. He didn't want to lose yet another important person in his life. Losing his parents had shaped his entire outlook. He didn't think he'd survive another emotional hit like that.

''I thought this consulting job was going to be your big break,'' he reminded her, grasping desperately at straws. ''That's what Destiny led me to believe. Was she wrong?''

''No, she wasn't wrong.'' Her gaze remained unflinching. ''I'll find another big break, Richard, one without the complications.''

Richard heard the finality in her voice and nodded slowly, not even trying to hide his reluctance to let this be the last word on the subject. ''You're sure?''

She chuckled. ''As sure as I've been about anything since the day we met. Things have been a bit confusing since then.''

''Tell me about it,'' he responded.

''Maybe you're the one who needs to think about this trip you have planned. Are you sure? You're not a man who's big on complications, and this could be a huge one.''

Richard grinned at her assessment. It had been true once, not all that long ago. He'd hated sticky situations, especially of a personal nature. But he was definitely looking forward to this one. For the first time ever he saw the possibility of a real future for a relationship, something more than satisfying sex.

He stood up and walked around his desk to stand in front of her. "I'm sure about this one," he said with quiet assurance. "I don't know how it happened, but I can't get you out of my head."

Her gaze narrowed suspiciously. "Are you hoping this weekend will purge me from your system? Because if that's the case, let's call the whole thing off. We can forget about the trip, the phony engagement, all of it. I'll return all this stuff and take all the blame with Destiny."

The possibility that she could turn her back on him so easily grated. Richard looked directly into her eyes. "I appreciate the offer, but that's not how it's going to happen."

She bristled visibly at his tone. "Oh?" she asked, as if daring him to utter another order.

"Here's what we're going to do. We're going to the cottage. We're going to put all of this other nonsense aside for the next few days. We're going to make love until we're exhausted, then maybe do it a few more times just to be sure we're getting it right."

"Were you an activities director at one of those singles resorts in another life?"

Richard chuckled at the totally incongruous suggestion. "I seriously doubt it. Are we clear about the plans?"

For a minute he seriously thought she might balk, but she finally met his gaze.

"Okay," she said quietly but firmly. There was no apparent doubt in her eyes or in her tone.

His heart soared. So did his libido. He was wise

enough not to let her know about either reaction. "Good, then. I'll pick you up in an hour."

"We're going tonight?"

"No time like the present. My desk is clear. Yours?"

"Clear enough," she admitted. "I have plans with Destiny day after tomorrow."

"I'll take care of that. I'll tell her we're going on a romantic getaway before all the wedding frenzy takes over our lives. She'll be delighted."

"Maybe you can convince her not to do anything precipitous without us," Melanie suggested hopefully. "Tell her we want to be a part of every decision. That way there's a slight chance we won't come back and find that every detail has been hammered out and nailed down with ironclad contracts."

Richard nodded at the sensible suggestion. "Good idea. I'll call now. You'd better get moving if you intend to be ready in an hour."

She gave him a long, measuring look, then scooped up the negligee that made his mouth go dry, let it dangle sexily from a finger, and said, "How much packing will I need to do, if this is all you expect me to wear?"

Richard was still trying to form a coherent thought when she sashayed past him. Given that remark, he wondered if it was possible they could be on the road in thirty minutes. Of course, with his body in a state of complete and total arousal, it might be very wise not to leave his office for a while.

Melanie arrived back at her house to find Becky sitting at her desk, staring glumly at her computer screen.

"What are you doing here?"

"I came in because I needed to talk to a friend. Where were you?" she asked accusingly. "You told me you'd be working today."

"Long story," Melanie said, regarding Becky with concern, her own plans forgotten for the moment. "What's wrong? They were all out of your size at Nordstrom's?"

"I didn't go shopping."

That was so startling Melanie sank down in her own chair. "Why not?"

"I broke up with Jason."

"Again? Why?"

"He's been cheating on me."

All of Melanie's good feelings toward the man vanished at once. "How did you find out? Are you sure?" she asked, sharing Becky's indignation.

"I spotted him with a woman in the men's department," Becky said. "Trust me, I recognized all the signs. She was practically drooling over him." She regarded Melanie with obvious misery. "And that was after he'd told me he'd rather be carved up into itty-bitty pieces than go shopping right after Christmas. He *knew* where I was going. He *wanted* me to see them together. The coward. It was easier than being honest with me."

"You're right. It was a cowardly thing to do," Melanie agreed. "But, Becky, wouldn't you rather know the truth?"

"No," Becky said at once, then sighed. "Okay, yes, but it's the holiday season. Who will I be with on New Year's Eve?" She regarded Melanie hopefully. "We could do something. There's still time to plan a party."

Melanie debated telling Richard they would have to be back for New Year's Eve, then decided against it. They had their own problems to sort through.

"I can't."

"You have a date?"

"In a way. Richard and I are going away."

Becky's mouth dropped open, her own sad plight momentarily forgotten. "You're kidding! Where? When?"

"We're going back to the cottage at the beach." She glanced at her watch. "In about twenty minutes. I need to pack."

"Then go. Don't worry about me."

Melanie hesitated. It didn't seem right to abandon her friend now. "Will you be all right?"

Becky gave her a brave smile. "Aren't I always? It's not like this will be the first New Year's Eve I've ever spent alone."

"Don't spend it alone," Melanie urged her. "Promise me you'll call someone, go out to dinner, go to a movie, something. Do not stay at home and cry over Jason the jerk."

Becky squared her shoulders. "Don't worry. I've shed my last tears over him." Her expression brightened. "In fact, I think I'll go home right now and take a pair of scissors to all those expensive designer shirts of his."

"There you go," Melanie said. "He deserves that and more."

Becky's good mood promptly deflated. "Of course, that's probably just what he expects me to do. That's probably one more reason he was buying shirts on sale today."

"Doesn't matter," Melanie said. "You'll still feel

better once you've savored a little revenge. Just remember how he loves his wardrobe. I always thought there was something a little weird about that. The man spent more on clothes than we do.''

Becky yanked open a drawer in her desk and pulled out a pair of lethal-looking scissors. ''These are sharper than the ones I have at home,'' she said gleefully as she tucked them into her purse.

''Have fun,'' Melanie called after her.

Becky was barely out the door when Richard came in.

''You're not ready,'' he guessed after surveying the room for any evidence of a suitcase.

''Sorry. We had a crisis around here.''

''I assume that's why Becky went charging past me with a somewhat maniacal glint in her eyes.''

Melanie grinned. ''She's on the warpath.''

''Boyfriend?''

''Ex-boyfriend.''

''His life's not in danger, is it?''

''Nope. Just his wardrobe.''

Richard chuckled. ''Remind me never to make you angry.''

Melanie patted his cheek. ''You make me furious all the time,'' she reminded him. ''So far, though, your clothes are safe.''

''Too bad. I was rather looking forward to having you rip them off of me.''

Melanie gave him a considering look. ''An interesting idea. I'll give it some thought on the way to the cottage.''

''Don't think out loud,'' he warned. ''I'd hate to have to stop at one of those less-than-stellar motels on the way down.''

"No chance of that. I'm going to be enjoying testing your patience too much."

Richard's patience was hanging by a thread by the time they finally got to the cottage. If there was any clothes ripping to be done, he was likely to be the one doing it. He was still a bit surprised that his restraint was as strong as it evidently was.

"Do you want me to make a fire?" he asked when they'd carried everything inside, including several bags of gourmet food he'd brought from home and their luggage. For the first time in recent memory, his laptop computer wasn't among the possessions he'd brought along. A rather impressive, unopened box of condoms was.

Melanie met his gaze. "A fire would be romantic," she said, then grinned. "But it would take too long. Maybe later."

"Dinner?" he asked, his voice oddly choked.

She took a step closer, letting her coat fall from her shoulders into a heap on the floor. "Later."

"Wine?"

She shook her head, her gaze locked with his. "Uh-uh. I'm already a little giddy." She reached for the top button on his shirt. "You're a little too prim and proper for the setting."

His gaze narrowed. "Are you really sure you want to start this right here, right now?"

"Oh, yeah," she said fervently.

"I haven't even turned the heat up."

"We won't need it," she said confidently.

He grinned finally. "Well, then, I guess one of us has her priorities all sorted out."

"For the short term," she agreed.

The phrase hit Richard like a slap, reminding him that he was treading on very thin ice. Neither of them had said a thing about permanency. This was an experiment, at least in her eyes. He'd done nothing to suggest otherwise.

"Then let's make it memorable," he said, pulling her into his arms and settling his mouth on hers.

This time there was no holding back. There was nothing tentative or uncertain or exploratory about the kiss. They both already knew that a kiss had the power to stir them.

Melanie was restless in his embrace when he scooped her up and headed for the stairs.

"Where are we going?" she murmured against his lips.

"To bed," he told her. "I can forget about the fire, the food and the wine, but I am not going to make love to you for the first time in the middle of the living room floor."

She grinned. "Afraid of a little rug burn?"

He heard the laughing challenge in her voice. "No, just determined to treat you the way you deserve to be treated."

Her eyes turned dreamy. "Sometimes you say the sweetest things."

"Sometimes you inspire me," he admitted as he strode into his bedroom. It was like an icebox, making him regret his decision not to bother just yet with turning up the heat. "I really think I should run back downstairs and kick up the furnace."

Melanie slid her hand inside his shirt, then slipped lower till her fingers were grazing the bare skin just below his waist. "Still cold?" she inquired.

"As a matter of fact," he began, only to moan as

her deft fingers slipped a little lower. "Okay, now I'm hot."

"Told you," she said gleefully.

He met her gaze, his expression suddenly serious. "Do you have any idea how much I've thought about this?"

"You think too much," she responded, still exploring his body in a way she had to know was likely to drive him mad.

Richard swallowed hard, trying to maintain some control. "In other words, you'd prefer action?"

"At the moment, most definitely."

He nodded. "Okay, then. I was taught to always defer to a lady's wishes, at least in a situation like this."

"Who taught you that? Destiny?"

"No, Mack. He has a very successful track record."

"What did Destiny tell you when she taught you about the birds and the bees?"

"That sex is always better when you're in love," he said quietly, his gaze on her face.

Melanie's eyes filled with an emotion he couldn't quite fathom. He was getting better at reading her, but this was something new. Something tender. It gave him hope.

He wasn't certain enough of his footing here, though, to say the rest of what was in his heart, that this was the very first time he'd put that theory about sex and love to the test.

The game had just taken a serious turn. Melanie felt the shift somewhere deep inside and it terrified her. She'd come down here because she'd lost the last

shred of willpower and sense she possessed. She
wanted whatever this trip would bring. She wanted
memories to savor and cling to on the lonely nights
in the future when Richard was out of her life again.

That day would come eventually. She had no
doubts about that. He was obviously attracted to her,
but chemistry was a transitory thing. Eventually he'd
remember that she drove him nuts and they would
stage their breakup. That would be that. It was what
they'd agreed to, and Richard was known for not going back on his word. It was one of his most admirable qualities. Even her own preliminary press re-
leases said so.

At least the certainty of a breakup was what she'd
been counting on until about five seconds ago, when
the look in Richard's eyes had been so filled with heat
and emotion that it had shaken her. Until now she'd
had very little at stake. In fact, she'd believed the only
real thing she could lose was an important consulting
contract, which was why she'd tossed that aside earlier. It no longer complicated matters, and recent
weeks had proved to her that her professional ideas
and strategies had real worth. She would find other
clients. She'd felt relieved the minute she'd quit the
consulting job.

Now it was all personal. It all mattered. This heat
between them, the growing respect they had for each
other, her delight in Destiny and the rest of Richard's
family—all that had caught her off guard. She was
flat out in love with Richard, but she'd learned once
before that she couldn't trust herself to accurately as-
sess what a man was feeling. She'd been burned too
badly last time.

Play it light. Pretend none of it matters. Those were

the lessons she'd learned in her last disastrous relationship. She had to remember that now. She had to protect her heart at all costs. Until and unless Richard said something about calling off their fake engagement, until he suggested making it real instead, she had to operate under the belief that nothing had changed beyond their admission that the attraction between them was too hot to ignore.

"Why so serious?" he asked, his voice low, his gaze intense.

"I just got lost in thought for a minute," she said. She forced an impish grin. "Where were we?"

He took her hand, kissed the palm, then placed it low on his belly. "Right about here, as I recall." He gazed deep into her eyes. "And wandering."

"Ah, yes," she said, giving herself up to sensation again, thrilling to each touch she initiated, loving that he seemed willing to let her be in charge.

Richard's gasp was audible when she ventured further, discovering his body in all its masculine splendor. A glint in his eyes, he suddenly flipped her on her back and began deftly undoing buttons and snaps, until she was naked beneath him. The shift in power left her breathless and wanting more.

"Let me see if I understand the agenda you have in mind," he said, slowly working his way down her body.

Slow, exploratory caresses were followed by long, lingering kisses until she was writhing restlessly. There was definitely no need for external heat now. She was on fire from the inside out, a demanding, relentless fire that only he could quench. She could lose herself in flames like this.

"How long do you plan on tormenting me?" she

asked, wanting him buried inside her, needing that connection, that fullness as his body stretched hers.

"A bit longer," he said with another teasing stroke that was almost her undoing. "Let it go, Melanie."

She shook her head, stubborn even at a moment like this. "Not without you."

His gaze stayed on her face. "Please," he said quietly, touching her intimately, tormenting her until control was out of question.

It was the quiet plea that did it. Spasms rocked through her, delicious, unexpected sensations that should have satisfied, but made her crave more.

His look was smug, too smug. It drove her to drastic measures.

"You don't get to control everything," she said, fighting a grin as she executed a move she'd learned in a self-defense class that had Richard under her, shock in his eyes. The move wasn't quite as smooth as it had been in class, but it got the job done.

"Where the devil did you learn to do that?" he asked.

"Doesn't matter. It's just important that you know that I can do it." She tried to fight a satisfied grin of her own and lost. She'd never expected those time-consuming lessons to pay off in quite this way. "Now, then, tell me what you'd like me to do."

He reached up and captured her face with his hands, then drew her mouth down to his. "This," he murmured against her lips. "Just this."

"That's all?"

"And this."

He lifted her hips, then settled her again, filling her just the way she'd imagined. He held her steady, back in control, his gaze locked with hers. Melanie felt as if they were at war, but if this went the way she expected, they'd both win.

At last, he moved, thrusting up slowly, surely, then withdrawing until she had to bite her lip to keep from pleading with him.

Then there was no more question of control. They were both lost to sensation, slick and hot, hard and demanding, spiraling closer and closer to that elusive release.

When it came at last, it was shattering, leaving her weak and spent and filled with so much emotion she was scared to look into his eyes for fear he would see the truth—that she loved him beyond measure. She wasn't sure it was a truth either of them could live with.

Chapter Fourteen

It was nearly midnight when Richard crept out of bed and went downstairs to turn up the heat. Even with Melanie snuggled close, the frigid air in the room was beginning to penetrate all the way through to his bones.

Tonight had been a revelation. He'd never had a woman give to him so completely, so unselfishly, so enthusiastically. There was no question in his mind that Melanie was after his money or his power. She'd had access to both and had turned them down, seemingly without a backward glance. He believed with all his heart that her feelings were personal, and that was what he'd waited a lifetime to find without even realizing how desperately he wanted it.

So why was he still holding back? Why hadn't he told her what was in *his* heart, even though she hadn't said what was in hers? Was he such a coward that he feared rejection? He hated admitting it, but that was exactly it.

He could go into an election a few months from now and face rejection by the voters without batting an eye, but he was terrified of opening his heart to Melanie, only to discover that she intended to stick by the original rules and walk away. He knew too well what that kind of devastating loss felt like. True, his parents hadn't chosen to die and leave him and his brothers, but the effect had been traumatic just the same. If Melanie *chose* to go, it would be even worse. He knew that a man never completely recovered from a loss like that. His cowardice now was proof of that.

While he was downstairs, he took the food they'd brought with them from its freezer chest and put it into the refrigerator. Thankfully, it was still cold.

Then he flipped on a single light over the counter, brewed a pot of decaf coffee and sat down at the kitchen table to think. He thought about all the times Destiny had told him that he couldn't let his parents' deaths scare him away from love.

"Protecting your heart is self-defeating," she told him on a dark night when he'd awakened from a childhood nightmare in which he'd relived the loss of his parents. "At the end of the day you're just as lonely as if you'd loved and lost."

Richard had nodded his understanding, but the truth was he hadn't believed her. Surely nothing could be as painful as the void left when someone went away forever.

"You believe I love you, don't you?" she'd persisted.

He had nodded again, accepting the truth of that. She had been a steady, solid presence in his life from the day she'd breezed back from France and said she intended to stay and take care of him and his brothers. He trusted her—loved her—as he did few people, but there was a part of his heart he held back, protected. Slowly but surely he'd shielded himself from feeling anything for anyone.

"Are you scared I'll leave? Or that I'll die?"

Unable to voice such a terrible fear aloud, he'd merely nodded acknowledgment of that, too.

"Oh, sweetie, I will never leave," Destiny had vowed to him time and again. "It's true that I might die. We all do one day. But that doesn't mean we shouldn't love each other. Instead we should be grateful for every minute we have together. Life is meant to be lived. If I haven't taught you the importance of seizing the moment, of taking chances, of loving someone with everything that's in you, then I've failed you."

She'd tried so valiantly to instill that lesson in him—in all of them—yet Richard had been resistant. So had Mack and Ben in their own ways. Mack had filled his life with meaningless affairs. Ben had loved well but not wisely, and the pain of that loss had cemented all of his old fears. Richard wondered if Ben would ever open his heart again.

Richard had never risked anything at all. Until Melanie had come along, he'd been certain all his determined efforts to protect his heart had been successful. He'd believed he was completely incapable of real emotion.

He was on his second cup of coffee and still brooding when he heard Melanie's footsteps on the stairs. His pulse kicked up in anticipation, oblivious to all those old fears that had been tormenting him once more in the dark of night.

She wandered into the dimly lit kitchen wearing his shirt and looking sexily rumpled. "I missed you," she said sleepily, crossing the room and snuggling onto his lap in a totally trusting way that made his heart and his body ache.

Richard's arms went around her automatically. Instantly he was all too aware of her bare thighs against his own, of her bare bottom intimately pressed against his boxers. Whatever faint hope he'd held of regaining his equilibrium with her flew out the window.

"I came down to turn up the heat," he murmured against her ear, drinking in the faint scent of perfume that lingered on her skin.

"You should have turned up *my* heat," she said lightly.

He grinned at the saucy suggestion. "Now why didn't I think of that? Is it too late?" He skimmed a caress over her breast, saw the tip bead under the soft cotton of his shirt.

"We might be able to work something out," she teased. "But first you have to feed me. I'm starved."

"So many appetites," he said with amusement. "Are you absolutely certain food is what you want first?"

A gleam lit her eyes as his touch wandered. "You're making it very difficult, but yes. I want sustenance."

"Dinner? Breakfast? A sandwich?"

She moaned. "Don't make me think. I'm half-asleep. Surprise me."

"An intriguing notion," Richard said. "You going

to let me stand up, or am I expected to manage a
meal while holding you?''

She stretched—yet another torment—then rose
slowly and moved to another chair. She immediately
put her tousled head down on her arms on the table.
For all Richard could tell, she went straight back to
sleep. His gaze seemed to lock on the nape of her
neck. He wondered how she would taste there. It was
one of the few places he hadn't sampled earlier.

Resisting the urge to find out, he poked his head
into the refrigerator instead and retrieved the makings
for a chicken and avocado sandwich. He checked the
freezer and found a container of Destiny's homemade
vegetable soup he could zap in the microwave.

Melanie remained perfectly still as he worked, not
twitching so much as a muscle until he put the food
down in front of her. Then as if drawn by the spicy
scent of the hot soup, she sniffed delicately and lifted
her head.

"Oh, my," she whispered. "Tell me this is homemade."

He laughed. "It is, but I can't take the credit. Destiny always leaves some in the freezer."

"It smells heavenly." She took a spoonful, blew
on it to cool it, then put it in her mouth. "Tastes
heavenly, too." Wide-awake now, she glanced at the
sandwich. "Chicken and avocado on a baguette?
Very fancy."

"I will take credit for that," he said, amused by
her enthusiasm. "Do you really not cook anything?"

"I'll have you know I've never ruined a frozen
dinner."

"Now there's a culinary claim to be proud of," he

said, laughing, his earlier cares forgotten for the moment.

"Fortunately, I am not in your life because of my skill in the kitchen," she said. "If I were, you would be doomed to disappointment."

"You could never disappoint me," he said. Unless she went through with the breakup. That would tear him apart.

She caught his gaze, studied him intently. "You sure about that?" she asked. "You looked kind of funny there for a second, as if there was something you weren't saying."

Now, he thought, now would be the perfect time to open it all up, to tell her that everything had changed. He wanted to do it. He should do it. He even opened his mouth to speak, but in the end, he remained silent, a prisoner to his longstanding doubts and fears.

And as he saw Melanie's expression close down, saw the light in her eyes die at his silence, he knew that he'd lost what might have been his best chance for getting what he wanted for the rest of his life.

Melanie knew that something significant had happened during their late-night meal in the kitchen. She even guessed that Richard had wrestled with his demons and lost, but she had no idea what to do about it. Though she was assertive about so many things in her life, confident of her professional skills, even assured about most of her relationships, she'd lost that self-assurance when it came to matters of the heart.

Truthfully, she had been praying that allowing herself to be open and vulnerable would be enough, that she would never have to actually risk putting her feelings into words that could be thrown back into her face. She knew the power of words better than anyone. They could heal or wound, but once spoken they could never be undone.

Not entirely daunted by Richard's silence, she left herself open to what might transpire between now and whenever they went back to Alexandria. She could do that much. She'd come down here hoping for a chance to make this work. They'd made so much progress, achieved a whole new level of intimacy. It was too soon to give up on getting more.

In the morning, it seemed that Richard had reached a similar conclusion. He greeted her with a smile and a breakfast worthy of a gourmet chef in a country inn.

"You know I might reconsider marrying you for real if you promised me a meal like this every morning," she teased lightly.

"You've got it," he said just as lightly. "Of course, we'll both be waddling into the doctor's office with high cholesterol and high blood pressure before we hit forty."

She sighed as she took another bite of a fluffy omelette made with goat cheese and chives. "It might be worth it."

He gave her a once-over that told her he appreciated the way she looked right now. "So, what are we going to do to work off these calories?" he asked, an unmistakably hopeful note in his voice.

"Not that," she said decisively. She needed to reclaim a bit of distance this morning, gain some perspective on the night before.

"Too bad."

She grinned. "I'll give you a rain check. I want to go sight-seeing."

He regarded her with surprise. "You do?"

"I glanced through some of those brochures in the living room last time I was here. There's George Washington's birthplace, Robert E. Lee's birthplace, a winery. This could be fun."

"The winery holds a certain appeal. I'm not so sure about the rest. Destiny considered all that history to be part of our summer experience."

"You didn't enjoy it?"

"Maybe I didn't make myself clear," he said. "We went *every* summer."

"Ah." She grinned. "Then we won't need a guide, will we? You can tell me everything."

"I'm pretty sure I've blocked all the details."

"I'll get a book and test you," she responded, refusing to relent. "Now let's get moving."

"Now who's acting like an activities director?" he grumbled, but he did get up and stack the dishes in the dishwasher.

Melanie grinned at his attitude. She patted his cheek. "Don't pout. When we get home you can test me."

"On the history?"

"No, on my responsiveness to other commands."

His expression brightened at that. "Put on your walking shoes, darling. These are going to be lightning-fast tours."

Richard found to his amazement that he could put last night's disappointment and worries behind him and fall in with Melanie's playful mood. She soaked up the history lessons with astonishing attention, making him sift through years of tidbits for the most fascinating ones in his memory. He loved that she listened so intently, her expression as rapt as if he were divulging bits of current gossip about still-living neighbors.

"I know as a Yankee from Ohio, I shouldn't be so caught up with Robert E. Lee's family home," she said as they left Stratford Hall, "but the place is so beautiful and so fascinating. I wish I'd lived back then. Imagine having his family and the Washingtons for neighbors. Just think what the dinner conversations must have been like."

Richard grinned at her. "Not unlike the conversation at one of Destiny's dinner parties when she invites half of the power brokers in D.C. I'll have to make sure you're at the next one. Destiny likes to throw off a controversial spark and see what it ignites."

"Yes, I imagine that would delight her. She told me about the incredibly lively and intellectual gatherings she used to have in her studio in France."

Richard regarded her with surprise. "She did? She never talks about France with us."

"Really?" Melanie's expression turned thoughtful. "Maybe she doesn't want to sound as if she misses it."

"Why on earth would she be afraid to let us see that she had a life before she came home to us?" he asked, then sighed as the answer came to him. "Because she doesn't want us to think for a second that she made a sacrifice."

"I suspect that's it," Melanie said. "Maybe you should ask her about it sometime."

"I probably should," he admitted. "I wonder if she and Ben ever talk about it. That's when she was painting. It's what they have in common. They both love art. She nurtured his talent unselfishly, but I some-times wondered if she missed painting herself.'' He felt oddly left out to think that there was a part of Destiny she had kept from him, a part she might have shared with at least one of his brothers, a part she had definitely shared with Melanie, a comparative stranger at the time.

Melanie seemed to guess the direction of his thoughts. ''If she kept silent, it was because she didn't think you were ready to hear about the life she had in France, not because she loved you less.''

''I know that,'' he snapped impatiently.

''Do you really?'' Melanie asked quietly. ''I think what she did was one of the most unselfish acts I've ever heard about. She had a wonderful life, Richard. She was living a charmed life in a place she loved. She was madly in love. Her paintings were selling in Paris and along the French Riviera. She had friends. She was even a bit famous in her world. But when you, Mack and Ben needed her, she never gave any of it a second thought. She was here for you. For her, family came first. That's the only thing that really matters.''

It was true. Richard had always known that his aunt had made sacrifices for them, but he'd never guessed how many. Or maybe as a child he hadn't wanted to know. And as an adult, her presence was a given, something he no longer questioned. How astonishing that it had taken Melanie to make him see a whole other side to Destiny. For the first time he was seeing her as a remarkable woman, not just as his aunt.

''You're amazing,'' he said, pressing a kiss to Mel-anie's cheek, grateful to her for making him put Des-tiny's sacrifices into perspective.

"Thank you, but what did I do?"

"Opened my eyes." And his heart, he added silently.

The brief vacation from the world passed in a blissful haze. If it hadn't been for the one thing Richard hadn't said—that he loved her—Melanie would have been totally content and rapturously happy.

They stayed up late, watched movies and ate popcorn. They danced to oldies on the radio. They made love in front of the fire time and again. Each time was a revelation, showing her new insights into everything but his heart. She despaired of that ever changing.

On New Year's Eve at the stroke of midnight, she was cradled in his arms, spent but filled with contentment, when he gazed into her eyes, "There's something we need to discuss before we go home tomorrow," he said. "It's a new year, time for new beginnings."

There was hope to be found in his words, but his tone filled Melanie with a sense of dread. "What?"

He looked away from her. "The very public breakup I promised you."

"You've been thinking about that?" she asked dully. She'd dared to envision happily-ever-after, and he'd been focused on extricating himself from the lie, starting the new year fresh without her and all of the complications she represented.

"Haven't you?" he asked. "You said all along it was something we should do sooner rather than later. I think you were right. After what happened with Destiny the other day, all the shopping and planning, we can't let this continue."

"This is it, then," she said bravely, refusing to

allow one single traitorous tear to fall. "What do you have in mind?"

He met her gaze then, searching her face for something, but she was determined not to let him see the hurt ripping her apart. Instead, she fought to keep her gaze neutral.

"I thought you should decide," he said, his voice suddenly flat and emotionless.

Melanie nodded, because she didn't trust herself to speak.

"You'll think about it?" he prodded. "You'll let me know? I'll go along with whatever you want."

"Do you want to do this very soon?" she asked when she could keep her voice steady.

"I think that's best," he said, his gaze averted.

"So do I," she said. Then she could get on with the business of mending her broken heart.

Suddenly chilled to the bone, she reached for the chenille throw on the sofa, stood up and wrapped herself in it. "I'm going to bed," she said in a voice so choked she barely recognized it as her own.

Richard didn't reach for her, said nothing to stop her. Only when she was at the foot of the stairs did he call out softly.

"Happy new year, Melanie."

"Happy new year," she replied automatically, but her heart wasn't in it. If anything, this new year was off to the worst start ever.

Upstairs, she barely resisted the desire to throw things. Unless something hit Richard in the head and knocked some sense into him, what would be the point?

Couldn't he see what she saw? They could be happy together. She knew it. She could help him get wherever he wanted to go in life. She'd be the perfect match for a man who needed some balance for all the demands he put on himself. She'd keep him from being stodgy.

But her hope of any future had died the instant he'd brought up the great breakup scene. Despite the emotional and physical connection she'd experienced over the past few days, they were obviously in very different places. To him this had apparently been nothing more than an interlude, something inevitable that had been building between them, something neither of them could have ignored forever. It hadn't meant anything, at least not to Richard.

Melanie knew better than most that it was impossible to make someone fall in love. It was equally impossible to make them admit to love when they were too afraid to recognize the emotion. When it came to that, she was as cowardly as Richard.

So to protect her stupid pride and her heart, she would go back to Alexandria and throw herself into planning the party at which she would throw that damnable ring back in his face. She would make the scene so believable, so memorable, that it would haunt him forever. Richard might be willing to toss away what they'd had, but he'd never forget her.

Sadly, she wasn't likely to forget him, either.

Chapter Fifteen

Melanie hated the fact that she was deliberately going to ruin Destiny's engagement party for them by creating a scene, but Richard's aunt had virtually given her no choice. With her usual impulsiveness, Destiny had already been well into planning the event when Richard and Melanie returned from their get-away. With invitations already at the printer's, it had been too late to turn back.

Since Melanie and Richard had concluded it was best to end the charade before it went on too much longer, the party was the most public way of accomplishing that. This way everyone would find out at once that she and Richard were no longer together. She'd even invited Pete Forsythe so he could witness the end of the romance his sleazy reporting—albeit at Destiny's instigation—had triggered in the first place.

"Are you absolutely certain you don't want your

parents to fly over for the party?'' Destiny asked as they were doing one final check of the guest list. "I'm sure Richard would be happy to send the company jet for them.''

And have them here for this debacle? No way, Melanie thought. It was bad enough that they were likely to read about it in some wire service tidbit in their morning paper.

She had, however, insisted on having Becky at the party. She was going to need at least one friendly face in the crowd when things blew up.

"My parents hate flying,'' she told Destiny truthfully. It was just about the only honest thing to cross her lips lately. "And Dad can't get off work in the middle of the week to drive over. I'm sure they'll want to throw their own party in Ohio sometime down the road.''

Probably when she was forced to move back home because her career here had gone up in flames, she thought despondently.

"Melanie, is everything all right?'' Destiny asked, regarding her worriedly. "For a bride-to-be, you don't seem very happy. You've looked sad ever since you and Richard got back from your little romantic getaway.''

"I'm just tired,'' she assured Destiny. "We did too much and my desk was piled high when I got back, so I've been working a lot of late hours.''

Destiny seemed to accept the explanation. "Once you and Richard are married, you could stop working,'' she said carefully. "I know that's not a very modern attitude, but you certainly could afford to quit.''

"I love what I do," Melanie told her. And soon it was going to be the most important thing in her life.

"I know and you're good at it, but sometimes life forces us to prioritize. At some point your family might need to come first."

"The way it did for you?"

Destiny's expression remained neutral. "Yes," she said quietly. "The way it did for me."

"Have you ever regretted it?"

Destiny looked shocked. "How could I? Richard, Mack and Ben are like sons to me. They needed me," she said fiercely. "I could never have lived with any other choice."

Melanie heard the total conviction in her voice, even though she also thought she heard a faint note of wistfulness, something Destiny would never voice aloud. If there were regrets, she would clearly take them to her grave. It was not a burden she would place on her nephews.

"How do you know when the choice is right?" Melanie asked, her own wistfulness far more evident.

Destiny smiled at her. "You ask your heart. It will never lie to you, not about anything important." Then she added wryly, "Of course, sometimes you have to listen carefully to hear it through all the clatter going on around you."

Melanie wondered about that. Her heart seemed to have quite a track record of getting it wrong. Before she could pursue that thought, Richard came into the very feminine office that Destiny maintained at Carlton Industries. It was a stark contrast to the clean, modern lines in the other offices.

He came over and gave Destiny an absentminded peck on the cheek, then dropped an equally impersonal kiss on Melanie's lips to maintain the charade for the moment. Even knowing it meant nothing, Melanie still felt the touch curl her toes.

"What are you two up to?" he asked.

"Finalizing plans for the engagement party," Destiny said. "The invitations are going out this afternoon."

He met Melanie's gaze, his expression guarded. "Has Destiny roped you into inviting a cast of thousands?"

"Only hundreds," Melanie said. "I cut her off when we hit three hundred and fifty."

"A nice round number," he said wryly. "Any media?"

"Pete Forsythe," Melanie told him. "And his photographer."

Destiny shook her head. "Why you want to invite Forsythe is beyond me."

Richard regarded her with amusement. "I thought you were rather fond of Mr. Forsythe."

Destiny looked suitably appalled. Melanie was impressed by her ability to feign indignation.

"Why would you think such a thing?" Destiny inquired coolly.

"You did use him to get that item about my cozy little getaway with Melanie in the paper a few weeks back," he reminded her. "Why not give him the inside scoop on the resulting engagement?"

"Whatever," Destiny said airily.

"Indeed," Richard replied. Then he asked, "Mind if I steal Melanie away? We need to firm up some plans of our own."

"By all means," Destiny said eagerly.

Melanie reluctantly followed Richard back to his office. "Is this about the campaign?"

He shook his head. "You quit, remember?"

"That doesn't mean you can't ask me something in an unofficial capacity," she told him, regretting now that all their ties were about to be severed.

"Well, it's not about the campaign. I needed to ask you about something else. I have a business dinner to attend tonight. Will you come along?"

Melanie stared at him. "Under the circumstances, don't you think that's a bad idea?"

"Probably, but these people will be offended if you're not there. They've heard about you, and they're anxious to meet you before the big party."

Melanie hated this. How could she go out with Richard tonight and fake being deliriously happy in front of strangers when she was already plotting their breakup?

"Could we have a spat tonight and end things before dinner?" she inquired hopefully. "Then we wouldn't have to go through with the rest of this, not dinner tonight, not the party, none of it."

He regarded her curiously. "I thought you wanted the big scene. It was one of the conditions when we went into this phony engagement."

"Honestly, I'm losing my taste for it." She didn't want to humiliate him, any more than she was looking forward to embarrassing herself or spoiling Destiny's hope for the two of them. She just wanted it all over with.

She reached for her ring and tried to twist it off. "Let's end this quietly, here and now."

Unfortunately, the ring wasn't budging. Nor, judging from the grim scowl on Richard's face, was he.

"You picked the time and place," he reminded her. "Backing out now is out of the question."

"Why?"

"It just is," he said, his expression set stubbornly.

If she hadn't known better, she might have entertained the crazy thought that he was trying to buy himself a little more time. But of course that couldn't be.

He should have let Melanie have her way and ended things in his office the other day when she'd pleaded with him to get it over with, Richard thought as he forced himself to take out his tuxedo in preparation for the upcoming engagement party.

What idiotic part of his brain had thought that waiting another week was a good idea? If he'd been hoping that having dinner with a couple of business associates would change anything, he'd been sadly mistaken. That evening, much like this one was destined to be, had been a disaster. Melanie had been quiet and withdrawn. The other couples had been uncomfortable. He wouldn't be a bit surprised if the deal they'd been discussing fell apart. Not that he could manage to work up much dismay over that. All of his dismay seemed to be reserved for the prospect of losing the only women he'd ever allowed himself to love.

"Why so glum?" Mack asked, when he found Richard pouring himself a stiff drink. "Tonight's party is supposed to be a celebration."

"Oh, can it," Richard retorted. "We both know better than that."

Mack seemed genuinely surprised by his reminder. "But I thought—"

"What? That something had changed? That we really were going to go through with the engagement and the wedding?"

"Yes, as a matter of fact," Mack said. "All the signs were pointing in that direction, especially when the two of you slipped out of town for a romantic little getaway."

"Well, where Melanie and I are concerned, things often aren't what they seem to be. She chose that time to let me know that we were going through with the previous arrangement."

Mack gave him a hard look. "And you did what to persuade her not to?"

"What was I supposed to do?" Richard demanded. "She'd obviously made up her mind."

Mack groaned. "Did you tell her you loved her?"

Richard frowned at him.

"I'll take that as a no," Mack concluded. "What is wrong with you? Never mind. I know the answer to that. Believe me, I'm as gun-shy when it comes to romance as you are, but we're talking Melanie here, bro. The woman is crazy in love with you, and you're obviously in love with her. Don't let her slip through your fingers."

Richard wasn't ready to admit his feelings, not even to a man he trusted with his life. "You're forgetting one thing. This whole engagement thing has been a farce to prove something to Destiny."

Mack, damn him, laughed. "You still think Destiny doesn't know that? You're delusional. All of this may have started as a stupid, immature game—"

Richard's scowl deepened.

"Don't pull that look on me, big brother," Mack said, undaunted. "You can't intimidate me. The im-

portant thing here is to admit that the game is over
and try to fix everything before it's too late. Don't be
stubborn, Richard. Not about something this important. If you want to make the whole engagement thing
real, it's entirely possible that she does, too, but was
too scared to admit it given your ridiculous agreement
about an exit strategy.''

Richard stared at him, startled by Mack's insight.
Could it be that Mack was right? Had he simply
backed Melanie into a corner, the same way she'd
backed him into one, both of them unwilling to risk
being vulnerable?

"When did you get to be so smart, especially about
matters of the heart, Mack?"

"I'm not the stupid one, bro. You're the one who
hasn't seen the handwriting on the wall till now."

It seemed pointless to keep denying his feelings
when Mack wasn't buying it. "Then what do I do?"

"You'll think of something, some grandstand play,
and don't take no for an answer. Melanie can stage
her scene, then you stage yours. I'll put my money
on you."

With that kind of faith in his persuasiveness, how
could Richard say no? Not when it meant getting the
only thing he'd ever wanted this desperately. He
picked up the phone and called his jeweler, then
gazed at his brother.

"I have an idea, it just might work."

"Even if it doesn't, at least you'll know that you
did everything you could. That's a hell of a lot better
than giving up without a fight."

Mack was right, Richard concluded, feeling marginally better. He knew all about the importance of
seizing the initiative in a negotiation. Why the hell

had the tactic slipped his mind until now, when this was the most important deal he was ever likely to close?

Melanie was impatiently swiping at tears when Destiny found her in the ladies' room moments before she was supposed to break her engagement. Until now the party had been a rousing success. She should have been smiling. In fact, she had been smiling till her jaw ached. She'd come in here when she couldn't bear it a moment longer.

"Darling, is anything wrong?" Destiny asked, her expression oddly smug rather than worried or sympathetic.

Melanie studied Destiny's expression, then sighed. Mack had been right. Destiny knew exactly what she and Richard had been up to. "You've known all along, haven't you? You've known that it was a charade?"

"Of course I have," Destiny said cheerfully, as if she hadn't just blown a fortune to celebrate something that had never been. She patted Melanie's hand. "But I also know you're in love with my nephew and he's in love with you. I don't have a doubt in my mind about that."

Melanie didn't ask her how she knew that. She needed advice and she needed it in a hurry. "Then how do I fix this?"

"You don't," Destiny advised gently. "You let Richard fix it. There are some things men have to figure out for themselves. Otherwise the balance of power is always off."

"Do you think he will?" Melanie asked plaintively.

"If he's even half the man I think he is, you'll be walking down the aisle in a month," Destiny declared confidently. "And no one knows my nephew better than I do."

"Then I break up with him as planned?"

Destiny nodded. "He'll be expecting it. Don't disappoint him. Or if he's been counting on a last-minute change of heart, this will really shake him up."

An hour later Melanie took a deep breath and tossed a glass of champagne in Richard's face. It wasn't what she'd mentally scripted for the opening gambit in the scene, but it felt good. Sometimes the man was so dense, she could barely stand it. Maybe the champagne would snap him to his senses.

"What the hell was that for?" he demanded, looking genuinely shocked.

"I was hoping it would wash some of that fog away from your eyes so you'd start seeing things more clearly."

Suddenly, to her surprise, he chuckled. "Is that so?"

"Yes, it's so. For a supposedly smart man, you're dumber than dirt about some things." Okay, this wasn't the way Destiny had advised her to go, but Melanie was tired of leaving her fate in other people's hands. She'd left it to Destiny, Richard, the gods, for too long already. She'd forgotten that she was in charge of her own future, that no one cared more about the outcome of this relationship more than she did…unless it was Richard.

"Are you breaking up with me?" he inquired, clearly amused despite the large sea of stunned faces surrounding them.

"Yes," she said very firmly.

"Do I get the ring back?"

She held out her hand and considered the huge rock that she'd hated from the beginning. It sparkled brilliantly in the lights from the ballroom's fancy chandeliers. The stupid thing must be six carats, with perfect clarity and color. It was worth a fortune. "I don't think so. I think I'll pawn it to help me expand my company."

Behind her, she heard his brothers chuckle.

Richard shrugged, not nearly as outraged by that as she'd expected.

"Okay, then," he said mildly, "but I think you're going to want to take it off now."

Melanie faced him stubbornly. "Why would I do that?"

He pulled a velvet jeweler's box from his pocket. "I've got another one I think maybe you'll like better."

Melanie felt her mouth gape. "You're proposing to me? Here? Now? For real?"

She heard a delighted gasp behind her and whirled on Destiny. "Oh, put a sock in it. This is exactly what you were counting on from the beginning. You said you knew him better than anyone."

Destiny's eyes were filled with laughter. "Trust me, darling, I didn't know about this."

Richard grinned. "You should have guessed. You did put it all into motion, didn't you?"

"I can't take all the credit," she said with surprising modesty.

Richard didn't seem impressed by her sudden sense of humility. "You should know by now that Destiny always gets what she wants," he confided to Melanie.

Destiny beamed at Richard and Melanie, then

turned to his brothers, a sparkle of pure mischief in her eyes. "Something you two need to remember, too."

Mack and Ben, their expressions instantly horrified, suddenly melted into the crowd. Watching them disappear, Melanie turned to Richard. "When their turns come, whose side are you going to be on?"

"Destiny's, of course," he said without hesitation. "She's made me a believer in the power of love." He looked deep into Melanie's eyes. "You still haven't given me an answer, by the way."

Melanie smiled. "I should make you wait, maybe torment you a little."

She heard Destiny mutter something about the balance of power again and made up her mind. She knew what it had cost Richard to put his heart on the line in this room filled with people. He'd taken the risk. The least she could do was reciprocate here and now.

"I accept," she told him, her gaze locked with his.

Their obviously baffled guests, who'd come to celebrate an engagement, seen it broken, then back on again, cheered wildly, taking their cue from Destiny, who swept Melanie into a hug and congratulated her.

"I couldn't have asked for a better woman for Richard," she said.

Melanie chuckled. "You act surprised. We both know you handpicked me, though I've yet to figure out why."

"Oh, darling, that one's easy," Destiny said, turning her to face Richard, who was more at ease than Melanie had ever seen him. His eyes filled with emotion when he caught her looking his way.

"Can you see what I see?" Destiny asked.

"He's happy," Melanie realized, recognizing the signs because she was filled with jubilation herself.

"He's happy," Destiny confirmed. "Because of you."

Melanie gave her a fierce hug. "Maybe we should share the credit."

Destiny nodded, her expression smug. "Yes, perhaps we should for tonight, but I think over time the lion's share will go to you. I'll thank you in advance for that."

Melanie's gaze lingered on Richard. "He's able to love me at all because of you," she told Destiny honestly. "Your work here is done."

"Yes, I believe it is." She looked around the room. "Now where the dickens do you suppose Mack is?"

Melanie chuckled at Destiny's eagerness as she began moving through the crowd in search of Mack. "You probably ought to find your brother and warn him," she told Richard when he joined her.

"Hell no," Richard said. "Mack can take care of himself. In fact, it'll be a pleasure to watch him squirm for a change. Besides, I have more important things to do."

"Oh? Such as?"

"This," he said, lowering his head to capture her mouth.

"Definitely more important," Melanie murmured against his lips.

"Have I mentioned that I love you?" Richard asked when the kiss ended.

"Come to think of it, no," Melanie said. "But I thought it was implicit in your proposal."

He smiled. "I knew you could read my mind."

She sighed. "There was a while there when I was

sure I'd gotten it all wrong. From now on, though, I think I'll trust my instincts.''

"What are your instincts telling you now?" he asked.

She studied him thoughtfully, then grinned. "Shame on you," she scolded.

"Then you're not interested in blowing off this party and getting a room upstairs?"

"I didn't say I wasn't interested," she replied. "I can see you're going to have to work on reading my mind."

His expression sobered. "I'll make it my life's mission. That and loving you."

Melanie felt her heart swell. If he said it, she could bank on it. Richard Carlton always kept his promises. That was the backbone of his campaign strategy and, best of all, it was the truth.

* * * * *

PRICELESS

BY
SHERRYL WOODS

To Dee Adams, Betty Baderman and
Pat Morrissey/Havlin, enduring friends from
my days at Miami's Jackson Memorial Hospital.

And to Karen Strauss, RN, Nurse Manager, Paediatric
Haematology Oncology, Jackson Memorial Hospital,
with thanks for her medical expertise.
Any mistakes are my own.

Chapter One

Mack Carlton, who'd had more quick moves on a football field than any player in Washington, D.C., history, had been dodging his Aunt Destiny for the better part of a month. Unfortunately, Destiny was faster and sneakier than most of the defensive linemen he'd ever faced. She was also more highly motivated. It was a toss-up as to how long it would be before she caught up with him.

Ever since she'd succeeded in getting his older brother, Richard, married a few weeks back, Destiny had set her sights on Mack. She wasn't even subtle about it. A steady parade of women had been popping up all over the place. Not that that was an unusual occurrence in Mack's life—he did have a well-deserved reputation as a playboy, after all—but these women were not his type. They had "serious" and "happily ever after" written all over them. Mack didn't do serious. He didn't do permanent. Destiny, of all people, should know that.

Not that he had the same issues with love and loss that had kept his big brother off the emotional roller coaster. Mack preferred to think that his hang-ups had more to do with a desire to know lots and lots of women than any fear of eventual abandonment. Why limit himself to one particular dish when there was an entire buffet to be sampled? Sure, he'd been affected by the deaths of his parents in a small plane crash in the Blue Ridge Mountains when he was barely ten, but the trauma hadn't followed him into adulthood as it had Richard.

Not that Destiny or Richard believed that. Hell, even his younger brother, Ben, was convinced they were all emotionally messed up because of the crash, but Mack knew otherwise, at least in his own case. He just flat-out liked women. He appreciated their minds, their quick wits.

Okay, that was the politically correct thing to say, he conceded, even though there was nobody around who was privy to his private, all-too-male thoughts. Truthfully, what he really appreciated was the way they felt in his arms, their soft skin and passionate responses. While he enjoyed a lively conversation as much as the next man, he truly loved the intimacy of sex, however fleeting and illusional it might be.

Not that he was any kind of sex addict, but a little wholesome rustling of the sheets made a man feel alive. So maybe that was it, he thought with a sudden rush of insight. Maybe what he loved most about sex was that it made him feel alive after being reminded at a very young age that life was short and death was permanent. Maybe he had some emotional scars from that plane crash, after all.

He was still pondering the magnitude of that discovery when Destiny sashayed into his office at team headquarters, where he was now ensconced as part owner of the team for which he'd once played. He was so thoroughly startled by her unexpected appearance in this male bastion, he brought the legs of his chair crashing to the floor with such force it was a wonder the chair didn't shatter.

"You've been avoiding me," Destiny said pleasantly, sitting across from him in her pale-blue suit that mirrored the color of her eyes.

As always, Destiny looked as if she'd just walked out of a beauty salon, which was a far cry from some of the pictures around the house taken during her years as a painter in the south of France. In those she always appeared a bit rumpled and wildly exotic. Mack occasionally allowed himself to wonder if his aunt missed those days, if she missed the life she'd given up to come back to Virginia to care for him and his brothers after the plane crash.

As a child he'd never dared to ask because he'd feared that reminding Destiny of what she'd sacrificed might send her scurrying back to Europe to reclaim it. As he'd gotten older, he'd started taking her presence—and her contentment—for granted.

Now he gave his aunt a cool, unblinking look, determined not to let her see that her arrival had shaken him in any way. With Destiny it was best not to show any signs of weakness at all. "You're imagining things," he told her flatly.

Destiny chuckled. "I didn't imagine that it was your behind I saw scurrying out the back door at Richard

and Melanie's the other night, did I? I saw that backside in too many football huddles to mistake it.''

Damn. He thought he'd made a clean escape. Of
course, it was possible that his brother had blabbed.
Richard thought Mack had taken a little too much pleasure in Destiny's successful maneuvering of Richard
straight into Melanie's arms. He was more than capable
of going for a little payback to see that Mack met the
same fate.

"Did you really spot me, or did Richard rat me
out?'' he asked suspiciously. "I know he wants me to
fall into one of your snares the same way he did.''

"Your brother is not a tattler," she assured him.
"And my eyesight's twenty-twenty.'' She gave him a
measuring look. "What are you scared of, Mack?''

"I think we both know the answer to that one. I also
suspect it's the same thing that brought you to my office. What sort of devious scheme do you have up your
sleeve, Destiny? And before you answer, let's get one
thing straight, my social life is off-limits. I'm handling
it very well on my own.''

Destiny rolled her eyes. "Yes, I've seen how well
you're handling it in every gossip column in town. It's
unseemly, Mack. You may not be directly affiliated
with Carlton Industries, but the family does have a certain social standing in the community. You need to be
mindful of that, especially with Richard entering politics any day now.''

The family respectability card was a familiar one.
He was surprised she'd tried the tactic again, since it
had failed abysmally in the past. "Most people are ca-
pable of separating me from my brother. Besides that,
I'm an adult,'' he recited as he had so often in the past.
"So are the women I date. No harm, no foul.''

"And you're content with that?" Destiny asked, her skepticism plain.

"Absolutely," he insisted. "Couldn't be happier."

She nodded slowly. "Well, that's that then. Your happiness is all that's ever mattered to me, you know. Yours and your brothers'."

Mack studied her with a narrowed gaze. Surely she wasn't giving up that easily. Destiny was constitutionally incapable of surrendering before she'd even had a first skirmish. If she were so easily put off, Richard wouldn't be married right now. Mack needed to remember that.

"We appreciate that you love us," he said carefully. "And I'm glad you're willing to let me choose my own dates. It's a real relief, in fact."

She fought a smile. "Yes, I imagine it is, since the kind of woman *I* see you with is not the sort of mental and emotional lightweight you tend to choose."

He ignored the slap at his taste in women. He'd heard it before. "Anything else I can do for you while you're here?" he asked politely. "Do you need any team souvenirs for one of your charity auctions?"

"Not really. I just wanted to drop by and catch up," she claimed with a perfectly straight face. "Will you come to dinner soon?"

"Now that I know you've given up meddling in my social life, yes," he told her, deciding to give her the benefit of the doubt for the moment. "Is everyone coming for Sunday dinner?"

"Of course."

"Then I'll be there," he promised. At least there was some safety in numbers, in case Destiny had a change of heart between now and Sunday.

She stood up. "I'll be on my way, then."

Mack walked with her down the hall to the elevator,
struck anew by how small she was. She barely reached
his shoulder. She'd always seemed to be such a giant
force to be reckoned with that it gave the illusion she
was bigger. Then, again, he was six-two, so Destiny
was probably a perfectly average-size woman. Add in
her dynamic personality, and she had few equals of any
size among Washington's most powerful women.

She was about to step into the elevator when she
gave him her most winning smile, the one reserved for
suckering big bucks from an unwitting corporate CEO.
Seeing that smile immediately put Mack right back on
guard.

"Oh, darling, I almost forgot," she claimed, reaching into her purse and pulling out a note written on a
sheet of her pretty floral stationery. "Could you drop
by the hospital this afternoon? A Dr. Browning spoke
to me earlier and said one of the young patients in the
oncology unit has a very poor outlook. The boy is a
huge fan of yours, and the doctor feels certain that a
visit from you might boost his morale."

Despite the clamor of alarm bells ringing in his head,
Mack took the note. Whatever Destiny was really up
to, it was not the kind of request he could ignore. She
knew that, too. She'd instilled a strong sense of responsibility in all of her nephews. His football celebrity
had made fulfilling requests of this type a commonplace part of his life.

He glanced at his watch. "I have a business meeting
in a couple of hours, but I can swing by there on my
way."

"Thank you, darling. I knew I could count on you.
I told Dr. Browning you'd be by, that the other requests
must have gotten lost."

Mack felt his stomach twist into a knot. "There were other requests?"

"Several of them, I believe. I was a last resort."

He nodded grimly, his initial suspicions about his aunt's scheming vanishing. "I'll look into that. The staff around here knows that I do this kind of visit whenever possible, especially if there's a kid involved."

"I'm sure it was just some sort of oversight or mix-up," Destiny said. "The important thing is that you're going now. I'll say a prayer for the young boy. You can tell me all about your visit on Sunday. Perhaps there's more we could be doing for him."

Mack leaned down and kissed her cheek. "You ought to be the one going over there. A dose of your good cheer could improve anyone's spirits."

She regarded him with a surprised sparkle in her eyes. "What a lovely thing to say, Mack. That must explain why you're such a hit with the ladies."

Mack could have told her it wasn't his sweet-talk that won the hearts of the women he dated, but there were some things a man simply didn't say to his aunt. If she wanted to believe he owed his social life to being a nice guy, he was more than willing to let her. It might keep a few tart-tongued lectures at bay.

"It's a game, for heaven's sake," pediatric oncologist Beth Browning declared, earning a thoroughly disgusted look from her male colleagues at Children's Cancer Hospital. "A game played by grown men, who ought to be using their brains instead of their brawn—assuming of course that their brains haven't been scrambled."

"We're talking about professional football," radiologist Jason Morgan protested, as if she'd uttered blasphemy. "It's about winning and losing. It's a metaphor for good triumphing over evil."

"I don't hear the surgeons saying that when they're patching up some kid's broken bones after a Saturday game," Beth said.

"Football injuries are a rite of passage," Hal Watkins, the orthopedic physician, insisted.

"And a boon to your practice," she noted.

"Hey," he protested. "That's not fair. Nobody wants to see a kid get hurt."

"Then keep 'em off the field," Beth suggested.

Jason looked shocked. "Then who'd grow up to play professional sports?"

"Oh, please, why does anyone have to do that?" Beth retorted, warming to the topic. She'd read about Mack Carlton and his rise from star quarterback to team owner. The man had a law degree, for goodness' sakes. What a waste! Not that she was a huge admirer of lawyers, given the way their greediness had led to hikes in malpractice insurance.

"Because it's football, for crying out loud," Hal replied, as if the game were as essential for survival as air.

"Come on, guys. It's a game. Nothing more, nothing less." She turned to appeal to Peyton Lang, the hematologist, who'd been silent until now. "What do you think?"

He held up his hands. "You're not drawing me into this one. I'm ambivalent. I don't care that much about football, but I don't have a problem if anyone else happens to find it entertaining."

"Don't you think it's absurd that so much time,

money and energy is being wasted in pursuit of some stupid title?'' Beth countered.

"The winner of the Super Bowl rules!'' Jason insisted.

"Rules what?'' Beth asked.

"The world.''

"I wasn't aware they played football in most of the rest of the world. Let's face it, in this town it's about some rich guy who has enough money to buy the best players so he'll have something to get excited about on Sunday afternoons,'' she said scathingly. "If Mack Carlton had a life, if he had a family, if he had *anything* important to do, he wouldn't be wasting his money on a football team.''

Rather than the indignant protests she'd expected, Beth was stunned when every man around her in the hospital cafeteria fell silent. Guilty looks were exchanged, the kind that said humiliation was just around the corner.

"You sure you don't want to reconsider that remark?'' Jason asked, giving her an odd, almost pleading look.

"Why would I want to do that?''

"Because I'm pretty sure you mentioned when we started this discussion that you've been trying to get Mack Carlton in here to visit with Tony Vitale,'' Jason said. "The kid's crazy about him. You thought meeting Mack might lift his spirits, since the chemo hasn't been going that well.''

Her gaze narrowed. "So? This community-minded paragon of football virtue hasn't bothered to respond to even one of my calls.''

Jason cleared his throat and gestured behind her.

Oh, hell, she thought as she slowly turned and stared

up at the tall, broad-shouldered man in the custom-tailored suit who was regarding her with a solemn, steady gaze. He had a faint scar under one eye, but that did nothing to mar his good looks. In fact, it merely added character to a perfectly sculpted face and drew attention to eyes so dark, so enigmatic, that she trembled under the impact. Everything about his appearance spoke of money, taste and arrogance, except maybe the hairstyle, which had a Harrison Ford kind of spikiness to it.

"Dr. Browning?" he inquired in an incredulous tone that suggested he'd been expecting someone older and definitely someone male.

Despite the unspoken but definitely implied insult, his quiet, smooth voice eased through Beth, then delivered a belated punch. She tried to gather her wits and to form the apology he deserved, but the words wouldn't come. She'd never have deliberately insulted him to his face, even if she did have an abundance of scorn for men who wasted money on athletic pursuits that could be better spent on saving mankind.

"She'll be with you as soon as she gets her foot out of her mouth," Jason said, breaking the tension.

Grateful to the radiologist for helping her out, she managed to stand and offer her hand. "Mr. Carlton, I wasn't expecting you."

"Obviously," he said, his lips curving into a slow smile. "My aunt said you'd had trouble contacting me. My staff shouldn't have put you off. I apologize for that."

Beth had read that he was a heartbreaker. Now she knew why. If his gaze could render her speechless, that smile could set her on fire. Add in the unexpected touch of humility and the sincerity of his apology, and her first impression was pretty much smashed to bits. She'd never experienced a reaction to any man quite like this. She wasn't sure she liked it.

"Would you...?" Exasperated by her inability to gather her thoughts, she swallowed hard, took a deep breath, then tried again. "Would you like a cup of coffee?"

"Actually I'm on a tight schedule. I found myself near here and wanted to let you know that I haven't been deliberately blowing off your calls. I thought I'd take a chance that now would be a good time to meet Tony."

"Of course," she said at once, knowing what such a visit would mean even if regular visiting hours were later in the day. This was one instance when she didn't mind breaking the rules. "I'll take you to his room. He'll be thrilled."

Jason cleared his throat. At his pointed look, Beth realized that her colleagues were hoping for an introduction to the local football legend. Amazed that grown men could be as enamored of Mack Carlton as her twelve-year-old patient was, she paused and made the introductions.

When it seemed that the doctors were about to go over every great play the man had ever made on the football field, she cut them off.

"As much as you guys would probably like to discuss football for the rest of the day, Mr. Carlton is here to see Tony," she reminded them a bit curtly.

Mack Carlton gave her another of those smiles that could melt the polar ice cap. "Besides," he said, "we're probably boring Dr. Browning to tears."

Now there was a loaded statement if ever she'd heard one. She didn't dare admit to being bored and risk insulting him more than she had when he'd first arrived and overheard her. Nor was she inclined to lie. Instead she forced a smile. "You did say you had a tight schedule."

His grin spread. "So I did. Lead the way, Doctor."

Relieved to have something concrete to do, she set off briskly through the corridors to the unit where twelve-year-old Tony had spent far too much of his young life.

"Tell me about Tony," Mack suggested as they walked.

"He's twelve and he has leukemia," Beth told him, fighting to keep any trace of emotion from her voice. It was the kind of story she hated to tell, especially when the battle wasn't being won. "It's the third time it's come back. This time he's not responding so well to the chemotherapy. We'd hoped to get him ready for a bone marrow transplant, but we don't have the right donor marrow, and because of his difficulty with the chemo, I'm not so sure it would be feasible for him right now anyway."

Mack listened intently to everything she was saying. "His prognosis?"

"Not good," she said tersely.

"And you're taking it personally," he said quietly.

Beth promptly shook her head. "I know I can't win every battle," she said, as she had to the psychologist who'd expressed his concern about her state of mind earlier in the day. Few people knew just how personally she took a case like Tony's. She was surprised that Mack Carlton had guessed it so easily.

"But you hate losing," Mack said.

"When it's a matter of life and death, of course I

do," she said fiercely. "I went into medicine to save lives."

"Why?" Before she could reply, he added, "I know it's a noble profession, but dealing with sick kids has to be an emotional killer. Why you? Why this field?"

She was surprised that he actually seemed interested in her response. "I was drawn to it early on," she said, aware that she was being evasive by suggesting that it hadn't been the motivating force in her entire life. With any luck, Mack wouldn't realize it.

"Because?" he prodded, not accepting the response at face value and proving once more that he was a more insightful man than she'd expected him to be.

"Why does it matter to you?" she asked, still dodging a direct answer to his question.

His eyes studied her intently. "Because it obviously matters to you."

Once again his insight caught her off guard. It was evident he wasn't going to let this go until he'd heard at least some version of the truth. "Okay, here it is in a nutshell. I had an older brother who died of leukemia when I was ten," she told him, revealing more than she had to anyone other than her family. They knew all too well what her motivation had been for choosing medicine, and they didn't entirely approve of her choice, fearing she was doomed to have repeated heartaches. "I vowed to save other kids like him."

Mack regarded her with what appeared to be real sympathy. "Like I said, you take it personally."

She sighed at the assessment. "Yes, I suppose I do."

"How long do you think you can keep it up, if you take every case to heart?"

"As long as I have to," she insisted tightly. "I only see a few patients. Most of my time is spent in research. Our treatments are getting better and better all the time.'' Sadly, Tony wasn't responding well to any of them, which was why she'd taken such an intense interest in his case.

''But not with Tony,'' Mack said.

Beth fought against the salty sting of unexpected tears. ''Not with Tony, at least not yet,'' she admitted softly. Then she set her jaw and regarded Mack defiantly, blinking back those tell-tale tears. ''But we're going to win this battle, too.''

He gave her an admiring look. ''Yes, I think you will,'' he said quietly. ''Will my being here actually help Tony?''

''Hopefully it will improve his spirits,'' Beth assured him. ''He's been a little down lately, and sometimes boosting a child's morale is the most important thing we can do. We need to keep him from giving up on himself or on us.''

Mack nodded. ''Okay, then. Let's go in there and talk football.'' He gave her an impudent grin. ''I assume you won't be saying much.''

Beth laughed despite herself, liking Mack far more than she'd ever expected to. She could forgive a lot in a person who had a sense of humor, whether about her foibles or his own. ''Probably not.''

His expression sobered. ''Good. What I do for a living may not be medicine or rocket science, but I'd hate to have you dismiss it in front of a kid who thinks it matters.''

Beth stared at him as his point struck home. Her opinion of football or of Mack Carlton didn't matter right now. ''Touché, Mr. Carlton. I'll definitely refrain from comment. This is all about Tony.''

He winked. ''Call me Mack. My fans do.''

"I'm not one of your fans."

"Stick around," he taunted lightly. "You might be, after this."

Beth bit back a sigh. Yes, she could be, she admitted to herself. Not that Mighty Mack Carlton needed another conquest in his life. The gossip columns were littered with the names of women who thought they had the inside track in his life. She'd noticed that few of them ever got a second mention. She wasn't the least bit inclined to test her luck in an already crowded field.

"Don't hold your breath, Mr. Carlton. Besides, the only person whose adoration counts is Tony, and you've already got a lock on that."

"I wouldn't mind at least a hint of approval from you, too," he said, his gaze capturing hers and holding it.

Despite the obvious attempt to disconcert her, Beth felt herself falling under his spell. She found it irritating. "Why? Do you have to win over every woman you meet?"

He hesitated then, and an odd look that might have been confusion flickered in his eyes. "How well do you know my aunt?" he asked.

The out-of-the-blue question caught her off guard. "Your aunt?"

"Destiny Carlton, the woman you contacted who made sure I came over here today."

Beth shook her head. "I don't believe we've met," she said. "Though I recognize the name. I think she raises a lot of money for the hospital. I never spoke to her, though."

Mack seemed surprised. "You really don't know her?"

"No."

"And you didn't call her?"

"No. Why?"

He shook his head, obviously more puzzled than ever. "Doesn't matter."

Despite his denial, Beth got the distinct impression that it mattered a lot. She simply had no idea why.

Chapter Two

Mack had been in his share of hospital rooms. He'd had enough football injuries to guarantee that—including one final blown-out knee that had ended his career on the field. Granted, his life had never been on the line, but even so, he hated the antiseptic smell, the too-perky nurses, the beeps and whirring of machines, the evasiveness of the doctors who never looked you in the eye when the news was bad. If he'd hated it, how much worse must it be for a kid, especially a kid who had to face the possibility that he might not come out alive?

During his football career, Mack had made it a habit to visit children in this hospital and others. The smiles on their faces, knowing that for a few minutes, at least, he'd taken them away from their problems, made his own discomfort seem like a small thing.

Now that his own playing days were over, he made fewer of these visits. Most kids wanted to meet the current players, and from his position in the team's front office, he made sure it happened, even if it made some of the biggest, brawniest players in the league cry afterward. Men who took a lot for granted suddenly started counting their blessings after a hospital visit to cheer kids facing the toughest fights of their lives. Nothing he'd ever encountered had given him a better perspective on what mattered in life.

Outside Tony Vitale's door, he braced himself for what he'd find inside—a pale kid, maybe bald, his eyes haunted. Mack had seen it too many times not to expect the worst. It never failed to make his chest tighten and his throat close up. Forcing himself not to react visibly had been one of the hardest lessons he'd ever had to learn.

"You okay?" Beth asked, regarding him worriedly. "You're not going to walk in there and pass out on me, are you?"

Mack gave her a disbelieving look. "Hardly."

"You wouldn't be the first man who couldn't take seeing a kid this sick," she said.

"I've been here before."

She gave him a look filled with understanding and commiseration. "It's always hardest the first time. After that, it gets easier."

"I doubt that," Mack said.

Her gaze stayed on his face. "You ready?" she asked finally, as if she'd seen some minute change in his demeanor that had satisfied her.

"Let's do it."

Beth pushed open the door, a seemingly genuine smile on her face. "Hey, Tony," she called out cheerfully. "Have I got a surprise for you!"

"Ice cream?" a weak voice called back hopefully.

"Better than that," she said, then stood aside to allow Mack to enter.

Admiring her performance and determined not to let her or the boy down, Mack gave her a thumbs-up and strode into the room.

The boy lying amid a pile of pillows and stuffed animals was wearing a too-large football jersey with Mack's old number on it. He clutched a football against his scrawny chest. When he spotted Mack, he struggled to sit up, and for just an instant there was a glimmer of childish delight in his dull eyes before he fell back against the pillows, obviously too weak to sit upright.

"Mighty Mack!" he whispered incredulously, his gaze avidly following Mack's progress across the room. "You really came."

"Hey, when I get a call from a pretty doctor telling me that my biggest fan is in the hospital, I always show up," Mack said, swallowing the familiar tide of dismay that washed over him. The men who walked onto a football field every Sunday and allowed equally brawny men to tackle them and pound them into the dirt didn't know half as much about real bravery as this kid.

Tony nodded enthusiastically. "I'm your biggest fan, all right. I've got tapes of every game you ever played."

"That can't be that many. I had a short career."

"But you were awesome, the best ever."

Mack chuckled. "Better than Johnny Unitas in Baltimore? Better than Denver's John Elway? Better than Dan Marino in Miami?"

"Way better," Tony said loyally.

Mack turned to the lady doc. "The kid knows his sports legends."

She gave him a wry look. "Obviously, the two of you agree you're in a class by yourself."

"He is, Dr. Beth," Tony asserted. "Ask anyone."

"Why ask anyone else, when I can get it straight from the horse's—" she deliberately hesitated, her gaze on Mack steady before she finally added "—mouth?"

Mack had the distinct impression she would have preferred to mention the opposite end of the horse. He had definitely not won her over. Not yet, anyway. That was a challenge for another time, though, one he was surprisingly eager to pursue. For now, his focus had to be on Tony.

"How about I sign your football for you?" he suggested to Tony.

The boy's eyes lit up. "That'd be great! Wait till my mom comes tonight. She'll be so excited. She's watched all those tapes with me a million times. I'll bet she's the only mom around who knows all your stats."

Mack read between the lines, but managed to keep his expression neutral at the hint that there was no father in this boy's life. He reached in his pocket and pulled out a valuable football card from his rookie year that he'd brought along. "Want me to sign this for your mom or for you?"

"Oh, wow! I saw that card on the Internet. It was selling for way more than I could pay," Tony said, obviously struggling to do the right thing. "Sign it for my mom, I guess. She can show it to all her friends at work. She'll probably want to put it in a frame on her desk."

Mack grinned at him. "Good choice. I'll bring you your own on my next visit. I think I can come up with one from my MVP year that's even more valuable, especially when it's signed.''

"You'll come back?" Tony asked, his eyes wide with disbelief. "Really? And we can talk about all the guys you drafted for this season? We really need that defensive lineman you got."

"Tell me about it," Mack said.

"Has he signed yet?"

Mack grinned at his enthusiasm and his up-to-date knowledge. "Not yet. We're still bargaining."

"He'll sign," Tony said confidently. "Who wouldn't want to play for your team? What I don't get is why you didn't go after that punter at Ohio State."

Mack laughed. "Maybe I'll explain budgets and salary caps to you the next time I come."

"I can't believe you'll really come back," Tony said.

"I'll be back so often you'll get sick of me," Mack promised. "Nothing I like more than talking to someone who remembers all my great plays."

"And I do," Tony said. "Every one of them. That game against the Eagles, when you threw for a team record was the best ever, but I liked the way you scrambled for a winning touchdown against the Packers, when everybody said you ought to be off the field because of a shoulder injury."

Mack laughed. "That was a great one," he agreed. "I still get a twinge in that shoulder every time I think about it. I had to scramble, because I couldn't have thrown the ball if my life had depended on it."

"I knew it!" Tony said, obviously delighted to have his impression confirmed. "I told my mom before you ran that there was no way you were going to try a pass. How come the Packers' defense didn't get that?"

"Pure, dumb luck," Mack admitted. "And just so you know, I shouldn't have stayed on the field. I could have cost us the game."

"But you didn't. You won it," Tony said.

"That doesn't mean it was the smartest play. It means I was showing off."

"I don't care. It was a great play," Tony insisted.

Mack laughed at the kid's stubborn defense. "Too bad you weren't around to talk to the coach. He almost benched me for the next game because of that play."

Tony's eyes widened in disbelief. "Really? But that's so unfair."

Mack studied the boy's face and thought he looked even paler than he had when Mack had first arrived, despite his obvious excitement. Mack glanced at Beth and saw the lines of worry creasing her forehead. He was pretty good at reading cues and he definitely got this one. It was time to go.

"Listen, Tony, I've got to head to a meeting. You get some rest. Maybe next time we can go down to the cafeteria for some hot chocolate. I hear it's pretty decent."

"Really?" Tony asked, his voice fading as if he were falling asleep but struggling to fight it.

"If the doc okays it," Mack said, giving her a questioning look.

"No problem," Beth said, but she didn't seem too enthusiastic.

Mack took Tony's frail hand and gave it a squeeze. "Take good care of yourself, son."

By the time he released the boy's hand, Tony was already asleep.

A few seconds later Mack and Beth Browning were

back in the hall. She scowled at him with fire in her eyes.

"Why did you do that?" she demanded.

"Do what?" Mack asked, confused by the sudden return of overt hostility. He'd felt good about the way things had gone during the visit. He was sure he'd lifted Tony's spirits and gotten his mind off of his illness for a few minutes at least. Wasn't that the point of his being here?

"Why did you say you'd be back?" she asked.

Mack was annoyed by the implication that he'd made a promise he had no intention of keeping. "Because if I was reading the signals correctly, that boy doesn't have a dad, and he needs someone around to support him," he retorted. "Do you have a problem with that?"

"Tony's not alone. You heard how he talks about his mom. She's great with him."

Mack regarded her with a steady look. "And I think that's fantastic, but now he has me, too."

Beth's expression faltered as the sincerity of his intentions finally sank in. "You actually mean that, don't you?"

"Yes."

"Why?"

"Because I know what it's like to grow up without a dad," Mack said honestly. "That was bad enough. To grow up sick and terrified without a dad must be a thousand times worse. If I can help by coming to visit, then that's what I intend to do. Any objections, Dr. Browning?"

She hesitated, her gaze locked with his, then finally she shook her head. "None, as long as you don't let him down."

"You concentrate on getting him well, Doc. I'll concentrate on giving him a few extra reasons to live."

That said, he turned and walked away, not sure whether he was more upset by Tony's situation or by the doctor who doubted his own good intentions.

Not until he was on his way to his business meeting did Mack allow himself to consider Beth's earlier claim that she had never spoken to Destiny. Was she telling him the truth? He couldn't imagine any reason she'd have to lie.

Destiny, to the contrary, might well be inclined to lie if this was another of her matchmaking plots as he'd initially suspected. The instant he'd met the doctor—pretty, brainy, serious—his suspicions had been aroused all over again. The fact that Destiny had never mentioned Dr. Browning being a woman raised all sorts of red flags, as well.

As he drove across town, he voice activated his cell phone and called Destiny.

"Darling, I didn't expect to hear from you again so soon," she said. "How did things go at the hospital? Were you able to meet Tony?"

"Yes. He's in rough shape."

"Then I'm sure your visit meant a lot. I'm so proud of you for taking the time to stop by."

"It's the least I can do." He hesitated, debating whether it was wise to ask his aunt any question at all about Beth Browning. She might make way too much of his curiosity. Still, he wanted to know what he was up against. Had she schemed to bring the two of them together? If so, she had to know that it was an unlikely match. The woman didn't even like football, much less understand it, and the game was an integral part of his life. And she seemed to have formed some very negative opinions about the kind of man he was.

"By the way, your Dr. Browning is not exactly a huge fan of the game," he said eventually.

"Really?" Destiny said.

He listened for a false note in her voice, but didn't detect one. "You didn't know?" he pressed.

"How would I know?"

"You did say you'd talked to her."

"Did I say that? Actually your secretary passed along all those messages."

Now she was getting her stories mixed up. Mack knew he was on to something. "Destiny, it's not like you to forget what tale you've told. What's the real scoop here?"

"I have no idea what you're talking about. I asked you to do a good deed. You did it. That's the end of it, isn't it?" Now she hesitated. "Or did you find Dr. Browning attractive?"

"In a quiet, no-frills sort of way," he said, considering that to be a bit generous. She had nice, warm eyes, pale blond hair in a chin-length style and lovely skin, but she didn't do much to accentuate her femininity, not like most of the women he knew. All of that made it much harder for him to understand the little frisson of attraction he'd felt toward her. Maybe it was nothing more than the obvious challenge she represented.

"Mack, didn't I teach you that the packaging is not what counts with a woman?" Destiny chided.

He laughed at that. "You tried."

"Perhaps you should reconsider the lesson. It was a good one."

"I'll keep that in mind."

"Well, if that's all, Mack, I've got to run. I have a million things to do before my dinner guest arrives."

"Anyone I know?" Maybe if his aunt had a social life of her own, she'd stop messing with his.

"No. This is just someone with whom I've recently become acquainted."

"A man?" he pressed.

"If you must know, no."

"Too bad. I could introduce you to some eligible bachelors anytime you say the word," he said, warming to the idea.

Destiny laughed. "Most of the men you know are half my age. As flattering as I might find that, I doubt it's very wise. There's nothing worse than a foolish old woman trying to be something she's not."

"I do know a lot of rich, powerful men who own their own companies," Mack retorted. "Though, frankly, I think a guy my age might find you more fascinating and challenging than some of the women they're currently dating."

"Ah, there's that silver tongue of yours again," she said, chuckling. "Thank you, darling. I must run, though."

Mack said goodbye, then went over the conversation a few more times in his head. Had Destiny actually admitted to knowing Beth or not? He had a hunch it was something he needed to know before he got sucked right smack into the middle of one of her schemes. Forewarned was forearmed with his aunt.

Beth studied the older woman seated across the elegant dinner table from her. So, this was Destiny Carlton.

Beth had been caught completely off guard when

she'd returned to her office after Mack's visit to find a message from his aunt inviting her to dinner. Curiosity had compelled her to accept. Maybe tonight she'd learn why Mack had seemed so sure that Beth and his aunt were already acquainted.

So far, though, the evening had been filled with idle chitchat. Beth was growing increasingly impatient. She put down her fork and met Destiny's penetrating gaze.

"Pardon me for being direct, Ms. Carlton, but why am I here?"

Destiny's blue eyes sparkled with merriment. "I was wondering when you were going to ask that. I'd heard you were direct."

Beth wasn't sure what to make of that. Surely there hadn't been time for Mack to report back to his aunt. "Oh?"

"No need to look so worried," Destiny said. "As I'm sure you know, I do a lot of fund-raising for the hospital. I tend to hear about the rising stars on the medical and research staff. Your name has come up rather frequently in recent months. When I heard about your messages for my nephew, I decided it was time we met."

"I see." Beth was still a bit confused. "Are you interested in funding some of the research at the hospital?"

"Always, but my interest here has more to do with Mack. What did you think of him?"

"I'm not sure I understand what you're asking," Beth responded cautiously.

"Come, dear," Destiny said with a hint of amusement in her voice. "From all reports, you're an exceedingly brilliant doctor. Surely you have some idea of what I'm asking."

"Not really," Beth insisted, not sure she wanted to go down the path Destiny seemed determined to explore.

"Women have a tendency to fall all over themselves when they first meet Mack," Destiny said.

"I don't doubt that," Beth said, not that she intended to be one of them. She didn't have time for a man who took so little seriously. Even as that thought entered her head, she recalled just how seriously Mack had taken Tony's situation. Maybe he wasn't as much of a lightweight as she'd assumed, but that still didn't make him her type.

Not that she had a type, she amended. Not anymore. Not since she'd discovered that the kind of man she'd always been drawn to, men who loved medicine as much as she did, often had an ego that couldn't stand the competition from a woman in the same field.

That was how she'd lost her fiancé. Her team had inadvertently applied for the same research grant Thomas had applied for, and she'd won it. He had not taken the news well. Not only had she lost him, but a month later the grant had been withdrawn because of a vicious rumor he'd deliberately spun about her research methodology. Beth had been crushed by the betrayal, but she'd learned a valuable lesson about not mixing her professional and personal life.

"But you weren't impressed by Mack," Destiny guessed.

Now there was a minefield, Beth thought. Insulting him to his face was bad enough. Insulting him to his doting aunt, who raised millions for the hospital, was something else. Beth wasn't the most politically savvy creature on earth, but she knew better than to offend a major donor.

"Actually I didn't spend that much time with him," Beth said truthfully.

Destiny's lips twitched as if she were fighting a smile. "Very diplomatic. I like that."

"Are you trying to set me up with your nephew?" Beth asked bluntly.

Destiny's eyes widened in a totally phony display of innocence. "How could I do that? You and Mack have already met. Either something clicked or it didn't. I'm sure you know as much about chemistry as I do, perhaps more."

Beth chuckled. "Some forms of chemistry, yes. The male-female thing is definitely not my area of expertise."

"My nephew might make an excellent teacher," Destiny suggested slyly.

"I don't think so." Beth grinned at the determined woman. "Does Mack know you're sneaking around behind his back trying to fix him up?"

"As I said, how could I fix him up with you since you've met? You're two consenting adults capable of making your own decisions," Destiny said, as if the thought had never crossed her obviously devious mind.

"But a little nudge from you wouldn't be out of the question, would it?" Beth suddenly recalled Mack's earlier suspicion that she and his aunt knew each other. "He's on to you, isn't he? He thinks you deliberately got him over to the hospital today to meet me. Seeing Tony was simply a means to an end."

"You called his office," Destiny reminded her. "He came over there to meet Tony at your request."

Beth couldn't argue with that. "Would you have been as quick to intercede if the request had come from one of my male colleagues?"

"Of course," Destiny claimed. "We're talking about a sick child."

Beth wasn't entirely sure she believed her. Nor, she suspected, would Mack.

"Look, Ms. Carlton—"

"Please call me Destiny. I insist."

"I appreciate what you're trying to do, Destiny, or at least what I think you're trying to do, but it's a bad idea," Beth said emphatically. "I'm not interested. Mack's not interested. Let's just leave it at that."

Rather than the disappointment Beth had anticipated, Destiny's expression brightened.

"Perfect," Destiny said.

"I beg your pardon."

"I said that was the perfect response. You're going to be a challenge," Destiny explained. "I love that. More important, it is exactly what my nephew needs in his life. Most women are all too eager to fall right into his bed."

"I don't have time to be the challenge your nephew needs," Beth said, beginning to feel a little frantic. She had a hunch that Destiny Carlton was a force to be reckoned with once her mind was set on something. Besides that, the whole image of falling into Mack's bed was a little too attractive. She needed to stay away from these two. They had money. They had power. And one of them at least had a plan for the rest of Beth's life, a plan she wasn't one bit happy about.

"Of course, you have the time," Destiny said blithely. "Everyone has time for love."

Love? *Love?* Sweet heaven, how had they gone from talking about the prospect of her even having a date with Mack to falling in love with him?

"Not me," Beth said fiercely. "I definitely do not

have time for a relationship. Really, Destiny. I don't have a second to spare. My days are crammed. There are simply not enough hours for all the work I have to do."

"You made time to have dinner with me at the last minute," Destiny reminded her. "You could just as easily make time for Mack. Keep that in mind when he asks you out."

"He is not going to ask me out," Beth said confidently. "And if he does, the answer will be no." A resounding no, she thought to herself. Bad enough to have to fight that little twinge of attraction she'd felt for him. She did not need to waste her time trying to fend off his aunt's machinations as well.

Destiny's smile spread.

"Stop that," Beth said. She could practically read the woman's mind. She was going back to that challenge thing again. "I am not saying no just to play hard to get. I am saying it because I am not interested. Period. That isn't going to change. I suspect your nephew has enough women saying yes that he won't waste too much time mourning my rejection, assuming he even asks me out in the first place. We didn't exactly get off on the best foot. I was being very insulting about him, and he happened to overhear me."

Destiny looked vaguely shocked by that. "You insulted him?"

"I never meant for him to hear me," Beth said in her own defense.

"But all the same," Destiny said. "He really is a fine man."

"I'm sure you believe that," Beth said, trying to extricate herself from the increasingly deep and murky waters of this conversation. "I only pointed out what he'd heard so you would understand why I don't think he's likely to ask me on a date.''

"Oh, Mack has a thick enough hide. He has to, after being in the public eye for so long. He'll ask you out. He won't let a little unwitting insult stop him," Destiny said confidently. "All I ask is that you give the invitation some thought."

"Why me?" Beth asked, completely bemused that a woman she'd barely even met seemed so certain Beth was right for her obviously beloved nephew.

"I think that will become clear in time," Destiny said enigmatically. "Just promise me you won't close any doors."

"I can't promise that," Beth said honestly. In fact, at the moment, with panic spreading through her, she was pretty sure that slamming the door on Mack Carlton and his meddling aunt, then bolting it tight, would be the smartest thing she could do.

Then again, she couldn't recall the last time she'd felt this little *zing* of anticipation humming through her veins. Sadly, it wasn't altogether unpleasant. Just dangerous.

Chapter Three

Mack Carlton was as good as his word. It began to seem as if every time Beth went into Tony's room in late afternoon, Mack was there. It was evident he'd become a quiet, comforting, dependable presence in Tony's life, just as he'd promised he would. She began to feel the first faint hint of respect for him, despite her determination to keep her guard up.

Sometimes he sat quietly reading a book while the boy slept. Beth couldn't help noticing that Mack's taste ran to thrillers, rather than to the sports books she would have guessed. She even caught him totally absorbed by a recently released presidential biography. He rose another notch in her estimation that day. She tried to smother the reaction by reminding herself that she couldn't weaken, not with Destiny Carlton scheming in the wings.

Sometimes Beth arrived to find Tony in a spirited

argument with Mack over the best football players ever. Mack listened intently to whatever case Tony made, and even when he disagreed, he did it in a respectful way that seemed to make Tony sit a little taller in bed, pride shining in his eyes at being taken so seriously by a man he idolized.

On more than one occasion, they played one of the electronic games that Mack provided. When they were caught up in the competition, they barely spared Beth a glance. That gave her a chance to observe the two of them a bit more closely. To her amusement, it was evident that Mack was having as much fun as Tony and was every bit as determined to win, not giving the boy an inch out of pity.

There was something a little too appealing about Mack with his hair mussed, his collar open, his expression totally focused as he concentrated on that little screen with such intensity.

To Beth's surprise Mack was also sensitive to Tony's level of exhaustion and his shifts in mood. Mack seemed to know just when to encourage a nap and just when to initiate some distracting activity. And he always left shortly after Tony's mother arrived, clearly attuned to Maria Vitale's need to spend time alone with her son.

The first time Beth saw Mack in the hallway outside Tony's room consoling an obviously shaken Maria, she caught herself looking for evidence of the kind of chemistry that Destiny Carlton had been talking about over dinner. If her reaction had involved anyone other than Mack, she might have labeled it a ridiculous twinge of jealousy, but with Mack that would be absurd. There was absolutely nothing between her and the ex-football star. Her interest was purely clinical, a chance to study how the male-female-chemistry thing worked.

After all, Mack was a virile man with a reputation for appreciating beautiful women. Maria was a gorgeous woman with a flawless olive complexion, a lush body and flowing waves of black hair. Only the exhaustion that was clearly visible in and around her eyes marred her beauty. For some men, Beth thought, that evidence of vulnerability would make her seem even more attractive. Beth couldn't help wondering if Mack was one of those men.

But despite her intense curiosity, Beth never saw the slightest sign that Mack was interested in the single mom. Even his attempts to comfort her were verbal, not physical. And rather than any hint of a growing closeness between the two, more often than not, he left mother and son together and sought Beth out when he left Tony's room.

In little more than a week, Beth had come to count on him dropping by far more than she should. While he'd shown no evidence of being attracted to her, he was giving her more attention than she'd expected from him.

Now, at the rap on her office door near the research lab, Beth glanced at the clock and saw that it was just past six. That was when Mack usually stopped in.

"Yes?" she said, fighting the little flash of heat that licked through her as she anticipated seeing him for a few minutes.

Her office door cracked open and, as expected, Mack peered around the edge. "Busy?"

Just this once she should tell him yes. That would be the smart thing to do. These brief little visits were beginning to feel too right, as if her day would be somehow incomplete without them.

"I have a few minutes," she said instead, telling herself that there was nothing wrong with indulging herself in the company of a sexy man in the privacy of her office. It didn't mean a thing. It just proved she was a woman, something she tended to forget when she was caught up in the whirlwind of her job.

"Long enough to go for coffee?" he asked, his expression hopeful. "I could really use a jolt of caffeine. It's been a long day, and I still have a dinner thing at eight."

This was something new. Beth wasn't sure what to make of the invitation. In her office, on her turf, she felt confident and in control of the situation. Even in a setting as thoroughly unromantic as the hospital cafeteria, with Mack buying her coffee she had a feeling that the balance of power between them would somehow shift.

Mack grinned at her hesitation. "I'm asking you to go for coffee, Doc. I swear I won't try to seduce you behind the vending machines."

"I was just thinking about everything I have to do before I can get out of here tonight," she fibbed.

Mack's grin spread. "If you're going to make a long night of it, then you need the coffee as much as I do."

"You're right," she said, telling herself that any other reply would make her seem churlish and ungrateful. After all, this man was coming here almost daily to bolster the spirits of one of her patients. The least she could do in return was share a cup of coffee with him. "I'll buy."

Her offer seemed to amuse him, but he stood aside

as she brushed past him, then he closed her office door behind them.

As they walked through the hospital corridors, Beth noticed the stares of the nurses, which were accompanied by more than a few whispers. This, she realized, was what she'd feared about being seen with Mack. She needed to command respect among the staff, not be the subject of speculative gossip.

"Doesn't that sort of thing get old?" she asked as they passed another cluster of gaping females.

"What?" Mack asked blankly.

"The women staring at you, speculating about you, looking you over as if you were a piece of meat."

He shrugged. "I don't really notice it anymore."

Beth couldn't decide if that was ego talking or a weird kind of humility. In fact, she was beginning to think there were a lot of fascinating contradictions in Mack Carlton. Worse, she was beginning to want to unravel them.

He studied her with a penetrating look. "I'm sorry if it bothers you. It didn't occur to me that you being seen with me around here might stir up talk. Would you rather go somewhere else?"

She shook her head. "No, the cafeteria's fine. I don't have time for anything else."

As they approached the line, he regarded her with concern. "Have you eaten?"

"No, but I'll grab something later or take a sandwich back to my office."

He glanced at the board of specials. "Come on. They have meat loaf. How can you pass that up?"

Beth chuckled. "I've had it before. Trust me, it is not like anything you ever had at home."

"Ah, then no to the meat loaf." He glanced along

the display of prepared foods. "The salads look fresh." Before she could decline, he reached for two and put them on a tray, then added two bowls of soup. "Crackers?"

Giving up the fight, Beth nodded. "Sure, but I thought you were going to dinner at eight."

"I am. Rubber chicken and a lot of schmoozing. I'll be lucky to get a couple of bites. Believe me, this is a lot more appetizing, and the company is a thousand percent better."

Beth tried not to feel flattered by the compliment, but it warmed her just the same. No wonder Mack had women falling at his feet. His charm was instinctive and natural, not the phony kind of lines she would have expected him to utter. He was slipping right past her natural wariness.

When he'd added apple pie and two cups of coffee to the tray as well, he brushed off her offer to buy and paid the cashier himself, then led the way to a table in a far corner of the room where there were fewer people around.

Once they were seated, Beth regarded him with curiosity. "Do you always get your own way?"

He seemed genuinely surprised by the question. "No, why?"

"You just steamrolled right over me back there," she said.

"I figured you were trying to be a lady."

She studied him with a narrowed gaze. "Meaning?" she asked, expecting some totally chauvinistic remark that would permit her to dislike him again.

"When it comes to food, my experience is that most women would rather starve than admit to a man that they're hungry. They seem to think we'll worry that they're about to start putting on weight. Personally I like a woman with a healthy appetite and a little meat on her bones.''

Beth bit back her impulse to point out that she had neither. She should have known Mack wouldn't be so reticent.

He gave her a thorough once-over, then added, ''You could use a few more pounds, Doc. People might take you more seriously if you didn't look as if a strong wind could blow you away.''

''The people who count seem to take me fairly seriously already,'' she said.

''But it's important to get lots of vitamins and minerals from food, right?'' he said, placing her food in front of her. ''Munching on a couple of vitamin caplets and drinking an energy shake does not constitute a healthy diet.''

Beth almost choked on her first spoonful of soup. How the heck did he know what she usually ate? ''What have you been doing? Lurking outside my office door at mealtime?''

''Nope. No need to. The industrial-size vitamin bottle's in plain view on your desk and the trash is littered with empty shake cans. If you ask me, that's a sure way to end up sick.''

''What made you an expert on nutrition?'' she asked irritably, because he was right and she didn't want to admit it.

''Destiny pretty much drilled the basics into us, but anything she missed, I got from the team doctors when I was playing football,'' he explained. ''Food is fuel. Without the right fuel, the body isn't going to run properly, not for long, anyway.''

She gave him a wry look. ''I'll keep that in mind.''

"You should," Mack said, his expression serious. "Tony and a lot of other kids are counting on you, Doc. You won't be able to help them if you get sick yourself."

"Point accepted," Beth said, deliberately taking a bite of salad to prove she'd gotten the message.

They ate in silence for several minutes, then Mack asked, "How's Tony doing? Any change?"

"You've probably seen for yourself that he's getting weaker every day. We're doing everything we can to build him back up so we can try another round of chemo, but nothing's working," she admitted, her frustration evident in her voice. "Maybe you could work some of your nutritional magic with him. He's not eating."

"I'm on it," he said at once. "Anything he can't have?"

"No."

"And I won't be breaking any rules by carting in takeout?"

"I'll save you from the food police around here, if you can just get him to eat," Beth promised.

"Consider it done. I think I have a pretty good idea what might tempt a twelve-year-old kid to eat. And I can always give him the same spiel I gave you about the body needing fuel."

"Thanks," Beth said sincerely. "These days he's much more likely to listen to you than me."

"It's a guy thing." Mack grinned. "Of course, I might have to insist that you stop by to split a pizza with us or maybe some tacos. Kids learn best by example."

Beth chuckled despite herself. "Still trying to fatten me up?"

"Just a little."

"It seems to me the women I usually see on your arm are all model thin."

Mack's expression darkened a bit. "Don't believe everything you see in the paper, Doc."

"Are you saying the pictures lie? How can that be?"

"Put an ambitious female and a sleazy photographer in the same room and all it takes is the click of a shutter to create a false impression," he said with an unmistakable touch of bitterness.

Before Beth could comment, he waved off the topic. "Let's not talk about that. Anything on the search for a bone marrow donor?"

Beth wasn't sure what to make of the quick change in subject, but she accepted that Mack didn't intend to say another word about the women in his life. Instead, she tried to answer his question about Tony honestly. "He's on the list, but we haven't been pushing because he's not a good candidate right now."

"Anything I can do?" Mack asked.

"Just keep coming to see him. It's the only time I ever hear him laugh," she said quietly.

Mack studied her intently. "What about you, Doc? How are you doing? This is getting to you, isn't it? I mean even more than it was before. You're scared, aren't you?"

Beth struggled with the emotions she tried to keep tamped down so they wouldn't overwhelm her. Mack had a way of bringing them right back to the surface, of forcing her to confront them.

"Terrified," she admitted finally.

Mack reached for her hand. "You know, even doctors are allowed to have feelings."

"No, we're not," she said, jerking her hand away

from the comfort it would be far too easy to accept. "We have to stay focused and objective."

"Why?"

"It's the only way we can do our jobs."

"Without falling apart, you mean?"

She nodded, her throat tight. Now she was the one who was uncomfortable with the turn the conversation had taken. "Can we talk about something else, please? I can't do this, not tonight."

Mack sat back in his chair. "Sure. We can talk about whatever you like." He grinned. "Want to talk about football?"

She relaxed at the teasing note in his voice. "It would have to be a brief conversation, unless you intend to do all the talking."

"You know us jocks. We can go on and on about sports at the drop of a hat," he taunted. "But I'll spare you. How about politics? Any opinions?"

"I saw in the paper that your brother finally announced he's running for city council in Alexandria."

Mack's expression darkened a bit. "Yep, Richard's fulfilling the legacy our father left for him."

Beth heard the edgy note in his voice and studied him curiously. "You don't seem pleased by that."

"If it were what my brother really wanted, I'd be all for it, but the truth is Richard has spent his whole life living up to these expectations that were drilled into him when we were boys. Running Carlton Industries is one thing. That's the family legacy and he loves it. He was clearly destined for it. But politics? I'm not convinced it's what he wants. He'll do it, though, out of a sense of duty to a man who's been gone for more than twenty years, and he'll do it well."

"Have you told him how you feel?"

He gave her a rueful look. "Nah. You don't tell Richard anything. He's the one who tells the rest of us what to do."

"Do you resent that?"

"Good grief, no. If he hadn't taken the pressure off the rest of us years ago, I'd probably be behind some desk at Carlton Industries pushing a pencil. I'd not only be totally miserable, but I'd probably bring down the company."

"Singlehandedly?" Beth asked skeptically.

"No, I imagine Ben, our younger brother, would be even worse at it than me."

"I think I read somewhere that he's an artist. Is that right?"

Mack's eyes twinkled with knowing amusement. "Checking us out, Doc?"

"No, it's just hard to avoid the mention of the Carlton name in the local media. Even your reportedly reclusive younger brother's name pops up from time to time."

"If you say so."

"Why would I bother checking you out?" Beth inquired irritably.

"Some women think we're pretty fascinating men," Mack responded with a straight face.

"I'm not one of them."

"So you only tolerate me hanging around for Tony's sake?"

"Yes," she said.

His skeptical gaze caught hers and held until she flushed under the intensity. Only when he was apparently satisfied that he'd rattled her and proved his point did he finally glance away.

Relieved to be out from under that disconcerting

gaze, Beth drew in a shaky breath. No man had ever unnerved her the way Mack Carlton did. For the life of her, she couldn't figure out why that was. Sure, he had the kind of body that would look great on a beefcake calendar. Sure, he even showed evidence of being kind and sensitive, two traits she admired in a man. He had a killer smile, an agile brain and a charming personality. With all of that added together, the question shouldn't have been why he unnerved her, but why she hadn't thrown herself straight into his arms.

That she could answer. Mack Carlton was a rich, exjock playboy, who didn't take anything seriously. His affairs were played out publicly, and she was a very private woman with a reputation to protect. So even if that glimmer of heat she thought she saw in his eyes from time to time was real, even if these brief hospital encounters implied a certain fascination on his part, she couldn't allow any of it to lead anywhere—assuming he even wanted to pursue it himself beyond the occasional cup of coffee or idle conversation at the end of the day.

Too bad, she thought, barely containing a sigh. Because something told her that Mack had the kind of moves that could make a woman not only forget every last bit of common sense she possessed, but could send her right up into flames.

A couple of days after his fascinating cafeteria dinner with Beth, Mack was sitting in the hospital waiting room while the doctors examined Tony when he looked up to see Richard striding toward him.

"What are you doing here?" he asked, standing to give his brother a hug. He glanced pointedly around the empty room. "No prospective voters in here to impress."

"Very funny. Actually I was in the neighborhood, and Destiny told me you might be here," Richard said. "What's going on? What are you doing hanging out in a hospital waiting room?"

Mack shrugged. "There's a sick kid I've been coming to see," he said as if it were no big deal.

Richard studied him intently. "You're here every day from what I hear. You getting too emotionally involved with this boy?"

"This isn't about me," Mack said defensively. "The boy doesn't have a dad to hang out with. He likes football. The least I can do is come by for an hour or so."

"I admire you for taking an interest, but is it really all about the kid?"

Mack stared at him, instantly suspicious. "What exactly did Destiny say to you?"

Richard's serious expression finally cracked. A grin spread across his face. "She mentioned that the boy's doctor is a very pretty woman with a brilliant scientific mind. Which hooked you, bro? Her body or her mind?"

"I am not hooked on anybody," Mack retorted defensively. "That's ridiculous. Next time you talk to her, tell Destiny to mind her own damn business."

"Ha," Richard said. "What are the odds of that ever happening?"

Mack scowled at his brother. "So the real reason you dropped by is to gloat. You think I'm about to get reeled smack into the middle of one of Destiny's schemes."

"That's what I'm thinking," Richard agreed unre-

pentantly. "If so, I want to be around to witness every
second of your downfall."

"Destiny claims she doesn't even know Beth
Browning," Mack said. "Beth said the same thing."

"Ever heard of the little white lie?" Richard asked.
"What kind of manipulator would our aunt be if she
didn't make liberal use of whatever tactic serves her
purposes? She wasn't entirely honest with me or Melanie, either. She sucked us both right in and never suffered a moment's remorse because of it."

"Well, there's nothing like that going on here,"
Mack insisted. "I'm not the doc's type. She's not my
type, either. If Destiny really is behind all of this, she
got it wrong this time."

"We'll see," Richard said. "Any chance the doctor
will be by anytime soon? I'd like to get a good look
at her. Melanie will have questions."

"Too bad. I'm pretty sure Dr. Browning is at a medical conference on the other side of the universe today," Mack said just in time to see the very woman
in question strolling their way. He sighed heavily. "On
the other hand, she could be back."

Richard's eyes widened with appreciation and he let
out a very soft whistle. "Not your type, huh? Maybe
you should get your eyes checked."

Mack took another look at Beth and tried to see what
his brother saw. She was pretty enough in a natural,
wholesome way, but compared to the beauties he usually dated, she was fairly unimpressive. Her hair was
straight and cut in a severe, simple style that clearly
required little fuss. Her simple, tailored clothes did
nothing to flatter a figure he'd already assessed as too
thin. Her low-heeled shoes, a necessity for a woman
on the run all day long, did nothing to enhance her

legs. Mack was really, really partial to women in strappy spike heels that made their legs look endless. He simply didn't get whatever it was Richard obviously saw.

Eventually his gaze made its way to Beth's eyes, which were regarding him with a perplexed expression. He blinked and looked away guiltily.

"I thought you'd want to know that it's okay to go back in to see Tony now," she said.

"Thanks."

Richard looked from Beth to Mack and back again, then shrugged. "Dr. Browning, I'm Mack's brother Richard. He seems to have lost his tongue. It happens sometimes. I can understand it in your case. I imagine you render him speechless a lot."

Beth gave Richard a startled look and a blush tinted her cheeks. "Not that I've noticed."

Richard grinned at Mack. "Then it must be something I said."

Before Richard could explain that remark and further embarrass him, Mack clapped his brother on the back a little more forcefully than necessary. "Thanks for stopping by to pass on the message," he said. "I know how busy you are, though, so feel free to take off. Give Melanie a kiss for me. Go win over a few voters or raise a few million for your campaign. You're going to need it, since I intend to vote for whoever runs against you."

Richard barely managed to contain a laugh at the brush-off. "If it comes down to one vote costing me the election, I didn't deserve to win in the first place," his brother said, unperturbed. "And I'm in no hurry. I can hang here awhile."

"No you can't," Mack said, his voice a little tighter. "I'll walk you out."

He spun Richard around and aimed him toward the door. As they were leaving, he called back to Beth. "Let Tony know I'll be back in a minute."

"Sure," she said, staring after them with a puzzled expression.

Not until they were in the elevator did Mack face his brother, staring him down with a look meant to intimidate. "Don't get any ideas, big brother. None, you hear me?"

Richard returned his glare with a look of pure innocence. "I can't imagine what you're talking about. I just wanted to get to know your new friend."

"You say that as if you'd caught me on the playground with some girl in pigtails," Mack grumbled.

"Believe me, I am well aware that you're past being infatuated with a kid. Those are definitely grown-up sparks flying between you and the doc."

"You're crazy."

"I don't think so," Richard said. "Maybe I'll have Melanie give her a call and set up dinner."

"You do and you're a dead man," Mack said fiercely. He didn't want his brother, his aunt or anyone else messing with Beth's head—or his, for that matter. "Leave it alone. This is not like that. Beth and I chat from time to time. We have coffee. It's no big deal, and I don't want to turn it into one."

Richard's gaze narrowed. "You really mean that, don't you?"

"What was your first clue?" Mack retorted.

To his consternation, Richard burst out laughing. "I'll be damned," he said. "Destiny's done it again."

SHERRYL WOODS 55

"Destiny hasn't done a thing," Mack shouted after him as Richard strolled off.

Unfortunately, it was evident that his protest hadn't done a thing to convince his brother. Heck, he wasn't so sure he was buying it himself anymore.

Chapter Four

After his disconcerting encounter with his brother, Mack realized that he hadn't been out on anything that qualified as a real date in several weeks. Maybe that was why he was feeling so edgy and out of sorts. Maybe that was why he was spending so much time seeking out Beth for a few minutes of female companionship at the end of the day.

Beth was quiet and undemanding and most definitely female. Seeing her casually at the hospital was a comfortable pattern to have fallen into. In fact, her total lack of personal interest in him was a relief after the pressure of too many feminine expectations and after his own misguided attempts to live up to the public perception that he was some sort of football-celebrity playboy. There had been a time when he hadn't minded being labeled that way, but it had grown old recently.

Very recently. In fact, it had happened when he'd realized it had shaped Beth's view of him.

Consoled by the notion that his attentions toward Beth had nothing to do with an interest in the doctor herself, he vowed to rectify the situation as quickly as possible before anyone other than Richard started getting ideas. It would be especially bad if Destiny got wind of his nightly chats with the doc.

Rather than going directly back inside the hospital, Mack pulled out his cell phone in the parking lot and called an attractive stockbroker with whom he'd done a little professional business and a whole lot of off-the-clock deal-making of a personal nature.

Ten minutes later he'd scheduled a dinner date for later in the evening at her place. Given their usual pattern, they'd spend most of their time concentrating on dessert.

Satisfied with the proof that Richard was dead wrong about Mack's interest in Beth, he went back to Tony's room to play a few quick video games before his date. When he opened the door, though, he caught Beth with the hand-held computer, a little furrow of concentration on her brow as she tried to master the fast-paced game. His heart seemed to do an odd little stutter at the sight. He had no idea why.

"Come on, Dr. Beth," Tony encouraged. "It's not that hard."

"Tell it to someone who'll buy it," she grumbled, not taking her eyes off of the small screen. "You hustled me, kid. You told me this was easy."

Tony laughed. "It is," he insisted, his gaze moving to Mack, who stood frozen in the doorway still trying to understand his unexpected reaction. "Show her, Mack."

"I don't need his help," Beth retorted.

Tony rolled his eyes. "She keeps getting killed at level one."

"Uh-oh, that's not good," Mack said, shaking off the disconcerting mood and moving across the room to stand behind her.

He leaned down to whisper a few tips in her ear, but the scent of a faintly sexy, musky perfume caught him by surprise. He was pretty sure she usually smelled of antiseptic and something vaguely flowery. This was something new. He wasn't sure he liked it. It made his thoughts stray directly toward rumpled sheets and pillow talk. He mentally cursed his brother for planting that idea in his head.

"Go away," Beth said, not even glancing at him. "I can do this."

Mack chuckled at the display of independence. "If you say so," he said, moving to sit on the edge of Tony's bed. He glanced at the boy, who was grinning broadly.

"Women," Mack said with a hint of exasperation. "You can't tell them anything. That's a lesson you need to learn at an early age, Tony."

Beth did look up then, and the hand-held computer beeped and whistled as she went down in an apparent burst of video flames. She glared at it, then scowled at Mack.

"Tony, do not listen to a thing this man tells you about women," she lectured primly.

"How come?" Tony asked. "Have you seen the babes he dates?"

At Beth's sour expression, Mack bit back the chuckle that crept up his throat. He sensed that now was not a good time to reinforce Tony's enthusiasm for Mack's well-publicized social life. Nor was a denial that he had a stable of "babes" likely to be believed by either of them.

"I think what the doctor is trying to say is that I might not be the best example for you to follow when it comes to matters of the heart," Mack said.

Tony stared at him. "Huh?"

Mack tried to control a grin and failed. "Yeah, I don't get it either, but women are funny about things like this. We'll have a man-to-man talk on the subject another time."

"Not on my watch," Beth said grimly. "Tony, you need to get some rest."

"But I'm not tired," Tony protested.

"I think she wants to get me alone," Mack explained to him. "She probably wants to chew me out for being a bad influence."

"Oh, give it a rest," Beth muttered. "This isn't about you. It's about Tony not getting overly tired."

"Hey, Doc, you were the one in here playing video games. I just got here," Mack reminded her.

Frowning at him, Beth marched to the door and held it open, giving Mack a pointed look until he finally shrugged. He bent down to ruffle Tony's hair, promised he'd be back tomorrow, then followed her from the room.

"Mind telling me what that was all about?" he inquired, regarding her with amusement. "Are you just a sore loser?"

"Don't be ridiculous."

"Jealous?" he suggested, surprisingly intrigued by that particular scenario.

She gave him a look that could have melted steel. "I don't think so."

"There must be some reason you don't want me talking to Tony about women."

"How about the fact that it's inappropriate? It's not your place. Besides that, he's twelve, for goodness' sakes. He doesn't need to start thinking about girls in that way for a while."

"I had a girlfriend when I was twelve," Mack said, recalling the blue-eyed imp with curly hair rather fondly.

"Why doesn't that surprise me?" Beth responded irritably.

Mack smothered a laugh. "Something tells me you were not dating at twelve."

"I wasn't dating at twenty," she snapped. "That's hardly the point."

"Then what is the point?" He studied her closely. "And why did you wait so long to date? You're not bad-looking." He deliberately chose the massive understatement just to see the flags of color brighten her pale-as-cream cheeks.

She opened her mouth to respond, then snapped it shut again.

"Not sure?" he taunted.

The fire in her eyes died slowly. She regarded him with a vaguely chagrined expression. "Not entirely, no."

"Yeah, that happens to me sometimes, too. I lose track of what point I was trying to make. Of course, it usually only happens when a really sexy woman catches me off guard. Is that what happened here? I got to you in there, the adrenaline started rushing around, and you kinda lost track of things?"

The fire came back with a vengeance then. "In your dreams, bud."

She whirled around and stalked off, leaving Mack to stare after, oddly aroused by the whole exchange.

''Hey, you didn't tell me why you were such a late bloomer,'' he called after her.

She pointedly ignored him, her spine rigid as she rounded a corner and disappeared from view. Only when she was out of sight did he stop and question exactly which one of them had actually won this latest little skirmish. Since he was standing here all hot and bothered, he had a feeling Beth had triumphed without even realizing the game they were playing.

Every positive point Mack had accumulated in recent days flew out the window as Beth walked away from his taunting gaze. The man was maddening. He was an immature, skirt-chasing rogue. Worse, he prided himself on it.

Giving Tony advice on women? Please! What was he thinking? If Maria Vitale heard about that, she'd probably ban Mack from ever seeing her son again.

Then, again, maybe she wouldn't, Beth concluded with a sigh. Mack was good for Tony, inappropriate remarks and all. He made the boy laugh, and under current circumstances, even Beth could forgive him a lot for accomplishing that miracle.

That didn't mean she had to like Mack or spend another minute in his company. She'd simply steer clear of him. It shouldn't be that difficult. It wasn't as if he was underfoot at the hospital all day long.

He had a job, an important job in the view of some people, even if she wasn't among them. He had a family, even if at least one member of that family was in part responsible for pushing Mack into Beth's life. He had a lot of community obligations. And, goodness

knows, he had a social life. Given all that, it was astonishing that he spent any time at all at the hospital.
Avoiding him should be a breeze.

Satisfied with her plan, Beth had barely made it back
to her office when Mack appeared in the doorway.

"You!" she muttered, not sure whether she was
more annoyed at him or at herself for not anticipating
that he'd be right on her heels.

Mack chuckled. "You didn't actually think we'd finished talking, did you?"

"I had high hopes that we had," she told him.
"Don't you have a date or something?"

"As a matter of fact, I do," he responded. "But I
have time for this."

"For what?" Beth asked warily as he strode across
her office.

"This," he said, lowering his head to touch his lips
to hers.

It began as a gentle, exploratory kiss, maybe meant
to tease, maybe to shock. Beth reached up to shove
him away, but instead found herself clutching his jacket
just to hold herself upright. Her knees were suddenly
unsteady, her heartbeat frantic. In some distant part of
her brain, she heard herself saying that this was crazy,
that it was stupid, that it was dangerous. The litany of
warnings went on and on, as did the kiss until her brain
shut off and her senses took over.

She heard a soft moan of pleasure and realized it
came from her as Mack's mouth plundered hers, making her blood sing and her head reel. This was bad.
Really, really bad.

But oh, so good, she thought with a whimper of
dismay as he slowly pulled away, one arm still firmly
behind her back, one hand gently cupping her chin.

As her eyes fluttered open, she was looking into his steady, turbulent gaze. She couldn't have looked away if her life depended on it.

"What the hell just happened here?" Mack murmured under his breath.

Beth had a hunch he was asking the question more of himself than of her. Even so, she was tempted to offer Destiny's explanation of chemistry, which she was pretty sure she totally understood for the first time in her life. She wondered how Mack would react to the idea that she and his aunt had had a little tête-à-tête about sexual attraction. She had a hunch he'd be more stunned and exasperated than he already seemed to be.

"I'm actually asking," he said, when Beth remained silent. "What just happened here?"

Something in his tone irked her even more than his assumption that he could walk into her office and kiss her senseless. "I would think a man of your worldliness and sophistication would recognize a kiss that got out of hand better than most," she snapped, jerking away and moving to stand behind her desk. It wasn't much of a defense, but she'd take anything she could get. "I think you should leave now."

To her annoyance, Mack seemed vaguely amused by her response, or maybe by her actions.

"Retreating to a neutral corner, Doc?"

"No, trying to get some work done. I've already wasted enough time on you for one day."

"A great kiss is never a waste of time," he told her, his lips curving into a smile. "Especially for a woman who didn't start dating till after she turned twenty. You have a lot of time to make up for."

Great? He thought the kiss was *great?* Beth had certainly thought so herself, but as he'd just reminded her, she sure as heck didn't have his level of expertise on the subject. How flattering was that? One of the region's most eligible, sought-after bachelors thought she was a great kisser. It almost made her exasperation with him fade.

"Go away," she said, because she was pretty certain that letting him stay another second was a bad idea. She just might be tempted to throw herself at him to see if the kissing could get even better.

Suddenly she recalled what Mack had said when he'd first entered her office. He had a date. The man had a date and he'd been kissing her. Maybe that was par for the course in his life, but not in hers. It seemed a little sleazy, in fact. No, a *lot* sleazy. She frowned at him.

"Go away," she repeated more emphatically. "I wouldn't want you to be late for your date."

"Date?" he echoed blankly.

"You told me you had a date," she said tightly.

He muttered an expletive and got out his cell phone.

"You can't use that in the hospital," she told him.

He muttered something else, then picked up her phone and dialed, punching in the numbers so hard the phone practically bounced on her desk.

With his gaze locked with Beth's, he offered some sort of halfhearted excuse to whoever was on the other end of the line, then hung up.

Beth stared at him. "You broke your date?" she asked incredulously.

"I broke the damn date," he said, not sounding especially happy about it.

"Why?"

"Because I'm taking you to dinner instead."

She bristled at the assumption. "I don't think so."

"Oh, yes," he said. "I just broke a date for you. The least you can do is have dinner with me. You don't want me to spend the evening alone, do you?"

Beth couldn't decide which part of his recitation to react to first. "Okay, let's get something straight," she began. "You did not break that date for me. I didn't ask you to do it."

"No, but after that kiss we shared, you'd have been furious if I'd gone through with it," he said.

"Furious? I don't think so. I might have thought you a little sleazy," she admitted, "but then I don't have a very high opinion of you to begin with, so that shouldn't be too worrisome for you."

"Cute."

"I'm not finished," she said. "Whether or not you spend the evening alone or with a steady stream of willing women has nothing whatsoever to do with me."

"I didn't think so, either, at least not until a few minutes ago," he agreed pleasantly.

"What happened a few minutes ago?" she asked cautiously.

"I kissed you and decided I'd rather take a chance on getting to do that again instead of going out with a sure thing." He settled down in the chair beside her desk. "If you have things to do, I can wait."

Beth sorted through his latest outrageous claim and tried to decide whether to be flattered. Since listening to flattery was dangerous around Mack, she concluded it was smarter to ignore it.

"I could be a long while," she told him to test his determination. "A really long while."

He picked up a medical journal from the corner of

her desk. "Take your time. This doesn't look like fast reading. It ought to keep me occupied for hours."

She stared at him, thoroughly bemused. "You're really not going to leave, are you?"

"Not without you," he said, already flipping through the journal.

"I don't understand you," she said plaintively.

Mack looked up and met her gaze, looking almost as bemused as she felt. "To tell you the honest truth, Doc, I'm not real sure I understand what's going on here, either."

Beth's pulse did a crazy little lurch. "I suppose I can spare an hour for dinner," she said ungraciously. "Not one second more."

Mack dropped the journal on her desk, his eyes filled with something that might have been relief. "Let's go, then."

He steered her out of her office, a hand possessively placed in the center of her back. Beth liked the touch more than she cared to admit.

When they turned toward the front of the building, rather than toward the cafeteria, she regarded him curiously. "I thought we were going to the cafeteria."

"Not tonight," he said tightly.

"We only have an hour," she reminded him.

"Believe me, you have made the timetable abundantly clear. It may take a little finesse, but I will have you back at your desk in an hour."

A few minutes later they pulled up in front of one of the hottest new restaurants in Washington. The gossip columns were filled with lists of society bigshots and power brokers who'd been turned away each evening. Mack had barely stopped the car, however, when the valet parkers converged, gave him a ticket and ush-ered Beth to the curb.

"I'll need the car back here in front in fifty-five minutes," Mack told the valet.

The man checked his watch, made a note on the ticket, then said, "No problem, Mr. Carlton. It'll be here when you're ready to leave."

Inside the crowded foyer, Mack spoke to the maître d' in a hushed tone that Beth couldn't hear. Two minute later they were seated and practically no time after that two steaming meals were placed in front of them, along with a chilled bottle of sparkling water.

"Since you're going back to the hospital, I took a chance that you wouldn't want champagne," Mack said.

Beth nodded slowly. "The water's perfect." She looked at the grilled salmon on her plate, the tiny Red Bliss potatoes with parsley, the perfectly steamed green beans, then lifted her gaze to Mack's. "So is the meal. How did you manage this in…?" She glanced at her watch. "Less than five minutes."

Mack shrugged. "No big deal. In a place like this, it's all about who you know."

"And you know the maître d'?"

"Among others," he said.

"The owner?"

"Yes."

Beth shook her head in amazement. "Given that crush of people out there waiting to get in, I know we took someone else's reserved table. Are there other din-ers in here who are still waiting for these particular meals to appear?" she asked, glancing around wor-riedly.

He grinned. "Don't feel guilty, sweetheart. They're probably having wine to tide them over."

"Probably?" She regarded him incredulously as the reality of the extremes to which he'd gone sank in. She wasn't sure whether to laugh or cry at the absurdity of it. "You really did steal someone else's dinners? And you bribed them with a bottle of wine?"

"Not me," he claimed with suitable indignation. "I never left your side."

"You know what I mean."

"Eat up, Doc," he encouraged, clearly unwilling to be drawn into the discussion. "That clock of yours is ticking and I, for one, intend to have the crème brulée for dessert. I'd recommend the chocolate soufflé, but we're a little short on time for that."

"Unless, of course, some unwary couple already happens to have their order in," Beth teased, not sure how she felt about a man who could snap his fingers and make this happen, apparently without offending anyone. In some ways, that was the most astonishing thing of all.

"Good point," Mack said, and immediately beckoned for their waiter.

"Mack, don't you dare," Beth said.

"You'll settle for the crème brulée?"

"I think that's best," she said, even though she was sorely tempted to throw caution to the wind and opt for the chocolate soufflé. "Otherwise we're liable to start a riot."

Mack grinned. "I guess it will be the crème brulée for dessert, John. Give us about twenty minutes, though, okay?"

"Sure thing, Mr. Carlton." He leaned down to whisper conspiratorially. "Of course, if you're on a tight timetable, there's a soufflé that should be ready in a half hour. I could put in another order for those diners and put this one in one of our takeout containers. Would that work?''

Mack glanced at Beth. "What do you say? Dessert at your desk?''

There were a lot of things in life that Beth could resist. Chocolate wasn't one of them, and a warm chocolate soufflé just out of the oven had the power to smash her resistance to smithereens. There were many things she might not like about Mack, many more things about which she had serious reservations, but if he could get her that dessert, she was willing to forgive a lot.

Giving in to temptation, she said, "The chocolate, definitely.''

Mack regarded her with fascination as the waiter walked away. "Good to know," he murmured, his gaze on her filled with heat.

"What?'' she asked, her voice surprisingly shaky.

"That your weak spot is chocolate.''

"That's one of them," Beth agreed, since there seemed little point in denying the obvious, not when she'd just caved and renounced several of her scruples to get a soufflé for dessert.

Mack lifted his glass of water. "To discovering the rest,'' he said, his tone soft and his gaze serious.

Beth returned his gaze and tried not to notice that her heart and her stomach were turning cartwheels. Sweet heaven, was there any female on the face of the earth who could remain immune to this man once he set out to be charming? She certainly prayed she'd turn out to be one of the rare ones, but right at this moment she didn't give herself a chance in hell.

Chapter Five

Mack had absolutely no idea how his evening had taken such an unexpected shift the night before. One minute he'd been looking forward to his date with a woman who undoubtedly would never speak to him again now. The next minute he'd been irresistibly drawn to Beth's office just for the simple pleasure of stealing a kiss. It didn't make a lick of sense.

Something about her revelation that she'd hardly dated as a teenager had stirred some kind of purely male reaction in him. If he hadn't known himself better, he might have thought it was some sort of weird attraction to the virginal nature of the admission, which was ridiculous. Not only had Beth not said anything at all about *still* being innocent, he definitely preferred women who knew the score.

But that hadn't stopped him from hightailing it after her like some sort of overheated jerk intent on making a conquest. He was damn lucky she hadn't guessed all of the undercurrents behind that kiss and leveled him with some sort of sedative, the way a vet took care of an unruly animal.

Okay, he thought as he unintentionally snapped a pencil in two, that explained the kiss. The assessment wasn't pretty, nor did it speak well of him, but it was honest. It did not, however, give him a clue about what had happened during and after the kiss.

The woman had made his supposedly rehabilitated knees weak. When in hell was the last time that had happened? Maybe never. He never lost control of a situation the way he had last night. From the minute his lips had touched Beth's, he'd been transported to some other dimension, a place where he wanted to take risks and give pleasure, not in some casual, meaningless way, but something real and lasting.

Which was absurd. Totally and utterly absurd, he decided as another pencil broke in two in his grip. He stared at the little pile of wood and lead and concluded he needed to get out of his office and away from all this unfamiliar introspection before it led him down a dangerous path or at least before he destroyed most of his office supplies. Wasn't he the one who was always going on and on around here about wasting everything from bandages to paper clips?

Outside and in his car, a recently developed habit made him turn in the direction of the hospital, but he overrode the instinct and headed instead to Virginia. He hadn't been out to Ben's farm in a while. Being around his artistic brother was usually soothing. Ben was an accepting guy. He took people as they came. He didn't ask a lot of probing questions, especially since his own life was such a mess. Nor was he the least bit inclined to meddle. Yep, visiting Ben was definitely a good choice. Mack would be able to chill out for a couple of hours and forget all about that disconcerting encounter with Beth.

As Mack approached the farm, the rolling Virginia countryside slowly began to work its magic. Mack found himself unwinding and understanding for the first time what had drawn Ben out here after the tragedy that had shaken him to his core. It was hard to feel anything here except for an appreciation of nature's beauty in the distant purple haze of the Blue Ridge Mountains, the soft green of the grass, the canopy of towering oaks and the majestic stature of the horses grazing behind pristine white fences.

Because Ben was always hungry, rarely paused to eat and never stocked his refrigerator with any decent junk food, Mack stopped at a coffee shop in town and picked up sandwiches, sodas and chips to take along as a peace offering for interrupting his brother's work. He grabbed a few freshly baked chocolate-chip cookies while he was at it. Those would go a long way in diverting Ben's attention away from the reason for Mack's unexpected visit.

By the time he finally reached the gate to his brother's place, Mack had pushed aside all thoughts of his own tumultuous emotions, if not the image of Beth herself.

Mack parked in the shade of an oak tree and headed directly to Ben's studio in the converted old red barn. No one responded to his knock, but that was fairly common. Ben wouldn't hear a herd of Black Angus cattle approaching if he was absorbed in one of his paintings.

As he stepped into the barn, Mack noted it was a

good ten degrees cooler inside, despite the sun shining through a skylight overhead. As Mack had expected, Ben was staring at a half-finished canvas, his brush poised in midair, a faraway look in his eyes. Something told Mack that look had less to do with the work on his easel than with a sad memory of the tragedy that had sent him scurrying to the country in the first place.

"Hey, bro," Mack said, startling Ben, who took a long moment to shake off his mood before he finally met Mack's gaze.

"Has the sky started to fall?" Ben inquired. "Surely that must be the case for you to drive all the way out here on a weekday."

"Nope. As far as I know, the sky's still in place. I'm here on an impulse." He performed a visual search of the studio, then gave an exaggerated sigh of disappointment. "I was hoping you'd have a naked model in your studio."

His brother grinned, the last shadows finally disappearing from his eyes. "I paint landscapes," Ben reminded him. "Which you would know if you weren't such a culturally deprived human being."

"Hey, I appreciate art," Mack objected. "Especially yours. I have a sketch you did of me on my refrigerator door."

"How flattering! I believe I was six when I did that."

"Yes, but you showed promise even then," Mack said with total sincerity, then had to ruin it by adding, "And I'm sure when you're really, really famous that little scrap of paper will be worth a fortune."

"Not if you get mustard and ketchup all over it," Ben retorted, then caught sight of the bag in Mack's hand. "You brought food. I take back every mean thing

I said to you, if that's lunch for me. I had an idea when I woke up this morning and skipped breakfast to come straight out here.''

Mack glanced at the canvas. As Ben had said, he was no expert, but this didn't look like his brother's usual style. "How's the idea working out?" he inquired carefully.

"Not quite the way I envisioned it," Ben admitted. "Now hand over the food. If one of those sandwiches is roast beef, it's mine."

"Which is why I got two roast beef," Mack said. "I'm tired of you stealing mine."

Ben chuckled. "Took you long enough to catch on. Did you get orange soda?"

Mack regarded him innocently. "I thought you liked grape."

"Very funny. Hand it over."

"Damn, but you're greedy. What happened to the whole starving artist thing?"

"I was never a starving artist. I can thank our parents for that. I'm famished. There's a difference." Ben took a bite out of the thick roast beef, lettuce and tomato sandwich and sighed with obvious pleasure. "Nothing on earth better than a fresh tomato in midsummer."

"Unless it's corn on the cob," Mack countered, falling into the familiar debate. "Dripping with butter."

"Or summer squash cooked with onion and browned."

Mack regarded his brother wistfully. "Do you suppose we could plant an idea in Destiny's head and get her to cook all our favorites this Sunday?"

"You mean, could *I* plant the idea in her head?" Ben guessed.

"You are the one she loves best," Mack pointed out,

drawing a sour look. Ben refused to admit that their aunt was partial to him, and Destiny would deny it with her dying breath. "Besides, she thinks you don't eat enough. She'd have pity on you. It would just take one little word."

Ben regarded him curiously. "Since when has the cat got your tongue? Nothing's ever stopped you from pleading with our aunt to fix you something special."

"Truthfully, I'm trying to avoid Destiny these days," Mack said casually.

"Won't that make eating all these goodies you want a bit tricky?"

"I was kinda hoping you'd pack up some leftovers and bring 'em to me," Mack admitted.

Ben chuckled. "Don't tell me. She's found a woman for you. What's wrong with Destiny's selection? Does she have buckteeth and wear glasses? Or is she simply not up to a ten on the Mack-o-meter for beauty?"

"I am not that shallow," Mack protested. "And there's nothing wrong with the woman. Nothing at all."

Ben studied him quietly. "I see," he said slowly, fighting a grin. "In other words, Destiny got it just right and you're running scared."

"Go suck an egg," Mack suggested mildly.

"Want to talk about it?"

"Nope."

"But panic is what brought you flying out here bearing gifts," Ben surmised.

"Can't a guy go visit his brother without getting cross-examined about ulterior motives?"

"Sure, but since you haven't been here in weeks, you'll have to excuse me for being a little suspicious."

Mack frowned at him. "We could talk about your social life."

Ben's expression immediately shut down. "No, we couldn't," he said tightly.

Mack instantly felt guilty for turning the tables on Ben. "I'm sorry. I was only teasing, but I should know better. The wound's still too raw, isn't it?"

"Drop it," Ben said, his tone angry, his eyes dull.

Mack regarded his brother helplessly. "Maybe I shouldn't. Maybe it would help if we all made you talk about it."

"Graciela's dead, dammit! What's to talk about?" Ben all but shouted in a fierce tone rarely used by Mack's soft-spoken brother. "Why the hell doesn't anyone get that?"

Mack barely resisted the urge to go to his brother, but Ben wouldn't appreciate any gesture of sympathy. Ben still blamed himself for Graciela's death and was convinced he wasn't deserving of sympathy. He only resented anyone's attempt to assuage his grief or his guilt.

"I'm sorry," Mack said again quietly. "I didn't mean to stir up the pain. That was the very last thing I wanted when I came out here."

Ben gave him a haunted look. "You didn't stir up anything," he told him. "It never goes away."

Telling Ben that Graciela wasn't worthy of the kind of guilt or misery Ben heaped on himself wouldn't help. Mack knew that much by now. He wasn't sure what it would take to finally shake Ben out of the dark, brooding mood which kept him isolated out here at his farm, but he prayed it would happen soon. Ben's on-going despondency worried the whole family. Once in a while they caught glimmers of the old, easygoing Ben, but those reminders were all too rare.

Mack studied his brother. "Anything I can do?"

"Nah," Ben said, obviously fighting to shake off his mood before Mack could make too much more of it. "Just keep coming around despite my general crankiness."

"That's a promise," Mack assured him.

Ben glanced across the table and his expression brightened. "You gonna finish that sandwich?"

Mack chuckled. "I thought the big, hulking football player in the family was supposed to be the one with the insatiable appetite," he grumbled even as he shoved the other half of his sandwich toward his brother. "Take the chips, too. I have to hit the road."

"Big date tonight?"

"No."

"Damn. You know I live vicariously through what I read about you in the papers."

"Sorry to disappoint you, but I'm living life in the slow lane right now."

"There has to be a story there," Ben guessed.

"None I intend to share."

"But it does have to do with that woman Destiny picked out for you, right?" Ben prodded.

"I came out here because you never pry," Mack grumbled.

"But this news is too good to pass up," Ben told him.

Mack frowned at him. "Get back to your canvas. Right now it looks a lot like a squashed pumpkin. Is that what you were going for?"

Ben groaned. "Heathen!"

"Hey, I have a good eye."

"For women, maybe."

Mack deliberately squinted intently at the half-finished painting. "The very large rear of a woman in an orange two-piece bathing suit?"

Ben laughed. "You were closer with the pumpkin."

"Well, what the hell is it?"

"Since you're having so much fun guessing, I think I'll let you wait till it's finished. Then you can try again."

"I'm usually better at this," Mack said. "Then again, you usually paint recognizable fields and trees and streams."

"This was an experiment," Ben reminded him.

Mack regarded him seriously. "A word of advice?"

Ben nodded, his expression wary.

"Stick to what you know," Mack said, then dodged when Ben tossed his empty soda bottle straight at his head. For an artsy kind of a guy, his brother had dead-accurate aim.

Better yet, for most of an entire hour, Ben had kept Mack's mind off one very disconcerting lady doctor.

"I'm not happy with Tony Vitale's blood count," the hematologist sitting across from Beth said. "He's not responding the way I'd hoped. I think we ought to consider a transfusion before he gets any weaker."

Beth bit back a sigh. She didn't have a good argument against that, but she was afraid that scheduling a transfusion would be demoralizing for Tony and for his mom. They would both know that all the other steps being taken weren't working. Transfusions were commonplace enough with kids in Tony's situation, but none of them were crazy about the process, even if they felt temporarily better in the end.

"Do you disagree?" Peyton Lang asked.

"Not really, but I know how discouraged Tony and his mother will be. I was really hoping that this last medicine and the food Mack's been bringing by for him would do the trick and get his blood count back up again, at least for the short term."

"Believe me, so was I," Peyton said. "We're running out of options."

"We can't give up on him," Beth said, unable to keep the frantic note out of her voice.

Peyton gave her a sharp look. "We may not win this one. You know that, Beth. It's time you started accepting the possibility. Maybe you need to pull back a little, let someone else step in as Tony's attending physician."

"Absolutely not. Besides, losing Tony is just a possibility," Beth said fiercely. "And I refuse to accept it until there are no other options. He's such a brave kid. He doesn't deserve this."

Peyton gave her a sad look. "None of them do."

"No, they don't, do they?" she said wearily. "Okay, then. Schedule the transfusion for first thing in the morning. I'll talk to Tony's mom tonight."

The hematologist looked as if he wanted to say more, but he finally shrugged and left without another word. Some things just couldn't be said aloud, even though they both might be thinking them. And no doctor ever wanted to acknowledge that a fight might be nearing an end.

A once-familiar sense of outrage and anger stirred in Beth's chest. She needed to get back in the lab and look over the latest test results from her current research one more time. The first batch hadn't held much promise, but this recent round was looking more hopeful. She needed more time, dammit. More time to get it right, so she could help Tony and some of the other kids who were at the end of the line with current treatments.

She was at the door, about to open it, when Mack appeared. He took one look at her and steered her right back inside her office.

"What's wrong?" he demanded at once. "Sit down. You look like hell."

"Just what every woman wants to hear," she muttered, even as she gratefully sank back onto her chair. The longer she could postpone seeing Maria and Tony, the better.

"I'm not here to flatter you."

"Obviously not. Why are you here?"

"I just saw Tony. He's not looking so good."

Beth nodded. If it was apparent even to a layman, then her decision a few minutes ago was the right one. "He needs a transfusion to buy him a little time," she admitted bleakly.

Mack looked stunned by the blunt assessment. "A little time?" he echoed warily. "What are we talking here, Beth? Days? Weeks?"

"No more than that."

"What about the bone marrow transplant?"

"He's not a candidate right now. It would be too risky."

"You just said he's only got a few days or weeks. Isn't it about time to start taking a few risks?"

"There's protocol," she began, only to have him cut her off with a curse. She looked into his eyes and saw the same torment she'd been feeling before his arrival. "I'm sorry, Mack."

"I won't accept this."

"We don't have a choice."

"I have a choice," he all but shouted. "We'll find another doctor, another treatment. That boy is not dying unless we've exhausted everything available."

Beth tried not to feel hurt that Mack didn't think she knew what was best, that he didn't think she was up to the task of saving Tony. She understood the kind of powerless rage he was feeling all too well. If she'd thought for a second that another doctor or another course of treatment might improve Tony's odds, she would have called for the consultation herself.

"Mack, right here at this hospital, we are his best hope," she said quietly.

"But you're giving up," he protested.

"No," she said vehemently. "Never. I'm just trying to be realistic."

"Damn being realistic," he said heatedly, then sighed and gave her an apologetic look. "I'm sorry. I know I shouldn't take this out on you. I know how hard you're working on his behalf. I know how much he matters to you."

"It's okay. Believe me, I understand your frustration."

"And I see now why you looked so beat when I got here." He met her gaze. "What's the plan?"

"A transfusion in the morning and then we wait to see if it helps," Beth explained. "A little prayer wouldn't be misplaced, either."

Mack nodded. "Okay, then." He held out his hand. "Want to go with me to pay Tony a visit?"

"I was on my way when you got here," she said, taking his hand because right now she desperately needed the contact with someone who shared her dismay. She also needed the little spark that came with it, the reminder that no matter what happened with Tony she was alive, that she would still be here fighting for other kids down the road.

Mack gave her hand a squeeze. "How about we take a little detour to the chapel on the way?"

She met his gaze. "You read my mind."

It was a habit of his that she was starting to take for granted. Moreover, instead of making her uncomfortable, it was beginning to feel very, very good to have that kind of connection with someone.

"Dr. Beth's really pretty, don't you think so, Mack?" Tony's huge eyes were focused intently on Mack's face.

Mack tried to ignore the question. He wasn't getting drawn into that discussion with yet another matchmaker. Instead he held up the assortment of comic books he'd brought with him. "Look at these, Tony. I had no idea there were so many cool new superheroes out there."

Tony's gaze remained unrelenting. "You didn't answer my question, Mack. Don't you think Dr. Beth is really pretty?"

Mack sighed. "Yes, she is."

"Maybe you should ask her on a date or something. I'll bet she'd go."

Mack had enough trouble convincing Beth to slip out of the hospital for an occasional meal on the run. An actual honest-to-goodness date was probably out of the question. He didn't want to ruin his image with Tony by admitting that, though.

Tony studied him worriedly. "She didn't turn you down already, did she? Did you say something to make her mad?"

"No, kid, I haven't bombed out entirely with the doc, but she's pretty busy, you know. She has a lot of responsibilities around here."

"I know. That's why I think she needs a date, to get her mind off things, you know what I mean? Sometimes she seems real sad."

"I've noticed," Mack said. In fact, some days he wondered how she stood it. Today had to be one of the worst since they'd met. Even he was shaken by the grim outlook for Tony's future.

Earlier, when they'd been on their way from the chapel to Tony's room, she'd gotten a beep and had taken off at a run with a terse apology and no explanation. He was dawdling in Tony's room now, hoping she'd eventually turn up. If that beep meant the kind of emergency he suspected, he thought she might be in need of some company this evening, maybe even another dinner someplace that wouldn't remind her of the hospital.

He turned his attention back to Tony, whose energy had obviously faded. He was resting against the pillows, which were barely a shade whiter than his pale complexion.

"How are you feeling, pal?"

"Kinda tired," Tony confessed.

Mack was taken aback by the rare admission. Usually Tony was all bluster when it came to his health. For him to admit that he was feeling tired meant he had to be exhausted. Mack recalled what Beth had said about a transfusion, but he knew the word on that hadn't gotten to Tony yet.

"Get some sleep. You want to be rested when your mom gets here after work," Mack told him.

"But you just got here," Tony protested weakly. "And you brought all those awesome comics."

"They'll be here when you wake up, and so will I," Mack promised. "Now close your eyes and take a nap."

Tony struggled to keep his eyes open. "Hey, Mack."

"What, pal?"

"Could you maybe sit here next to me?"

"Sure," he said, lowering himself carefully to the edge of the bed. He'd noticed that too much movement seemed to make the boy wince. It was yet another sign that his condition was worsening.

Mack was barely seated when he felt Tony's hand slip into his and hang on tight. Tears immediately stung the backs of his eyes.

"It's okay," he said softly. "You can sleep. I'm right here."

"Can I tell you something?" Tony asked sleepily.

"Anything, pal."

"You won't tell my mom or Dr. Beth?"

"No," Mack promised.

"Sometimes I'm scared to close my eyes," Tony whispered. "'Cause I'm afraid I won't wake up."

Ah, hell, Mack thought, blinking back tears.

"You don't need to worry about that now," Mack said, his voice choked. "Nothing's going to happen while I'm here with you."

Tony's eyes blinked open and his expression turned serious. "It could, Mack. So if it does, will you tell my mom I love her?"

Mack struggled to maintain his composure. If this boy could lie here so bravely facing death, then surely he could give Tony the reassurance he needed to hear.

''I think your mom already knows that,'' he told Tony. ''But I'll tell her.''

Tony sighed then and finally allowed himself to fall asleep, his hand still clinging to Mack's.

And somewhere deep inside, Mack's heart broke.

Chapter Six

When Beth finally finished dealing with the emergency that had sent her racing away from Mack, she felt as if she'd been through an emotional wringer. The young patient who'd come in with a severe reaction to her chemotherapy had finally been stabilized and sent to a room. Beth would have given just about anything to go home to her own room, to spend an hour soaking in a hot bath and then to crawl beneath the covers and sleep for a month.

Instead, she drew in a deep breath, steadied her nerves and headed to Tony's room to break the news about the transfusion scheduled for morning. She was not looking forward to the meeting with Mrs. Vitale. Maria had had just about all the bad news she could handle lately.

As Beth turned the corner toward Tony's room, she spotted Mack in the hall, shoulders slumped, eyes closed. He was leaning against a wall, looking about as wiped-out as she felt.

"You okay?" she asked.

He blinked as if he'd been a million miles away, then smiled weakly. "How the hell do you do this every day?" he asked, his voice filled with respect.

Beth instinctively glanced at the door to Tony's room. "A tough night in there?"

Mack nodded, his expression bleak. "You could say that. Tony asked me to tell his mom he loved her if he died during his nap."

"Oh, no," Beth whispered, her heart aching for him and for Tony. "I'm so sorry, Mack."

"Don't be sorry for me," he said fiercely. "Be sorry for Tony. No kid should ever have to say something like that. He shouldn't have that kind of weight on his shoulders. My God, how does he bear it?"

Beth put her hand on his arm, felt the muscle jerk beneath her touch. "I couldn't agree with you more, but sometimes life simply isn't fair or just. If you can't accept that, then you'd better not choose medicine as a career."

"Then you accept it?" he asked skeptically.

"I have to," she said. "It's not easy, but what else can I do? I have to focus on the times we win, not on the times we lose."

"I don't envy you. Compared to this, getting pummeled on a football field on Sundays was a piece of cake."

She managed a weak smile. "Maybe I should give that a try sometime."

He grinned. "I imagine you have some pretty tricky moves, Doc. How's your throwing arm?"

"Like a girl's."

"Yeah, it figures." His expression sobered and his gaze sought hers. "You know what else was on Tony's mind tonight?"

She was almost afraid to ask. "What?"

"He thought I should ask you on a date." Mack shook his head. "The kid is sick as a dog and he's matchmaking."

Beth grinned, despite the sorrow eating at her. "More proof that life goes on. Even a kid like Tony sees that." She studied Mack's tense expression and decided he'd gotten a whole lot more than he'd bargained for when he'd befriended Tony. "Tell you what. I'm going to break a vow and ask you on a date."

Mack regarded her with surprise. "You made a vow never to ask me out?"

"I made a vow never to ask any man out," she corrected.

"Any particular reason?"

"It tends to give a man the illusion that he has the upper hand," she explained.

"And you don't like relinquishing control?"

"Not especially."

"But you're willing to make an exception for me?"

"Yes, and don't make me regret it by reacting predictably and letting your ego get out of hand. It's dinner, Mack. Nothing more."

Mack chuckled. "I think I can control my ego." He gave her a thorough once-over with a devilish twinkle in his eye. "And my hormones, if it comes to that."

She gave him a stern look. "You're determined to cross a line, aren't you? I could take back the invitation."

"You won't, though. You're feeling sorry for me.

Besides, I'm not determined to cross any lines, just considering the possibilities," he replied. "Especially since mentioning them has put some color back in your cheeks."

Beth frowned at him, and he managed to look suitably chastened. It was probably an act, but she let it pass. "Okay, then. Can you stick around while I speak to Mrs. Vitale? Then I'll take you someplace for dinner."

He regarded her with a hopeful expression. "Home?" he inquired. "That's where I feel like being tonight. Yours. Mine. It doesn't matter. I just don't feel like being around a lot of people."

Beth totally understood what he was saying. Being under a microscope must be hard enough when life was perfect. Being subjected to scrutiny when you'd been through an emotional wringer as Mack had been tonight would be unbearable.

She tried to imagine what in her kitchen might be edible, given the way she tended to ignore things like grocery shopping, then nodded. "There's bound to be something I can throw together that won't kill us both."

"Works for me," he said.

"I'll just be a few minutes."

"Take your time." He gave her a faint smile. "If you want to make Tony's day, tell him you're taking me home with you."

Beth laughed despite the somber mood and her exhaustion. "I think that might encourage his matchmaking efforts a little too much."

Mack was still a little stunned that Beth had invited him to her place. He must have looked like the emo-

tional wreck he was if she'd felt the need to take pity
on him. Despite the obvious reason for the invitation,
he couldn't help looking forward to the opportunity to
get a look at where she lived and maybe discover a
few more details that would tell him what made her
tick. His curiosity about her seemed to deepen with
each encounter.

A woman with Beth's sort of dedication and commitment to her work, with the compassion to treat kids
in Tony's dire straits, was a rarity in his world. His
admiration for her grew with every minute he spent
around her and the kids to whom she'd devoted her
life. He'd done his share of good deeds and small kind-
nesses in his time, but Beth did Herculean good deeds
every day.

When she finally emerged from Tony's room, she
gave him a distracted look and beckoned for him to
follow her. "We can get out of here as soon as I get
my purse and keys," she told him. "I'll jot down my
address for you."

A few minutes later she gave him an address on the
fringes of Georgetown. He had a hunch she'd chosen
it less for the prestige of the neighborhood than for its
proximity to the hospital and the short commute required in an emergency.

"See you there in ten minutes," she told him when
they'd reached her car in the hospital parking lot. Mack
had insisted on walking her there, though his own car
was in the visitor's lot. She seemed about to say something more, then hesitated, her expression thoughtful.

"What?" Mack prodded.

"Just trying to remember if there's any wine in the
house. Probably not. If you want some, you'll need to

stop and pick up a bottle,'' she said as she got behind the wheel of her small SUV.

''I'm too wiped-out for wine,'' he told her. ''Unless you want some?''

She shook her head. ''Not unless you don't mind me falling sound asleep in whatever pot of food I'm fixing.''

He studied her weary, fragile features. ''Look, Beth, I really appreciate the invitation, but we don't have to do this tonight.''

''We both need to eat,'' she said, sounding exactly like the dictatorial doctor he knew her capable of being. ''Don't dawdle along the way or I'll make you eat spinach.''

Mack laughed. ''I happen to love spinach.''

''Oh, my, your aunt really did train you well, didn't she?''

''Let's leave Destiny out of this. See you in a few,'' he said, dropping a quick kiss on her forehead before closing the door of her car. ''Drive safely.''

He loped out of the employee parking lot toward his own car half a block away feeling surprisingly energized all of a sudden, enough to motivate him to make a quick stop by the florist's so that when he showed up on Beth's doorstep he was carrying a huge bouquet of flowers.

As he rang the doorbell of her small brick town house, he realized he was anticipating the rest of the evening in a way he hadn't looked forward to a date in a very long time. The knowledge that this impromptu date had been initiated by a woman to whom he supposedly wasn't the least bit attracted didn't seem to matter. Nor did the fact that sex clearly wasn't on the agenda. He was content with the prospect of food and some intelligent conversation, anything that might delay going home, where he was certain to be plagued by dreams about Tony's sad situation.

When Beth opened the door, her eyes widening in delight at the sight of the flowers, Mack felt something shift inside him. He had the funniest feeling that few men had ever bestowed such a simple gift on her before, probably because they mistook her cool, professional demeanor to mean that she didn't appreciate the more feminine pleasures in life.

"Oh, Mack," she said softly, burying her nose in the flowers. "What on earth made you think to do this?"

"A gentleman caller always brings something for his hostess," he recited, grinning at her.

"Remind me to thank your aunt for drilling those manners into you," she said. "I hope I have a vase big enough for all these. Did you buy out the shop?"

Actually he had. The man had been ready to close and had given him a deal on all of the bunches that remained in the cooler. There had been lilies and roses, baby's breath, snapdragons and some other colorful, fragrant blooms he couldn't identify. Impulse had made him take them all. If anyone on earth deserved to be pampered a bit, it was Beth after a day like today. He only wished flowers could brighten his mood as easily. Better to concentrate on Beth.

He could think of all sorts of ways she ought to be indulged. Maybe he'd get her one of those spa days he'd heard women talking about, one with a facial, massages, wraps and who knew what else went on behind those discreet doors.

"Mack?"

"Hmm?"

"Where'd you go just then?" she asked.

"I got a little lost envisioning you in a seaweed wrap," he said just to watch the color in her cheeks deepen.

"What an odd imagination you have," she said, leading the way into the kitchen.

"Have you ever had one?" he asked.

"My time and my budget don't really run to seaweed wraps," she said, clearly amused. "Have you had one?"

He shuddered. "Hell, no, but I hear women talking about that kind of stuff. I thought you might like it."

"Who knows? Maybe one of these years, if I ever get a whole day off, I'll try one," she said. "Seems like a waste of money to me."

"Being pampered is never a waste of money, especially not with the kind of work you do. You need to take better care of yourself."

She regarded him curiously. "Is this some new mission you're on? It's not enough that you cheer up Tony, now you're intent on cheering me up, too?"

He thought about it and decided it was. It didn't have to mean he was falling for her or anything. It was just common decency to worry about someone who spent her life worrying about others. "Yep," he said. "I'm making you my project."

"Don't you have an entire football team to worry about? That's what? Eleven men?"

He chuckled. "On the field at any given moment. There are a lot more on the bench. Remind me to get you a manual explaining the basics."

"It would be wasted. Besides, you're missing my point that you have your own responsibilities. Those should keep you busy enough."

"Not the same thing," he told her. "Besides, those guys have trainers who worry about whether they're eating properly, getting enough exercise and generally staying fit. Who worries about you?"

She shook her head as she poured him a glass of iced tea. "I'm an adult and a doctor. I can pretty much look after myself."

"But do you?"

"Of course I do."

"When was the last time you took a day off?"

She hesitated so long, he knew she was having to really think about it. *"Ding,"* he said as if calling time in a game. "Too long. That must mean it's been weeks, if not months."

She frowned. "Actually I was off last Saturday," she retorted, then sighed. "But I got called in around eleven-thirty and never got away."

"That's exactly what I'm talking about. You're not invincible. What happens if you get so worn down, you get sick?"

"I don't get sick." She gave him an exasperated look. "I appreciate your concern. I really do, but it's misguided." She poked her head in the refrigerator. "Your choices are scrambled eggs or..." Her voice became muffled until she withdrew and gave him a chagrined look. "Or poached eggs or an omelet, assuming this cheddar isn't too hard to grate." She held up a pitiful-looking block of cheese.

Mack shook his head. "Where's your phone?"

"Right behind you on the wall," she said. "Why?"

He was already punching in a familiar number. "Do you have some sort of aversion to meat?" he asked her as the phone rang.

"No," she said, regarding him curiously. "What are you doing?"

"Isn't it obvious? How about baked potatoes?"

"Love them."

Mack nodded. "Hey, William, can you throw together a couple of filet mignons, baked potatoes with sour cream and butter, caesar salads and something decadently chocolate?"

"Absolutely, Mr. Carlton," the chef at one of the Carlton Industries steak-house restaurants in Georgetown said at once. "Is this for your house?"

"No." He gave the man Beth's address. "Will a half hour be too much of a rush?"

"Of course not. I'll send it right over."

"Thanks, William. You're a lifesaver."

"It's my pleasure, sir."

"Oh, and one more thing, William."

"Yes, sir."

"Could you at least wait till morning before you call Destiny and tell her about this?"

"Sir, I do not report to your aunt," the chef said indignantly.

"Not officially, no," Mack said. "But she does have a way of wheedling information out of you, doesn't she?"

William chuckled. "Your aunt is a very clever woman," he admitted. "She does have a way of getting whatever information she wants. Most men find her irresistible."

"Irresistible or not, try not to let her get hold of this little tidbit to chew on, okay? She'll make my life a living nightmare."

"Only because she cares about you and your brothers," William said. "You're very lucky to have such a fine woman in your lives. I'm not sure any of you appreciate that.''

"Your scolding is duly noted, William."

"As it should be, sir. I'll have your dinner there shortly.''

Mack sighed, almost regretting the can of worms he'd opened by making that particular call. Unfortunately, despite his tendency to blab what he knew to Destiny, William served the best steaks in town.

As he hung up, he saw Beth studying him with a bemused expression. "Was that William of William's Steak House?"

Mack nodded.

"And he's going to send over takeout in thirty minutes?"

"Yes."

"And then, most likely, report back to your aunt?"

Mack nodded again.

"You live in a very fascinating world."

He grinned. "It has its moments." He regarded her with interest. "I suppose your family is totally normal.''

An odd look that Mack couldn't quite interpret passed across Beth's face. "Not so normal?" he pressed.

"I guess that depends on your view of normal," she hedged.

"I mostly grew up with an aunt who regards life as one gigantic adventure and who has turned meddling into a fine art," he said. "Believe me, I have a very loose definition of what constitutes normal. Do you have brothers and sisters?"

A shadow darkened her eyes and he immediately recalled the brother who'd died during a childhood bout with leukemia. "I'm sorry. I forgot about your brother."

"That's okay. Sometimes it feels as if it happened several lifetimes ago."

"Because every time you face losing a patient, it's like going through it all over again," Mack guessed.

"In a way, though at the time I was so young, I was only aware that someone I loved very much was really, really sick and then he died. It left this huge void in my life, because Tommy was all I had in some ways."

"You mean because he was your only sibling?" Mack asked.

Beth shook her head. "Because after he died, my parents retreated even more deeply into their work. They were research scientists, too. They were never very outgoing, demonstrative people, but after Tommy died, it got worse. They were driven to find answers. Most nights they got home long after I'd gone to bed, and they were usually gone when I got up in the morning. I rarely saw them."

Mack heard the hurt behind the factual recitation, and another piece of the puzzle clicked into place. "So your work isn't really all about your brother, is it? It's also a connection to your parents."

She seemed startled by the comment, then relieved when the doorbell rang to prevent her from having to answer.

Mack looked her in the eye as he stood up to go to the door. "I'm not forgetting about this conversation," he warned as he left the kitchen.

When he returned a moment later, Beth was busy setting the table. She never even looked up to meet his gaze until after he'd set out the dishes from the restaurant.

"It smells heavenly," she said a little too brightly, taking her place at the table. "You must order from William a lot to get such incredible service."

"I do, but it's also a company restaurant in some division or another."

She studied him curiously. "You really don't care about all that, do you?"

"Only when it's convenient, like tonight," he admitted. "Thank God I don't need to think about it. The company is totally and completely Richard's bailiwick."

"You never had the slightest inclination to claim your part of the family legacy?"

"Nope," he said readily. "I made my own money playing football, even though my career was brief. I made some sound investments, then used those to buy a share of the team. I love football. I get it. When I was on the field, I enjoyed the competitiveness, the physical demands of the game. I still like the strategy involved. I don't care about manufacturing widgets or running restaurants or whatever else Carlton Industries is into."

He waved a finger under her nose. "And don't try to get me off track. I haven't forgotten that we were talking about your family."

Her expression immediately closed down. "There's not much more to say."

"Are you trying to prove something to them? Maybe finally earn the attention they denied you growing up?"

She deliberately put a bite of meat in her mouth and chewed slowly, her expression thoughtful. "Probably," she said at last, surprising him with the admission.

"But didn't you learn anything from them?" he asked.

"Sure," she said at once. "I learned all about dedication and focus."

Mack regarded her impatiently. "But they hurt you, Beth. Call it benign neglect, if you want to be generous, but it was neglect. Is that how you want to live your life, being oblivious to the people around you, not having any sort of personal life?"

She stared at him in shock. "Is that what you think? Do you think I don't date much, because I'm trying to emulate my parents?"

"It looks plain as day to me."

"Well, who died and named you Freud?" she inquired tartly.

"Are you denying it?"

"Of course I'm denying it. I work hard because I love what I do, because it matters."

"I'm sure your folks thought the same thing. Did that make you cry any less when you went to bed at night without them there to read you a story or tuck you in?"

"You don't know what you're talking about," she insisted stubbornly. "I was ten when my brother died, much too old for stories."

"But not for a kiss before bed," Mack said, recalling how Destiny had insisted on tucking them all in, even when they protested that they were much too old. He and Ben had loved it. Richard had grumbled loudest of all, but Mack realized now that he'd needed Destiny's attention most of all, and she had instinctively known that and ignored all their complaints.

"It wasn't important," Beth insisted.

Mack shrugged. "If you say so." He met her gaze

and saw the confusion and vulnerability she was trying so hard not to let him see. "You know, Beth, when you look at my life, you see a life of privilege, right?"

She nodded.

"Because my family has money?"

"Of course."

He shook his head. "The money's there, no question about it. And it's made a lot of things easier, there's no doubt about that, either. But you know what really made our lives rich?"

"What?"

"Having an aunt who was willing to give up a life she loved, even a man she loved, to come back to the States to take care of three little boys she barely knew just because they needed her. After our folks died, Destiny was there every single night to tuck us in and reassure us that we'd be okay. She taught us by example that there was still joy to be had in living life to its fullest. She didn't retreat into some other place and hide out, leaving us to struggle to figure out how the hell to heal from the hurt."

Beth carefully put her fork down and met his gaze. "Your aunt sounds remarkable, but my parents did the best they could," she claimed, though there wasn't much conviction behind her defense of them.

"Well, if you ask me, it sure as hell wasn't good enough," he said angrily, thinking about how terrified and lonely she must have been after her brother died, how she must have feared the same thing could happen to her. Had they reassured her about that much, at least? Probably not. In their self-absorbed world, they'd probably never even noticed she needed the reassurance, or maybe they'd even dismissed it as a weakness in a way that had stopped her from even voicing her fears.

"You don't have any right to say that," she said, her lower lip quivering. "None. You weren't there. You don't know what it was like for any of us."

Mack sighed. "No, I don't suppose I do, but imagining what it must have been like for you kills me."

"I was okay," she said, but the tears welling up in the corners of her eyes said otherwise.

"Ah, Beth," Mack whispered, standing up and pulling her into his arms. "I'm sorry. I may hate what they did to you, but I never meant to make you cry."

"I'm not crying," she insisted, sniffing, her face pressed against his chest.

"If you say so," he said, even though he could feel the dampness of tears through his shirt.

"I *never* cry," she said staunchly.

He had a feeling she'd spent a lifetime trying to get the lie to come out so adamantly. "I know," he said, holding her tight and wondering how someone so emotionally fragile ever managed to get through the kind of days she had to endure. She had more real strength than some of the three-hundred-pound players on his team, certainly more than he had.

When she lifted her gaze to his, the tears were still shimmering in her eyes and clinging to her dark lashes. Mack couldn't seem to help himself. He leaned down to kiss a streak of dampness on first one cheek and then the other. The salty tears, the petal-soft skin were wildly intoxicating, far more so than any wine might have been. He needed to resist the temptation, needed to release her before the evening took a turn neither of them had anticipated.

But then with the tiniest shift of her head, Beth's mouth found his, and he was lost.

Chapter Seven

Beth had never been so hungry for a man's touch. That it was Mack's touch she craved was a shock, but right now all she could think about was the way his mouth felt on hers, about the way his hands covered her breasts and stroked the sensitive peaks into tight buds of exquisite pleasure.

"Don't stop," she pleaded when he pulled back, his breath ragged. He looked as stunned as she was feeling, maybe more so.

"Beth, are you sure about this?" he asked with obvious worry. "It's been a long, stressful day, and I've just put you through an emotional wringer. I don't want to take advantage of you. I don't want us to do something you'll be sorry about in the morning. Hell, up until a few minutes ago, I wasn't even sure you liked me very much."

"Guess we both know better than that now," she said wryly.

Thanks to the unmistakable concern she heard in his voice, Beth felt more certain than ever that this was right. What Mack had said was true. He had put her through hell with all his questions about her uneasy relationship with her parents. He'd managed to open up too many old wounds and leave them raw.

But no one else had ever cared deeply enough to dig past the facade she put on for the world. She felt connected to Mack in some weird way that didn't bear close scrutiny. And tonight, most of all, she needed to go with her senses for once, and not her head. Her senses were practically screaming for more of Mack's touches.

She looked deep into his eyes. "I want this," she reassured him, reveling in the sandpapery feel of his cheek beneath her lips. "I need to feel alive, Mack. I know you do, too. Please give that to me, to *us*."

She saw by the sudden spark of heat in his eyes that she'd said exactly the right thing. After the turmoil of the day, after listening to Tony's sad request that Mack relay his love to Maria, Mack understood better than most the need to feel excitement and anticipation, rather than dread and despair, to revel in the here and now and tomorrow be damned.

His answer was in the touch of his lips against hers, tender for an instant and then greedy, his tongue plunging deep in her mouth in a dark, sensual assault that filled her body with heat and made her senses spin.

Beth had known he would be good at this—the media made him out to be some sort of expert, after all—but she hadn't expected him to know just how to move her. It was as if their bodies knew something their brains did not, as if there was a mystical connection that ran so deep that one touch was all it took to unlock it.

"Bedroom?" he murmured, his breath ragged.

"No, now," she said, the urgency of her need stunning her as it must be shocking him. She wanted to forget the world and this was the way, the only way. She was already tugging at the buckle of his belt, fumbling for his zipper. She didn't want time to think, time to reconsider, not so much as a second to wonder if this was an act of desperation she would live to regret.

Mack caught her frenzy. Buttons flew as he pushed aside her blouse, then caught the peak of her breast in his mouth, sucking, using lips, tongue and teeth until she was writhing against him, certain that she would fly apart from that touch alone.

With a clever flick, her bra disappeared and then her skirt was hiked up to her waist, her panties stripped away. His fingers found her moist heat and dove inside, making her cry out with the sheer wonder of it as wave after wave of pulsing pleasure washed over her.

That quick, violent release should have been enough to slake the need, but she wanted more, so much more. She tugged at the zipper she'd forgotten in the swirl of wild sensations he'd stirred in her. There was something wild and totally uninhibited in control of her now, a need so great, so demanding that she couldn't have turned away from it even if the thought had crossed her mind. Not that it did. Stopping wasn't an option.

She looked deep into Mack's eyes and saw the answering hunger, the same desperate need even as he rolled on a condom, then lifted her and drove himself into her, filling her, taking her right here, right now with her back pressed against the kitchen wall, her legs wrapped tightly around him as he thrust into her. Her last conscious thought was that she was just beginning to fully appreciate the advantages of a man with the well-toned body and strength of an athlete.

Sensations ripped through her—the cool hardness of the wall at her back, Mack's rough breathing in her ear, the slick slip-slide of him inside her, the rigid tension of his muscles where she clung to him, the scent of aftershave and sex. It was all so sweet, so powerful, so amazing…and shocking in its unexpected intensity.

When the hard, throbbing waves of a second release finally crashed over her, Beth felt as weak as if she'd been thrown on shore after a storm at sea. But she was exhilarated, too, as if she'd had one exquisite chance to touch the sky.

Slowly, oh, so slowly, she fought her way back to earth, back to the here and now, back to her own kitchen, which would never, ever feel the same again. There were clothes strewn everywhere, a plate had somehow ended up on the floor, a glass of tea had toppled over leaving melting ice cubes sitting in puddles on the table.

Before she realized his intention, Mack reached for one of the cubes of ice and lightly swirled it across the tip of her breast, then lower, his clever mouth following the same intimate path. The shock of cold, the heat of Mack against her still-sensitive skin sent her off into another totally unexpected whirl of mind-blowing sensation. Shattered, all she could do was cling to him and let the ride take her where it would.

Afterward, she struggled with embarrassment, looking everywhere except at Mack until he touched a finger to her chin and forced her to meet his gaze.

"You know, Doc, if I'd just hit that many highs with anyone else, I'd worry about dying on the spot."

Relieved by the flash of humor in his eyes, she said, "But not with me?"

"Nope. I figure you know CPR and you'd be highly motivated to save me so we can do this again."

Her lips curved at the purely male arrogance of the suggestion. "Again?"

"Definitely again." He grinned sheepishly as he tugged up the briefs and pants pooled at his ankles. "Maybe not in the next ten minutes," he conceded, "but most definitely again."

Her own grin spread, along with a heady dose of feminine satisfaction. "In that case, maybe I'd better tell you where the bedroom is, after all."

Lying next to Beth in the middle of the night, Mack was pretty sure he wouldn't have been more stunned by the way the night had unfolded if Beth had stripped naked and run through the hospital. Under all that starch and propriety, the woman had a wild streak. Since she seemed almost as shocked as he did, he couldn't help wondering if she'd known about it all along or if this was something he'd managed to unleash in her. He rather liked that scenario, probably more than he should.

Unfortunately, he also knew that what seemed right and inevitable tonight was going to prove worrisome in the morning, most likely for both of them, no matter how many disclaimers each of them had uttered. He wondered if it wouldn't be smart to slip away before daybreak, but dismissed the idea on several counts. First, it was cowardly. Second, the image of her face when she discovered he'd run out would nag at him.

And third, he was pretty sure he couldn't crawl out of her bed even if he wanted to. He might have just enough energy to make love to her one more time before morning, and that seemed infinitely preferable to wasting it sneaking out of her house as if he—as if *they*—had committed some unpardonable sin here tonight.

Right now she was plastered across his chest, exactly where she'd collapsed after riding him to another explosive climax once they'd come upstairs to her room. Mack was just as beat as she was, maybe even more so, but he was also energized in a totally unexpected way. He was filled with a whole new sense of curiosity about this woman who'd once expressed disdain for him and everything he stood for. Apparently she'd concluded he wasn't such a bad guy, after all. Either that or she'd simply been as desperate for human contact tonight as he had been.

Slamming up against the mortality wall had shaken him, especially since the person involved was a twelve-year-old boy he'd grown to love. Usually his life revolved around fun. Even work was something he enjoyed, not something with life-or-death consequences. Since meeting Tony, it had been harder and harder to maintain that devil-may-care attitude. Tonight he'd pretty much snapped.

Beth sighed and snuggled more tightly against him, her head tucked under his chin, her hand distressingly close to a part of him that he was trying hard to ignore so she could get some obviously much-needed sleep.

She shifted again, tormenting him further, but then as if the contact finally sent an electrical charge straight to her brain, her eyes snapped open. She would have scrambled away from him, if he hadn't kept his arm firmly around her waist.

"Where do you think you're going?" Mack asked lightly.

"Over...um, to my side of the bed," she mumbled finally.

"I like sharing the middle," he teased.

She finally met his gaze. "Really?" she asked, looking surprised. "I'm not bothering you?"

"Oh, you are definitely bothering me," he said. "I think that's evident."

She followed the direction of his gaze, then blushed. "I had no idea."

"That I wanted you again?"

"That it was even possible for you to want me again," she said.

Her comment told Mack all he'd wanted to know about the kind of experiences she'd had in the past. Whatever jealous twinges he might have felt about the man who'd hurt her so long ago vanished. "Not to make too big a deal about it, but a guy would have to be made of stone to get his fill of you after just a couple of tastes."

A spark of amusement lit her eyes as she glanced pointedly downward. "I'm not sure the analogy works," she said. "You're obviously rock hard at the moment. And, for the record, it was more than a couple of times."

He feigned shock at the observation. "Why, so it was and so I am. Since you're awake and counting, maybe we ought to do something about that."

"Medically speaking, that's what I'd prescribe," she said agreeably, already shifting to accommodate him.

It was no surprise to him that she was as ready and

eager as he was. She'd already proved that her sexual appetite was a more than even match for his. What amazed him was her willingness to let him see this neediness in her, this slight hint of vulnerability that came from sharing something so intimate. He would have been less surprised if she'd kicked him to the curb after that first time downstairs.

The heat between them flared again, this time more slowly, more sweetly, as if the discoveries they'd made earlier gave them the leisure to savor each touch. Instead of urgency, Mack felt his body taking an exquisitely lazy ride to the top of yet another cliff. Gazing into Beth's eyes, he saw every emotion as she made her way to the same peak.

Only when they were there together, their bodies damp with perspiration, their senses razor sharp so that the mere flick of a tongue, the sweep of a caress worked magic, did they fly over the edge.

Only then, still trembling from that incredible release of passion, did Mack close his eyes and give himself over to sleep, with Beth still cradled in his arms. For the first time in months, maybe years, he wasn't falling asleep after sex, worried that he'd just made a terrible mistake. In fact he felt as if he'd finally done something very right. He was pretty sure that this was the first time that what he'd done could only be described as making love.

Beth wasn't a morning person by nature. Only rigid self-discipline made her reach for the alarm clock to hit the off button and start to roll out of bed in the same fluid movement. When she ran smack into a hard, obviously male body as she was about to make her half-asleep flight from bed, she felt as if she'd suddenly touched a live wire.

Mack! The memory of the night before slammed into her. Every single touch, every single amazing release replayed itself, not only in her mind but in the sudden humming of the blood through her veins. She had to smother a smile. This was better than any alarm clock—bells, buzzers or cheery beeps—she'd ever tried. She was completely, totally, instantly awake. Too bad there wasn't time to do anything about it.

Filled with regrets, she found a way to extricate herself from Mack's embrace. To her astonishment he slept on. It was the dead-to-the-world sleep of the truly exhausted. She smothered another grin at the realization that she'd done that to him. Imagine that! She had left a physically fit, professional athlete—a *playboy*— too wiped out to move. She was still gloating when she climbed into the shower.

The icy water meant to revive her had barely hit her overheated skin when the shower curtain was swept aside and Mack climbed in with her.

Beth stared at him in shock, not sure she was ready for quite this much intimacy, even after the night they'd just shared. "What do you think you're doing?"

"The bed got lonely without you. Besides, I can't let you go sneaking off without so much as a morning kiss."

She gave his body a thorough once-over. "Something tells me you're after more than a kiss."

He grinned and backed her against the tile. "I'm open to negotiations."

"You're a Carlton. Negotiating is second nature to you. I'm sure you always get the terms you want." She hooked a leg around his. "Let's just cut to the chase."

He laughed. "Works for me."

Fifteen minutes later Beth's knees were wobbly and her body still sizzled with so much heat she was amazed the bathroom wasn't filled with steam despite the icy temperature of the water flowing over them. She gazed into Mack's eyes. "What have you done to me?" she asked. "I'm used to starting my day with oatmeal."

"This is healthier," Mack said.

"I'm not so sure about that. I feel a little faint."

He looked pleased with himself at her admission. "You get dressed. I'll fix breakfast. Eggs, I think. You obviously need the protein."

"I don't have time," she said as she scrambled from the shower, wrapped herself in a towel and ran into the bedroom. One frantic glance at the clock proved how true that was. She was running well behind schedule.

"Make time. Breakfast is the most important meal of the day," Mack said, wandering in after her. "You'd think a fine doctor would know that."

"I do know it. I also know I have a jam-packed day ahead of me and I'm already late."

"Then ten more minutes won't make any difference, will it?" he said.

Beth tried not to stare as he pulled on his briefs over his excellent backside, then turned his pants right side out and climbed into those. He didn't bother to button them at the waist. Since they were the only clothes that had actually made it upstairs, Beth was treated to one more excellent view of his muscles as he left her room without wasting another word arguing with her. She sighed heavily after his exit.

As soon as he was gone, she dived into her closet, dragged out the first skirt and blouse she came to, then dressed in the kind of rush with which she was all too familiar.

A quick flick of her brush through hair that had a surprising hint of curl to it—no time to tame it into submission—a touch of lipstick and she was done. By the time she walked into the kitchen, she'd figuratively drawn her protective professional cloak around her. Other than those wayward curls, there was no hint of the wanton woman she'd been during the night.

True to his word, Mack had juice on the table and a plate of perfectly scrambled eggs in his hand. He'd put on his shirt, but thankfully he hadn't buttoned it. She liked the sexily rumpled look. In fact, she was fairly certain she could become addicted to it. She'd have to remind herself later how dangerous and ill advised that would be.

"Sit," he ordered, his expression uncompromising.

The order was a bit less attractive, but the protectiveness behind it had its charm. "Five minutes," she muttered, because it was easier than arguing with him. Besides, she was starved and *her* eggs never looked that good.

The toaster popped up, and she stared at it in surprise. "You found bread?"

"In the freezer," he said, then added wryly, "you should look in there sometime." He put the buttered toast in front of her, then took his own place opposite her with only a cup of coffee in hand.

"You're not eating?" she asked.

"Not enough eggs. I'll grab something at my place when I go home to change."

"I could share," she said, shoving the plate in his direction.

"Nope. I fixed those for you with my own secret ingredient."

She frowned at the eggs. "You didn't find any poison around, did you?"

His lips twitched at the outrageous suggestion. "Why would I want to kill you?"

"So I can never tell about the night you spent in the arms of a woman who isn't some glamorous model or sexy actress," she said, exposing a hint of vulnerability. She'd been attacked by self-doubt almost from the second he'd left her room. It was running rampant now.

Mack regarded her with disbelief. "Are you crazy? Believe me, letting the world know I slept with a brilliant, dedicated doctor would probably do more for my reputation than you can imagine. This is something worth bragging about, not hiding." He grinned. "Not that I will, of course."

Beth faltered at his acknowledgment that he wasn't ashamed of the time they'd spent together. She hadn't gone looking for any kind of compliment, but she was ridiculously pleased that he'd offered one.

"How?" she asked, unable to resist pursuing it.

"People might finally accept that I have half a brain."

She'd never considered that one aspect of his football and playboy celebrity might mean that people didn't take him seriously. She should have, too. Until she'd gotten to know him, wasn't that how she'd seen him, as a mental lightweight with few scruples? Not even his law degree was that impressive, since he wasn't using it. On some level she'd wondered if he hadn't cruised through law school simply because of who he was. Thankfully she'd never said such a thing. Her cheeks still burned when she thought of the comments he'd overheard her making the first time he'd come to the hospital to meet Tony.

"I'm sorry," she said. "I never looked at all the gossip from your point of view."

He shrugged. "Why would you? It's not as if I ever shied away from it. The image worked for me."

"How so?"

"Because if I ever let anyone take me too seriously—any woman, that is—I might have to deal with real emotions," he said easily.

The comment and his tone were fair warning. Beth couldn't mistake the message he was sending. "Last night didn't give me any expectations where you're concerned," she reassured him, surprised by just how empty those words made her feel. "It was nothing more than two people who were hurting reaching out for each other."

Mack's gaze lingered on hers, his expression wary. "And you don't have a problem with that?"

She forced herself to shrug. "Why would I?"

"I just thought you might," he said.

"Hey, it was no big deal, Mack. Nothing you need to worry about."

He nodded slowly. "Good to know."

Beth expected to see relief in his eyes, to hear it in his voice, but it wasn't there. In fact, if her imagination wasn't playing tricks on her, what she heard instead was disappointment.

Or maybe she was merely projecting, because right this second she felt more of an emotional letdown than she'd ever felt in her life. If she weren't so late, she'd sit right here and try to figure out why.

Then again, the prospect of spending one more second with Mack right now, when she was feeling totally vulnerable and exposed, was too much to bear.

"Gotta run," she said, taking one last bite of toast, then standing up. "Lock up when you leave."

Before Mack could even react, she grabbed her purse and keys and tore out the door. She wanted to be safely in her car and on the road before the first traitorous tear fell.

Chapter Eight

Mack sat at Beth's kitchen table for a very long time after she'd gone, staring into space, trying to figure out why, after such an incredible night, he felt so damned lousy. Surely it wasn't because he'd been honest with her, warned her not to make too much of what had happened between them. He'd had the same conversation dozens of times with dozens of women. It was a part of his spiel, as routine as the flirting that came second nature to him. It usually filled him with relief to know that things had been clarified.

But Beth was not in the same sophisticated, blasé league as all those women. They knew the score from the moment Mack met them, understood the rules going in and accepted them. In fact, they had rules of their own about the level of emotional attachment they were interested in pursuing...or not pursuing.

With Beth, despite that brave, nonchalant front she'd

put on, he felt as if he'd just kicked a friendly puppy. There had been a brittle edge to her voice, the slightest hint that she might suddenly shatter if pushed. And in those expressive eyes of hers, he'd seen the faint shadow of genuine hurt.

For the first time in a very long time, Mack wasn't proud of himself and his brand of so-called honesty. He saw it as the cop-out it was, a way to extricate himself from guilt over doing whatever the hell he wanted to do. Something told him if his aunt ever found out about this encounter, she'd tear a strip out of his hide for treating Beth in such a cavalier way. Not that Destiny was likely to berate him any more than he was berating himself at the moment.

Sure, he and Beth were consenting adults. Sure, she'd wanted last night to happen every bit as much as he had. But looking into her eyes this morning, he couldn't help but conclude that it had really meant something to her. Hell, it had meant something to him, too, but he wasn't about to acknowledge that to her or to act on it in the future. At the first warning sign that he might become emotionally involved with someone, he generally took off without a backward glance.

In fact, his usual panic was already telling him that if he had half a brain, he'd immediately start making himself scarce around the hospital. He wouldn't stop seeing Tony, but he was familiar enough with Beth's routine to avoid running into her. No more casual little drop-ins at her office just to catch a glimpse of her. No more coffee breaks in the cafeteria. No more dinners just to get her away from the hospital for a bit. He was pretty sure she'd gotten the message this morning, but just in case, his actions would reinforce it. That was what he *should* do, what he always did.

And, he realized with a sinking sensation, if he followed his usual pattern, he would feel like an even worse heel than he felt like right at this moment. He wasn't sure he had it in him to do the smart thing this time.

When Beth's phone rang, Mack stared at it. With her running late, it could be the hospital calling. It could be an emergency, and at least he could alert whoever was on the other end that Beth was on her way in. Did that outweigh whatever gossip might arise from having a man answer her phone? How would she see it?

With the phone still ringing insistently, he finally grabbed it. "Hello, Dr. Browning's residence."

His greeting was met with silence.

"Hello," he prompted.

"Who the hell is this and why are you answering Beth's phone?" a very possessive-sounding male voice demanded with open hostility.

Now there was a question that could lead down a path Mack didn't want to travel, especially with some stranger who hadn't even bothered identifying himself.

"I'm a friend of Dr. Browning's," he said cautiously. "She just left for the hospital. Can I take a message for her?"

His reply was greeted by another hesitation.

"Well?" Mack prodded.

"No. I'll speak to her when she gets here," the man said. "I intend to tell her I spoke to you."

Mack grinned despite himself at the tattle-tale tenor of the warning. "You do that," he said, then hung up.

He wasn't entirely sure whether to be amused or worried by the threat. He'd know soon enough. His intention to avoid Beth had flown right out the window the instant he'd heard that trace of possessiveness in the caller's voice. If some other man had the right to think of Beth as his, then what the devil had she been doing in Mack's arms the night before? He wasn't crazy about the streak of jealousy that had shot through him. He did know that since it was a first in his life, he had no intention of ignoring it.

Beth spent her first two hours at the hospital racing from one crisis to another. She was beginning to wonder if she'd ever get another minute to spend in her lab with the research that was so important to her. She was also having trouble staying focused, which wasn't like her at all. When it came to medicine and her patients, she rarely allowed anything to distract her. Today, though, images of Mack and the way they'd parted this morning kept intruding.

At eleven-thirty she'd finally had enough of fighting the distraction. She needed a break. She needed caffeine. Caffeine *and* chocolate, she decided en route to the cafeteria. Maybe a lot of chocolate.

After loading up on candy bars and a large takeout coffee, she found a quiet table, spread her loot out on the table and debated about which chocolate to eat first. Snickers had nuts and caramel, but a chunk of plain old Hershey bar melting on her tongue had its own allure. Then there was the Kit Kat or the Peanut M&M's or maybe the Milky Way.

"Boy, your diet really has taken a turn right off the nutritional charts, hasn't it?" Jason commented, sliding into the chair opposite her.

Beth glared at the radiologist. "Keep your snide comments to yourself."

"Tough morning?" he asked, then struggled with a grin as he added, "Or a tough night?"

She stared at him trying to gauge what on earth he knew or thought he knew. "If you have something on your mind, just spit it out. I'm in no mood for games."

"Yes, I can see that," Jason said, his grin spreading. "The chocolate's a dead giveaway, especially before lunch. Usually you don't have one of these attacks till around four, right after rounds." He gestured toward the little pile of candy. "Even for you this is a bit over the top."

Beth was not half as amused by his observations as he clearly was. "Did you come over here to hassle me or is something else on your mind?"

The radiologist regarded her innocently. "Can't I do both?"

"Not if you expect to live," Beth said sourly, tearing open the M&M candies and popping several into her mouth.

Unfortunately, Jason didn't look daunted. If anything, the level of amusement in his eyes increased. "Called your house looking for you earlier," he said. "You were running late. I got worried. Beth Browning is never late. She never misses an important meeting."

Her gaze flew to his. "What meeting?"

"Peyton called one to talk about Tony. He wanted to go over a few things with our entire oncology team before Tony's transfusion this morning. You `didn't know?"

"Oh, hell," Beth moaned. "Yes, I knew. It completely slipped my mind. Was he furious?"

"Actually, I think he was relieved. It was the first sign any of us have ever had that you're human and fallible."

Beth covered her face with her hands. "What is wrong with me? How could I forget a meeting like that?"

"Maybe it had something to do with that man who answered the phone at your house when I called," Jason suggested mildly. "Could that be?"

Beth had honestly thought it impossible to be any more embarrassed, but with her cheeks burning and her stomach churning, she discovered she'd been wrong. This was a thousand times worse.

"You, um…" She gazed into Jason's laughing eyes, then sucked in a breath. "You spoke to my house-guest?" There, that was a good, safe, anonymous description of Mack, though she intended to be sure that he was never her guest again.

"That I did," Jason said gleefully. "Funny thing, too. He wasn't much more communicative about his identity than you're being."

"Maybe because it's none of your business who he is," she replied testily.

"My money's on Mack Carlton," Jason responded.

Beth fought the panic creeping up the back of her throat. "Why on earth would you think that?"

"Informed guess," Jason told her. "And the fact that I recognized his voice."

"From meeting him once?" she asked incredulously.

Jason laughed. "For the moment I'll ignore the fact that you as much as admitted it was Mack and say that his voice is familiar because he's interviewed on TV about every ten seconds during football season." His expression suddenly sobered. "You sure you know what you're doing, Beth? This guy has a reputation, you know."

"Tell me about it," she said glumly.

"Don't get in over your head."

Because she desperately needed someone to talk to, because she could use a male point of view and because she trusted Jason to keep his mouth shut, she muttered, "Too late for that, I'm afraid."

Jason regarded her with shock. "You're not actually falling for him, are you?"

"No!" she said so fiercely that Jason whistled in disbelief. She scowled at him. "Oh, shove a sock in it."

"That will severely limit my attempt to give you some well-meaning advice."

Beth sighed heavily. "Okay, then, talk, but try not to sound smug or disgustingly macho. Remember, I'm your friend and your colleague. Mack's just some football idol you met once."

Jason opened his mouth, then clamped it shut again, his expression going blank.

"Jason?" Beth prodded.

"I think the cat's got Jason's tongue," Mack said, pulling up a chair to join them. "Isn't that right, Jason?"

"Pretty much," Jason said. "I think I'll go take some X rays or do some radiation treatments or maybe lock myself in a convenient closet."

Mack gave him an approving look. "Thanks. Nice talking to you earlier. That was you on the phone, I assume."

"Yep," Jason said.

Then he took off like the little weasel he was. Beth had expected better of him. Hadn't he just warned her about Mack? Then why would Jason turn right around and leave her alone with the man? It must be some tacit, male, nonpoaching, noninterference agreement that women weren't privy to.

"You answered my phone this morning," she said accusingly, frowning at Mack. "What possessed you to do that?"

He shrugged. "It was ringing. I thought it might be important."

He sounded so blasted reasonable, she wanted to strangle him. "And it never occurred to you that it could prove embarrassing for me?"

"I thought it would be more embarrassing if you missed being notified of an emergency."

"If it had been an emergency, someone would have beeped me," she said.

"Never thought of that." He nodded in the direction in which Jason had gone. "He sounded a little miffed to find me there. Something going on between you two that I should know about? Until this morning I had the impression you were just friends."

She could claim there was and put an end to things with Mack right here and now, but then he'd wonder about what kind of woman she was to sleep with him while she had some sort of relationship with Jason. She might accept that there wasn't ever going to be anything more between her and Mack, but she didn't want him to think badly of her. She had too much self-respect to leave him with an impression like that, as convenient as it might be at the moment.

"Jason is a friend," she confirmed finally. "If he implied it was anything more, it was only because he's worried that I'm in over my head with you."

"It wasn't anything he said," Mack admitted. "Just something in his tone. He sounded possessive."

Something in *Mack's* tone sounded a wee bit possessive, as well. Beth studied his expression for a minute before it sank in what was going on in his head. He was jealous. At least for one tiny fraction of a second Mighty Mack Carlton, of the date-a-night gossip, was actually jealous that there might be another man in her life. She had to fight to keep from chuckling aloud. This was definitely a twist she hadn't anticipated.

Unfortunately, the twist felt a little too welcome, especially after she had spent most of the morning warning herself to cut Mack out of her life before she got burned. Heck, she was sitting here downing chocolate before lunch to forget about him.

"Jason and I have known each other since med school. He's protective, not possessive. There's a difference."

"He thinks you need protection from me?"

She grinned at his vaguely incredulous expression. "Don't you?"

"I'm not going to hurt you," he said sharply.

Beth leveled a look straight into his eyes. "Too late," she said quietly.

Then, before he could react, she stood up and headed for the nearest exit at a clip that few people could keep up with. Mack, of course, could have caught her in a few long strides had he wanted to. That he didn't even try told her all she needed to know.

Or at least she thought the message was pretty plain, until she walked into her office an hour later and found a little mound of candy bars in the middle of her desk. She recognized them as the ones she'd left behind in her haste to leave the cafeteria. More disconcerting was the sight of Mack sprawled out on the sofa where she caught catnaps on the nights she couldn't get away from the hospital. He had an open medical journal on his chest, but his eyes were shut tight. The steady rise and fall of his chest suggested he was sound asleep.

Beth stood there staring at him in consternation. The memory of waking in his arms just a few hours ago was still a little too fresh in her mind. A part of her wanted to crawl onto that sofa with him and recapture that amazing feeling.

Because of that, she deliberately walked behind her desk and sat down, cursing the loud creaking in her old chair. Mack's eyes promptly snapped open.

"Ah, you're back," he said, "I figured you'd turn up here sooner or later."

"Good guess, since it *is* my office," she said tartly. "What are you doing here?"

He gave her an oddly bemused look that made her heart flip over.

"Not sure entirely," he admitted.

"That must be a first."

"It is," he said. He met her gaze. "You confuse me."

She found his honesty a little *too* charming. Maybe it was part of some game he played. "I'm a fairly straightforward kind of woman."

"I get that," he said.

"You are not a straightforward kind of man," she added bluntly.

"I'm trying to be, at least with you."

"Why?" she asked.

"I wish to hell I knew. I sat there after you'd left the house this morning and tried to figure it out, but I still don't entirely get it."

Beth lost patience. She was in over her head with Mack and she didn't like it. That she'd slept with him at all was probably a huge mistake. That she wanted to do it again was pure insanity. Hearing that he was beset with uncertainties was not reassuring. One of them surely needed to know what the hell they were doing.

"Well, since it's such an obvious struggle for you to figure it out, maybe you should just stop trying," she said. "We spent one night together, Mack. We didn't make a commitment. You don't do commitment. From what I've read in the paper, you don't even go out with the same woman twice. I get that. My time is up."

He frowned at her. "You're making this hard."

"What am I making hard?" she asked, unable to hide her growing exasperation. "I just let you completely off the hook. No harm, no foul. Go forth and do whatever the hell you do without giving me another thought."

"That would be the sensible thing for me to do," he agreed.

"Then do it."

He shook his head. "Can't."

"Why not? There's the door. Walk out and that's that. No big deal." She held her breath waiting for him to take her advice and go. Instead, he sat right where he was, his expression glum. Beth sighed. "Mack, what is going on?"

"Have you had lunch yet?"

"I've had coffee and candy. In my book that qualifies."

"Not in mine. Let's go."

"I don't have time."

"You do for this," he coaxed, his lips twitching

when her stomach growled. "I'll have you back in an hour, like always."

"It's twelve-thirty. There's not a decent restaurant anywhere that won't be mobbed at this hour."

"I'll have you back in an hour," he repeated.

Since he'd never before broken that promise, Beth finally gave in. And since the coffee and caffeine definitely hadn't done what she'd intended—taken her mind off Mack—maybe another hour in his annoying company would do the trick. At least she'd be well fed at the end of it.

"Okay," she relented. "One hour, and we don't talk about us."

"Deal," he said.

Once again, the instant they reached the very popular crab house on the Potomac River, a table magically appeared. Their food arrived moments later—a dozen steamed and spiced crabs with coleslaw and potato salad.

Mack handed her a wooden mallet with a grin. "Pretend you're bashing me upside the head, and you'll get through these in no time."

Cracking crabs was messy work, but the succulent meat was worth the effort. And thinking of each red shell as Mack's hard head did give her a certain amount of perverse pleasure as she hammered away. She uttered a little sigh when she'd finished the last one. Only then did she realize that Mack had eaten very little.

"Weren't you hungry? This is the second time today when you've sat there and watched me eat."

"I'm trying to fatten you up," he said.

"Planning to have me slaughtered like a pig?"

"Nope. Looking for a little more flesh to hang on to."

The comment brought an immediate flush to her cheeks. "Mack!"

"Sorry," he said at once, though he didn't look especially repentant. "I promised you we wouldn't talk about us. I suppose that precludes any talk of sex, as well."

"There is no us," she said flatly, refusing to get drawn into any discussion of sex.

"Yeah, you would have thought so, wouldn't you?"

She stared at him, not sure how to take the wry note in his voice. "Meaning?"

"We're not much alike. You're serious. I'm not. You're brilliant—"

"So are you," she said impatiently, tired of him using his own stereotypical image as some sort of cop-out. "Stop denigrating your intelligence. You have a law degree, which you earned while playing professional football. You can't juggle all that without being smart. And it must take some intelligence to run a successful football franchise, even if I don't happen to get why you'd want to."

"Thank you," he said. "I think."

"Since you're busy laying out all our differences, how about this one? I'm a struggling researcher and physician and you're very, very rich."

He grinned. "Too obvious and not that important, unless, of course, you're trying to decide whether to go after me for my money."

Beth smiled as she was struck by a brilliant idea to get her research project moving along at a swifter pace. Maybe she should test the waters and see if he was open to the idea. Hopefully he wouldn't conclude that she really was in this just for the money. "Actually

I'm trying to decide whether to get you to fund a new research project," she retorted cheerfully.

"Just tell me what you need," he said matter-of-factly.

She stared at him in shock, totally unprepared for his immediate agreement. "I was joking," she protested. "Or at least half joking."

"I wasn't."

"Oh my God," she whispered, not quite daring to believe he was as serious as he sounded. She had grants, but with just a little more funding she could hire the kind of assistant who would enable her to move her research along much more quickly.

"While it's always nice to show your appreciation of a Higher Power, in this instance you should really thank football and wise investments," he teased. "Of course, if you can't bear the thought of taking any money earned playing such a stupid game..."

"I'll give it some thought," she replied oh, so seriously, then added a quick, "Yes. When it comes to saving more kids, I'm not proud. If you're really serious about this, I'll get together with my team and put a proposal together by the end of the week."

Mack nodded. "I'll be in to pick it up."

She studied him intently, then shook her head at the unexpected turn the day had taken. It was yet more proof that she had seriously misjudged Mack. If the sex had been predictably incredible, then this gesture was equally mind-boggling in its unpredictability and its generosity.

"You're not at all what I expected," she admitted.

"Not so dumb?"

She flushed. "I thought we'd already established that as a lie. More important, you're amazingly kind to

Tony. And this whole playboy thing, I'm beginning to
think maybe that's more an image you've created for
the media than a fact.''

"You think that after last night?" he asked, regarding her with evident surprise. "And all that fancy foot-
work I danced through this morning?"

Beth thought about it and finally nodded slowly.
"Yes. Now that I look back over the last few weeks,
I realize that you never seem to have a date. You've
been spending every evening at the hospital."

He gave her long, simmering look that made her
pulse race.

"What do you think you and I have been doing?"
he asked quietly. "I mean even before last night."

"Grabbing a quick meal on the run," she said, confused by the hint of amusement in his eyes.

"You with an eligible man. Me with a beautiful,
intelligent woman. In my book, those are dates." His
grin spread. "And just look where they led."

She sat back, stunned. "Well, I'll be damned."
Somehow she'd dismissed all that earlier stuff as casual, friendly, inconsequential get-togethers, while he'd
seen it as some sort of foreplay.

"I doubt you'll be damned, unless of course you let
me take advantage of you," he taunted. "Any possibility of that happening again? Not right this second,
of course, but sometime when you're not due back at
the hospital in less than five minutes?"

Before last night, Beth would have said there wasn't
a snowball's chance in hell of her letting that happen.
Even this morning, with his stinging reminder that he
wasn't to be taken seriously, she would have said a flat
no.

Now, seeing the faint vulnerability in his eyes as he

awaited her reply, guessing that he was stepping far outside of his own relationship comfort zone to even ask such a thing, she was tempted to see where this could lead.

With her heart hammering in her chest, she met his gaze evenly. "You never know."

Mack laughed, as if he'd never expected a different answer. "I'll take that as a yes."

"Has any woman ever actually said no to you?" she asked curiously.

"More than you might imagine. Then again, I've probably asked the question a lot less than you've imagined."

To Beth's very real regret, she wanted to believe that far more than was wise. She wanted to believe that the media had gotten it all wrong, but even she was savvy enough to accept that where there was smoke, there was usually fire. Or in this case, that if gossip paired Mack with a different woman every night, then more than likely he'd done something to foster that impression.

But maybe, just maybe, he'd done it as a defense mechanism to keep from having to put his heart on the line. That was a scenario Beth very much wanted to believe. In fact, she wanted it so much it should have sent her scurrying right straight out of Mack's life before she got her own heart well and truly broken.

It should have, but she very much feared she wasn't going anywhere.

Chapter Nine

When Mack wandered into the Carlton Industries offices after dropping Beth off at the hospital, he headed straight for Destiny's office. She rarely put in an appearance there, but a few calls had assured him she was in this afternoon. He'd been drawn there because his aunt had a way of clarifying things for him when he was faced with uncertainty. Since meeting Beth, he'd spent a lot of time feeling completely off-kilter.

It had been a most enlightening lunch. He'd discovered that Beth was more of a risk taker than he'd imagined. He'd expected her to turn him down flat when he'd suggested they spend another passionate night together, especially after the way they'd parted just this morning. That she hadn't said an immediate no had left him turned on and more intrigued than ever.

He wasn't entirely sure what conclusions Beth had reached about him or about their prospects for the future. Given his confusion on that point, dropping by Destiny's office to solicit advice probably wasn't really a wise thing to do, but he was feeling a bit reckless.

He was also feeling somewhat in Destiny's debt for steering Beth into his life. Not that he intended to tell Destiny that—in fact, he'd probably claim just the opposite, if she pressed him—but he didn't doubt for a second that she was smart enough to read between the lines of whatever he did say. He doubted his aunt would be the least bit surprised that he was finding himself more than a little conflicted where Beth Browning was concerned.

"I haven't seen much of you lately, Mack," Destiny scolded, after he'd dropped a kiss on her smooth cheek. "Where have you been spending your evenings?"

He poured himself a cup of her special-blend coffee, then lounged in a chair opposite her while he contemplated just how much to tell her. She was bound to take a certain amount of gloating satisfaction in whatever he revealed. He decided to take the cagey route and see what she already knew.

"As if you didn't know," he said finally, regarding her with amusement. She was damned good at the innocent act, but he wasn't buying it. Getting her to confess her involvement in this matchmaking plot could be highly entertaining. Matching wits with Destiny and avoiding her romantic snares had been a lifelong challenge for him and his brothers. He was usually quite good at it. Maybe that was another reason he found Beth so fascinating. She was the first woman he'd met who challenged him mentally with the same deft skill as his aunt.

"Would I be asking if I did?" Destiny inquired tartly, sticking to the charade.

"Of course, you would. You want me to reveal all, so you'll have a reason to gloat."

Her innocent look was priceless. "I have no idea what you're talking about, Mack."

"Were you or were you not the one who insisted that I go over to the hospital a few weeks ago to see that sick kid?" he coached, watching her carefully for any hint of a reaction. She kept her expression perfectly bland.

"Tony Vitale?" she asked after a thoughtful pause.

He grinned at the well-honed act, knowing full well that the name had been on the tip of her tongue. She probably got daily updates from the hospital. Lord knew she had sources everywhere. "Precisely."

"Then you have continued to visit him? That's wonderful," she said, regarding him with evident approval. "I'm sure that's helped his morale considerably. Darling, I'm so proud of you for taking an interest in him."

"He's having a rough time," Mack said, momentarily distracted from his mission to exasperate his aunt. "He's such a tough kid. It breaks my heart to see him so sick."

"When I first spoke to his doctor, she said things hadn't been going well. Has there been any change at all?"

"Only for the worse," Mack said.

"Oh, I'm so sorry," Destiny said with genuine sympathy. "His mother must be completely distraught. Surely they'll be able to turn things around."

"I hope so." He met her gaze with an innocent look of his own. "Since you've shown such an interest in his case, I imagine you'll be willing to match the research donation I'm making in his name," he said.

His aunt's eyebrows rose, suggesting that he really had caught her by surprise this time.

"You're funding a research project?" she asked. "Mack, that's wonderful! What a generous thing for you to do. Of course, I'll match it. Which doctor is in charge?"

Mack laughed. "I suspect you can pull that name out of thin air in another second or two."

She looked momentarily perplexed. "I'm sure I have no idea," she claimed. "There are many fine doctors there."

"Try," he pressed.

She appeared to give it some thought. "It wouldn't be that lovely Beth Browning, would it?"

He lifted his coffee cup in a congratulatory toast. "Bingo."

"I understand she's very dedicated," Destiny said smoothly, not giving away by so much as the blink of an eyelash that she'd all but hand picked the woman for Mack, most likely because of Beth's dedication and brilliance.

"And very beautiful and very available, but then that never crossed your mind when you sent me scampering over there, did it?" he asked.

Destiny looked for a moment as if she might try to keep up the charade, but eventually she simply shrugged, conceding the game. "It might have crossed my mind," she conceded.

Mack laughed at her total lack of chagrin. "Oh, give it up, Destiny. You've been meddling again, and you're damned proud of it."

She leveled a look directly into his eyes. "Do you honestly have a problem with that, Mack? It worked rather well with Richard, didn't it? He and Melanie are deliriously happy.''

"But I'm not in the market for a wife," Mack pointed out, though with considerably less vehemence than he might have a few short weeks ago.

"Neither was Richard," she reminded him.

"Why are you so blasted anxious to marry us all off?'' he asked curiously. "Do you have someplace you'd like to be besides here? Are you thinking of going back to France and taking up your Bohemian lifestyle once we're all settled? Is that what the rush is all about?''

"This isn't about me," she said. "It's about you. Not a one of you has learned the first thing about love. I simply can't understand how I failed so abysmally at teaching you the most important lesson of all. I decided it was past time I did something about it.''

Mack heard the genuine frustration in her voice and regretted that he couldn't give her what she wanted. "I know you think we won't be happy without wives and children, but there are other measures of happiness, Destiny.''

"Name one," she challenged.

"I can do better than that," he claimed, then ticked them off for her. "Success, friendships, family.''

"Family is exactly what I'm talking about," she retorted impatiently.

"We have each other and we have you." He gave her a penetrating look. "Unless, as I said, you're anxious to leave after all these years and want to be sure we have someone in our lives to take your place.''

"Don't be ridiculous," she snapped. "I'm perfectly content with my life just the way it is.''

He gave her a wide-eyed look. "How can that be? There's no man in your life."

She frowned at having her own argument tossed back in her face. "There is no need to be snide, Mack."

"Just pointing out the obvious flaw in your case for marrying us off."

"If you are so fiercely determined never to marry, why are you still seeing Beth?" she asked.

He honestly didn't have an answer for that. As they'd discussed at lunch, Beth wasn't at all like the women he usually dated. She wasn't wild or carefree. She was serious and thoughtful and took far too many of her patients' problems to heart.

In recent weeks he'd often felt ashamed at how little he took seriously and how easy his life was. He'd always been conscientious about good deeds—Destiny has raised him and his brothers with a strong sense of their obligation to give back to the community—but he hadn't taken it to heart the way Beth did. She genuinely cared about people. She had a passion for her work. More important, it was work that truly mattered. What he did was frivolous by comparison. Even his visits to Tony were window dressing. They weren't the thing that would ultimately save the boy. Only Beth and her team could do that.

Mack cared about his brothers and his aunt. He even cared about Tony Vitale and other kids like him. But in general he'd learned to keep the world at a distance. Losing his parents so young had made him wary about loving anyone too much. It was too hard to tell when fate might snatch them away. He was terrified that the simple act of loving someone might doom them in some weird way. He knew it was a kid's reaction to loss, but more and more lately he'd come to realize that he'd never entirely gotten past it. Faced with his growing feelings for Beth and his attachment to Tony and the fears they'd stirred in him, he was coming to accept that he was as haunted by it as his other brothers had been.

"Mack," Destiny coaxed gently. "You don't go out with a woman like Beth Browning unless you're serious about her. She's not one of those clever, worldly women you can toss aside with no harm done."

Mack nodded, accepting the truth of that despite Beth's own claims to the contrary. "I know that."

Acknowledging that meant he ought to give Beth up now. It was the right thing to do, the noble, self-sacrificing thing to do. He'd been telling himself that all day. It hadn't kept him from making another date with her.

The sad truth was, when he thought about how empty his life would be without her, he couldn't begin to contemplate doing the right thing.

"Well, then?" Destiny prodded.

He met his aunt's gaze and made a decision. "I'd like to bring her to dinner one of these days. How would you feel about that?"

Destiny's eyes glowed with immediate excitement. "I'd be delighted. You know that I love meeting your friends. I'm free tonight. Will that work?"

He concluded he might as well get it over with. Maybe after seeing him and Beth together, Destiny could help him sort out his feelings. "Tonight's fine for me. I'll check with Beth and get back to you in an hour or so."

"Perfect."

He studied the glint of anticipation in her eyes warily. "You won't make too much of it?" he asked. "I rarely bring a woman to dinner, because you always get this gleam in your eyes—the one that's there right now, by the way—and start imagining wedding bells."

"I will make Beth feel welcome, and I will not bring out a single bridal magazine," Destiny promised. "I won't even leave one conspicuously lying around the living room."

He knew there were a million other sneaky ways to get the same message across. "And you won't drag out Richard's wedding pictures?" he asked, naming one of them.

"Heavens, no," she said with suitable indignation. "I certainly know better than to force someone to look at family photos. That can be so tedious." She grinned. "Though there is one of you in the bathtub at two that I think is awfully cute. Few women could resist it. In fact, it might plant a few ideas about how absolutely adorable your babies will be."

Mack gave her a genuinely horrified look. "I just changed my mind. I'm not bringing Beth anywhere near you."

Destiny laughed merrily. "I was teasing, darling. I won't embarrass you."

"You swear?"

Destiny sketched a cross over her heart. "Not one inappropriate word," she vowed.

Mack frowned. "Why doesn't that reassure me?"

"Because you have a cynical nature," she told him. "Anything in particular you'd like me to cook? One of my Provençal specialties perhaps?"

"Anything," he said, wondering if he was making a huge mistake in exposing Beth to Destiny's probing gaze and clever questions. "Just keep in mind that I'm lucky to steal her away from the hospital for an hour. This can't be one of your long, drawn-out, five-course meals.''

''Fine dining can't be rushed, darling. You know that.''

''I also know that Beth will refuse to come if she thinks this is going to be some sort of formal occasion. It has to be just the three of us, and it can't be one of your dressed-to-the-nines nights. She'll probably have to come straight from the hospital and then go right back there.''

His aunt scowled at that. ''If you insist. Would you like hot dogs and baked beans? Those are quick and easy,'' Destiny said tartly.

Mack knew she wasn't entirely kidding. She had her standards when it came to the way someone in their position should entertain. ''I think you can do better than that,'' he told her. ''In fact, I'm counting on it.''

She studied him intently, then finally nodded. ''Okay then, but may I ask one thing?''

''Sure.''

''Why does this dinner mean so much, Mack, if Beth's not becoming important to you?''

''Can't we just have a nice meal together without turning it into a precursor to an engagement?'' he asked plaintively.

''I can do that,'' Destiny agreed readily, then gave him a far too knowing look. ''Can you?''

Because he didn't have a ready answer to that, Mack merely frowned and headed for the door. ''See you tonight.''

''I'm looking forward to it, darling,'' Destiny said cheerfully.

''Yeah, I'll bet,'' Mack muttered, already regretting

the impulse that had caused him to make the arrangements for this little get-together.

He'd told himself that he wanted Destiny's insights and impressions of the relationship, but maybe the truth was something else entirely. Maybe he was hoping that exposing sensible, down-to-earth Beth to the realities of life with a Carlton would scare her off and he'd never have to break her heart by doing what he always did...walking away.

Beth's day had gone from bad to worse. A patient had swatted away a bottle of bright-orange antiseptic, sending most of it cascading over Beth's blouse. Though there had been a faint hint of amusement lurking in his eyes, Peyton had soundly scolded her for missing the morning meeting. And Tony had regarded her with a hurt expression for not being there for his transfusion.

"You know it hurts less when you're the one who has to stick me with a needle," Tony said accusingly. "I was counting on you."

"Oh, sweetie, I know and I'm sorry," she said, although somewhat relieved to hear the feistiness in his voice and to finally see some color in his cheeks.

"Where were you?" Tony asked.

"I've had one crisis after another today," she told him. "But that's no excuse. I should have been here."

"Mack wasn't here, either."

She regarded Tony with surprise. Since she had seen Mack, she'd assumed Tony would have, too. "Mack hasn't been by all day?"

"Not once," Tony confirmed. "He said he'd be here, too."

That made no sense at all. Mack had been in the

hospital most of the morning. She sighed as she realized that he'd spent the better part of that time with
her. "If Mack said he'd be here, then he'll be here,"
she reassured Tony. "He's never once broken his word
to you, has he?"

"No." Tony gave her a curious look. "Do you like
Mack?"

"He's been a wonderful friend to you," she responded carefully.

"But do *you* like him?" Tony pressed. Before she
could respond, he added, "I think maybe he likes
you."

Beth had to fight a grin at the latest round of matchmaking. She'd been warned about Tony's interest in
her relationship with Mack, but even so, the questions
surprised her.

"I was kinda hoping he'd fall for my mom," Tony
admitted. "That would be so awesome, but he hardly
gives her a second look. If he can't be my stepdad,
then it would be really great if he was with you, Dr.
Beth. You're way prettier than those flashy babes with
him in those pictures in the paper. You're real, you
know what I mean?"

She laughed at the compliment. "Thanks, Tony. I
appreciate the loyalty, but I don't think I can compete
with a supermodel."

"Sure you can," a much deeper voice chimed in.

Beth whirled around to find Mack in the doorway, a
grin on his face. "How long have you been eaves-
dropping?" she asked testily.

"Long enough to hear my pal Tony here trying to
set us up again." He gave her an impudent look. "So,
how about it, Doc? You want to have dinner tonight
with my aunt?"

Beth gaped at him. He was inviting her to Destiny's? "Maybe we should discuss this outside."

"Just say yes, Dr. Beth," Tony encouraged. "It's not every day you get asked out by a guy like Mighty Mack."

"I'll say," she muttered, then forced a smile for Tony's benefit. "Could I see you in the hallway for a moment, Mack?"

Mack winked at Tony. "I hope she's not going to turn me down. Rejection really sucks, you know."

Tony nodded knowingly.

Beth rolled her eyes at the pair of them. In the hallway, she frowned at Mack. "Why did you put me on the spot in front of Tony?"

"Because Destiny invited us for tonight, and I told her I'd have an answer for her in an hour. I wasn't sure I'd be able to track you down once you got away from Tony's room. Besides, what's the big deal? Hearing me ask you out obviously made his day."

"That's what worries me. Tony has expectations for us now. And your aunt?" She shook her head. "Are you really sure you want to do this?"

"Truthfully, it was my idea," he admitted.

She regarded him with surprise. "You're willingly going to subject yourself and me to your aunt's matchmaking? I thought you said she was like some sort of grand master manipulator. Why would you want to put ideas into her head?"

"The ideas are already there," Mack pointed out.

Beth thought back to her private dinner with Destiny and knew he was right. "Then how do you see this helping?"

"It might not. It might be a terrible mistake."

"Well, that makes me feel all warm and fuzzy about tonight," she said irritably. "I think I'll pass."

"And let Destiny think you're a coward? Or worse, convince her that you're already emotionally involved with me and trying to fight it?"

She regarded him blankly. "Huh? That's too convoluted even for me."

"Not for Destiny." Mack insisted. "I'm telling you, if you say no, it will open up a huge can of worms. This way we get the dreaded meeting over with. She might even conclude that we're a very bad match."

Suddenly Beth got it. She wasn't sure she liked it, but she understood exactly what Mack was up to. He was looking for an out, and he was hoping his beloved aunt would provide it by finding fault with Beth after all. If Destiny found Beth to be an unsuitable match for a Carlton, Mack would use that valued opinion to let himself off the hook.

She looked Mack directly in the eye. "Okay, here's what I'm hearing. You want Destiny to decide I'm wrong for you, so you can give yourself permission to stop seeing me," she said.

"You're crazy," he said just a little too quickly and vehemently.

"Am I?" she asked doubtfully. "Mack, if you're scared, I understand. If you want to call it quits, the way you're used to doing about now in a relationship, I understand that, too. Nobody's forcing you to be with me, certainly not me. I'm not exactly deliriously jumping up and down with joy at what's going on between us, either."

Mack frowned at that. "I'm not looking for an easy out," he claimed again.

"Aren't you? There's an attraction going on here,

but attractions come and go. They're not necessarily permanent. Instead of getting all panicky about the future, we both need to go with the flow or just get out now before things get complicated. I'm not going to freak out on you. I have enough self-confidence to weather your rejection. Heck, I won't even lump myself in with all those other women you dumped when you got scared."

She was about to go on, doing her best to let him off the hook and avoid the impending disaster, when he leaned down and covered her mouth with his own. Her words immediately died in her throat, and every sensible thought flew from her head.

When he finally pulled away, she stared at him through dazed eyes. "What was that for?"

"It was the only way I could think of to shut you up. You were thinking too much. Stop trying to guess what I'm feeling. If I don't know, you can't possibly know. We're still at the early stages of this thing."

Beth couldn't seem to drag herself back from the impact of that kiss to absorb what he was saying. Instead, she told him stiffly, "Kissing me outside of my patient's room where anyone could be passing by is inappropriate."

"Sorry."

She studied his expression for so much as a hint of sincere regret, but there was nothing. If anything, he looked a little smug at having rattled her.

His attitude, the conversation, the whole stupid dinner—it was all too much. She whirled around. "I have to go," she said, already striding away.

"Pick you up at six-thirty," he called after her.

"No."

"Be ready."

"I am not going to dinner."

"Sure you are."

She turned around and marched right back until she was in his face. If necessary, she would shout and make a total scene until he got the message.

"I am not going to dinner at your aunt's," she announced very firmly.

He studied her intently, then nodded. "Okay."

She faltered at his acquiescence. For some reason that irked her even more than his assumption that she would fall in with his plans. "Maybe I will go, after all."

"Okay." He looked as if he was struggling to bite back a grin.

"But I'll meet you there."

He frowned, but nodded. "Okay. I'll give you the address."

"No need," she said blithely, beaming at him. "I've been there."

He stared at her as if she'd announced a familiarity with the direct route to Mars. "When in the hell did you visit my aunt?"

"Weeks ago," she said.

"Before she sent me over here to meet Tony?" he asked suspiciously.

"No, after. Well, later that same day, to be precise. Your aunt has impeccable timing. She called me minutes after you left."

"She never said anything," he said, half to himself. He stared at Beth. "Neither did you."

"I'm sure your aunt doesn't run all of her social engagements past you," Beth told him. "And just so you know, I have no intention of doing that, either."

He shook his head. "Good to know."

"See you at seven," Beth told him. "Maybe I'll call Destiny and see if she'd mind if I bring a date."

"You do and he's a dead man," Mack said grimly.

Beth laughed. Once again she had made Mighty Mack Carlton jealous. Damn, but that felt good. She glanced at his fierce expression and concluded it might be wise not to test him too often, though.

She reached up and patted his cheek. "Okay then, it's just you and me, pal."

"I am not your *pal.* You can get over that idea right now."

"Oh? Then how would you describe yourself?"

"I'm the man you're currently driving stark raving mad," he said. Suddenly a grin spread across his face. "Of course, if you play your cards right over dinner, I can be driving you a little crazy by ten."

She nodded slowly. "A fascinating prospect," she noted. "I'll definitely keep it in mind."

He pressed another hard, sizzling kiss to her mouth, then released her. "Just a little something to tide you over," he said.

He was whistling when he walked back into Tony's room. Beth waited until the door was firmly shut behind him before sagging against the wall. The arrogant, impossible man had once again made her knees weak. She could only pray he never figured out just how easily he could accomplish that. Then again, given how well he understood women, he probably already knew.

Chapter Ten

Mack paced around Destiny's den like a caged tiger. Where the devil was Beth? He'd called the hospital an hour ago and been told that she'd left at five-thirty. He'd assumed she'd gone home to change, especially since her blouse had been stained with some god-awful orange stuff, but how long did it take for a woman to put on a new outfit and drive across the bridge into Alexandria? He was surprisingly inexperienced when it came to knowing such things, which just proved how little he'd ever discovered about the personal habits and idiosyncrasies of the many women he'd dated.

It was nearly seven-thirty now. For a woman as punctual as Beth tried to be, running a half hour late or more was totally out of character.

"Will you sit down, please?" Destiny said, her exasperation evident. "You're giving me a headache. Beth said she'll be here, and I'm sure she will be."

"She was supposed to be here thirty minutes ago."

"Darling, I'm sure she wouldn't stand you up."

Mack took note of the distinction, implying that *he* was the only one with any cause for worry. Besides, he wasn't so sure Destiny was right about Beth not ditching him at the last minute. It would be just like her to do something so completely unpredictable to annoy him. He hadn't guessed about that perverse streak in her until that conversation they'd had in the hallway this afternoon. He was still trying to decide how he felt about it, especially that belated revelation about her prior meeting with Destiny.

"She wasn't that enthused about coming," he admitted in what had to be the most massive understatement he'd ever uttered.

Destiny regarded him solemnly. "But she has very lovely manners, Mack. She might not contact you if you've somehow offended her, but she would call me if she intended to cancel."

He scowled at the suggestion that he was somehow at fault. "I didn't offend her. And how would you know about her manners?" he asked. Then, without waiting for a response he added, "Oh, yes, that would be because of the cozy little dinner you two shared not long ago, the dinner you neglected to mention when we spoke earlier today."

Destiny regarded him with surprise. "She told you about that?"

"Gloated about it, in fact," he said, then added sourly, "I thought it was great that someone finally thought to bring me into the loop."

Destiny's expression grew thoughtful. "Isn't that interesting?"

"What's so blasted interesting about her finally

'fessing up to the fact that the two of you were sneaking around behind my back? For all I know, you've been in cahoots with her for months. This little admission could be the tip of the iceberg.''

His aunt frowned at him. "Don't be melodramatic, darling. It was dinner, nothing more. It's not as if we hatched some plot to reel you in. You're obviously a man who makes up his own mind about these things. You don't believe I would set a trap for you, do you?''

He scowled right back at her. "Oh, please. I learned a long time ago never to underestimate you. You might not be successful at setting me up with a woman I'd walk down the aisle, but you're not above trying.''

"Do you think Beth is so spineless that she would go along with a scheme of mine?''

He considered that and knew it was unlikely. If there was one thing he was certain of it was that Beth had a very strong sense of herself. Spineless was the last thing she was. Heaven knew, she didn't hesitate to tell him what was on her mind. He doubted she'd be any less forthcoming with Destiny. If his aunt had approached her about Mack, Beth most likely would have laughed in her face.

"No," he finally conceded to Destiny.

"You know, Mack, I'm a little surprised you decided to go through with dinner tonight once you found out about my previous meeting with Beth. Since you obviously see a conspiracy around every corner where I'm concerned, is there some particular reason you chose not to back out?''

He had a pretty good idea what she was driving at, but he decided to give her the satisfaction of making her point. "Such as?''

"Are you looking for some evidence that Beth doesn't fit in here?"

He started to deny it, but Destiny knew him too well. Besides, Beth had had the exact same suspicion. Obviously, these two people, who knew him better than most, could see straight through him.

"It crossed my mind that she might come to that conclusion," he conceded eventually.

"And then what?" Destiny kept her gaze on his face while she awaited his reply. When he said nothing, she asked, "Surely you weren't hoping that she'd dump you?" At his continued silence, she regarded him incredulously. "That's exactly what you were hoping, isn't it?"

"It's not like I'm this incredible prize," he said defensively, "especially for a woman who hopes to marry and have a family."

"Oh, please, this is no time for false modesty," his aunt said, dismissing the comment as ridiculous. "Besides, has Beth said anything about getting married?"

"No."

"Is she ready to start a family?"

"She hasn't mentioned it, no."

"Then aren't you jumping ahead a bit prematurely?" She regarded him intently. "Or is that the point? Are you the one who's beginning to think about marriage?" Amusement sparkled in her eyes. "Oh my," she said happily. "No wonder you're terrified and looking for the fastest exit. Even worse, since you're not sure you'll take it, you're obviously hoping to push Beth through it."

Mack's head was spinning from Destiny's convoluted logic. He couldn't cope with that and his concern over Beth's whereabouts at the same time. "Maybe I

should call her cell phone. She could be stuck in traffic.''

"Avoiding the question won't make it go away,"
Destiny chided. "And if she were stuck in traffic, don't
you think she'd call?"

"Do you have an answer for everything?" he grumbled.

Destiny smiled happily. "I like to think so," she said
as the doorbell rang. "Why don't you get that, Mack?
And try to wipe that scowl off your face before you
get there. You don't want to scare the woman to death
before she even crosses the threshold." Her smile
spread. "Or do you?"

When he reached the front door, his temper was still
simmering, though whether his irritation was directed
toward his impossible aunt or Beth was hard to say.
He flung open the door, took one look at Beth's disheveled appearance and immediately forgot all about
his lousy mood.

"What on earth happened to you?" he demanded,
noting that before she'd ruined them, her clothes were
very feminine and flattering compared to the tailored
look he'd grown accustomed to. She'd really made an
effort for tonight's dinner.

"Flat tire," she said succinctly.

Judging from the grease all over her, she had
changed it herself. "Didn't it occur to you to call a
garage or me?"

She gave him an impatient look. "I know how to
change a tire. I figured it would be faster to do it myself
than to wait for a tow truck to get there in the middle
of rush hour. I should have gone back home to change
again, but I was already so late, I decided I'd better
come on over."

Still not reassured, he studied her from head to toe. "You didn't hurt yourself, did you?"

She rolled her eyes and held out her arms for his inspection. "See, no blood. No bruises. Just grease. Do you suppose I could use a bathroom to clean up?"

"Come with me," he said, and led the way toward the kitchen instead. "The soap in the bathroom isn't going to do it. Ben used to have a snazzy little car he worked on in the garage. Believe me, this house is no stranger to grease and oil. There's bound to be something in the garage we can use to get off the worst of this, though I'm not sure anything will help with the clothes."

She glanced down at her flowery silk dress and groaned. "This was brand-new."

Mack shook his head. She could have seriously injured herself wrestling with the damn tire and she was worried about her dress. "I'll buy you another one," he said impatiently.

She regarded him with a withering glance. "I can buy another dress myself."

"But that doesn't solve the immediate problem." He handed her some rags and a can of cleanser. "You get started on the grease and oil and I'll speak to Destiny. I'm sure she has something you can put on. You're about the same size. I'll be right back to show you where the downstairs powder room is."

Once he'd explained the problem to his aunt, Destiny immediately hurried off to find something suitable in her closet. When she returned, Mack started to take the clothes from her, but she brushed him off. "You don't get to help her undress in my house."

He chuckled at the unexpected display of propriety.

"I would have thought you'd be inclined to encourage me to do just that."

She frowned at him. "You can check the oven and make sure dinner isn't burning. Turn it down to low."

"Yes, ma'am."

"And Mack…"

"Yes?"

She gave him a warm, reassuring smile. "I told you she wouldn't stand you up."

He sighed, not even attempting to hide how relieved he'd been to realize that for himself.

Beth kept touching the fine fabric of the cardigan Destiny had given her to slip on over a sleeveless silk top. She was amazed at what a difference there was in the quality from her usual wardrobe. She'd always believed it was ridiculous to spend a fortune on clothes, but now she understood why people who had the money did just that. She was fairly certain she never wanted to take this off.

"I think you should keep the sweater," Destiny said, regarding her with amusement. "That soft pink color is very becoming on you. Don't you agree, Mack?"

Mack nodded distractedly. He'd been in an odd mood ever since Beth's arrival. She couldn't quite pin down what was wrong. He'd been so anxious for her to come tonight and he'd looked so relieved when he'd opened the door. He'd looked even more relieved when he'd assured himself that she wasn't hurt. It had been some time, though, since he'd entered into the dinner conversation.

Not that it had made things awkward. Destiny was perfectly capable of keeping the talk lively. She had a million and one questions about Tony and about Beth's work.

"Mack tells me he's going to fund a research project," Destiny said eventually. "I hope you'll accept a donation from me, as well."

Beth stared at her, overcome with gratitude. "That's very generous of you," she said when she'd gathered her composure. "I know you already give quite a bit to the hospital. Are you sure you want to do more?"

"Absolutely. As soon as you have your proposal put together, Mack and I will sit down and discuss the details with our attorneys. Carlton Industries will participate, as well. Your research should be quite adequately funded."

"Did I hear some mention of the family company in connection with giving away money?" Richard asked, walking into the dining room with his wife just as it was time for dessert.

"Yes," Destiny said. "And no penny-pinching, either. Beth's work is important."

"Are you sure you're not just trying to buy her for Mack?" he teased.

The comment drew an immediate rebuke from the petite woman accompanying him.

"What?" Richard asked. "It's not as if Destiny is above such a thing."

"I don't need anyone buying a woman for me," Mack countered indignantly. "If anything I usually have more than I can handle."

"None of them appropriate," Destiny retorted.

Richard's wife gave Beth a commiserating look. "Don't mind them. I've been really looking forward to meeting you," Melanie said.

Surprised that Melanie Carlton even knew about her, Beth merely said, "Oh?"

"I wanted to express my heartfelt sympathy."

"Sympathy?" Beth asked, puzzled.

Melanie directed an impudent look toward Destiny. "If I'm not mistaken, you're the latest target of the Carlton steamroller. If it gets to be too much for you, give me a call. I'll be sure to give you my number. I may not be able to save you, but we can discuss a few evasive maneuvers."

Beth regarded Richard's wife with an immediate sense of camaraderie. "Been there, done that?" she inquired.

"In spades," Melanie said, casting another pointed look toward Destiny.

"I really don't see that you have a thing to complain about," Destiny said, a glint of amusement in her eyes proving that Melanie's teasing hadn't offended her.

"Not now," Melanie agreed, linking her arm through Richard's. "It all turned out rather well in the end, once we caved in and did what Destiny had wanted all along."

Mack had remained silent, his expression gloomy, during most of this exchange, but he finally frowned at his brother. "So, what brings you by tonight? Did you just have a sudden impulse while driving by?"

Richard grinned. "Actually we were invited for dessert."

"Really?" Mack said, frowning at his aunt. "Which part of just the three of us did you not understand, Destiny?"

"It's my home," she chided. "I'm entitled to include your brother and his wife, if I so choose. I thought it was time they had a chance to meet Beth."

Mack gave her a wry look. "Then Richard didn't mention that he'd taken the bait you tossed out weeks ago? He came scurrying right over to the hospital to meet her. I would have thought he'd give you a full report long before now."

Destiny looked genuinely surprised. "Really? What brought that on? Surely not some casual remark I might have made."

"He came to gloat," Mack said before his brother could speak. "Seems he'd figured out you were up to your eyeballs in planning my life and wanted to see for himself how it was working out."

Beth turned to Melanie. "Was it this bad with you?"

"Worse," Melanie said with heartfelt sincerity. "Richard was the first part of Destiny's grand scheme. She really had something to prove with us."

Beth buried her face in her hands. She'd had no idea things were going to spin this far out of control so quickly. She finally drew in a deep breath and looked up. "I think it's time for me to get back to the hospital."

"I agree," Mack said at once, practically knocking over his chair in his eagerness.

"You don't need to come," she told him. "I have my own car, remember?"

"It's got a spare tire on, probably one of those little doughnut things. At the very least, you need to let me follow you to make sure you don't have another problem."

Beth's chin set stubbornly. "It's not necessary."

Mack's set just as firmly. "Yes, it is."

She realized he wasn't going to bend on this, either out of a real sense of protectiveness toward her or out of desperation to make his own escape. She might as well give in gracefully.

"Fine, then," she relented. She faced Destiny. "Thanks so much for a lovely dinner. And I apologize again for being so late. I'll get your clothes back to you."

"I still think you should keep them," Destiny said. "They're very becoming."

Beth shook her head. She wasn't about to owe this clever woman for another thing. "I couldn't."

"Your decision, of course," Destiny said, giving in. "I do wish you wouldn't run off, though. I made something chocolate for dessert. I understand you're partial to it."

"So am I," Melanie said, then added eagerly, "I'll eat her share."

"And probably Mack's as well," Richard said, regarding her indulgently. "Before you two leave, you should know that Melanie and I have an announcement to make."

Everyone turned to stare at them expectantly.

Eyes shining, Melanie said, "We're going to have a baby."

"Well, I'll be damned," Mack said, grabbing his brother and enthusiastically slapping him on the back. "Congratulations!"

Tears spilled down Destiny's cheeks as she embraced first Melanie and then her nephew.

Melanie winked at Beth. "There, that should take the heat off you for a bit. Run now, while you have the chance."

"Not until we drink a toast," Destiny insisted. "Let me get some sparkling cider for Melanie and the rest of us can have champagne."

Not willing to spoil Melanie and Richard's moment, Beth nodded. "We can wait just a minute, but make mine sparkling cider as well, since I'm heading back to work."

"What the heck," Mack told his aunt. "Make it sparkling cider all around. I'm getting behind the wheel, so it's best if I don't have anything more to drink."

"Richard, darling, why don't you come into the kitchen with me?" Destiny suggested. "You can help me carry the glasses. And, Mack, you can clear the table and bring in dessert." She glanced toward Beth. "You might as well have that chocolate mousse now, too, don't you think?"

The temptation was too great to resist. Beth nodded. "Sure."

Destiny beamed. "I knew you could be tempted."

After they'd all disappeared into the kitchen, Melanie turned to Beth. "So, tell me, just how pressured are you feeling?"

Beth thought about it. She'd really only experienced one panicky moment earlier. "Actually it's not so bad. Mack and I are in the same place, I think. He's no more interested in marriage than I am."

Melanie chuckled. "Is that what you think?"

"It's the truth," Beth insisted.

"I'm sure he thinks it is," Melanie said agreeably. "And I know it's what you want to believe, but I just caught a glimpse of the way he looks at you. The man is head-over-heels in love with you."

"Mack? Don't be ridiculous." Beth retorted. "In lust, maybe."

"With the Carlton men, it's sometimes the same thing. I'm not talking about the casual kind of lust-at-

first-sight business. I'm talking about the can't-keep-
his-hands-off-you lust that doesn't quit and gets more
intense with every day that passes."

Beth was embarrassed by Melanie's frankness and
by her ability to see the desire that Beth had been trying
very hard to conceal all night. Even when Mack had
been at his most exasperating, all she'd been able to
think about was his earlier promise to take her home
tonight and drive her a little crazy. When she'd announced her intention to return to work, she'd half expected never to make it there.

"Are you denying that that's what is going on with
you two?" Melanie asked.

"I really don't think we should be discussing this,"
Beth said, uncomfortable not only with the topic, but
with Melanie's accurate assessment of the situation.

"I've embarrassed you, haven't I? I'm sorry," Melanie apologized. "It's just that I've been down this
road, and I can see all the signs. When the Carlton men
finally fall, they fall hard. If you ever decide you do
want to talk about it, give me a call." She pulled a
Carlton Industries business card from her purse and
jotted a number on the back. "There. Now you have
my number at the office and at home. I mean it, Beth.
The only way for us to hold our own when the Carlton
steamroller gets into high gear is to stick together. I
know I'd have been happy to have the moral support
when I was in the same place you're in now."

Beth laughed. "Yes, I can see how that might help,"
she said, tucking the card into her pocket. She could
also imagine being friends with this open, energetic
woman who saw the Carltons so clearly. It had been
years and years since she'd had a woman friend to

confide in, years since she'd had anything to confide, for that matter.

Before either of them could say more, Destiny, Richard and Mack came back with the drinks and dessert.

During the toast, Mack's gaze caught Beth's, and she felt herself responding to the barely banked heat in his eyes. Okay, she admitted, her hand trembling slightly, she was a little bit past being in lust herself.

But in love with the region's consummate playboy? No way. She simply couldn't allow it to happen.

Mack rolled over and stared down into Beth's face. She looked so peaceful, so beautiful with her cheeks still flushed from sex, her skin still glowing with a soft sheen of perspiration. He wondered if he'd ever get his fill of moments like this.

"Do you intend to spend the night watching me sleep?" she murmured.

"I didn't think you'd catch me. I thought you were actually asleep, rather than playing possum," Mack said, daring to reach out and tuck a curl behind her ear now that he knew he wouldn't be waking her. He let his fingers linger against her petal-soft skin.

"Faking it," she teased. "You wore me out. I needed a breather."

Mack laughed. "If anyone needs a breather, it should be me. I thought I was going to follow you back to work and leave you there, then go home and spend a quiet night all alone in my own bed. I still have a lot of recovering to do from the last night we spent together. It's a good thing I'm not in training any more. The coaches would have a lot to say about me being this wiped out."

"Ha!" she muttered. "You knew exactly where we

were heading the instant we left your aunt's. In fact, you were leading the way.''

He grinned. "Well, I was hopeful," he admitted. "I kept watching in my rearview mirror to see if you were going to turn off and head straight for the hospital, after all.''

"I thought about it," Beth said. "Then I thought about this. It was no contest.''

"Glad to know you find me more fascinating than your paperwork," he groused.

She regarded him with an impish expression. "Definitely better than paperwork, though my research might give you a run for your money.''

"Want to tell me about what you're working on?" he asked, realizing that he truly did want to understand every single thing that was important to her. He couldn't recall another time when he'd cared about anything more than the moment, when it came to a woman who was in his bed.

"It'll be in the grant proposal," she said. "Do you really want to hear me go on and on about it now?''

"I could listen to you go on and on about most anything," he said honestly, no less surprised than she was by that. "You're so passionate about what you do.''

"And you're not?''

"You said it yourself," he reminded her. "Football is just a game.''

She winced. "That was a really lousy thing for me to say. The important thing for anyone is to do work that they love. You're doing that. Who knows, maybe one of these days I'll even let you take me to a game and try to explain why all those huge, hulking men are running up and down the field.''

Mack stared at her, certain he couldn't be understanding her correctly. "You've *never* been to a football game?"

"Never."

"Watched one on TV?"

"Not if I could help it."

"So all that dismissive talk was based on absolutely no firsthand experience whatsoever?" he asked incredulously.

"Afraid so."

He shook his head. "If there's a football-for-complete-novices book, I'm buying it and giving it to you. Once you've learned a few things and been to a few games, we'll discuss this gap in your education again."

Beth chuckled. "Will there be a test? I'm very good at tests."

He heard the low, taunting note in her voice and his body immediately responded to the unspoken challenge. He reached for her.

"How about this test?" he murmured. "Are you ready for this?"

"Oh, yes," she said fervently.

And for the rest of the night, football, his meddling aunt and the future were the very last things on Mack's mind.

Chapter Eleven

When Beth walked into the hospital cafeteria at lunchtime the next day, she was greeted by an unexpected sea of guilty expressions. Jason immediately tried his best to slide a newspaper out of sight under the table. Three people rose, nodded a greeting and suddenly took off, leaving her with Jason and Peyton.

Since their odd reactions seemed to have something to do with that newspaper, Beth walked right up to Jason and plucked it out of his hand before he could safely stash it somewhere. "Something interesting in here?" she asked, holding it aloft and attempting to skim the headlines, a task made more difficult by Jason's urgent attempts to snatch it back. She gave him a withering look that finally caused him to retreat, albeit with obvious reluctance.

"It's no big deal," he muttered defensively. "It's just some silly item. Nothing important."

Unfortunately, he had the kind of open face that told Beth he was lying.

"Then why don't you want me to see it?" she asked reasonably. "Or is it some girlie club ad or an ad to end sexual dysfunction that you think will embarrass me?"

"Come on, Beth," Jason protested, his cheeks now flaming. "You know we wouldn't be looking at anything like that."

"What then?"

When he tried once again to make a grab for the newspaper, she held it out of his reach and glanced more thoroughly at the page that her colleagues had been so absorbed in reading. All she spotted was the daily gossip column by that sleazy tabloid-style reporter Pete Forsythe.

"You guys were reading the local gossip?" she asked incredulously. "I thought you were above such things. Don't you have all sorts of lofty medical journals you could be reading instead?"

"But this is lots more interesting and hits closer to home," Peyton said, a definite twinkle in his eyes.

It was so rare to see the serious-minded hematologist with a smile tugging at his lips, that Beth almost didn't care what was in the paper as long as it was responsible for that smile. Unfortunately, she had a hunch she couldn't dismiss it so lightly. She took a second look at the headline: Man-About-Town Missing In Action. She still didn't get the fascination. She gave the men a curious look. "So?"

"Did you read the first paragraph?" Jason finally asked, his expression resigned.

Beth scanned the beginning of the article, her jaw dropping as she read on.

Playboy jock Mack Carlton, who can normally be
spotted in every hot spot in town, always with a
glamorous beauty by his side, has vanished from
view lately. The lonely women are starting to ask
questions. Has some secret gal-pal snagged his attention and taken him out of the social whirl?

Well, we can answer that. Mighty Mack has
been spending a lot of time at a local hospital
lately, and the word is that he's not there for medical tests. A brilliant doc has caught his eye, and
he's been wooing her far from the prying eyes of
the local media.

Stay tuned, Mack watchers. We'll be the first
to report when the ex-quarterback and current
team owner scores his first marital touchdown.
Based on what we've heard, we'll give you odds
that it's going to happen before the football season
starts.

Beth reread the entire item again, her cheeks burning. Even though her name wasn't mentioned, the men
gathered around this table—including those who had
taken off at her arrival—all knew the article referred
to her. Otherwise they wouldn't have reacted so guiltily
or tried to keep it from her.

"Sorry," Jason said. "I was hoping you wouldn't
see it. It's just a silly little item, Beth. Not anything to
get upset about."

"Hardly anybody reads that junk," Peyton chimed
in.

"Oh, please. If you guys—who are oblivious to most
of this so-called junk—read it, then obviously the entire
metropolitan Washington region has seen it by now,"
Beth said grimly. "Actually, I'm glad you brought it

to my attention, albeit reluctantly. Now I have time to do a little damage control.''

Jason regarded her with alarm. "What are you going to do?"

"I'm not going to kill Pete Forsythe, if that's what you're worried about,'' she said.

"And you're not going to break up with Mack, are you?" Jason asked with evident dismay. "I've been counting on this lasting at least through football season, so maybe you can snag a pair of tickets for me.''

"How thoughtful of you to put my reputation first," Beth said.

"Your reputation is just fine," Peyton pointed out. "Your name was never mentioned. Only a few people know you're the doctor in question."

"Sure. Just you guys, Mack's entire family, anyone who's seen us together around here and a half-dozen maître d's around town. How long do you think it will be before one of them fills in the blanks for Forsythe? People love to share inside information.''

"What difference does it make?" Peyton persisted. "It's not as if either of you is married. You're dating. So what?"

Beth knew what he was saying was perfectly reasonable, but she wasn't feeling especially reasonable. She wanted to string up whoever had planted this item with the gossip columnist. She wanted to strangle Mack for ever giving her a second glance. And, come to think of it, she wasn't all that happy with herself at the moment.

She'd known this was one of the risks of getting involved with a high-profile playboy. But once she'd drifted into a real relationship with Mack, her concerns and good sense had flown right out the window. All she'd thought about lately was how alive she felt in his arms. She hadn't given a moment's consideration to how their relationship might blow up in her face. If she'd found the stares disconcerting before, they were going to be even more humiliating now, just as they had been after her ex-fiancé had spread his lies about her.

"I have to do something," she insisted. "I have to put an end to this before things get any worse."

"What can you do that won't make it worse?" Peyton asked.

"He's right," Jason said. "If you call Forsythe, you'll be giving him exactly the information he needs to print another item."

Because even she could see that there wasn't much she could do about any of it, Beth finally sighed heavily and sat down. Jason regarded her warily, then stood.

"Chocolate?" he asked, his expression filled with concern.

"As much as the vending machine has," she said, feeling defeated. Even if the vending machine had been filled just that morning, it probably wouldn't be enough. She reached for her purse.

"No, I'll buy," Jason said. "I feel responsible for setting off this chocolate attack."

"I'll chip in, too," Peyton said, tossing a few dollar bills to Jason.

"I'm depressed, not suicidal," Beth said, a faint flicker of amusement sneaking in at their sudden show of protectiveness. "Besides, maybe we should use some of that money to buy up all the newspapers in the machines around the hospital."

"Too late for that," Peyton said. "The way the rumor mill fires up in this place, it takes only one person with the inside scoop to have the news spread far and wide by lunchtime.''

Beth scowled at his bleak outlook, but she knew he was right. The only news medium faster than the hospital grapevine was *CNN*.

Jason was already loping off toward the vending machine when she called after him. "Bring me chips, too.''

Peyton regarded her worriedly. "Chips? You never eat chips.''

"I'm feeling reckless.''

"Junk food is not the answer,'' he scolded, looking more like his somber self.

"Any idea what might be?''

"That depends.''

"On?''

"Whether you're in love with Mack Carlton.''

Shocked that a man so totally absorbed in his work might have taken note of the attraction, she felt compelled to deny it. "Of course I'm not in love with Mack,'' she said, though her protest wasn't nearly as fierce as it had been the night before.

Peyton shook his head. "Not convincing, Beth. For it to be believable, you must sound certain, not miserable.''

"Why do I have to convince you?''

His lips twitched. "Not me. Yourself.''

Ah, Beth thought. He had a point. She wasn't buying her own protests anymore, either.

Mack was seething when he saw the gossip column that someone on the team's administrative staff had thoughtfully left on his desk first thing this morning.

Beth was going to be fit to be tied. He could sympa-
thize, but at least he was used to seeing his name in
the paper. He'd become accustomed to the half-truths
and innuendoes that made up a column like Pete Forsythe's. He'd learned to shrug it off as a cost of celebrity. Beth wouldn't have any such defense mechanisms.

It didn't matter that her name hadn't been mentioned. It was only a matter of time before it would be.
Too many people could fill in that particular blank. He
hadn't realized how much he valued the lack of media
attention vis-à-vis this relationship until now, when his
peace and quiet were being threatened.

He picked up the phone and tried Beth's office. He
left a voice mail on her machine, then beeped her. It
was ten minutes before she finally returned his call, ten
of the longest minutes of his life that left him wondering if she was too furious to ever speak to him again.

"I'm sorry," he said the instant he heard her voice
and the edginess in it. "I should have warned you
something like this could happen."

She sighed. "I should have known," she said. "After all, isn't that the column where I spotted your name
all the time? That's how I formed my rather jaundiced
view of you."

"Maybe so, but I'd thought we were being discreet.
I never wanted to drag you into the spotlight."

"Not your fault," she said.

To his relief, she sounded sincere. She wasn't blaming him. "Thank you," he said.

"For?"

"Letting me off the hook. I probably don't deserve
it."

"Look, Mack, I know we've been discreet, but it's
not as if we've never been anywhere at all together.

We've just avoided your usual haunts in prime time, so to speak. We should have expected something like this to happen sooner or later.''

''I can't get over the fact that you're not more upset.''

''At you? No. I'm not crazy about this, believe me. Jason and Peyton had to buy all the chocolate in the vending machine to calm me down, but they've finally convinced me it could have been much worse.''

''It could still get worse,'' Mack warned her. ''Once Forsythe's on the scent of a scoop, he can be relentless. Ask Melanie to fill you in on the role he played in her relationship with Richard.''

''Actually, now that you mention it, I remember that. I wonder who put Forsythe onto this particular scent,'' Beth asked. ''I'm a boring doctor, not your usual high-profile date.''

''Which is exactly why he probably finds it so intriguing,'' Mack told her, then was suddenly struck by something that was so obvious, he should have suspected it right off. ''Damn!''

''What?''

''Look, I'll see you later, okay? There's something I need to do right now.''

''What's so important that you don't want to finish this conversation?'' she asked, her voice filled with suspicion.

''I'm going to have a chat with Forsythe's informed source,'' he said grimly.

''You know who spilled the beans?'' Beth demanded

''Not with absolutely certainty,'' he said. ''But I'd give you Vegas odds I can name the culprit in one guess.''

''Who?''

"Destiny, of course."

"She wouldn't," Beth said, sounding genuinely shocked.

"Darling, this is vintage Destiny. She's been stirring our particular pot for weeks now. After last night's dinner, she's obviously decided it needs a little something to spice it up a notch. Pete Forsythe has been her chosen messenger before. Hell, she probably has his private fax number memorized after spilling all those juicy little tidbits about Richard and Melanie to him."

"Are you serious? She was behind those?"

"Oh, yes, and proud of it," Mack said. "You know the expression 'All's fair in love and war'? Well, Destiny thinks she's fighting a war for romance. Believe me, Forsythe's column is just one of her weapons of choice."

"Are you going over there?"

"The instant we hang up."

"Pick me up on your way," she said. "I want a piece of this. I have more at stake than you do."

Mack laughed at her out-for-blood tone. "I'll be there in twenty minutes."

"I'll be out front," she said, then hung up.

"Oh, Destiny," Mack murmured, not even bothering to hide his anticipation. "You have really gone and stepped in it this time."

For once, he wasn't going to have to say a single word to his aunt about her meddling. He could sit back and let Beth do all the dirty work. Damn, this was going to be more fun than watching a couple of sexy women get down and dirty in the mud.

Unfortunately, Destiny Carlton was nowhere to be found. Beth's frustration grew with every call Mack made on his cell phone only to be told that he'd just missed his aunt.

"She's lying low," he finally concluded.

"Smart woman," Beth said with a trace of admiration. Destiny was clearly a worthy adversary. No doubt that was why her nephews hadn't succeeded in foiling her meddling yet.

"Want to have lunch?" Mack asked.

"In public?" she responded, not even attempting to hide her horror at the prospect.

He chuckled. "Oh, I think I can pull it off so that we don't get caught by the paparazzi."

"How?"

"Watch a master at work," he said, making a few calls, then heading through Washington's crowded roads at a pace few race-car drivers would have attempted. He turned into a back alley, pulled up beside an unmarked door and told her to sit tight. "I'll be right back."

Beth looked around warily. "Are you sure it's safe here?"

"From everything except rats, most likely," he said,

She shuddered. "Hurry."

"Five minutes," he promised.

The entire time he was gone—which seemed like an eternity—Beth's gaze darted in every direction, on the lookout for lurking dangers. To her relief he was back before she'd spotted so much as a rodent of any kind. The aromas drifting from the cooler he was carrying were worth all the moments of anxiety she'd suffered.

"Garlic," she whispered happily. "Tomatoes. Oh, my God, what did you get? There was no sign over that door you slipped through."

"The best pasta you will ever put in your mouth," he told her. "Your place?"

She sniffed greedily even as she nodded. "And step on it," she told him. "My mouth is watering."

Mack gave her a sideways glance. "I gather Italian food ranks right up there with chocolate on your personal aphrodisiac scale."

"Oh, yes."

"Does this mean I'm going to get lucky this afternoon?" he inquired, his expression hopeful.

Beth considered the proposition for about fifteen seconds. "If there's time," she said conscientiously. "I do have to get back to work, you know. Peyton and Jason are covering for me now, but at some point people might start to wonder why I'm not on duty."

Mack took the corner on two wheels and was parked behind her town house in three minutes flat.

"Ever consider trying out for NASCAR?" she asked as she got out, still clutching the cooler.

"Nah, too tame," he teased. "I like the challenge of maneuvering through rush hour."

"You just like a challenge, period," she guessed.

"That, too."

Even as she put the food on the kitchen table, she studied him closely. "Is that what I am, Mack? A challenge?"

Rather than the flip response she'd anticipated, he seemed to take the question seriously. "Not the way you mean," he said eventually.

"How, then?"

"I'm not sure I can explain."

Because his serious expression and tone told her this could be really important, she met his gaze. "Try," she said.

His expression turned thoughtful, and he took his time answering. "Okay, here's what I think. It's never been about winning your heart or getting you into bed just to prove I could," he told her. His gaze met hers. "In some weird way it's been about seeing just how involved I dared to get before the panic set in."

Beth wasn't sure how to take that, wasn't even sure she fully understood it. "And?"

He regarded her with a hint of surprise in his eyes. It was there in his voice, too. "Hasn't happened yet," he admitted.

Beth's heart beat unsteadily at what he wasn't saying. "Why do you suppose that is?"

Mack sighed then and finally looked away. "I don't know, Beth. I honestly don't know, but I will tell you this." He once again looked directly into her eyes. "Considering the possibilities scares the hell out of me."

Try as she might, Beth couldn't shake that conversation as she went about her duties at the hospital that afternoon. What was Mack most afraid of? That she was winning his heart, despite all the defenses he'd erected around it? Or that even after all of the incredible sex and growing intimacy, he was incapable of feeling anything more?

Forget Mack for a minute. What did *she* want? The lines on that had blurred a lot lately, too. If only Destiny hadn't planted that stupid item with Pete Forsythe. It was going to force them out into the real world before either of them was ready. And the real world had a way of taking the edge off the excitement, a way of stripping away pretenses and forcing an examination of the core feelings behind an involvement.

Wasn't that what had happened to her before? That grant application, which had brought the real world smack into the middle of her relationship, had exposed wounds and clashing egos in a way that might otherwise never have happened. Not that she wasn't grateful now to have made the discovery about her ex-fiancé's competitiveness, insecurities and cruelty before they married, but it had been a bitter blow at the time.

She was very much afraid that her relationship with Mack wouldn't weather this current storm any more smoothly.

When she opened the door to Tony's room, she was surprised to find Mack there. She thought he'd left after dropping her off, but there he was, leafing through a comic book while Tony slept.

"Heavy reading?" she teased. "I'm beginning to think that's why you keep coming around—because it gives you an excuse to read all those comics."

"Afraid not," he said, his gaze steady on hers. "You keep me coming around, Doc. I thought you understood that after the conversation we had earlier."

She opened her mouth to respond, then caught a flicker of Tony's eyelids that suggested he was playing possum and listening to every word. "We'll finish this conversation later," she told Mack.

"Aw, come on, Dr. Beth, it was just getting good," Tony protested, opening his eyes.

Mack whirled around to stare at him. "I thought you were asleep."

"I was, but then I woke up," Tony said. He grinned impishly at Mack. "I knew you liked Dr. Beth. I could tell. I even told my mom."

"You know, kid, my love life is none of your business," Mack scolded.

"Why not?" Tony asked. "I thought we were all friends."

"We are, but most adults like to figure things out for themselves," Beth told him.

"But you guys are taking way too long," Tony said.

"Says who?" Mack asked.

Tony gave him a feisty look. "Says me. You know I don't exactly have forever."

Tony uttered the horrific words with a blithe acceptance of the reality, but Mack looked as if someone had slugged him. Even Beth was taken aback by Tony's matter-of-fact statement about his own prospects.

"You don't know that," she said fiercely, struggling against the tears stinging her eyes. She could not cry in front of Tony, or in front of Mack, for that matter. "I will not let you give up on yourself."

Tony reached her hand. "It's okay, Dr. Beth. I don't blame you."

"That's not the point. You *are* going to get better, Tony. You need to believe that."

Tony gave her a stubborn look. "It's not like I want to die," he said seriously. "But sometimes you just gotta face facts."

"And the fact is that we don't know what's going to happen," Beth said. "Only God knows that. And in the meantime, you have Peyton and me, your mom and Mack, and a whole lot of other people rooting for you." Desperate to get through to him, she gestured toward a colorful mural that had been painted by the kids at his school and which hung now on the wall across from his bed. "Look at that. All of your classmates are behind you, too."

Tony sighed wearily and lay back against the pillows. "I know, but sometimes it feels like it's time to let go." He looked plaintively at Mack. "You know what I mean?"

Though he was clearly as shaken as Beth, Mack moved to the edge of the bed and took Tony's frail hand in his big one. "It takes a very brave person to fight this illness," Mack told him quietly. "And, Tony, you're the bravest person I ever met." He glanced at Beth. "But there's no shame in saying 'enough' if it gets to be too much. No one will blame you."

Beth wanted to scream at Mack for saying such a thing, but she knew he was right, knew it was exactly what Tony needed to hear from his hero. She held her breath, praying he would say more, praying he would tell Tony that that time hadn't yet come.

Mack gave Tony's hand a squeeze and reached up to settle his cap more firmly on his bald head. "But you know what?" he said gently. "I've got to believe that Dr. Beth here knows what she's talking about. It's too soon to give up."

A faint glimmer of hope lit Tony's eyes. "You think so?"

"I really do," Mack said. "I think there's a lot more fight in you, Tony. And I promise you that I'll be right here with you every step of the way. If the day comes when you can't bear one more treatment or one more needle, you say the word. Okay?"

Tony nodded. "And you won't let my mom be too sad?"

Mack cleared his throat, carefully avoiding Beth's gaze. She could tell that he, too, was fighting tears.

"That's the thing about moms," Mack told him. "There's no way to keep them from being sad, but they always, always understand."

Tony struggled up and threw himself into Mack's arms. "I love you," he whispered.

Beth saw Mack's arms tighten around the boy, but his words were muffled when he responded. She didn't have to hear them, though, to know that he'd once more said exactly the right thing.

And in that moment of deepest despair, when her heart was breaking for Tony, she also felt it fill with something else and was finally forced to admit that she was wildly, madly—and totally unexpectedly—in love with Mack Carlton.

Chapter Twelve

Mack left Tony's room half-blinded by tears he was struggling not to shed. Oblivious to everything, he strode down the hall, took the stairs two at a time and left the hospital, needing to escape from the overwhelming emotions, needing fresh air and…hell, he didn't know what else. He'd never felt like this before, completely and utterly helpless. He hated discovering such weakness in himself.

He was also shocked to discover just how cleverly Tony had slipped past all of his defenses. What had begun as a good deed, what had continued as a way to keep seeing Beth, had turned into genuine affection for the boy. No, even more than that, he loved the feisty kid with the smart mouth and the brave heart. And today he'd fully realized for the first time that he actually could lose him.

He was halfway to his car when he finally heard

Beth's cries and realized she'd been chasing after him the whole way. He stood in the parking lot and waited for her to catch up.

"I can't talk about this," he said flatly when she was still several yards away.

His warning apparently fell on deaf ears, because she faced him with a stubborn set to her jaw and compassion in her eyes.

"I know you're upset by what happened in there," she began. "Who wouldn't be?"

"Beth, I told you, I am not discussing it," he said again. He didn't think he could bear it. He didn't want the raw emotions reduced to words, didn't want to hash it all out in a calm, reasonable way. Facts couldn't possibly tell the story. Nothing she said, however hopeful, could give a guaranteed future to Tony.

"Mack, I know you must have a thousand thoughts running through your head about what just happened in there, but you handled it exactly right," she continued, talking right over his objection. "You were wonderful. You were encouraging and reassuring, but you didn't sugarcoat anything. Most important, you didn't dismiss what Tony had to say. It's not easy to hear, but Tony needs someone he can be honest with, someone who won't flinch when he says what he's really feeling. He is so lucky to have you."

Lucky? If she thought Tony was lucky in any way at all, much less just because Mack was around, she was crazy. Tony didn't need Mack. He needed a miracle.

Trying to comprehend where she was coming from, Mack stared at her through his sunglasses. They were hardly necessary with dusk falling, but they were the only shield he had to keep her from seeing the despair

that must be in his eyes. Even so, he could tell that she
understood, that she was desperately trying to reassure
him, when it should have been the other way around.
He should be the one bolstering her up. That conversation couldn't have been easy for her to hear, either.

He drew in a deep breath and forced himself to
speak. "You have no idea what it took for me not to
sit there and curse God and medicine and everything
else right there in front of him," he admitted finally.

"Oh, but I do," Beth said. "Don't you think I feel
like that a hundred times a day, a few thousand times
a year? But I can't focus on what's going on with me.
It's only about the kids and what they're feeling. The
worst thing anyone can do is make them feel even more
isolated by refusing to listen to their fears. Often, their
parents don't want to face the truth, so there's this awful silence that just builds and builds. I think it's worst
of all when that silence is never broken and no one has
ever had the chance to say goodbye."

Mack sighed, recognizing the sorrow and regrets she
must deal with every day. "Do you have any idea how
much admiration and respect I have for you?" he
asked, fighting the desire to reach for her because he
was one more person needing her comfort. He couldn't
be sure how much strength she had to go around, and
it wasn't fair for him to be one of those demanding a
share of that incredible emotional resource. He was
hurting, but the kids and their parents must be in far
worse shape. He needed to let her conserve her strength
for them.

He met her gaze. "It's not just that what you do is
important, it's that you handle it with such grace, the
ups and, more importantly, the downs."

"You haven't been around to count the number of

mugs I go through in a year,'' she told him, her expression rueful. "It's a good thing my office is off the beaten path, since I break so much pottery."

He knew she was trying to lighten the mood, but he felt even sadder at the admission of her lonely battle against desolation. "Does it help?"

"Not a bit."

"Does anything?"

"The success stories," she said at once. "Every tiny victory keeps me going till the next time."

"Tony could use a victory about now," Mack said, unable to keep the wistful note out of his voice.

"He'll have it," Beth said. "I truly believe that, Mack."

"In your heart?" he asked, studying her intently. "Or because it's the only way you can get out of bed in the morning?"

She sighed. "Maybe a little of both." She searched his face. "Is there anything I can do for you? Would you like to come over for dinner? Or we could go to a movie, some action flick that will block out reality for a couple of hours."

Mack shook his head. He could have used the comfort of her presence, maybe even needed it, but that need scared him. Like Beth, he was used to dealing with his emotions on his own. Of course, that usually meant ignoring them, but she didn't need to know that.

Beth nodded, her expression filled with understanding. "Call me if you change your mind."

"Thanks," he said, then bent down to press a soft kiss to her forehead. He had to resist the urge to take more. "Get some sleep tonight. I'll speak to you in the morning."

He knew she was still there, watching him, her eyes

filled with concern, when he pulled out of the parking
lot a few minutes later. He was tempted to go back and
get her. He knew she was hurting as badly as he was.
She was simply more accustomed to covering it.

If he weakened and went back, they could cling to
each other, maybe even feel a little better for it, but in
the end it wouldn't be what either of them really
needed tonight. What they truly needed was some
glimmer of real hope for Tony.

Or the strength to bear it if they lost him.

Beth watched Mack drive off with her heart aching.
She understood his need to go off by himself, but he
looked so unbearably alone. On impulse, she reached
in her pocket and pulled out her cell phone along with
Melanie Carlton's business card.

"Beth!" Melanie said cheerfully when she took the
call. "I hadn't expected to hear from you so soon."

"Actually I called because I need a favor," Beth told
her. She explained what had happened with Tony and
the way it had affected Mack. "Think you could get
Richard to check on him? He said he wanted to be
alone, but I think he could use his brother about now."

"Absolutely," Melanie said without hesitation.
"Can you hold on a sec while I call Richard? Then
you and I can make some plans. Something tells me
you could use a friendly ear, too."

"Thanks," Beth said, grateful for the immediate understanding.

It was only a couple of minutes before Melanie came
back on the line. "That's taken care of," she said
briskly. "Richard's already calling Ben, and then he'll
track Mack down. He won't let Mack put them off."

Beth sighed. "I knew I could count on you."

"Anytime," Melanie assured her. "And since the guys are going to be tied up, why don't you join me for dinner? I imagine that Mack's not the only one who needs cheering up."

The invitation was unexpected and Beth was exhausted, but turning down this chance to get a better sense of the man she'd all but handed her heart to was too good to pass up. Besides, Melanie was exactly right. She was in desperate need of company. Once again she had the sense that Melanie was going to be a good friend.

"Tell me where and when," she said.

"I'll come to you. There's a place in Georgetown Richard and I love." She named a restaurant within a few blocks of Beth's town house. "I could meet you there around six. Would that work?"

"It's perfect."

"And, Beth, just so you know, I won't pry," Melanie said. "Of course, if there's anything you do want to tell me about you and Mack, I'll be happy to listen."

Beth laughed at Melanie's feeble attempt to bank her obvious curiosity. "I'll hold you to that."

"Well, hell," Melanie said. "I'll just have to ply you with alcohol till you forget my promise."

"I knew it wasn't going to last, anyway," Beth told her.

"And yet you've still agreed to meet me," Melanie retorted. "Brave woman."

"Not so brave. Just confident I can handle you. Destiny might be another story."

"Then I won't suggest we include her," Melanie teased. "Besides, just for once, it will feel good to know something that's going on in this family before she does. I swear the woman has eyes and ears everywhere.''

''Speaking of that, remind me to ask you about Pete Forsythe,'' Beth said.

''Oh, that one's so easy, I can tell you right now. You can blame Destiny for that item,'' Melanie said confidently. ''I'd stake my firstborn baby on that—something I don't say lightly in my current condition.''

''Mack was equally sure it was Destiny. We tried to find her today, but she was cleverly absent every place we looked.''

Melanie chuckled. ''I doubt that. I imagine she bribed the help to say she was out. Everyone who works for her adores her. They'll all protect her with their dying breath—even from her own family. I wonder what it's like to instill that kind of loyalty in people.''

''She's obviously a remarkable woman.''

''Remarkable and sneaky,'' Melanie confirmed. ''You're definitely no match for her, especially not when you're in this vulnerable condition. We'll work on toughening you up over dinner. I'll see you soon.''

Feeling better than she had all day, Beth hung up and headed back to Tony's room for one last check. She always liked to make sure that Maria Vitale was there before she left the hospital for the night.

She cracked open the door to the room and saw that Maria and Tony were playing a quiet game of Scrabble. They didn't see her, so she closed the door gently and leaned against it, relieved that she could escape without another harrowing confrontation.

Tomorrow, with all of its uncertainties, would come soon enough.

* * *

The minute he heard from Richard, Mack suspected that Beth was behind it. Richard never called out of the blue to suggest a guys' night out, not since he'd gotten married, and rarely enough before that. As for Ben, it took a crisis of major proportions or a command from Destiny to get him away from the isolated farm in Middleburg where he was living these days.

Because Richard presented the evening's plans as a fait accompli, Mack accepted grudgingly and drove to the crowded chain restaurant that was partway between Alexandria and Middleburg, smack in the middle of what had once been the region's wildly successful high-tech corridor.

"Why are we here?" he asked, wincing at the noise level as he found his older brother at a table in the back. Ben hadn't yet arrived.

"Because Ben wanted Chinese and I figured he deserved some consideration for agreeing to drive in on short notice," Richard explained. "Besides, it's impossible to have a heavy conversation in a place like this. We'll be reduced to idle chitchat." He gave Mack an intense look. "I thought you might prefer that."

Mack nodded. "The more mundane, the better," he agreed, relieved that his brother knew him so well.

"Sure you don't want to tell me what's going on in your life before Ben gets here?"

"Nope," Mack said firmly. "What I want is a drink."

Richard immediately beckoned for their waitress. "Scotch?" he asked Mack.

"A double," Mack confirmed.

When the waitress had gone, Richard opened his mouth, probably to deliver a lecture about the dangers of overindulgence, but Ben arrived just then.

"The things I do for you," he muttered as he sat down. He regarded Mack with the same intense look Richard had given him earlier. "You okay?"

Mack nodded. "And I'll make you a deal. I won't ask a single question about how you're doing if you'll drop all the questions about my life."

"Deal," Ben said at once, clearly eager to forgo an examination of his own recovery from the tragedy that had nearly destroyed him.

Richard shook his head. "I'll bet you Melanie and Beth are spilling their guts to each other by now and here we sit, reduced to talking about what? Football? Political corruption? Terrorism?"

Mack regarded him with shock. "Beth is out with your wife?"

"Oh, yes," Richard said, looking pleased as punch at having been the bearer of that news. "Melanie could hardly wait. She's anticipating great revelations."

Ben grinned at Mack. "You're doomed, bro. Just accept it and start looking at china patterns."

"Bite me," Mack retorted. "Besides, it's not as if she's out with Destiny. That would be terrifying." He suddenly recalled Beth's current anger toward their aunt. "Then again, that little stunt Destiny pulled by planting an item about us with Pete Forsythe got Beth pretty stirred up. I imagine she could more than hold her own with Destiny about now."

"I'd pay to see that," Richard said.

"If the occasion actually arises, I'll get you a seat in the front row," Mack promised him.

He was about to down the rest of his drink when he saw Ben's eyes widen and Richard's mouth drop open. He turned slowly and spotted a very buxom model he'd stopped seeing several months ago heading their way.

Cassandra was gorgeous, scantily clad and brash. She walked up and planted a kiss on him that would have melted his zipper not all that long ago.

"Hey, darlin'," she whispered huskily, ignoring his brothers as if they weren't even there. "I've missed you."

Mack tried to extricate himself from the hand that was sliding directly toward his belt buckle. "Cass, I'd like you to meet my brothers," he said pointedly. "Richard, Ben, this is Cassandra."

She blinked at the distinct lack of welcome in his tone, studied his face for a moment, then turned to his brothers. "Gentlemen, it's nice to meet you." She gave them both a considering look, then shrugged at the lack of response from either one. "See you around, Mack."

A pout on her full lips, she turned and sashayed off, her skimpy skirt barely covering her extraordinary derriere. Richard and Ben stared after her, then turned back to Mack, their eyes filled with amusement.

"It must be hell to be you," Richard said.

"The women, the attention, the media." Ben shook his head pityingly. "A curse. A definite curse."

Mack glowered at them, then lifted his glass. "You know, you two, I could drink at home and get a whole lot less attitude."

"But why would you want to?" Richard asked, grinning. "This way you get brotherly love, Chinese food and an excellent floor show."

"One woman stopping by the table does not constitute a floor show," Mack protested.

"Then how about three?" Ben asked, nodding in the direction of two more women heading their way. "Damn, but this is fun."

Mack scowled fiercely at the women and they turned

away. At least those two were strangers who wouldn't go away pouting, their feelings hurt.

Mack loved his brothers. He even appreciated that this evening was meant to cheer him up, but he'd had all he could take. He should have taken Beth up on her offer of dinner or a movie. Maybe it wasn't too late. Maybe he could get Beth to send Melanie over here to her traitorous husband. Then he could meet Beth at her place.

Great plan, he concluded, but little chance of success. Beth wasn't like him. She wouldn't dump the person she was with to be with someone else. That didn't mean he had to stick around.

He pushed back his chair and stood up. "Guys, I love you both and I appreciate that you came here to cheer me up, but I've gotta go."

"Go where?" Richard demanded.

"Anyplace besides this hotbed of women on the prowl," he said bluntly.

Both men stared at him in shock.

"He really is in love," Ben concluded.

"Seems that way to me," Richard agreed sagely.

"Bite me," Mack said again.

Only when he'd made his escape did he stop long enough to admit to himself that his brothers had gotten it exactly right. He was in love with Beth. He waited after making the admission, expecting real panic to set in, but all he felt was this amazing sense of relief that he'd finally recognized the emotion for what it really was. He grinned as he got behind the wheel.

"Well, I'll be damned," he said as he headed for home. Maybe Destiny had gotten it right after all. But given how irritated he was with her at the moment, it would take a stack of snowballs in hell before he told her that.

Mack was still sound asleep when the phone beside the bed jarred him awake. "Yeah, what?" he growled.

"What on earth were you thinking?" Destiny demanded, snapping him awake with the genuine dismay in her voice.

"What?" he asked, sitting up in bed.

"You haven't seen the morning paper?"

"You woke me out of a sound sleep. What do you think?" he retorted more sharply than he should have. He might be irritated with his aunt, but she didn't deserve rudeness.

"Get your paper and call me back after you've read Pete Forsythe's column," she said, and hung up on him.

Mack stared at the phone, then finally returned it to its cradle. He couldn't recall the last time he'd heard his aunt so furious. Nor could he imagine anything he might have done to set her off.

Yanking on a pair of jeans, he went to the front door and picked up the paper, turning immediately to the gossip column.

"Mack's back!" screamed the headline, as if he'd been recovered from space aliens.

His heart thudding dully he began to read.

"Maybe reports of Mighty Mack Carlton's fascination with a prominent lady doctor were premature," Forsythe had written. "Just last night Mack was spotted by our photographer out on the town with an old flame, supermodel Cassandra Wells."

Mack stared at the photo accompanying the article. Sure enough, there he was with Cassandra draped all over him. The photographer had managed to shoot from an angle that completely blocked out his brothers. He finally understood Destiny's indignation. He was pretty damn livid himself, especially since he knew what had gone on last night...and what hadn't.

He picked up the phone and dialed Destiny. "It's not what it looks like," he said at once.

"They doctored the photo?" she asked in a scathing tone. "Please, Mack, don't even try to suggest such a thing."

"No, but they managed to take the picture or crop it so that Richard and Ben weren't in it," he told her.

She paused then. "Your brothers were there?" she asked in a tone that sounded slightly less irate.

"Yes."

Instead of sounding relieved, Destiny muttered, "I think I'd better speak to both of them about appropriate behavior in a public place."

If she hadn't sounded so serious, Mack might have laughed. "Destiny, I think we're all a little too old for that particular lecture."

"Obviously not," she huffed. "How are you going to explain this to Beth? She must be devastated. You've publicly humiliated her. Just yesterday—"

Mack cut her off. "Destiny, you really don't want to go there. If anyone is responsible for Beth being humiliated, I think we can agree that it's you. Pete Forsythe wouldn't know about her at all, if you hadn't tipped him off."

She sighed heavily. "You're right," she said, giving up the fight gracefully. "It was probably a mistake to try that particular tactic."

"Probably? It *was* a mistake," Mack said emphatically.

"Darling, I'll ask you again, then. Why are you still seeing her? I was so hopeful that it was getting serious and here you are running around with an old flame."

"Didn't you hear a word I just said? I wasn't running around. Cassandra was at my table for less than a minute, long enough to plant that kiss and get her picture snapped. It had nothing to do with Beth," Mack insisted. "Though after this debacle, I'll be lucky if she ever speaks to me again."

"Can I help?"

"No. I think you've done quite enough. I'll handle this."

"Mack, before you see Beth, really think about what you want. It's not fair to lead her on, if you don't intend to truly open your heart and let her in. She'd be better off if you simply let her go now."

"You want me to break up with her?"

"No, of course that's not what I want, but it might be for the best. As for this business last night, I'm sorry if I jumped to the wrong conclusion," Destiny apologized. "It just made me so angry to see you taking up with that little nobody when you could have a woman of substance like Beth in your life. In the end, though, it is your decision."

Mack grinned at the dismissal of Cassandra as a "little nobody." She was on the cover of half the high-fashion magazines in the world.

"I appreciate your concern," Mack told his aunt. "But maybe you should let me handle this from here on out, okay?"

"Whatever you think is best," she said meekly.

"Thank you," Mack said, figuring that submissiveness would last for no more than twenty-four hours. "Love you."

"Love you, too, darling."

As soon as he'd hung up from speaking to Destiny, he called a florist and ordered a dozen white roses to be sent to Beth at the hospital. It might not be much, but as peace offerings went he figured it was a decent start.

Of course, there was always the slim possibility that Beth hadn't even seen this morning's paper and would have no idea why he felt the need to apologize in the first place. In that case, those roses might even buy him enough points to get another night in her bed, rather than the crack of a vase over his head.

Chapter Thirteen

Beth returned to her office from morning rounds to find a huge bouquet of perfect white roses in a crystal vase on her desk and Jason sitting in her chair with his feet propped up and a grim look on his face.

Jason's expression was somber enough, and his mere presence at this hour was sufficient to distract her momentarily from the flowers.

"What's wrong? Nothing's happened to one of the kids, has it? I just finished seeing most of them. Everyone seemed to be stable."

He shook his head. "I'm not here about the kids."

"What then?"

"I think you should sit down."

She lifted a brow and pointedly stared at him. When he didn't get the hint, she told him, "You're in my chair."

He guiltily scrambled up and moved out of her way.

As he settled on the edge of the spare seat next to her desk, he cast a sour look at the flowers.

"Okay, now I'm sitting," Beth said, studying him and trying to make sense of his odd mood. "What's going on, Jason? It's not like you to be so mysterious."

"I think we need to talk about Mack," he said, regarding her seriously.

The announcement was so unexpected, so totally unlike Jason, that Beth merely stared. "You want to talk about Mack?" she repeated slowly. "Is this about those tickets you're so hot to get?"

"Forget about the damn tickets!" he said heatedly. "I think you should stop seeing him."

Beth couldn't have been more surprised if he'd announced a desire to marry her himself. "Why do you suddenly care if I continue to see Mack? In fact, I thought that was exactly what you wanted. The other day you all but begged me not to break up with him, at least not until after football season."

In the way of most males who took a contradictory position five seconds after battling over something, he shrugged. "I changed my mind."

"Are you going to tell me why?"

Like a kid being forced to tattle, he made a face. "Do I have to?"

"Yes, Jason," she said patiently. "If you want me to stop seeing Mack, you need to tell me why. Obviously you have a reason. What's the agenda here?"

"He's no good for you. You're a decent person, Beth. A great person, in fact. He's…" He seemed stuck for a suitable word. "Okay, he's a playboy, a scoundrel and…what's that other word? A rogue. That's what he is, a rogue."

Beth chuckled. "That's hardly news. I thought we

were all well aware of that before he ever set foot in this hospital.''

''I mean he's *still* a playboy,'' Jason said, looking miserable. ''Even though he supposedly has something going on with you.''

Her heartbeat seemed to slow down as Jason's message finally sank in. Mack was still playing around, despite how close she thought they'd gotten, despite the fact that she had feelings for him and he claimed to have feelings for her. In fact, most likely, it was precisely because he was starting to care for her that he'd started running around with another woman... assuming Jason was to be believed.

''And you know this because?'' she asked.

He pulled a folded-up section of the newspaper from his pocket and handed it to her. ''Something tells me this explains the flowers,'' he said quietly.

Beth stared at the photo, apparently taken the night before, when she'd assumed Mack was with his brothers. Apparently, he'd found a far more effective way to cheer himself up. She felt sick inside at the sight of the buxom woman draped all over him.

To cover her reaction, she immediately balled up the paper and tossed it in the trash, then regarded Jason with a bland expression. Pride demanded that she put on a very convincing act, even with this man who was a good friend.

''So?'' she said, managing what she considered to be a respectably nonchalant tone.

''You don't care that he was out with some model?'' Jason asked incredulously.

''He hasn't made any kind of commitment to me,'' she replied reasonably, even though her heart was breaking into little pieces. "Besides, there could be some perfectly innocent explanation."

"Then why send flowers? That's guilt talking, Beth. I know how men think."

She frowned at the bouquet. They *were* tantamount to an admission of some kind, no question about it. If Jason hadn't been here, she might have tossed them across the room just to hear the satisfying crash of that expensive crystal vase. Then again, it might be nice to keep it whole until she could use it on Mack's hard head.

Before she could come up with a less demonstrative response, her cell phone rang. She glanced at the display and immediately recognized Mack's number. Taking the call right now, with Jason watching her worriedly, was not an option.

"Aren't you going to get that?" Jason asked.

"No."

"It's Mack, isn't it?"

She saw little point in denying it. It was obvious if it had been another physician or a parent, she would have taken it at once. "Yes."

"Avoiding him won't help," Jason told her.

"Then what do you suggest?" she asked angrily. "That I take the call and tell him he's low-down, no-good scum, without even giving him a chance to explain? That's about the only thing I could say with you sitting here listening to every word. Anything else and you'd lose respect for me."

Jason looked shocked. "No, I wouldn't. I'm your friend, no matter what you decide to do. I hate this, in fact, because for a few weeks now you've seemed happier than I've ever seen you before. Even though you being with Mack caught me by surprise after the way things went that first day, I wanted it to work out for you.''

Beth managed a shrug. ''Yes, well, we all knew I wasn't exactly Mack's usual type. The fact that we had a few lovely weeks together is probably something of a miracle, but they had to end sooner or later. Unsuitable people are often drawn together during a crisis. It rarely lasts.''

If only she hadn't been so sure that this would last, Beth thought wearily. She'd been so certain—especially after everything Melanie Carlton had said to her the night before—that she and Mack were starting something special.

''Can you really be that calm and accepting about this?'' Jason asked skeptically.

She gave him a tired smile and the only truthful answer she could offer. ''I have to be, don't I?'' Killing the man would be highly unprofessional.

Mack was chomping at the bit with frustration. Beth wasn't taking his calls, which meant she'd seen the photo and that even after getting his peace offering, she was still absolutely livid. He couldn't blame her, but not being able to get away from the office to get over there and talk things out was making him a little crazy. If the attorney and agent seated across from him hadn't been there to finalize terms for a much-needed defensive player for the team, he'd have cut the meeting short and excused himself. Thankfully, they were finally down to the last few sticking points.

He glanced across the table, then looked down at the figures on the paper in front of him. He could probably bargain the numbers down a few thousand here and there, but right at this moment, he didn't care enough to bother.

Looking up, he met the agent's gaze. "Gentlemen, I think we have a deal."

Both men looked momentarily startled, then exuberant.

"Damn, I thought you were going to fight us for every penny," celebrity sports agent Lawrence Miller told him. "Nice to have you on the other side of the table. You bring a pro-player perspective to the negotiations."

"In other words, I let you put the screws to me," Mack said, chuckling. "Don't worry. It won't happen again. Now, if you'll excuse me, I have someplace I need to be."

"A pleasure doing business with you," attorney Jerry Warren said. "You just got yourself one hell of a ballplayer."

"Don't think I don't recognize that," Mack told him. He winked at the agent. "In fact, before you start gloating too badly, you should know I was prepared to offer another million as a signing bonus."

Before they could react, he walked from the room and headed straight for the elevator. It was almost four. If he hurried, he could probably catch up with Beth in Tony's room, where she'd be unlikely to ask for his head on a platter.

Beth glanced up from her examination of Tony's vital signs to see Mack standing in the doorway. Her heart did a little hop, skip and jump, even though she'd been firmly telling herself all day that he'd never really mattered to her.

"You'll have to come back later," she told him stiffly.

"Aw, Dr. Beth, don't send Mack away," Tony protested weakly. "I've been waiting all day for him to get here."

"I'll be right outside," Mack promised. "I'll come in the second Doc gives me the all-clear."

Beth heard the message intended for her, as well. She wasn't going to get rid of him so easily, especially not after ducking his calls all day.

"Oh, come on in," she said grudgingly. "I'm almost finished anyway."

"Are you sure?" Mack asked, studying her intently.

"Sure, why not?" she said, hoping she sounded totally unconcerned about his presence.

The minute he stepped inside, though, her pulse rate escalated predictably. He looked so darn good. He was dressed in one of those light-gray perfectly tailored custom suits of his with a silk-blend shirt with monogrammed cuffs and a tie in a slightly darker tone of the same dusky blue. He was the epitome of the successful businessman with the well-honed body of a trained athlete. She'd never realized before meeting Mack just how incredibly sexy that combination could be. She almost sighed with regret that he was no longer hers.

Not that he'd ever been, she reminded herself sharply. That was something she shouldn't forget. Recent weeks, all that time they'd spent together, had been no more solid than an illusion.

She finished up her quick examination of Tony, made a few notes in his chart and turned to leave. Mack stood directly in her path.

"Did you get the flowers?" he asked.

"You sent flowers to Dr. Beth?" Tony asked, his

eyes bright with excitement. "That is so awesome. How come you didn't tell me, Dr. Beth?"

Mack grinned at him. "Maybe she thought her personal business was none of *your* business," Mack teased.

"Or maybe I didn't think it was any big deal," she said, gazing directly into Mack's eyes.

She saw that he immediately got the message. Guilt and regret darkened his eyes.

"We need to talk," he said in a lowered voice.

"I don't think there's anything left to say," she replied.

"Beth, don't do this," he said with surprising urgency. "You owe me a chance to explain."

She regarded him quizzically. "I *owe* you a chance to explain?"

"Yes. You owe it to both of us. How about if I come over in an hour or so? I'll bring dinner. We can talk privately and get this settled, before the whole ridiculous thing gets out of hand."

Beth wanted to turn him down flat. She wanted to protect what was left of her tattered pride, but fairness dictated that she needed to hear him out, even if she couldn't imagine that he had anything to say worth hearing.

"Forget dinner, but you can come by," she said eventually. "I don't expect it to change anything, though."

"Maybe not, but I have to try." Mack tucked a finger under her chin and met her gaze. "This is important, Beth. Really important."

Her skin tingled at the innocent touch, proving that even as hurt and angry as she was, he still had the power to get to her. She should have told him no, should have protected her heart better. The only problem with that was that it was already way too late.

Mack had been talking nonstop since he walked through the door. Beth had heard every word he said, but she was trying so damn hard to fight the desire to give in and accept his apology. It didn't help that he kept touching her—casual, innocent touches it was impossible to protest but that managed to inflame.

"Is any of this getting through to you?" he asked eventually. "What happened last night was totally innocent. I was not out with Cassandra. She was barely at the table more than a minute, and Ben and Richard were right there. They'll back me up."

"You've explained that," she said, trying not to take too much comfort from it. "But it's going to happen again, Mack. This Cassandra person is just the tip of the iceberg when it comes to your past. I'm not sure I can live with that kind of attention. I don't want to wake up every morning and wonder what I'm going to see in some newspaper gossip column."

He nodded slowly. "I can understand how that would get old," he admitted. "Even if it's not through any wrongdoing on my part." He regarded her with obvious misery. "Maybe Destiny was right."

"About?"

"I spoke to her earlier today after she saw that picture. She was furious. She knew you would be upset. As a result there's been an unexpected shift in her position."

"Regarding?"

"Us."

"What kind of shift?" Beth asked, feeling a faint chill stir inside her. Destiny had been the staunchest supporter of their relationship. Heck, she'd been the primary instigator behind that first meeting. If she'd had second thoughts, then there really was little hope. No one knew Mack better than Destiny did, not even Beth.

"Basically she reminded me that I shouldn't be playing games with you, that you're not like the other women I've dated, all things she'd said before," Mack said. "But this time she seems genuinely concerned that I'm going to break your heart. She doesn't want that to happen. Obviously, she's concluded that I'm a bad risk in the romance department, after all."

Beth's muscles grew even tighter, despite Mack's deft touch. She was less interested in Destiny's concern for her than she was in Mack's intentions now that his aunt had shifted positions on their relationship. She met his gaze directly. "Leaving the incident last night aside, what do you think? Have you been playing games? I thought we'd clarified that, but maybe something's changed."

He abandoned the massage to come around and hunker down in front of her, taking her hands in his, his expression serious. "I honestly don't think so, but I probably need to make my position really clear in case I haven't done that before. I don't do the long haul, Beth. I can't. Not even for you, and, believe me, I am tempted to try."

She fought the dismay that crawled up the back of her throat. "That's hardly a shock," she admitted, forcing out the calm, measured words. "Your track record alone would give anyone that impression, wouldn't it?" She'd been wondering for some time now, though, if impressions were to be believed. Now she had her answer. In Mack's case, they were dead-on accurate.

"It's the truth, not just an impression," he said flatly, confirming her conclusion.

Beth stared straight into his eyes and saw the real torment there. Ironically now, with everything out on the table, she wasn't sure that letting go to avoid more hurt was the right choice for either of them.

"This is all because you lost your parents and you're afraid if you care too much about someone else, you'll lose them, too," she said quietly. "That's why you won't take a chance."

He didn't seem surprised that she'd put the pieces of the puzzle together. He merely nodded.

"I always thought I was immune to whatever damage their deaths had caused, but I guess I'm not," Mack said. "Lord knows, I've always found some reason to move on every time a relationship started to get serious. I thought it was different with you. I know how I feel about you. This morning when I thought I might lose you over that stupid photo in the paper, I panicked, but at the same time I can't see myself taking the next step."

"Meaning what? Marriage?"

He nodded. "My stomach starts churning just hearing you say the word," he admitted. "How can I not consider the probability that it's because of that early loss?"

Beth struggled with the dismay spreading through her, but no one knew better than she did the hole that was left in a heart after losing someone. Hers had healed, but that didn't mean Mack had to recover on the same kind of timetable. At least he was trying desperately to be honest with her. She had to respect him for that.

"Fair enough," she said, making up her mind not to

let this matter. She'd known all along that their match wasn't made in heaven, even though it had begun to feel so right. She'd been taken by surprise from the moment they met. It struck her as a little sad that this was the one time he hadn't surprised her, but rather acted totally predictably—reaching out only to yank his hand back before it could get burned.

"We should stop seeing each other," he said when she remained silent. "Now, before I can hurt you any more than I already have."

"Is that what you want?" she asked dully, her heart in her throat. If it was, she would have to accept it and move on. She had too much pride to do anything less.

"No," he admitted.

Relief nearly overwhelmed her. Sometime soon she would have to examine why that was, but not tonight. Tonight she needed to feel Mack's arms around her again. She needed the connection to him that had made her feel alive these past few weeks. In time she might have to let go but not yet.

"Okay then," she said briskly, to cover her emotional reaction. "Neither do I. And you seem to have forgotten that I've lost someone I loved, too—my brother. I know exactly how devastating and life-altering that experience can be."

"But—"

Beth cut him off. "You've been honest with me, Mack. That's all you owe me. I'm a grown woman. I can decide when the risk is too high. It's not your decision to make, at least not on my behalf, only for yourself."

His expression still troubled, he touched her cheek. "But I couldn't bear it if I hurt you or let you down. You don't deserve that."

"You might do both," she told him, then slid out of the chair to wrap her arms around him and rest her cheek against his. "But not tonight. Not unless you go away without making love to me."

He studied her intently, then a smile tugged at his lips. "Guess there's no chance of that, darlin'. No chance at all."

A few days later Mack sat in his office contemplating the turn of events that had kept Beth in his life. For a few minutes he'd thought it was all over, thought it needed to be over. It had stunned him how much that had dismayed him.

Until Destiny had spilled the beans to Pete Forsythe, Beth had been the first woman that the media hadn't caught on to in Mack's life. Now that the days of being out of the limelight were pretty much over, Mack appreciated them more than ever. It had been surprisingly nice to actually have a private life that was his alone.

At least so far, his warnings to his aunt had kept Beth's identity a secret. He'd thought maybe that photo had been a boon, after all, that it would throw Forsythe off the scent, but he'd been mistaken about that. In fact, according to the indignant call he'd received a half hour ago from Jason, the columnist had been poking around at the hospital this morning.

Fortunately, most of those who knew about the two of them were as interested in protecting Beth as Mack was. Jason had reassured him that he, Peyton and the other doctors and nurses who worked around Tony would never say a word. Tony might happily give away the secret, but so far the hospital public relations department had been dedicated to protecting the identity of the sick child Mack came to visit so regularly.

Yesterday, when a reporter had caught up with Mack outside the hospital, he'd uttered nothing more than "No comment," then hurried inside, beyond the reach of the reporters and photographers who were staking out the public areas outside hoping for details of the secret romance in his life. He knew that the terse reply would only stir curiosity. Until now he'd been well-known for cooperating with the media. Until now he hadn't even viewed them as adversaries, but rather as a condition of celebrity.

Of course, until now, the women he'd been with had sought the spotlight that shone on them because of him. Maybe that's why he felt so completely off-kilter. Beth didn't crave the media attention. She was with him despite it, in fact.

Just as important, his relationship with Beth was his alone, not the media's and not his fans'. He was stunned to discover he could be with a woman out of the spotlight for weeks on end without growing bored or restless. They had an endless supply of things to talk about besides football, and that was a relief, too. His brain was getting a workout keeping up with Beth, and rather than being intimidated by that, he was delighting in it.

He was pondering the meaning of all that when his secretary buzzed him.

"Dr. Browning on line one. She says it's urgent."

Heart pounding, he picked up the phone. "Beth? What is it? Are you okay?"

"It's Tony," she said, her voice oddly cool and detached. "He's taken a turn for the worse."

When? How? Was this it, then, after all that struggle? A million and one questions nagged at him, but he could tell from Beth's tone that now was not the time to ask them.

"I'm on my way," Mack promised, his heart pounding. "Hang in there, sweetheart. And tell Tony to hang on, too."

"Hurry, Mack."

Chapter Fourteen

"Without that donor marrow, he doesn't stand a chance," an unfamiliar doctor was telling Beth when Mack arrived. Peyton and Jason were beside her, their expressions equally bleak. "If we could get that transplant lined up, we could go ahead with the high-dose chemo and prep him. It's our only shot at this point."

"No hits on the donor list?" Beth asked in that same detached tone she'd used on the phone. She could have been talking about someone she'd barely met rather than a boy that Mack knew she loved as much as he did.

Mack studied her worriedly. There was no color in her cheeks, and her eyes were dulled by fatigue and anguish. Her demeanor might be calm and professional, but he didn't think it could possibly be healthy. She had to be as torn up by the news as he was.

Jason caught his eye and gestured for him to join

them. Mack walked up beside Beth, put a reassuring hand on her shoulder and squeezed. She gave him a quick, grateful glance, but her eyes were haunted.

When Beth went back to her consultation with the other doctors, Mack looked down the hall and spotted Maria Vitale outside of Tony's door, her shoulders shaking with silent sobs, her forehead resting against the cool tiles on the wall. He'd never seen anyone look so utterly sad and alone. Because there was nothing he could do here at the moment, he decided to go offer his support to Maria.

He leaned down and whispered to Beth that he was going to speak to Maria. "I'll be right there if you need me."

Again she regarded him with gratitude, but her focus remained with the other doctors.

Reluctantly Mack left her and went to Tony's mother. He spoke softly. "Maria?"

She looked up at him, tears streaming down her face. "Oh, Mack, I'm so glad you're here. I don't think I can bear it. He's giving up. He told me you would understand, that you would make me see that it's time for him to let go, but I can't let him do that. He's my baby. How can I let him go?"

Mack hadn't spent nearly enough time in church, had never had a reason to bargain with God. It had been too late when news of his parents' plane crash had been delivered. Prayers had been useless then. He searched his heart for the right words now, trying to balance comfort against hope.

"Maria, it's out of your hands," he reminded her gently. "Maybe it's always been out of your hands. God has a plan for Tony. He's the only one who'll decide this."

"How could God want my boy?" she demanded angrily, choking back another sob. "Tony is all I have."

Mack was helpless to answer that. "What did Dr. Browning tell you?"

"That without a bone marrow transplant very soon, there is no hope." She gave him an anguished look. "There is no donor. I would give my boy my own life, but they say the match is not good enough. His father…" She gestured dismissively. "He's given Tony nothing, not since the day he was born. I don't even know where he is."

"Are there other family members?"

"None close enough to help," she said bleakly.

Mack finally saw the one thing he could do. He should have thought of it weeks ago, but for some reason it had never struck him that he could help in this way. He gave Maria's hand a squeeze. "Then let me see if I can buy Tony a little hope. Go back in there, Maria. Talk to him. Tell him you love him. Tell him I'll be in soon, too. He needs to know you're there beside him and that there are a lot of people around who care about him."

She nodded and wiped her tears. Her shoulders squared. "I left because I didn't want him to see me crying. He asked me not to cry for him. That's the kind of boy he is, concerned for me and not himself."

"Then, no more tears," Mack said. "Not until all hope is gone."

Maria regarded him with a sad smile. "You've been a good friend, Mack. I will never forget that you've been here for him every day. It has been like the fulfillment of a dream for him. If these are his last days, you've made them happy ones."

Mack shrugged off his effort. "Let me see if I can't do something for him that really matters."

When Maria had stepped back inside the room, Mack ducked in behind her for just a glimpse of Tony. He was paler than ever, his eyes closed. He looked so frail it didn't seem possible that there was even a breath of life left in him. Mack's heart ached, but his resolve strengthened.

Closing the door quietly behind him, he headed for an exit so he could use his cell phone. Maybe it was too late, but he had to do something. This wasn't happening to just any kid. It was happening to Tony, and over the past weeks, Mack had come to love that boy as if he were his own son. He couldn't lose him. It simply wasn't an option.

Mack was suddenly a boy again, listening to a stranger tell him, Richard and Ben that their parents were dead. The housekeeper had stood silently weeping at the stark recitation of the facts about the plane crash in the fog-shrouded mountains. Ben had cried with her, but Richard had stood stoically silent, looking dazed. Mack knew about death, but he'd never experienced its finality. He hadn't really understood what the full implications were at the time. He'd had no idea how horribly alone they were.

Only after the funeral had it begun to sink in that his mother and father would never be there with them again. Only when Destiny had moved into the house, trying in her own unexpected way to make things normal, had he fully grasped that things had changed forever. His aunt was such a dramatic change from their parents, and in some ways a welcome one. She was always laughing, always unpredictable, always ready for a new experience. It had been easier after a while to simply pretend that his world was okay.

But it hadn't been. He could see now that it had never been okay, that the scar from losing his folks ran deep, shaping him in ways he hadn't had to confront until he contemplated losing first Beth over something foolish and now Tony through a ravaging illness. He was terrified right down to his soul that he would never recover from this loss, that he would never dare to risk his heart again.

He wasn't thinking just of himself now, either. He didn't want Maria Vitale to have to face the feelings that had shaped his life. Nor could he handle watching Beth struggle so hard to bear that loss, that stark reminder of another boy—her beloved brother—who had died of the same devastating illness.

Filled with a sense of urgency, he made a mental checklist as he went down the hall. As he passed Beth, she gave him a questioning look. He mouthed that he would be outside, and she nodded. Then she and the other doctors kept on talking, struggling for answers that could buy Tony a few more days, or even a few more hours.

It was a half hour later and Mack was still on the phone when Beth finally broke free and came outside looking for him. He reached for her hand and gave her a tired smile as he wrapped up this one last call. She looked as wiped out as he felt.

"You okay?" she asked when he'd finished and stuck the cell phone back in his pocket.

"How could I be?" he asked, astounded that she had enough strength to worry about him, when she so clearly needed comfort herself.

She raised a hand, rested it against his cheek. "Don't take it so hard, Mack. We knew this could happen."

Her quiet acceptance, her defeatist attitude, grated. "We can't let it happen," he said angrily, shrugging off her touch and her words. "I won't listen to you give up on him."

"Sometimes you do everything you can and it's not enough," she said pragmatically.

"I can't accept that," he stated flatly. "I've made some calls."

"To?"

"The team."

She gave him a bewildered look. "Why?"

"He needs a bone marrow transplant, right? That's his only hope?"

She nodded. "But the chances—"

He cut her off. He wouldn't listen to any more doubts. "I've got just about everyone I know coming in here to be tested as potential donors. Can the lab handle that?"

She stared at him, her expression filled with disbelief and maybe just a tiny hint of hope. "Yes," she said at once. "I'll alert them right away, but are you sure? Did you explain to them that it's not just a simple little blood test?"

"They get it," Mack assured her. "They understand the important part, that it's a chance to save a boy's life." He met her gaze. "You can start right now with me. I should have done it weeks ago. It never even occurred to me that it was the one thing I should do that might really make a difference."

Sudden tears welled up in her eyes. "Oh, Mack."

He squeezed her hand. "Let's get started. That boy has to live, Beth. He has to."

What he couldn't say was how terrified he was of losing not only Tony but Beth. The two were so connected by now, he didn't think he could bear it if he lost either one.

Beth would have sworn that she'd already shed all the tears she possibly could, way back when her brother had died. Since then she'd maintained a stoic kind of calm in the face of each and every loss that had come her way. She might be shaken when she lost a patient, she might feel like a failure, but she never shed a tear. Even today, when she'd been forced to accept that the end was all but inevitable for Tony, her eyes had remained dry.

Now, though, as she watched one brawny football player after another appear to be tested as a prospective bone marrow donor, she kept bursting into tears. Mack had finally gone to the gift shop and brought back the biggest box of tissues the store offered.

She blinked away a fresh batch of tears when she spotted Mack's brother Richard, accompanied by a man who could only be another Carlton, the reclusive artist, Ben. Her eyes grew even mistier when she saw that Destiny was with them.

Mack opened his arms to his aunt. "You didn't have to come. I just wanted you to get in touch with Richard and Ben for me."

"Of course I had to come," Destiny insisted, reaching for Beth's hand and giving it a squeeze. "I intend to be tested, too."

"Destiny, no," Beth protested.

"Why on earth not? Is there some reason I should be disqualified?" Destiny inquired.

"No, but no one would expect you to do this."

"Then isn't it a good thing that I expect it of myself," Destiny said briskly. "Where do we need to go?"

Beth looked up at Mack, expecting him to protest, but he merely gave his aunt another fierce hug.

"Have I ever told you how much I admire you?" he asked her quietly.

"You've never had to say the words," she told him. "None of you have. I know you think I'm impossible sometimes, that I'm annoying, that I'm a romantic meddler, but I also know that you love me."

"This isn't just about loving you," Mack said. "That's a given. Admiration and respect are something you've earned quite aside from that."

"He's right," Ben said. "You're a remarkable woman, Destiny."

"Oh, stop it," she said, clearly flustered. She grabbed one of Beth's tissues and dabbed at her eyes. "See what you've gone and made me do? I'm crying."

"And we know how you hate to spoil your makeup," Richard teased.

"Especially in a place like this," Destiny responded tartly. "With all these handsome doctors around, I want to look my best."

Beth chuckled. "Shall I take you someplace to powder your nose on the way to the lab?" She leaned in to confide, "Peyton Lang is quite something and he's single."

Destiny's eyes immediately brightened. "Really?" She winked at Mack. "See, darling, this isn't nearly the unselfish act you were making it out to be."

"You can't fool me, Destiny," he countered. "This is not about meeting a doctor. You already have half the available men in Washington falling at your feet and you never give most of them a second glance.''

"Politicians and bankers,'' she said dismissively. "There is something so impressive about a man in a white coat, don't you think so?'' she asked, linking her arm through Beth's. "It's reassuring.''

To Beth's amusement, Mack rolled his eyes.

"I think I'll wait here,'' Mack said. "I'm not sure I can bear to watch my aunt in there batting her eyelashes at Peyton.''

"Neither can I,'' Ben said. "I'll wait with Mack till they're ready for me.'' He glanced up at Richard. "And before you say one single word, big brother, no, I'm not trying to back out. I said I'd do this and I will.''

"Never doubted it,'' Richard said. He turned to Mack. "Just in case, be prepared to escort him down there. You know how Ben is about needles.''

Ben feigned a horrified expression. "There are needles involved in this test?''

"Big ones,'' Mack confirmed.

Beth laughed, despite the dire situation that had brought them all here. "Ben, don't let them get to you. Mack's acting all brave and superior now, but even he turned pea-green during the procedure.''

"Oh, that's reassuring,'' Ben said dryly, then squared his shoulders. "Hell, I might as well get this over with. Come on, Beth, lead the way. If a wuss like Mack can do this, then anybody can.''

"Hey, I'll do just about anything for a lollipop and one of Beth's kisses,'' Mack said. "The rest of you will have to content yourselves with the candy.''

Beth grinned at him. "Not necessarily. Right now I'm in the mood to dispense a lot of very grateful kisses.''

Mack shook his head. "Then isn't it a damn good thing that most of the team has come and gone?" he grumbled.

"Jealous, bro?" Ben taunted.

"Damn straight," Mack shot back without hesitation.

Beth's heart filled with unexpected joy. Life was an amazing thing, she concluded. Just when you were very near the depths of despair, it could turn around.

Maybe they would find a match from today's testing or maybe not, but she doubted she would ever forget the astonishing parade of people who had come here at Mack's request. Only an incredible man could garner such an outpouring of generosity with a few phone calls.

Whatever happened with Tony, however heartbreaking the outcome might be, she would always think of this as the precise moment when she'd realized that she could never let Mack go, not without a fight.

After the last of the volunteers had gone, after his family had said goodbye and left for home, Mack paced the halls of the hospital waiting for word on the test results. Surely someone would be a match. Granted, the odds weren't in their favor—Beth and Peyton had made that clear—but Mack couldn't stop himself from hoping and praying that the news would be good.

"You should go home," Beth told him. "It could be a while before we know anything for certain."

"Are you leaving?" he'd asked.

"No."

"Then neither am I. How about some coffee?"

"I don't think I could drink one more cup," she told

him honestly. "I'm jittery enough. But some chocolate would be good. I'll come to the cafeteria with you."

"You need something more substantial than chocolate," Mack coaxed when they were in the cafeteria. "How about a salad? Or some soup?"

"Something tells me you got me down here under false pretenses," she teased with feigned indignation. "You never wanted coffee at all, did you? You wanted to get me to eat."

He shrugged, not even trying to deny it. "It's been a long day and I know you haven't eaten anything."

"I'm used to that," she insisted.

"Well, you shouldn't be," he said, piling food onto a tray as she trailed along beside him. "The pie looks good. What do you think? Blueberry or lemon meringue?"

"Mack, if I eat all that, I'll be up half the night."

"Something tells me we're going to be up half the night anyway," he said, undaunted by her protest. "I'll get both. You can try some of each."

He put both pieces of pie on the already loaded tray, then carried it to the cashier, who beamed at him.

"I heard what you did for that boy today, Mr. Carlton." The woman regarded Beth with a more serious expression. "I hope there's a match, Dr. Browning. If not, maybe there will be one tomorrow."

"Tomorrow?" Beth repeated, looking confused.

"Didn't you see the news tonight?" the cashier asked. "It was all over about how Mack got the whole team over here to be tested. The news guys are challenging the community to come in, too. One of the operators told me the phone lines have been lit up all night with volunteers calling for information. The bone marrow registry is going to be flooded with new people.''

Beth gazed up at Mack, her eyes shimmering with tears. "I had no idea."

"Neither did I," he said honestly. "But that's a good thing, right? There are other people waiting for marrow donors, too, aren't there?"

"Yes."

Suddenly, before he realized what she intended, she stood on tiptoe and kissed him—a hard, breath-stealing kiss that drew cheers from the few people in the cafeteria at that hour.

When she finally released him, Mack regarded her with surprise. "What was that for?"

"For doing something so incredible. I will never complain about all the media that circles around you again."

Mack thought about it and realized that for once his celebrity had been a good thing, giving Tony and maybe even others a fighting chance.

"Neither will I," he said. "Heck, maybe I'll even send a bottle of scotch to Pete Forsythe as a peace offering."

Beth frowned at that. "Don't get *too* carried away."

Mack led the way to a table across the cafeteria, then sat back and watched to make sure that Beth actually ate something, instead of just moving the food around on the plate. She was almost finished with her pie when Peyton walked in, his expression elated.

"We have a match," he called out from halfway across the cafeteria.

The announcement drew cheers. Mack felt his eyes fill with tears and saw that Beth's cheeks were damp, as well.

222   *PRICELESS*

"Who?" she said.

"Me? One of the players?" Mack asked, hoping in a way that he could be the one, not because he wanted credit for the heroics, but because it would give him a permanent link to Tony.

Peyton shook his head, his gaze on Mack. "It's your aunt, Mack. Destiny is the match."

Chapter Fifteen

Mack was still in shock at the unexpected twist fate had taken. Destiny—the woman who had saved him and his brothers from despair after the loss of their parents—was in a position to save another little boy, this time from almost certain death. He should have guessed that his aunt would be the one to keep Tony alive.

He couldn't help worrying, though, whether she was physically up to it. Destiny would laugh in his face at any hint that she was old, and, truthfully, in her early fifties, she was in better health than many women much younger. Still, he was concerned.

"Peyton, are you sure this won't be too much for her?" he asked.

"We'll have to do a more complete assessment, of course, but I see no reason why she won't be able to do this,'' Peyton told him. ''If she's willing, of course. Is there some reason why she might not be?''

''Absolutely not,'' Mack said with total confidence. ''She'll want to go ahead. There's no doubt about that. I just need to be sure there's no risk.''

''Any risk is minimal,'' Peyton reassured him. ''Do you want to call and tell her or should I? We'll have to get her back in here as soon as possible for a complete physical before we can go ahead with Tony's intensive chemotherapy and schedule the transplant.''

''I'll go over there and tell her tonight,'' Mack said. He glanced at Beth. ''Do you want to come? It'll probably take both of us to keep her from running straight back over here the second she hears.''

Beth nodded at once. ''I'm sure we can convince her that tomorrow morning will be soon enough.'' She turned to her colleague. ''What about Mrs. Vitale? Have you told her the good news yet?''

Peyton shook his head. ''I thought you two might want to come along. It's because of you that we have a real hope of saving Tony now.''

''Oh, yes,'' Beth said fervently. ''Mack?''

Suddenly it was all too much. Mack felt this overwhelming desire to shout with joy and at the same time he wanted to cry. He was ecstatic at the promise of a future for Tony, yet fearful for his aunt. ''Maybe you should go without me,'' he said. ''I'm not sure I can hold it together in there.''

Beth reached for his hand. ''You don't have to. This is a miracle, Mack. Even hardened football players are allowed to cry over miracles.''

''Doctors, too,'' Peyton said, his gaze on Beth filled with understanding.

''Later, when Tony is out of the woods. Besides,

I've shed more than my share of tears today,'' she said, avoiding his gaze. ''Now I just want to get on with things.''

Peyton gave her a knowing look that only another physician could fully understand. Mack wasn't entirely sure how to interpret it.

''Is there something you two aren't telling me?'' he asked.

''No,'' Beth assured him at once. ''There's every reason to believe Tony is finally going to turn the corner. The bone marrow transplant should put him into remission, and with luck he'll stay there. He'll be watched closely and given frequent blood tests to make sure his white count stays up, but this is absolutely his best shot at a normal future.''

Mack wasn't sure whether to believe her, but he had little choice. Besides, he'd endured about all the doubts and fears he could handle for one day.

Upstairs, he hung back while Beth and Peyton broke the news to Maria Vitale. When it finally sank in that her son truly had hope, she ran to Mack and clung to him. He hadn't expected the emotional outburst, and once again he found himself fighting tears. After a moment, though, he let them fall unashamedly.

''Maria, don't thank me,'' he pleaded, uncomfortable with the outpouring of gratitude. ''I didn't do anything.''

''You got those people to come here,'' she insisted fiercely. ''And it is your aunt who is the one who will save my boy. With my dying breath, I will thank her and you.''

''The important thing is that now Tony has a fighting chance,'' Mack said. ''I couldn't be happier about that.''

"What will happen now?" Maria asked Beth.

"I think I'll let Dr. Lang explain that to you. Mack and I are going to go to see Destiny and tell her the good news, then prepare her for what happens next."

As they were about to leave, Maria came to Mack and met his gaze. "Please tell her for me that I will ask God to bless her."

"I will, Maria."

Mack was silent on the drive to Destiny's. Beth kept making halfhearted attempts at conversation, but he was too drained to respond until she finally asked, "Mack, are you having second thoughts about this?"

He stared at her in shock. "Why would I have second thoughts? Besides, it's not my call. It's in Destiny's hands now."

"It's just that you're not saying anything. I was afraid you might be worrying that something will happen to her and it will be your fault. No one would blame you for feeling that way. I feel scared every time I recommend a risky treatment to someone, even if it's their only hope. It's a perfectly natural reaction."

"I can't tell you that I'm not concerned, but I don't doubt that it's the right thing to do," Mack said. "If Destiny wants to go ahead, I'm behind her one hundred percent."

"Nothing's going to go wrong," Beth told him.

"Sweetheart, we both know there are no guarantees, but I can't look back. I won't. Tony has to have his chance to live."

Beth tucked her hand in his. "Can I tell you something without you getting all crazy?"

Mack fought a grin. "Try me."

"I love you, Mack. If I hadn't before today, I would now," she said quietly.

Mack wanted to say the words back. They were on the very tip of his tongue, but somehow he couldn't get them out.

Beth met his gaze and smiled. "It's okay. I know."

He studied her face for a minute, then nodded. She did know. That was the remarkable thing about Beth. She seemed to know what was in his heart, even when he couldn't explain it.

One of these days, though, he was going to have to find the words. She deserved to hear them.

And their future depended on them.

"I simply don't understand why there's so much commotion over this," Destiny said when the entire family had gathered for dinner a few nights later. "It's a simple, uncomplicated procedure. That handsome Dr. Lang explained that to all of us at the hospital today."

"It's simple and uncomplicated if you're a doctor who does it routinely," Mack said dryly. "*You've* never done it before."

"Well, fortunately I'll have very experienced doctors doing the hard part," Destiny told him. "Now stop it, all of you. I've made up my mind. If I hadn't before, that visit to Tony today would have clinched it. What an amazing boy he is. I look forward to having him in my life after this."

"I'm glad you're looking ahead," Richard said, "but I don't think any of us could live with ourselves if something happened to you."

"Then we'll make sure that nothing does," Destiny told him firmly. She looked pointedly toward Melanie. "How are you feeling? Any morning sickness?"

Mack sat back and sighed. So did Ben and Richard. It was evident that the topic of the transplant was over and done with for the evening. Destiny had made up her mind days ago as soon as she'd been told that she was a good match. She intended to be at the hospital at 6:00 a.m., no matter what any of them said. The wheels had been put into motion. Tony had received the high-dose chemo and was pronounced ready for the procedure. There would be no turning back now. A part of Mack was relieved, a part of him still terrified.

"I'm feeling fit as a fiddle," Melanie said, going along with Destiny's attempt to change the subject. "Of course, maybe that's because Richard hasn't let me pick up anything heavier than a glass since we got the news."

"Enjoy it while you can," Destiny told her. "Once the baby comes, Richard will fall back into his old workaholic patterns, and you'll be left to fend for yourself."

Destiny pushed aside her plate. "I want you all to know that I appreciate you coming over tonight, but I need to get my beauty sleep if I'm going to be up before dawn. I'll say good-night now. I'll see you at the hospital in the morning."

"I'm staying," Ben said, regarding her defiantly.

"So are we," Richard added.

Destiny returned their stubborn expressions with an impatient look, then finally uttered a sigh of her own. "Whatever makes you happy." She gazed at Mack. "Since I'm going to be so well looked after, why don't you go on over to Beth's? I'm sure she could use some company tonight. I'm still not sure I understand why she turned down my dinner invitation."

"She thought you should concentrate on family tonight," Mack said.

"She's family, too," Destiny replied. "Or she will be if someone we know doesn't blow it."

Mack shook his head. "Stop with the matchmaking, Destiny. It's already worked."

Her expression brightened. "Really?"

"As if you would have allowed it to turn out any other way," Ben remarked.

Mack bent down and kissed his aunt's cheek. "I owe you one."

She grinned at him. "You usually do. Good night, darling. Give Beth my love and tell her I'm counting on her bringing both Tony and me through all of this with flying colors."

"How would you like to have that pressure hanging over you?" Richard commented. "If I were you, I'd keep that to myself, Mack."

"Believe me, I'm not going over to Beth's to lay a guilt trip on her."

"Gee, bro, what are you going over there to do?" Ben inquired.

Destiny frowned at him. "That is none of your business, young man. I thought I raised you better than that."

"Sometimes these wild urges to poke around in Mack's personal life just overtake me," Ben said unrepentantly. "I live vicariously through him."

Destiny gave him a considering look. Mack could almost read her mind. If Ben was looking for vicarious thrills, then maybe, at long last, he was ready for another love affair of his own.

"You've stepped in it now," Mack taunted him. "I predict Destiny will have fixed you up with a nurse before she's out of surgery tomorrow."

Ben shuddered dramatically. "I don't think so," he said. "After all, Mack, she's not quite finished with you yet, is she?"

"You're sure you want to do this?" Beth asked Destiny for the tenth time, still unable to believe that a miracle was so close at hand. She felt compelled to keep asking, even though Destiny was losing patience with her.

"Don't you dare start in on me, too. I got enough of this from my nephews last night. It's not as if there's another option," Destiny said, giving Beth's hand a squeeze. She looked at her nephew. "I've known for months now that our lives were going to be forever intertwined. I think Mack finally understands the significance of that, too, don't you, darling?"

Mack gave her one of his irrepressible grins. "Stop trying to propose for me, Destiny. I'll handle that part myself, and I won't be doing it with you lying here on a hospital bed listening to every word."

Beth's head snapped around to stare at him. "What is she talking about?"

"We'll discuss it a little later," he said. "Let's get Tony well again, okay?"

"Some things are too important to wait," Destiny scolded.

Mack gave her an impatient look, seemed to reach some conclusion, then reached in his pocket. "I suppose I might as well get on with this," he told Beth, looking vaguely apologetic. "She's not going into that operating room until she sees this on your finger."

Beth stared at him, not comprehending the sudden turn the conversation had taken. Or maybe she was just a little terrified that she understood it too well and wasn't ready to hear it.

"Mack, what's going on?" she asked warily.

He looked into her eyes, holding her gaze until the room, Destiny, everything else seemed to fade into the background. It was as if they were completely alone.

"Finding out that we could lose Tony made me realize that life is far too short to waste a single minute on what-ifs," Mack told her quietly. "We don't know what's going to happen next year, next month or even tomorrow."

Beth's heart began to pound erratically. Surely he wasn't really going to do this, not here, not now. A part of her wanted him to get on with it so badly it terrified her. Another part was screaming that she wasn't ready.

"I do know that I want you at my side whatever happens. I love you, Beth. And I always will," Mack said, then waited.

"Well?" Destiny prodded, giving Beth an unsubtle poke. "He's waiting, Beth. Answer the man."

Beth's mouth gaped, her gaze never leaving Mack's face. "You're asking me to marry you?"

Destiny chuckled. "Maybe I'm biased, but I, for one, thought he was pretty clear about that. Don't make him ask twice. He could get cold feet."

"Not a chance," Mack said. "Not when it's this important. I'll ask as often as I have to."

Beth studied Mack intently and saw the certainty in his eyes. Instantly her heart was filled with the same conviction. If he could take this leap of faith, then she certainly could. "Yes," she whispered, choking back tears of joy. She shouldn't feel this happy when so much about this day was filled with uncertainty. "Yes."

"Put the ring on her finger, Mack," Destiny coached.

He gave her an irritated look. "I think I can take it from here. I got her to say yes, didn't I?"

"But time's awasting," Destiny retorted. "They're about to wheel me out of here, and I want this deal closed before I leave."

Mack took Beth's hand in his, then slid the simple diamond on her finger. "Now it's official, Doc."

Beth stared at the ring, then met his gaze. "You never back out of a deal, do you?"

"Never," he said solemnly. "Carltons are men of integrity and honor."

Beth beamed at him. "I think I knew that all along."

"Maybe not all along," Mack reminded her. "But you got the message when it counted." He winked at her. "I think I'll go give Tony the good news before he goes into the operating room. I promised him if you said yes, he could be best man at our wedding."

"You told him about this?" Beth asked incredulously.

"Hey, Destiny might have kicked off this relationship, but Tony was a critical player. He deserved to know it was all paying off."

"You could have told him after surgery," Beth reminded him quietly.

Mack nodded, his expression suddenly sad. "I know, but just in case…"

Beth went to him. "No doubts, Mack. Tony's a fighter. He'll dance at our wedding. I'm counting on it."

Slowly Mack's expression brightened. "Okay, Doc. That's good enough for me."

* * *

It was an eternity before Beth and Peyton finally emerged and pronounced the bone marrow transplant complete. Until then Mack, his brothers and Melanie huddled in the waiting room with Maria Vitale, passing the time with lousy coffee and prayers.

"They're both okay?" Mack asked, his gaze locked with Beth's. If there had been any unexpected twists, he would see it at once in her eyes, but they were clear and filled with an optimistic glint.

"Perfect," she assured him.

"How long will it be before we know if it was a success and that Tony's out of the woods?" he asked her.

"A while," she confessed. "But there's every reason for optimism."

Mack thought about his promise to Tony that he could be best man at their wedding. He pulled Beth aside and regarded her closely. "Do we need to set a wedding date soon?"

She studied him with surprise. "Are you anxious to get married for some reason?"

"You know what I'm asking, Beth."

"And I've told you, we have every reason to be optimistic. I'm not covering anything up, Mack. I swear it."

He nodded slowly and finally allowed himself to feel the first faint stirring of relief. He grinned then. "Maybe we shouldn't put the wedding off, anyway."

"Oh?"

"I'd hate to have you change your mind once the crisis is over."

"No chance of that," she assured him. "If anything, I'm the one who ought to be worried."

Mack pulled her into his arms and held her tight. For

the first time in his life, he genuinely felt complete. "Sweetheart, you have nothing to be worried about. I told you earlier that I've never reneged on a major deal in my life."

"The Carlton integrity," she said.

"That," he agreed, then tilted her chin up until he could look directly into her eyes. "And the fact that this is the most important deal I ever closed."

A smile tugged at her lips. "Better than that defensive player you hired a couple of weeks ago?" she asked.

He stared at her in shock. "You know about that?"

"Hey, I read the sports pages."

Mack laughed. "Since when?"

"Since I fell in love with this celebrity jock, whose name is in there nearly every day. I can't have the entire world knowing more about you than I do."

"Never happen, darlin'. Never happen."

Epilogue

It was the first Friday in October when Dr. Beth Browning married Mighty Mack Carlton before a crowd of dedicated doctors, somber scientists, raucous football players, loving family and still-stunned friends. Outside the church a throng of well-wishers had turned out, tipped off to the occasion by Pete Forsythe's column. Naturally he'd learned all of the supposedly secret details, though for once Destiny claimed total innocence.

Tony Vitale was the best man. His hair had grown back, his skin had a healthy glow and his smile was huge as he waited in front of the altar with Mack by his side.

When Tony whispered something, Mack leaned down to listen, then his gaze shot to the back of the candlelit church where Beth was waiting. A smile spread across his face, as well.

Beth heard the start of the organ music, but before she took her first step, she took a good, long look at her two guys, her heart in her throat. If Tony had a hopeful prognosis for a long and healthy life, it was thanks to Mack, as well as Destiny. This family she was marrying into was a remarkable one.

Destiny sat beside Maria Vitale in the front of the church. The two had become fast friends since the transplant. Destiny was now dedicated to mothering both Maria and Tony to ensure their lives were a bit easier.

Richard and Ben stood next to Mack and Tony, looking handsome in their tuxes, though Ben had a slightly wary expression, as if he were all too aware that his days as a bachelor were likely to be short-lived now that Mack was about to be married.

Only a brief ceremony stood between Beth and the future she'd never anticipated on that long-ago day in the hospital cafeteria when Mack Carlton had walked into her life. A ceremony and a honeymoon, she thought, her blood suddenly humming.

The honeymoon had required a major concession on her part. Because neither of them had wanted to delay getting married until after the official football season ended in January, the honeymoon was built around the team's upcoming road trip, a week in San Francisco, followed by a week in St. Louis. Beth had bought a book on the finer points of football and ten scientific journals to read during the games.

The rest of the time she had other plans for Mack. It hardly mattered what city they were in. She didn't intend to leave the hotel suite until an hour before game time.

She met Mack's gaze and held back a smug grin. Something told her if she played her cards right, they might even miss the kickoff.

*   *   *   *   *

TREASURED

BY
SHERRYL WOODS

Chapter One

It had been one of those Friday-night gallery receptions that made Kathleen Dugan wonder if she'd been wrong not to take a job teaching art in the local school system. Maybe putting finger paints in the hands of five-year-old kids would be more rewarding than trying to introduce the bold, vibrant works of an amazingly talented young artist to people who preferred bland and insipid.

Of course, it hadn't helped that Boris Ostronovich spoke little English and took the temperamental-artist stereotype to new heights. He'd been sulking in a corner for the last two hours, a glass of vodka in one hand and a cigarette in the other. The cigarette had remained unlit only because Kathleen had threatened to close the show if he lit it up in direct defiance of fire codes, no-smoking policies and a whole list of personal objections.

All in all, the evening had pretty much been a disaster. Kathleen was willing to take responsibility for that. She hadn't gauged correctly just how important it was for the artist to mingle and make small talk. She'd thought Boris's work would sell itself. She'd discovered, instead, that people on the fence about a purchase were inclined to pass when they hadn't exchanged so much as a civil word with the artist. In another minute or two, when the few remaining guests had cleared out of her gallery, Kathleen was inclined to join Boris in a good, old-fashioned, well-deserved funk. She might even have a couple of burning shots of straight vodka, assuming there was any left by then.

"Bad night, dear?"

Kathleen turned to find Destiny Carlton regarding her with sympathy. Destiny was not only an artist herself, she was a regular at Kathleen's gallery in historic Old Town Alexandria, Virginia. Kathleen had been trying to wheedle a few of Destiny's more recent paintings from her to sell, but so far Destiny had resisted all of her overtures.

Destiny considered herself a patron of the arts these days, not a painter. She said she merely dabbled on those increasingly rare occasions when she picked up a brush at all. She was adamant that she hadn't done any work worthy of a showing since she'd closed her studio in the south of France over two decades ago.

Despite her disappointment, Kathleen considered Destiny to be a good friend. She could always be counted on to attend a show, if not to buy. And her understanding of the art world and her contacts had proven invaluable time and again as Kathleen worked to get her galley established.

"The worst," Kathleen said, something she would never have admitted to anyone else.

"Don't be discouraged. It happens that way sometimes. Not everyone appreciates genius when they first see it."

Kathleen immediately brightened. "Then it isn't just me? Boris's work really is incredible?"

"Of course," Destiny said with convincing enthusiasm. "It's just not to everyone's taste. He'll find his audience and do rather well, I suspect. In fact, I was speaking to the paper's art critic before he left. I think he plans to write something quite positive. You'll be inundated with sales by this time next week. At the first whiff of a major new discovery, collectors will jump on the bandwagon, including some of those who left here tonight without buying anything."

Kathleen sighed. "Thank you so much for saying that. I thought for a minute I'd completely lost my touch. Tonight was every gallery owner's worst nightmare."

"Only a momentary blip," Destiny assured her. She glanced toward Boris. "How is he taking it?"

"Since he's barely said two words all evening, even before the night was officially declared a disaster, it's hard to tell," Kathleen said. "Either he's pining for his homeland or he had a lousy disposition even before the show. My guess is the latter. Until tonight I had no idea how important the artist's charm could be."

Destiny gave her a consoling look. "In the end it won't matter. In fact, the instant the critics declare Boris a true modern-art genius, all those people he put off tonight will brag to their friends about the night they met the sullen, eccentric artist."

Kathleen gave Destiny a warm hug. "Thank you so much for staying behind to tell me that."

"Actually, I lingered till the others had gone because I wanted a moment alone with you."

"Oh?"

"What are your plans for Thanksgiving, Kathleen? Are you going to Providence to visit your family?"

Kathleen frowned. She'd had a very tense conversation with her wealthy, socialite mother on that very topic earlier in the day, when she'd announced her intention to stay right here in Alexandria. She'd been reminded that all three current generations of Dugans gathered religiously for all major holidays. She'd been told that her absence was an affront to the family, a precursor to the breakdown of tradition. And on and on and on. It had been incredibly tedious and totally expected, which was why she'd put off making the call until this morning. Prudence Dugan was not put off easily, but Kathleen had held her ground for once.

"Actually I'm staying in town," she told Destiny. "I have a lot of work to catch up on. And I don't really want to close the gallery for the holiday weekend. I think business could be brisk on Friday and Saturday."

Destiny beamed at her. "Then I would love it if you would spend Thanksgiving day with my family. We'll all be at Ben's farm. It's lovely in Middleburg this time of year."

Kathleen regarded her friend suspiciously. While they had become rather well acquainted in recent years, this was the first time Destiny had sought to include her in a family gathering.

"Won't I be intruding?" she asked.

"Absolutely not. It will be a very low-key dinner for family and a few close friends. And it will give you a chance to see my nephew's paintings and give me a professional opinion.''

Kathleen's suspicions mounted. She knew for a fact that Destiny's eye for art was every bit as good as her own. She also knew that Ben Carlton considered his painting to be little more than a hobby, something he loved to do. In fact, as far as she knew, he'd never sold his work. She suspected there was a good reason for that, that even he knew it wasn't of the caliber needed to make a splash in the art world.

Every article she'd ever read about the three Carlton men had said very little about the reclusive youngest brother. Ben stayed out of the spotlight, which shone on businessman and politician Richard Carlton and football great Mack Carlton. There were rumors of a tragic love affair that had sent Ben into hiding, but none of those rumors had ever been publicly confirmed. However, *brooding* was the adjective that was most often applied whenever his name was mentioned.

''Is he thinking of selling his works?'' Kathleen asked carefully, trying to figure out just what her friend was up to. Being first in line for a chance to show them would, indeed, be a major coup. There was bound to be a lot of curiosity about the Carlton who chose to stay out of the public eye, whether his paintings were any good or not.

''Heavens, no,'' Destiny said, though there was a hint of dismay in her voice. ''He's very stubborn on that point, but I'd like to persuade him that a talent like his shouldn't be hidden away in that drafty old barn of a studio out there.''

''And you think I might be able to change his mind when *you* haven't succeeded?'' Kathleen asked, her skepticism plain. Destiny had lots of practice wheedling million-dollar donations to her pet charities. Surely she could persuade her own nephew that he was talented.

"Perhaps. At the very least, you'll give him another perspective. He thinks I'm totally biased."

Never able to resist the chance that she might discover an exciting new talent, Kathleen finally nodded. She assured herself it was because she wanted a glimpse of the work, not the mysterious man. "I'd love to come for Thanksgiving. Where and when?"

Destiny beamed at her. "I'll send over directions and the details first thing in the morning." She headed for the door, looking oddly smug. "Oh, and wear that bright red silk tunic of yours, the one you had on at the Carlucci show. You looked stunning that night."

Destiny was gone before Kathleen could think of a response, but the comment had set off alarm bells. Everyone in certain social circles in the Washington Metropolitan region knew about Destiny's matchmaking schemes. While her behind-the-scenes plots had never made their way into the engagement or wedding announcements for Richard or Mack, they were hot gossip among the well-connected. And everyone was waiting to see what she would do to see Ben take the walk down the aisle.

Kathleen stared after her. "Oh, no, you don't," she whispered to Destiny's retreating back. "I am not looking for a husband, especially not some wounded, artistic type."

It was a type she knew all too well. It was the type she'd married, fought with and divorced. And while that had made her eminently qualified to run an art gallery and cope with artistic temperament, it had also strengthened her resolve never, ever, to be swept off her feet by another artist.

Tim Radnor had been kind and sensitive when they'd first met. He'd adored Kathleen, claiming she was his muse. But when his work faltered, she'd discovered that he had a cruel streak. There had been flashes of temper and stormy torrents of hurtful words. He'd never laid a hand on her, but his verbal abuse had been just as intolerable. Her marriage had been over within months. Healing had taken much longer.

As a result of that tumultuous marriage, she could deal with the craziness when it came to business, but not when it affected her heart.

If romance was on Destiny's mind, she was doomed to disappointment, Kathleen thought, already steeling her resolve. Ben Carlton could be the sexiest, most charming and most talented artist on the planet and it wouldn't matter. She would remain immune, because she knew all too well the dark side of an artistic temperament.

Firm words. Powerful resolve. She had 'em both. But just in case, Kathleen gazed skyward. "Help me out here, okay?"

"Is trouble?" a deep male voice asked quizzically.

Kathleen jumped. She'd forgotten all about Boris. Turning, she faced him and forced a smile. "No trouble, Boris. None at all." She would see to it.

Only a faint, pale hint of sunlight streamed across the canvas, but Ben Carlton was hardly aware that night was falling. It was like this when a painting was nearing completion. All he could see was what was in front of his eyes, the layers of color, the image slowly unfolding, capturing a moment in time, an impression he was terrified would be lost if he let it go before the last stroke was done. When natural light faded, he automatically adjusted the artificial light without really thinking about it.

"I should have known," a faintly exasperated female voice said, cutting through the silence.

He blinked at the interruption. No one came to his studio when he was working, not without risking his wrath. It was the one rule in a family that tended to defy rules.

"Go away," he muttered, his own impatience as evident as the annoyance in his aunt's voice.

"I most certainly will not go away," Destiny said. "Have you forgotten what day this is? What time it is?"

He struggled to hold on to the image in his head, but it fluttered like a snapshot caught by a breeze, then vanished. He sighed, then slowly turned to face his aunt.

"It's Thursday," he said to prove that he was not as oblivious as she'd assumed.

Destiny Carlton gave him a look filled with tolerant amusement. "Any particular Thursday?"

Ben dragged a hand through his hair and tried to remember what might be the least bit special about this particular Thursday. He was not the kind of man who paid attention to details, unless they were the sort of details going into one of his paintings. Then he could remember every nuance of light and texture.

"A holiday," she hinted. "One when the entire family gathers together to give thanks, a family that is currently waiting for their host while the turkey gets cold and the rolls burn."

"Aw, hell," he muttered. "I forgot all about Thanksgiving. Everyone's here already?"

"They have been for some time. Your brothers threatened to eat every bite of the holiday feast and leave you nothing, but I convinced them to let me try to drag you away from your painting." She stepped closer and eyed the canvas with a critical eye. "It's amazing, Ben. No one captures the beauty of this part of the world the way you do."

He grinned at the high praise. "Not even you? You taught me everything I know."

"When you were eight, I put a brush in your hand and taught you technique. You have the natural talent. It's extraordinary. I dabbled. You're a genius."

"Oh, please," he said, waving off the praise.

Painting had always given him peace of mind, a sense of control over the chaotic world around him. When his parents had died in a plane crash, he'd needed to find something that made sense, something that wouldn't abandon him. Destiny had bought him his first set of paints, taken him with her to a sidewalk near the family home on a charming, shaded street in Old Town Alexandria and told him to paint what he saw.

That first crude attempt still hung in the old town house where she continued to live alone now that he and his brothers had moved on with their lives. She insisted it was her most prized possession because it showed the promise of what he could become. She'd squirreled away some of Richard's early business plans and Mack's football trophies for the same reason. Destiny could be cool and calculating when necessary, but for the most part she was ruled by sentiment.

Richard had been clever with money and business.

Mack was athletic. Ben had felt neither an interest in
the family company nor in sports. Even when his parents were alive, he'd felt desperately alone, a sensitive
misfit in a family of achievers. The day Destiny had
handed him those paints, his aunt had given him a
sense of pride and purpose. She'd told him that, like
her, he brought another dimension to the well-respected
family name and that he was never to dismiss the importance of what he could do that the others couldn't.
After that, it had been easier to take his brothers' teasing and to dish out a fair amount of his own. He imagined he was going to be in for a ton of it this evening
for missing his own party.

Having the holiday dinner at his place in the country
had been Destiny's idea. Ben didn't entertain. He knew
his way around a kitchen well enough to keep from
starving, but certainly not well enough to foist what he
cooked on to unsuspecting company. Destiny had dismissed every objection and arrived three days ago to
take charge, bringing along the family's longtime
housekeeper to clean and to prepare the meal.

If anyone else had tried taking over his life that way,
Ben would have rebelled, but he owed his aunt too
much. Besides, she understood his need for solitude
better than anyone. Ever since Graciela's death, Ben
had immersed himself in his art. The canvas and paints
didn't make judgments. They didn't place blame. He
could control them, as he couldn't control his own
thoughts or his own sense of guilt over Graciela's accident on that awful night three years ago.

But if Destiny understood all that, she also seemed
to know instinctively when he'd buried himself in his
work for too long. That's when she'd dream up some
excuse to take him away from his studio and draw him

back into the real world. Tonight's holiday celebration was meant to be one of those occasions. Her one slipup had been not reminding him this morning that today was the day company was coming.

"Give me ten minutes," he told her now. "I'll clean up."

"Too late for that. Melanie is pregnant and starving. She'll eat the flower arrangement if we don't offer an alternative soon. Besides, the company is beginning to wonder if we've just taken over some stranger's house. They need to meet you. You'll make up in charm what you lack in sartorial splendor."

"I have paint on my clothes," he protested, then gave her a hard look as what she'd said finally sank in. "Company? You mean besides Richard and Mack and their wives? Did you say anything about company when you badgered me into having Thanksgiving here?"

"I'm sure I did," she said blithely.

She hadn't, and they both knew it, which meant she was scheming about something more than relieving his solitude. When they reached the house, Ben immediately understood what she was up to.

"And, darling, this is Kathleen Dugan," Destiny said, after introducing several other strangers who were part of the rag-tag group of people Destiny had collected because she knew they had no place else to spend the holiday. There was little question, judging from her tone, that this Kathleen was the pièce de résistance.

He gave his aunt a sharp look. Kathleen was young, beautiful and here alone, which suggested she was available. He'd known for some time now—since Mack's recent wedding, in fact—that Destiny had targeted him for her next matchmaking scheme. Here was his proof—a woman with a fringe of black hair in a pixie cut that emphasized her cheekbones and her amazing violet eyes. There wasn't an artist on earth who wouldn't want to capture that interesting, angular face on canvas. Not that Ben ever did portraits, but even he was tempted to break his hard-and-fast rule. She was stunning in a red silk tunic that skimmed over a slender figure. She wore it over black pants and accented it with a necklace of chunky beads in gold and red. The look was elegant and just a touch avant-garde.

"Lovely to meet you," Kathleen said with a soft smile that showed no hint of the awkwardness Ben was feeling. Clearly she hadn't caught on to the scheme yet.

Ben nodded. He politely shook her hand, felt a startling jolt of awareness, then took another look into her eyes to see if she'd felt the same little *zing*. She showed no evidence of it, thank heavens.

"If you'll excuse my totally inappropriate attire," Ben said, quickly turning away from her and addressing the others, "I gather dinner is ready to be served."

"We've time for another drink," Destiny insisted, apparently no longer worried about the delayed meal. "Richard, bring your brother something. He can spend at least a few minutes socializing before we sit down to eat."

Ben frowned at her. "I thought we were in a rush."

"Only to drag you in here," his very pregnant sister-in-law said as she came and linked an arm through his, drawing him out of the spotlight, even as she whispered conspiratorially, "Don't you know that you're the main attraction?"

He gave Melanie a sharp look. They'd formed a bond back when Richard had been fighting his attraction to her. Ben trusted her instincts. He wanted to hear her take on this gathering. "Oh?"

"You never come out of this lair of yours," Melanie explained. "When Destiny invited us here, we figured something was up."

"Oh?" he said again, waiting to see if she'd drawn the same conclusion about Kathleen's presence here that he had. "Such as?"

Melanie studied him intently. "You really don't know what Destiny is up to? You're as much in the dark as the rest of us?"

Ben glanced toward Kathleen, then. "Not as much as you might think," he said with a faint scowl.

Melanie gave the newcomer a knowing look. "Ah, so that's it. I wondered when Kathleen arrived if she was the chosen one. I figured it was going to be your turn soon. Destiny won't be entirely happy until all of her men are settled."

"I hope you're wrong about that," Ben said darkly. "I'd hate to disappoint her, but I am settled."

Richard overheard him and chuckled. "Oh, bro, if that's what you think, you're delusional." He, too, glanced toward Kathleen, whose head was tilted as she listened intently to something Destiny was saying. "I give you till May."

"June," Mack chimed in. "Destiny's been moping because none of us had a traditional June wedding. You're all she's got left, little brother. She won't allow you to let her down. I caught her out in the garden earlier. I think she was mentally seating the guests and envisioning the perfect area for the reception."

Ben shuddered. Richard and Mack had once been as fiercely adamant about not getting married as he was. Look at the two of them now. Richard even had a baby on the way, and Mack and Beth were talking about adopting one of the sick kids she worked with at the hospital. Maybe more. To his astonishment, those two seemed destined for a houseful. By this time next year, there would be the cries of children filling this house and any other place the Carlton family gathered. No one needed him adding to the clutter. He doubted Destiny saw it that way, though.

There were very few things that Ben wouldn't do for his aunt. Getting married was one of them. He liked his solitude. After the chaotic upheaval of his early years, he counted on the predictability of his quiet life in the country. Graciela had given him a reprieve from that, but then she, too, had died, and it had reinforced his commitment to go through life with his heart under the tightest possible wraps. Those who wrote that he was prone to dark moods and eccentricities had gotten it exactly right. There would be no more nicks in his armor, no more devastating pain to endure.

His resolve steady and sure, he risked another look at Kathleen Dugan, then belatedly saw the smug expression on his aunt's face when she caught him.

Ben sighed, then stood a little straighter, stiffening his spine, giving Destiny a daunting look. She didn't bat so much as an eyelash. That was the trouble with his aunt. She rarely took no for an answer. She was persuasive and sneaky. If he didn't take a firm stand right here, right now, he was doomed.

Unfortunately, though, he couldn't think of a single way to make his position clear over turkey and dressing.

He could always say, "So glad you could come, Kathleen, but don't get any ideas."

Or, "Delighted to meet you, Ms. Dugan, but ignore

every word out of my aunt's mouth. She's devious and clever and not to be trusted.''

Or maybe he should simply say nothing at all, just ignore the woman and avoid his aunt. If he could endure the next couple of hours, they'd all be gone and that would be that. He could bar the gates and go back into seclusion.

Perfect, he concluded. That was definitely the way to go. No overt rudeness that would come back to haunt him. No throwing down of the gauntlet. Just passive acceptance of Kathleen's presence here tonight.

Satisfied with that solution, he turned his attention to the drink Richard had thrust in his hand. A sniff reassured him it was nonalcoholic. He hadn't touched a drop of anything stronger than beer since the night of Graciela's accident.

''Darling,'' Destiny said, her gaze on him as she crossed the room, Kathleen at her side. ''Did I mention earlier that Kathleen owns an art gallery?''

Next to him Melanie choked back a laugh. Richard and Mack smirked. Ben wanted nothing more than to pummel his brothers for getting so much enjoyment out of his discomfort at his aunt's obvious ploy. Kathleen was her handpicked choice for him, all right. There was no longer any question about that.

''Really?'' he said tightly.

''She has the most amazing work on display there now,'' Destiny continued blithely. ''You should stop by and take a look.''

Ben cast a helpless look in Kathleen's direction. She now looked every bit as uncomfortable as he felt. ''Maybe I will one of these days.'' When hell freezes over, he thought even as he muttered the polite words.

"I'd love to have your opinion," Kathleen said gamely.

"My opinion's not worth much," Ben said. "Destiny's the family expert."

Kathleen held his gaze. "But most artists have an eye for recognizing talent," she argued.

Ben barely contained a sigh. Surely Kathleen was smart enough not to fall into his aunt's trap. He wanted to warn her to run for her life, to skip the turkey, the dressing and the pumpkin pie and head back to Alexandria as quickly as possible and bar the door of her gallery from anyone named Carlton. He was tempted to point to Melanie and Beth and explain how they'd unwittingly fallen in with his aunt's schemes, but he doubted his sisters-in-law would appreciate the suggestion that their marriages were anything other than heaven-sent. They both seemed to have revised history to their liking after the wedding ceremonies.

Instead he merely said, "I'm not an artist."

"Of course you are," Destiny declared indignantly. "An exceptionally talented one at that. Why would you say such a thing, Ben?"

To get out of being drawn any further into this web, he very nearly shouted. He looked his aunt in the eye. "Are you an artist?"

"Not anymore," she said at once.

"Because you no longer paint?" he pressed.

Destiny frowned at him. "I still dabble."

"Then it must be because you don't show or sell your work," he said. "Is that why you're no longer an artist?"

"Yes," she said at once. "That's it exactly."

He gave Destiny a triumphant look. "Neither do I. No shows. No sales. I dabble." He found himself winking at Kathleen. "I guess we can forget about me offering a professional opinion on your current show."

A grin tugged at the corners of Kathleen's mouth. "Clever," she praised.

"Too clever for his own good," Destiny muttered.

"Uh-oh," Mack murmured, grinning broadly. "You've done it now, Ben. Destiny's on the warpath. You're doomed."

Funny, Ben thought, glancing around the room at the sea of amused expressions, that was the same conclusion he'd reached about an hour ago. He should have quit back then and saved himself the aggravation.

Chapter Two

Kathleen felt as if the undercurrents swirling around Ben Carlton's living room were about to drag her under. Every single suspicion she'd had about the real reason she'd been invited tonight was being confirmed with every subtle dig, every dark look between Ben and his aunt. Even his brothers and sisters-in-law seemed to be in on the game and were enjoying it thoroughly. In fact, she was the only one who didn't seem to get the rules. If she could have fled without appearing unbearably rude, she might have.

"Would you like to freshen up before dinner?" Beth Carlton asked, regarding her with sympathy.

If it meant escaping from this room, Kathleen would have agreed to join a trek across the still-green fields of winter wheat that stretched as far as the eye could see.

"Yes, please," she said gratefully.

"I'll show you where the powder room is," Beth said.

The minute they were out of earshot of the others, Beth gave her a warm smile. "Feel as if you're caught in an intricate web you didn't even realize was being spun?"

Kathleen nodded. "Worse, I have no idea how I got there. Am I some sort of sacrificial lamb?"

"Pretty much," Beth said. "Believe me, Melanie and I know exactly how you feel. We've been there. We were tangled up with Carlton men before we knew it."

"I don't suppose there's a way out?" Kathleen asked.

"Obviously neither of us found one," Beth said cheerfully. "Maybe you'll be the exception. Right now she's batting two for two, but Destiny's track record is bound to falter sooner or later."

Kathleen studied the pediatric oncologist who'd married Mack. Beth Carlton struck her as quiet, intelligent and lovely in an understated way, very much the opposite of Kathleen's eccentricity and flamboyance. It was hard to imagine that the same woman would have chosen them as potential marriage material for beloved nephews. Then, again, Ben was a far cry from his more outgoing, athletic brother. Destiny obviously knew her nephews well. As Beth had just noted, her knack for choosing the right women was outstanding.

"Then I'm not crazy," Kathleen ventured carefully. "Destiny is plotting to set me up with Ben? She didn't get me out here just to look at his art?"

Beth's grin spread. "Have you actually seen a single canvas since you arrived?"

"No."

"Were you asked to tag along when Destiny went to fetch Ben from his studio?"

"No."

Beth took a little bow, her expression amused. "I rest my case."

"But why me?" Kathleen couldn't keep the plaintive note out of her voice.

"Believe me, I asked the same thing when I realized what Destiny was up to with me and Mack. He was a professional football player, for heaven's sakes, and I'd never even watched a game. At least you and Ben have art in common. On the surface you're a much better match than Mack and I were."

"But Destiny got it right with the two of you, didn't she?" Kathleen concluded.

"Exactly right," Beth admitted happily. "She was absolutely on target with Richard and Melanie, too, though they fought it just as hard as Mack and I did. My advice is to go with the flow and see what happens. Assuming you ever want to get married, maybe having a woman with Destiny's intuition in your corner is not all bad."

"But I'm not looking for a husband," Kathleen protested. "Especially not an artist. I was married to one once. It did not turn out well."

Beth's expression turned thoughtful. "Does Destiny know about that?"

Kathleen shook her head. "I doubt it. I don't talk about it, and I took back my maiden name after the divorce."

"Let me think about this a minute," Beth said, then gestured toward a door. "The powder room's in there. I'll wait right here to show you the way to the dining room."

When Kathleen emerged a few minutes later, she found Beth and Melanie huddled together. They glanced up and beamed at her.

"So, here's the way we see it," Beth said. "Either Destiny knows about your past and figures that will make you a real challenge for Ben."

"Or she's made a serious miscalculation," Melanie said, grinning. "I like that one. Just once I'd like to see her get it wrong. No offense."

"None taken," Kathleen said, liking these two women immensely. She had a feeling their advice was going to be invaluable if she was to evade Destiny Carlton's snare. With any luck Ben would be equally appalled by this scheme, and the whole crazy thing would die for lack of participation by either one of them. He certainly hadn't looked especially happy earlier.

"We'd better go in to dinner before Destiny comes looking for us," Beth said, casting a worried look in the direction of the living room. "Destiny's allowed her conspiracies. Ours make her nervous."

"Why is that?" Kathleen asked.

"Because we're on to her," Melanie explained. "She was terrified I'd warn Beth away. Now she's equally worried that we might gang up and help you escape her clutches. I think she anticipates that the day will come when we'll get even with her, even though we're happy about the outcome of her machinations." She gave Kathleen the same sort of sympathetic look Beth had given her earlier. "We will, you know. If you need backup, just holler. We love Ben and we want to see him happy, but we also feel a certain amount of loyalty to any woman caught up in one of Destiny's matchmaking plots. It's a sisterhood thing."

Kathleen listened to the offer with amusement. Now that she'd been forewarned about the lengths to which Destiny might go, she felt much more confident that she was prepared to deal with her. "Don't worry. I think I can handle Destiny."

The declaration drew hoots of laughter. Despite her confidence in her own willpower and strength, that laughter gave Kathleen pause. That was the voice of experience responding. Two voices, in fact.

"Maybe I'd better get your phone numbers, just in case," she said as they walked toward the dining room where the other guests had now assembled.

In the doorway, Destiny gave them all a sharp look, then beamed at Kathleen. "Come, dear, I've seated you next to Ben."

Of course she had, Kathleen thought, fighting a renewed surge of panic. She avoided glancing at Melanie or Beth, afraid of the justifiable amusement she'd likely find in their eyes now. Instead she cast a look in Ben's direction, wondering what he thought of his aunt's blatant machinations. He had to find them as disquieting as she did.

Oddly enough, she thought he looked surprisingly relaxed. Maybe he was confident of his own ability to resist whatever trap Destiny was setting. Or maybe he hadn't figured out what she was up to. Doubtful, though, if he'd watched his brothers get snared one by one.

Kathleen took a closer look. He was every bit as handsome as she'd expected after seeing his brothers' pictures in the gossip columns of the local papers. There was no mistaking the fact that he was an artist, though. There were paint daubs in a variety of colors on his old jeans, a streak of vermilion on his cheek.

Kathleen couldn't help feeling a faint flicker of admiration for a man who could be so totally unselfconscious showing up at his own dinner party at less than his best.

What a contrast that was to her own insecurities. She'd spent her entire life trying to put her best foot forward, trying to impress, trying to overcome an upbringing that had been financially privileged but beyond that had had very little to redeem it. She'd spent a lifetime hiding secrets and shame, acceding to her mother's pleas not to rock the family boat. Art had brought beauty into her life, and she admired and respected those who could create it.

As she stepped into the dining room, her gaze shifted from Ben to the magnificent painting above the mantel. At the sight of it, she came to a sudden stop. All thoughts of Ben Carlton, Destiny's scheming and her own past flew out of her head. Her breath caught in her throat.

"Oh, my," she whispered.

The artist had captured the fall scene with both a brilliant use of color and a delicate touch that made it seem almost dreamlike, the way it might look in the mind's eye when remembered weeks or months later, too perfect to be real. There was a lone deer at the edge of a brook, traces of snow on the ground with leaves of gold, red and burnished bronze falling along with the last faint snowflakes. The deer was staring straight out of the painting, as if looking directly at the artist, but its keen eyes were serene and unafraid. Kathleen imagined it had been exactly like that when the artist had come upon the scene, then made himself a part of it in a way that protected and preserved the moment.

Destiny caught her rapt gaze. "One of Ben's. He

hated it when I insisted he hang it in here where his guests could enjoy it.''

''But it's spectacular,'' Kathleen said, dismayed that it might have been hidden away if not for Destiny's insistence. Work this amazing did belong in a gallery. ''I feel as if I looked out a window and saw exactly that scene.''

Destiny smiled, her expression smug. ''I just knew you would react that way. Tell my nephew that, please. He might actually believe it if it comes from you. He dismisses whatever I say. He's convinced I'm biased about his talent.''

Excitement rippled through Kathleen. Destiny hadn't been exaggerating about her nephew's extraordinary gift. ''There are more like this?'' she asked, knowing the answer but hardly daring to hope that this was the rule, rather than the exception.

''His studio is packed to the rafters,'' Destiny revealed. ''He's given a few to family and friends when we've begged, but for the most part, this is something he does strictly for himself.''

''I could make him rich,'' Kathleen said with certainty, eager to fight to do just that. She was well-known for overcoming objections, for persuading tight-fisted people to part with their money, and difficult artists to agree to showings in her small but prestigious gallery. All of Destiny's scheming meant nothing now. All that mattered was the art.

Destiny squeezed her hand. ''Ben is rich. You'll have to find some other lure, if you hope to do a showing.''

''Fame?'' What painter didn't secretly yearn to be this generation's Renoir or Picasso? Disclaimers aside, surely Ben had an artist's ego.

Destiny shook her head. "He thinks Richard and Mack have all the limelight that the Carlton family needs."

Frustration burned inside Kathleen. What else could she come up with that might appeal to a reclusive artist who had no need for money or fame?

She drew her gaze from the incredible painting and turned to the woman who knew Ben best. "Any ideas?" she asked Destiny.

The older woman patted her hand and gave her a serene, knowing look. "I'm sure you'll think of something if you put your mind to it."

Even though she'd suspected the plot all along, even though Melanie and Beth had all but confirmed it, Kathleen was taken aback by the determined glint in Destiny's eyes. In Destiny's mind the art and the man were intertwined. Any desire for one was bound to tie Kathleen to the other. It was a diabolical scheme.

Kathleen looked from the painting to Ben Carlton. She would gladly sell her soul to the devil for a chance to represent such incredible art. But if she was understanding Destiny's sly hint correctly, it wasn't her soul she was expected to sell.

One more glance at Ben, one more little frisson of awareness and she couldn't help thinking it might not be such a bad bargain.

Ben watched warily as his aunt guided Kathleen into the dining room. He saw the way the younger woman came to a sudden halt when she saw his painting, and despite his claim that he painted only for himself, his breath snagged in his throat as he tried to gauge her reaction. She seemed impressed, but without being able to hear what she said, he couldn't be sure. It irked him that he cared.

"You're amazingly talented," Kathleen said the instant she'd taken her seat beside him.

Relief washed over him. Because that annoyed him, too, he merely shrugged. "Thanks. That's Destiny's favorite."

"She has a good eye."

"Have you ever seen *her* work?"

"A few pieces," Kathleen said. "She won't let me sell them for her, though." She met his gaze. "Modesty must run in the family."

"I'm not modest," Ben assured her. "I'm just not interested in turning this into a career."

"Why not?"

His gaze challenged her. "Why should I? I don't need the money."

"Critical acclaim?"

"Not interested."

"Really?" she asked skeptically. "Or are you afraid your work won't measure up?"

He frowned at that. "Measure up to what? Some other artist's? Some artificial standard for technique or style or commercial success?"

"All of that," she said at once.

"None of it matters to me."

"Then why do you paint?"

"Because I enjoy it."

She stared at him in disbelief. "And that's enough?"

He grinned at her astonishment. "Isn't there anything you do, Ms. Dugan, just for the fun of it?"

"Of course," she said heatedly. "But you're wasting your talent, hiding it away from others who could take pleasure in seeing it or owning it."

He was astounded by the assessment. "You think I'm being selfish?"

"Absolutely."

Ben looked into her flashing violet eyes, and for an instant he lost his train of thought, lost his desire to argue with her. If they'd been alone, he might have been tempted to sweep her into his arms and kiss her until she forgot all about this silly debate over whether art was important if it wasn't on display for the masses.

"What are you passionate about?" he asked instead, clearly startling her.

"Art," she said at once.

"Nothing else?"

She flushed at the question. "Not really."

"Too bad. Don't you think that's taking a rather limited view of the world?"

"That from a man who's known far and wide as a recluse?" she retorted wryly.

Ben chuckled. "But a *passionate* recluse," he told her. "I love nature. I care about my family. I feel strongly about what I paint." He shot a look toward Richard. "I'm even starting to care just a little about politics." He turned toward Mack. "Not so much about football, though."

"Only because you could never catch a pass if your life had depended on it," Mack retorted amiably. He grinned at Kathleen. "He was afraid of breaking his fingers and not being able to hold a paint brush again."

"Then, even as a boy you loved painting?" Kathleen said. "It's always mattered to you?"

"It's what I enjoy doing," Ben confirmed. "It's not who I am."

"No ambition at all?"

He shook his head. "Sorry. None. Richard and Mack have more than enough for one family."

Kathleen set down her fork and regarded him with consternation. "How do you define yourself, if not as an artist?"

"A *reclusive* artist," Ben corrected, quoting the usual media description. "Why do I need to pin a label on myself?"

She seemed taken aback by that. "I don't suppose you do."

"How do you define who you are?" he asked.

"I own an art gallery. A very prestigious art gallery, in fact," she said with pride.

Ben studied her intently. He wondered if she had any idea how telling it was that she saw herself only in terms of what she did, not as a woman with any sort of hopes and dreams. A part of him wanted to unravel that particular puzzle and discover what had made her choose ambition over any sort of personal connection.

Because right here and now, surrounded by people absorbed in their own conversations, it was safe enough to ask, he gazed into her amazing eyes. "No man in your life?"

A shadow flitted across her face. "None."

"Why is that?"

Eyes flashing, she met his gaze. "Is there a woman in yours?"

Ben laughed. "Touché."

"Which isn't an answer, is it?"

"No, there is no woman in my life," he said, waiting for the twinge of guilt that usually accompanied that admission.

"Why not?" she asked, proving she was better at the game than he was.

"Because the only one who ever mattered died," he said quietly.

Sympathy immediately filled her eyes. "I'm sorry. I didn't know."

"I'm surprised Destiny didn't fill you in," he said, glancing in his aunt's direction. Though Destiny was engaged in conversation with Richard, it was obvious she was keeping one ear attuned to what was going on between him and Kathleen. She gave him a quizzical look.

"Nothing," Ben said for her benefit. He almost regretted letting the conversation veer away from the safe topic of art. But since Kathleen had sidestepped his question as neatly as he'd initially avoided hers, he went back to it. "Why is there no special man in your life?"

"I was married once. It didn't work out."

There was a story there. He could see it in her face, hear it in the sudden tension in her voice. "Was it so awful you decided never to try it again?"

"Worse," she said succinctly. She met his gaze. "We were doing better when we were sticking to art."

Ben laughed. "Yes, we were, weren't we? I was just thinking the same thing, though I imagine there are those who think all the small talk is just avoidance."

"Avoidance?"

"Two people dancing around what really matters."

Kathleen flushed. "I'm perfectly willing to avoid delving into my personal life. How about you?"

"Suits me," he said easily, though a part of him was filled with regret. "Want to debate about the talent of the Impressionists versus the Modernists?"

She frowned. "Not especially."

"Know anything about politics?"

"Not much."

"Environmental issues?"

"I think global warming is a real risk," she said at once.

"Good for you. Anything else?"

She held up a forkful of turkey. "The food's delicious."

"I was thinking more in terms of another environmental issue," he teased.

"Sorry. You're fresh out of luck. I could argue the merits of free-range turkey over the frozen kind," she suggested cheerfully. "Everyone says free-range is healthier, but they're just as dead, so how healthy is that?"

Ben chuckled. "Now there's a hot-button topic, if ever I heard one."

"You don't have to be sarcastic," she said. "I told you I have a one-track mind."

"And it's totally focused on art," Ben said. "I think I get that." He studied her thoughtfully. "This man you were married to, was he an artist?"

She stiffened visibly. "As a matter of fact, he was."

Ben should have taken comfort in that. If an artist had hurt Kathleen so badly that she wasn't the least bit interested in marriage, then he should be safe enough from all of Destiny's clever machinations. She'd miscalculated this time. Oddly, though, he didn't feel nearly as relieved as he should. In fact, he felt a powerful urge to go find this man who'd hurt Kathleen and wring his neck.

"People get over bad marriages and move on," he told her quietly.

"Have you gotten over losing the woman you loved?"

"No, but it's different."

"Different how?"

Ben hesitated. They were about to enter into an area he never discussed, not with anyone. Somehow, though, he felt compelled to tell Kathleen the truth. "I blame myself for her death," he said.

Kathleen looked momentarily startled by the admission. "Did you cause her death?"

He smiled sadly at the sudden hint of caution in her voice. "Not the way you mean, no, but I was responsible just the same."

"How?"

"We argued. She was drunk and I let her leave. She ran her car into a tree and died." He recited the bare facts without emotion, watching Kathleen's face. She didn't flinch. She didn't look shocked or horrified. Rather she looked indignant.

"You can't blame yourself for that," she said fiercely. "She was an adult. She should have known better than to get behind the wheel when she was upset and drunk."

"People who are drunk are not known for their logic. I could have stopped her. I *should* have," Ben countered as he had to every other person who'd tried to let him off the hook.

"Really? How? By taking away the car keys?"

"That would have done it," he said bleakly, thinking how simple it would have been to prevent the tragedy that had shaped the last three years of his adult life.

"Or she would have waited a bit, then found your keys and taken your car," Kathleen countered.

"It might have slowed her down, though, given her time to think."

"As you said yourself, it doesn't sound to me as if she was thinking all that rationally."

Ben sighed. No, Graciela hadn't been thinking rationally, but neither had he. He'd known her state of mind was irrational that night, that she was feeling defensive and cornered at having been caught with her lover. He'd told her to get out anyway. Not only hadn't he taken those car keys from her, he'd all but tossed her out the door and put her behind the wheel.

"It hardly matters now," he said at last. "I can't change that night."

Kathleen looked directly into his eyes. "No," she said softly. "You can't. The only thing you can do— the thing you *must* do—is put it behind you."

Ben wanted desperately to accept that, to let go of the past as his entire family had urged him to do, but blaming himself was too ingrained. Absolution from a woman he'd known a few hours counted for nothing.

He forced his gaze away from Kathleen and saw Destiny and his brothers watching him intently, as if they'd sensed or even heard what Ben and Kathleen had been discussing and were awaiting either an explosion or a sudden epiphany. He gave them neither.

Instead, he lifted his glass of water. "To good company and wonderful food. Thanks, Destiny."

"To Destiny," the others echoed.

Destiny beamed at him, evidently satisfied that things were working out exactly as she'd intended. "Happy Thanksgiving, everyone."

Ben drank to her toast, but even as he wished everyone a wonderful Thanksgiving, he couldn't help wondering when this dark, empty hole inside him would go away and he'd truly be able to count his blessings again. He gazed at Kathleen and thought he saw shadows in her eyes, as well, and guessed she was feeling much the same way.

He knew Destiny wanted something to come from this meeting today, but it wasn't in the cards. Whatever the whole story, Kathleen Dugan's soul was as shattered as his own.

Chapter Three

Kathleen waited impatiently through several courses of excellent food. She nibbled on pecan pie, then lingered over two cups of rich, dark coffee, hoping for an invitation to Ben's studio to go through the works that were stashed there. She desperately wanted to see for herself if the painting in the dining room was the exception or the rule.

Then again, it might be sheer torment, especially if each and every painting was extraordinary and Ben still flatly refused to allow her to show them.

When the meal finally ended and people started making their excuses and leaving, she lingered at the table with the family. She debated simply asking for a tour of the studio, but Ben's forbidding expression stopped her. Not even Destiny seemed inclined to broach the very subject that she claimed had been her reason for asking Kathleen to dinner. It was as if she, too, had read her nephew's mood and determined that he wouldn't be receptive.

Kathleen was about to accept a momentary defeat and leave, when Melanie stepped in.

"Kathleen, surely you're not going without looking at Ben's paintings," Melanie said, merriment sparkling in her eyes. "Isn't that why you came tonight?"

Ben looked as if he'd like to strangle his sister-in-law. Kathleen took her cue from that.

"Perhaps another time," she said before Ben could utter a word. She smiled at him. "I would love to come back sometime to see your studio, if you'll let me."

He regarded her with a faint frown. "Sure," he said, too polite to refuse outright.

"I'll call to set it up," Kathleen promised. She had no intention of doing that. She had a hunch she needed the element of surprise on her side. Meantime, though, let him get complacent, thinking that he'd have fair warning.

"There's no phone in the studio," Melanie chimed in.

"And Ben never checks his messages," Beth added.

"You should probably just pop in whenever the mood strikes," Melanie suggested.

Kathleen grinned. Obviously those two were on the same wavelength. They'd found a way to encourage her and warn Ben at the same time. Very clever.

"Perhaps I will," Kathleen said. She gave him a pointed look. "If Ben doesn't return my calls."

He rolled his eyes. "I return my calls." He gave his sisters-in-law a hard look. "At least to anyone important."

The two women laughed, not the least bit insulted by the innuendo.

"I guess you put us in our place," Melanie said, giving him a kiss. "Don't be a stranger. I expect you to come to dinner soon."

To Kathleen's surprise, his expression softened and he rested a hand on Melanie's huge belly. "I'd better hurry before this little one steals all your attention."

"We'll always have time for you," Melanie told him. "And we're counting on you to give the baby its first set of paints and plenty of free art lessons, just the way Destiny did for you. Mack's going to teach the baby the finer points of football."

"Even if it's a girl?" Ben inquired skeptically.

"There will be no gender discrimination in this family," Melanie retorted. "Right, Mack?"

"None," Mack agreed at once. "And if it is a girl and she's really, really good, I'll make her the first woman in the National Football League. Who cares about a few cuts and bruises and broken bones?"

"Hold it," Richard said, scowling at his brother. "Nobody gets to tackle any daughter of mine."

Beth nudged Mack in the ribs. "You knew your brother would forbid it, didn't you? Obviously you inherited Destiny's sneakiness. You sound very broad-minded since there's absolutely no risk that you'll ever have to pay up."

"Hey, my offer was genuine," Mack insisted, looking hurt that his wife would think otherwise. "Now let's get out of here. We've got some kids at the hospital we want to see tonight. I promised them pie for dessert."

Destiny stood up at once. "I have the pies all ready in the kitchen. I'll get them."

Melanie and Richard left as Mack, Beth and Destiny headed for the kitchen, leaving Kathleen alone with Ben.

"You have an amazing family," she told him.

"They're good people," Ben agreed, then regarded her curiously. "What about your family? Were they together today?"

"Of course. It's tradition." She knew there was no mistaking the harsh edge in her voice, but she was unable to contain it.

"But you weren't there," he noted.

"I'd had enough of tradition," she said succinctly. "I decided it was time to do my own thing."

"Something tells me there's a story there," he said.

"Not a very interesting one," she insisted, unwilling to air the Dugan family laundry to this man she barely knew.

He studied her so intently that she felt herself flush under his scrutiny.

"If you ever change your mind, I'm a good listener," he said eventually.

Kathleen didn't talk about that part of her past any more than she talked about her marriage. "I'll keep that in mind," she said with no intention of following up on it. Why reveal intimate secrets to a man she wanted to represent, not to date? Not that she'd ever shared any part of her family history with anyone. Keeping quiet had been ingrained in her from an early age.

"But you have no intention of talking to me about that or anything else personal, do you?" Ben guessed. "It's all about the art with you."

"Yes," she said, seeing little point in denying it.

"Even if I were to tell you that I'd let you take a look around my studio, if you'd open up to me?"

She gave him a sharp look. "Why would you do that?"

"I'm not sure," he responded slowly, looking faintly bewildered. "Maybe because I'm as fascinated with what you're holding back as you are with the paintings I'm keeping from you."

Kathleen was caught completely off guard by the admission. It was an opening, a chance to get what she wanted, but at what cost?

"I don't think so," she said at last.

"What are you afraid of?"

She wasn't about to answer that. She couldn't tell him that talking about the past would make her far too vulnerable, that it would create an illusion of intimacy that could be far too dangerous. There had been so many times in her life when she'd wanted to share all the secrets, to lean on someone stronger, but she'd kept her own counsel instead, because that was what Dugans did, damn them all.

"I'm not afraid of anything," she said fiercely, desperately wishing it were true. She was terrified of shadows, of people who weren't what they first seemed to be. Her faith in people, her trust had been shattered too many times to count, even by the mother and grandparents she was expected to respect and adore.

"Really?" Ben asked skeptically. "Nothing frightens you?"

"Absolutely nothing," she insisted, meeting his gaze, then faltering at the intensity in his blue eyes.

"Then I guess there's no reason at all not to do this," he said, cupping a hand behind her neck and covering her mouth with his own.

Fire shot through Kathleen's veins as if she'd been touched by flame. Every sensible cell in her brain told her to pull away from the heat, but like the moth tempting fate, she moved into the kiss instead, then moaned when Ben was the one who withdrew.

Feeling dazed, she stared into his eyes, saw the confusion and the passion and wondered what the devil had just happened. If anyone else had hit on her so abruptly, with so little warning, she would have been shaking with anger now. To her shock, while she was indeed trembling, it was because that kiss had touched a part of her she'd thought was forever dead.

"Why?" she asked, unable to form a longer, more coherent question. Besides, *why* pretty much covered it.

"I'm asking myself the same thing," Ben admitted. "Maybe I just wanted to challenge that confidence I heard in your voice."

"Or maybe you wanted to prove something to yourself," she responded irritably.

"Such as?"

"That Destiny had gotten it wrong this time."

"My aunt had nothing to do with that kiss," he said heatedly.

"Oh, really? Then you don't care that it was exactly what she was hoping would happen between us?"

"The damn kiss had nothing to do with Destiny," he said again, dragging his hand through his hair. "I am sorry, though. It shouldn't have happened."

Kathleen sighed. She agreed it had been a mistake, but she couldn't seem to regret it the way she knew she should.

"Let's just forget about it," she suggested mildly. "People kiss all the time and it means nothing." At least, other people did. It was a brand-new experience for her to be able to participate in a kiss without wildly overreacting, without a hint of panic clawing at her.

"Exactly," Ben said, sounding relieved.

"I should go. Please tell Destiny that I had a wonderful time. I'm sure I'll see her soon at the gallery."

"Tomorrow morning would be my guess," Ben said wryly.

Kathleen laughed despite herself. "Mine, too."

"Will you tell her about the kiss?"

"Heavens, no. Will you?"

"Are you crazy? Not a chance."

Kathleen looked into his eyes and made a swift decision. "I'm still coming back out here, you know. You haven't scared me off."

He gave her a vaguely chagrined look that told her she'd hit the mark. That kiss had been deliberate, after all, not the wicked impulse he'd wanted her to believe.

He shrugged. "It was worth a shot."

She laughed at having caught him. "I knew it. I knew that was what the kiss was about."

He gave her a long, lingering look that made her toes curl.

"Not entirely," he said, then grinned. "That should give you something to think about before you get into your car and head out this way again."

It was a dare, no question about it. If only he'd known Kathleen better, he'd have realized that it was a point of honor with her never to resist a challenge. She'd survived her past, and when she'd come through it, she'd vowed never to let another soul intimidate her or get the upper hand. She didn't intend to let Ben Carlton—despite his sexy looks, killer smile and devastating kisses—be the exception.

* * *

After that potent kiss, Ben was surprised and oddly disgruntled when Kathleen simply grabbed her coat and walked out without even waiting to say goodbye to Destiny or to Mack and Beth.

That was what he'd wanted, wasn't it? He'd wanted to scare her off. He should have felt nothing but relief that his plan had worked and his aunt's plotting hadn't succeeded, but he felt a little miffed, instead. That wasn't a good sign. All of the Carlton men loved a challenge.

Which probably meant that Destiny had advised Kathleen to go with her patented "always leave 'em wanting more" maxim. Alone with Destiny now, he gave his aunt a grim look.

"What are you up to?" he asked as she sat on the sofa, her feet tucked under her. With her soft cloud of brown hair and bright, clear brown eyes, she looked to be little more than a girl, though he knew perfectly well she was fifty-three.

Destiny sipped her brandy and regarded him without the slightest hint of guilt. "You're too suspicious, Ben. Why would I be up to anything?"

"Because it's what you do. You meddle. Ever since you decided Richard, Mack and I were old enough to settle down, you've systematically worked to make it happen."

"Of course I have. I love you. What's wrong with wanting to see you happy?"

"I am happy."

"You're alone. Ever since Graciela died, you've been terribly unhappy and guilt-ridden. It's time to put that behind you, Ben. What happened was not your fault."

"I'm not discussing Graciela," he said tightly.

"That's the problem," Destiny said, undaunted for once by his refusal to talk about what had happened. "You've never talked about her, and I think perhaps it's time you did. She wasn't the paragon of virtue you've built her up to be, Ben. That much has to be clear, even to you."

"Destiny, don't go there," Ben warned. He knew that his family had never held a high opinion of Graciela, but he'd refused to listen then, and he was equally adamant about not listening now, even with all of the facts still burning a graphic image in his head. He'd seen her with that polo player, dammit. He didn't need to be reminded of what were only rumors and speculation to everyone else.

"I will go there," Destiny said fiercely. "She was hardly a saint."

"Dammit, Destiny—"

She cut him off with a look that made her disapproval of his language plain. "Leaving her was the right thing to do, Ben. You're not responsible that she stormed off that night far too upset and drunk to be driving, and crashed her car into a tree. That was her doing, *hers*," she repeated emphatically. "Not yours."

Ben felt the words slamming into him, carrying him back to a place he didn't want to go, to a night he would never forget.

The argument had been heated, far more volatile than any that had gone before. He'd caught Graciela cheating on him that afternoon, found her with a neighboring Brazilian polo player, but she'd tried to explain away what he'd seen as if there could possibly be an innocent explanation.

In the past he would have accepted the lies, because it was easier, but he'd reached the end of his rope.

Loving her and forgiving her had worn him down, the cycle unending despite all the promises that she would change, that she would be faithful. He'd been foolish enough to believe them at first. He had loved her unconditionally and for a time had thought that accepting her flaws was a part of that.

Then he'd realized that what he felt wasn't love, but an obsessive need not to lose someone important again. He'd seen the truth with blinding clarity that afternoon. He'd realized finally that he'd never really had her anyway.

On that fateful night he'd told her to get out and he'd meant it. Her hold on him had finally snapped.

"You'll change your mind," she'd said confidently, slurring her words, her expression smug, beautiful even in her drunken state.

"Not this time," he'd told her coldly. "It's over, Graciela. I've had enough."

If that had been it, he could have moved on with his life, buried the repeated humiliations in the past and kept his heart hopeful that someone else would come along. But Graciela hadn't even made it out to the main highway when she'd crashed. He'd heard that awful sound and run outside, only to find the mangled wreckage, her body broken and bloody and trapped inside as the first flames had licked toward the gasoline spilling across the drive.

Frantic, he'd tried to drag her to safety, knowing even as he struggled that it was too late, that nothing he could do would save her.

From that moment on, as the car exploded into a fiery inferno, Ben had shut down emotionally. It had stirred the images that had haunted him from childhood of his parents' plane going down into the side of a mountain on a foggy night. He'd been so young back then that he'd barely understood what had happened. Everyone was careful to tiptoe around the details of that crash, so he'd filled in the blanks for himself, envisioning the kind of unbearable horrors that only a child with an active imagination could spin.

Now he shuddered and tried to push from his mind all of those memories, forever intertwined even though they'd occurred years apart.

"There's a huge difference between being alone and being lonely," he pointed out quietly. "No one should recognize that better than you. I don't see you trying to snag a husband now that your nest is empty, Destiny."

She frowned at the challenge. "It doesn't mean I wouldn't like to have companionship if the right man came along."

"There," he said triumphantly. "The *right* man, and nothing less."

"Well, of course." She gave him a sad smile. "I had that extraordinary experience once. I know what it's like. I won't accept anything less."

"Neither will I."

"But you won't find it, if you don't get out and look," she scolded.

"So you've decided to bring the likely candidate to my doorstep?"

She shrugged. "Sue me." Then she gave him a sly look. "It worked, didn't it? You're intrigued by Kathleen. I saw it in your eyes. You were watching her."

"Maybe I'd just like to paint her," he said, unwilling to admit to any more. Kathleen had been right, if Destiny knew about that kiss, he'd never hear the end of it. Who knew what she might do to capitalize on the impact of that kiss? Throwing them together at every opportunity would be the least of it.

Destiny chuckled. "You don't do portraits. If you are genuinely interested in painting her, I find that very telling, don't you?"

He refused to give her an inch. She would seize it and run with it for a mile. "Not particularly."

"Look at your choice of subjects, Benjamin," she said impatiently. "You're more comfortable with nature than you are with people. Ever since you lost your parents, you don't trust yourself to truly connect with anyone, much less to fall in love. Even Graciela was safe, because she was incapable of real love. You knew that from the start, and it suited you. You're afraid we'll all leave you."

"I fell in love with Graciela," he insisted.

"I don't believe that for a minute, but let's say it's true. In the end, she only reinforced the pain," Destiny said.

They'd been through this before. Ben had copped to it, so he saw no need to belabor the point. "Yes," he said tersely.

"I haven't left. Richard and Mack haven't left. And you're beginning to let yourself care for their wives, too. They're here for the long haul. I'll wager that you'll lose your heart to the children when they come along, as well."

"More than likely," he agreed. Each time he felt Melanie's baby kick, it set off an odd tug of longing inside him. He envied his brother the joy that awaited him, no question about it.

"Then why not open yourself to the possibility that there might be someone special out there for you as well?"

"I don't need anyone," he declared flatly.

"We all need someone. If I haven't taught you that, then I've failed you miserably."

"*You* don't seem to need anyone."

"But I have memories," she said sadly. "Wonderful memories."

"And those keep you warm at night?"

"They bring me peace," she said. "Life is for living, darling. Never forget that."

"Unless fate steps in," he said. "Tricky thing, fate. You never quite know when it's going to bite you in the butt."

She sighed, her expression suddenly nostalgic. "No, you don't, do you?"

Ben seized on the rare hint of melancholy in her voice. "You're thinking about what you gave up to come and take care of us, aren't you?" he said.

"You say that as if I have regrets. It wasn't a sacrifice," she insisted, just as she had on so many past occasions. "I did what I had to do. You boys have brought nothing but joy into my life."

"But nothing to equal the man you left behind," he pressed, wishing for once she would share that part of her life. If he had his hang-ups, they were nothing next to the secrets that Destiny clung to and kept hidden from them.

"Water under the bridge," she insisted. "I have no regrets, and that's the point. People move forward, take risks, let people in. Holing up and protecting your heart doesn't keep you safe. It keeps you lonely." She gave him one of her trademark penetrating, steady looks. "I could give you Kathleen's phone number, if you like."

"I'm surprised you haven't had it tattooed to my hand while I slept."

"Tattoos are too tacky," she teased. "Besides, if I happen to be wrong just this once, I'd hate for you to have to explain it away the rest of your life."

Ben grinned despite his exasperation. "I love you, you know that, don't you?"

"Yes," she said, her expression totally serene. "And in the end you'll do what I expect. You always do."

Sadly, she had that right. He could call Kathleen Dugan in the morning or he could hold out against the inevitable. In the end, though, he would see her again. Kiss her again.

He just wanted to make sure it was on his own terms.

Chapter Four

By noon on Friday, Kathleen's gallery was packed with customers who'd read a review of Boris's work in the morning paper. As Destiny had expected, the critic had raved about his bold style and predicted great things. Collectors who'd left without buying or even expressing much interest at the opening were now eagerly lining up to pay the premium prices Kathleen had put on tags the instant she'd seen the review. At this rate, the show would be a sell-out before the end of the day.

Which meant she would have to find another artist for the schedule, she realized as an image of Ben's painting slipped into her head. It would be awfully convenient if she could talk him into an immediate showing, but the likelihood of that was somewhere between slim and none. Winning him over was going to take time, patience and persistence, something she didn't have at the moment.

She'd just written up her last sale of the morning and drawn a deep breath at the prospect of a midday lull, when Destiny breezed into the gallery, resplendent in a trim red coat with a fake-fur collar and a matching hat.

"Good morning, Kathleen," she said, her gaze going to the walls, where red Sold stickers were on more than half of the price tags. Her expression immediately brightened. "Didn't I tell you that a favorable review would turn the tide for Boris? The show is obviously a resounding success, after all."

"It is," Kathleen said happily. "Now if only I had something to replace it, once the buyers come back to claim their pieces. I've been able to hold most of them off for the next week, but after that these walls could be bare." She gave Destiny a sly look. "I don't suppose you'd like to help me out?"

"You saw for yourself how difficult Ben can be. I doubt you'll be able to talk him into a show quickly enough," Destiny said.

It was obvious to Kathleen that Destiny was deliberately misunderstanding her question. "I agree, but there is another Carlton artist who's quite good." She met Destiny's gaze evenly. "And I think she owes me one, don't you?"

Destiny returned her gaze without so much as a flicker of an eyelash. "Why on earth would I owe you anything, my dear?"

"You got me out to your nephew's house under false pretenses, didn't you?"

"False pretenses?" Destiny echoed blankly. "I don't understand."

The woman was good, no doubt about it. She almost sounded convincing, and she'd managed to look downright wounded.

"It was never about Ben's art, was it?" Kathleen pressed. "You simply wanted me to meet him."

"And now you have," Destiny said brightly, as if attaching no significance to that meeting besides the obvious contact with an artist. "I'm sure in time you can persuade him to let you sell his paintings."

"How do I know there are more paintings?" Kathleen asked. "I never got to see them."

Destiny didn't look a bit uncomfortable at that reminder. "Yes, well, the timing seemed to be a bit off, after all. Perhaps in a few days or a few weeks things will settle down a bit and you can go back out there. I'd recommend waiting until after the first of the year."

"Nearly six weeks? My, my. Ben must be mad as hell at your scheming," Kathleen guessed.

Destiny waved off the suggestion. "He'll get over it. Just give him a little time."

"Which I don't have. I need something new and exciting to promote before Christmas." She gave Destiny another piercing look. "A few pieces by Destiny Carlton would be a huge draw before the holidays. We could do a lovely reception."

"Absolutely not," Destiny said flatly. "I no longer show my work."

"Just like someone else in the family," Kathleen scoffed. "Why not? I know you're good, Destiny. You've let me see your paintings."

"Painting was something I did professionally years ago. Now I merely dabble."

"The way Ben claims to dabble?"

"Ben's a genius!" Destiny said fiercely. "Concentrate on winning him over, my dear, and forget about me.''

"Hard to do, when you're here and he's not.''

"He'll come around in time. In the meantime, I'm sure you'll find something wonderful for the gallery for the holiday season," Destiny said. "Even at the last second, there are dozens of local artists who'd be thrilled by an invitation to show their works here. Ask one of them. They'll accept. You're very persuasive, after all.''

Kathleen gave her a wry look. "I don't seem to be doing so well with you. Maybe all Carltons are immune to my charms.''

"Maybe you simply need to formulate a new strategy and try a little harder," Destiny advised. Her expression turned thoughtful. "My nephew has a sweet tooth. Since you bake all those delicious little pastries you serve at your events here, I'm sure you could use that skill to your advantage.''

Apparently satisfied that she'd planted her seed for the day, Destiny glanced at her watch and feigned shock. "Oh, dear, look at the time. I'm late. I just wanted to stop by and tell you how delighted I was to see that review and to tell you again that I'm so glad you were able to join us yesterday.''

"Thanks for including me," Kathleen said, giving up the battle of wits with Destiny for now. A retreat seemed in order, since it seemed unlikely she'd be able to change Destiny's mind.

"I really enjoyed meeting the rest of your family," she added with total sincerity, "Beth and Melanie especially. Chatting with them was very enlightening.''

Destiny gave her a sharp look. "Don't believe everything you're told, Kathleen.''

Kathleen chuckled at her worried expression. "Yes, I can see why you wouldn't want me taking their advice at face value."

"What did those two tell you?" she asked, clearly ready to defend herself against all charges.

"Nothing I hadn't already figured out for myself," Kathleen said. "You're a clever woman, Destiny. And a force to be reckoned with."

Destiny squared her shoulders. "I'll take that as a compliment," she said.

"I thought you might," Kathleen said, her grin spreading. "I'm not entirely convinced they meant it that way, though."

"Those two have nothing to complain about," Destiny grumbled. "If it weren't for me giving them and my nephews a timely nudge, their lives would be very different."

"I'm sure they would all concede that," Kathleen agreed. "But may I give you a piece of advice?"

"Of course."

"Don't count on getting your way where Ben and I are concerned."

Destiny looked amused. "Because you're made of tougher stuff?"

"Precisely."

"Darling, that only means you'll fall even faster and harder."

Abandoning Kathleen to ponder that, she swept out of the gallery, leaving only the scent of her expensive perfume and her warning to linger in the air.

Ben slapped a heavy layer of dark, swirling paint on the canvas and regarded it bleakly. It pretty much mirrored his mood ever since Thanksgiving. Anyone looking at the painting would see nothing but turmoil and confusion. Some fool critic would probably look at it and see evidence of madness, and maybe he had gone a little mad from the moment he'd met Kathleen Dugan. Heaven knew, he couldn't get her out of his head, which was something he hadn't expected.

Nor had he been able to paint, not with the delicate touch required to translate nature into art. The fiasco in front of him had started out to be a painting of Canada geese heading north, but he'd messed it up so badly, he'd simply started layering coats of paint over the disaster, swirling together colors simply to rid himself of the restless desire to be doing something artistic even when his talent seemed to have deserted him. Who knew? Maybe he'd discover a whole new style. Looking at the canvas, though, it didn't seem likely.

He was about to put a fresh canvas on the easel and start over when he heard the slam of a car door. He glanced outside and saw Mack climbing out of his SUV. He figured his big brother had probably come to gloat. One look at the painting in front of Ben and even without an ounce of artistic talent of his own, Mack would recognize that his brother was in a funk. To avoid that, Ben took the still-damp canvas and shoved it out of sight, then grabbed a blank one and sat it on the easel.

Mack came in seconds later, carrying a bag filled with sandwiches and bottles of soda. He glanced at the pristine canvas and raised an eyebrow.

"Artist's block?" he inquired, barely containing a grin.

"Nope," Ben lied. "Just thinking about a new painting. Haven't even picked up my brush yet."

Mack's gaze immediately went to the palette of paints that had clearly been in use recently. "Oh?"

"I finished something earlier," Ben claimed, knowing he was only digging the hole deeper. Mack might not know art, but he knew his brother. He was also pretty deft at recognizing an evasion when he heard one.

"Can I see?" he asked, his expression innocent. His eyes betrayed him, though. They were filled with amusement.

"No. I tossed it out," Ben claimed. "It wasn't coming together right."

"Maybe you were too close to it. Could be you'd lost perspective. I could give you my opinion," Mack offered cheerfully, clearly not buying the elaborate tale.

"I'd rather you just dole out one of those sandwiches and leave the art critiques to people who know what they're talking about," Ben groused.

"You mean people like Kathleen Dugan?" Mack asked, his expression perfectly bland as he handed over a roast beef sandwich. "She seems knowledgeable."

"It'll be a cold day in hell before I let her near my paintings," Ben retorted.

"Because you don't think she knows the business or because Destiny introduced you?" Mack asked, grinning broadly. "Can't say I blame you for not trusting our aunt's motivation in inviting Kathleen out here."

"Yeah, well, you would know, wouldn't you?" Ben said.

"That I would."

"Why are you here, by the way?"

"Just thought I'd drop by and see how you're doing," Mack claimed.

"You were here Thursday. It's only Saturday. How much could happen in a couple of days?"

"I'd say that depends on how sneaky Destiny is being," Mack said cheerfully. "Has Kathleen popped up yet?"

"No sign of her," Ben admitted.

Mack studied him intently. "Are you relieved about that?"

"Of course."

"You don't sound especially happy. Seemed to me the two of you hit it off okay the other night. Maybe you were hoping she'd turn up to pester you by now."

Ben gave him a sour look. "We were polite."

"Then that kiss was just a polite gesture?" Mack asked.

Ben felt his face burn. "What kiss?" he asked with what he thought was a pretty good display of complete ignorance. Surely Mack was just guessing, adding up one man, one woman, a bit of chemistry and drawing his own conclusion about what had happened while he'd been out of the room. Maybe he was simply drawing on the knowledge of what he would have done if left alone with an attractive woman, pre-Beth, of course.

"The kiss I stumbled across when I came back into the dining room," Mack replied, disproving Ben's theory. "Looked pretty friendly to me."

Faced with the truth, indignation seemed the only route left to him. "What the hell were you doing? Spying on us?" Ben demanded.

"Nope," his brother said, clearly undaunted. "Destiny sent me in to ask how many pies you wanted her to leave for you, so she'd know how many to give Beth and me to take to the hospital."

"I didn't hear you come in," Ben said defensively.

"Obviously."

Ben scowled at his brother. "You didn't race right back in the kitchen and report what you'd seen, did you?"

"Absolutely not," Mack said, his indignation far more genuine than Ben's. "I just told Destiny you said you'd had all the pie you needed and I should take the rest."

"*That's* why I couldn't find so much as a crumb when I went looking for a late-night snack," Ben grumbled.

Mack gave him an unrepentant smile. "I figured you owed me for not blabbing."

Ben sighed. "You're right. It's a small enough price to pay for not getting Destiny's hopes up. Who knows what she'd dream up, if she thought round one had gone her way."

"Oh, I don't think you're off the hook, little brother, not by any means. In fact, if I were you, I'd be looking over my shoulder from here on out. Something tells me you'll be seeing Kathleen every time you turn around."

Ben decided not to tell Mack that he was already seeing her everywhere. The blasted woman had crawled into his head and wouldn't leave.

When it came to business, Kathleen wasn't especially patient. The art world was competitive and she'd learned early to go after what she wanted before someone else snapped it up.

Though Destiny had suggested prudence where Ben was concerned, Kathleen decided not to take any chances. If, by some fluke, word about his talent leaked out, she could be competing with a crowd for the chance to mount his first show, maybe even to represent his work. The fact that he intended to play hard-to-get simply made the game more interesting.

She was back out in the rolling hills of Middleburg by 7:00 a.m. on the Sunday after Thanksgiving. Leaves on the trees were falling fast, but there were still plenty of hints of the gold, red and burnished-bronze colors of fall. On this surprisingly warm, sunny morning, horses had been turned out to pasture behind white fences. It was little wonder that Ben painted nature, when he lived in a setting this spectacular.

Kathleen was armed for the occasion. She had two extralarge lattes from Starbucks with her, along with cranberry scones she'd baked the night before when she couldn't get to sleep for thinking about Ben and that stash of paintings his aunt had alluded to. She told herself those scones were not bribery, that she hadn't taken Destiny's advice about Ben's sweet tooth to heart. Rather they were simply a peace offering for intruding on his Sunday morning.

She was waiting in her car with the motor running when Ben emerged from the house, wearing yet another pair of disreputable jeans, a sweatshirt and sneakers. Unshaven, his hair shining but disheveled, he looked sexy as hell. All dressed up, he would be devastating.

But she wasn't here because Ben sent her hormones into high gear. She was here because his talent gave her goose bumps. Sometimes it was hard to separate the two reactions, but in general she steered clear of artists in her personal life. Most were too self-absorbed, the emotional ride too bumpy. If that was her basic philosophy, avoiding the dark, brooding types was her hard-and-fast rule, learned by bitter experience. Ben Carlton was off-limits to her heart. Period.

Seemingly, though, her heart hadn't quite gotten the message. It was doing little hops, skips and jumps at the sight of him.

She expected a quick dismissal and was prepared to argue. She wasn't prepared for the hopeful gleam in his eye the instant he spotted the coffee.

"If one of those is for me, I will forgive you for showing up here uninvited," he said, already reaching for a cup.

"If the coffee gets me inside your studio, what will these freshly baked scones get me?" She waved the bag under his nose.

"I'll call off the guard dogs," he said generously.

"There are no guard dogs," she said.

"You didn't see the sign posted at the gate?"

"I saw it. Your aunt told me it was for show."

"No wonder people come parading in here whenever they feel like it," he grumbled. "I'll have to talk to her about giving away my security secrets."

"Either that or go out and buy a rottweiler," Kathleen suggested, taking the fact that he hadn't actually sent her packing as an invitation to follow him into the studio, which had been converted from a barn.

The exterior of the old barn wasn't much, just faded red paint on weathered boards, but inside was an artist's paradise of natural light and space. The smell of oil paint and turpentine was faint, thanks to windows that had been left cracked open overnight. Ben moved methodically around the room to close them, then switched on a thermostat. Soon warm air was taking away the chill.

Kathleen had to stop herself from dumping everything in her hands and racing straight to the built-in racks that held literally hundreds of canvases. Instead, she bit back her impatience and set the bag of scones on the counter directly in front of Ben.

"All yours," she told him.

Apparently he was the kind of man who believed in savoring pleasure. He opened the bag slowly, sniffed deeply, then sighed. "You actually baked these?"

"With my own two hands," she confirmed.

"Is this something you do every Sunday, get a sudden urge to bake?"

"Actually this urge hit last night," she told him.

"Let's see if you're any good at it," he said as he retrieved one of the scones and broke off a bite. He put it in his mouth, then closed his eyes.

"Not bad," he said eventually, then gave her a sly look. "This will get you five minutes to look around. Promise to leave the bagful and you can stay for ten."

"There are a half-dozen scones in that bag. That ought to buy me a half hour at least," she bargained.

Ben regarded her suspiciously. "Are you here just to satisfy your curiosity?"

Kathleen hesitated on her way to the first stack of paintings that had caught her eye. She had a feeling if she told him the truth, he'd hustle her out the door before she got her first glimpse of those tantalizingly close canvases. If she lied, though, it would destroy whatever fragile trust she was going to need to get him to agree to do a show.

"Nope," she said at last. "Though what art dealer wouldn't be curious about a treasure trove of paintings?"

"Then you still have some crazy idea about getting me to do a showing at your gallery?"

Kathleen shrugged. "Perhaps, if your work is actually any good."

He frowned. "I don't care if you think I'm better than Monet, I'm not doing a show. And your ten minutes is ticking by while we argue."

She smiled at his fierce expression. "We'll see."

"It's not going to happen," he repeated. "So if that's your only interest, you're wasting your time."

"Discovering an incredible talent is never a waste of my time."

"In this case it is, at least if you expect to make money by showing or selling my paintings."

She walked back to the counter where he sat, now crumbling one of those scones into crumbs. "Why are you so vehemently opposed to letting others see your work, Ben?"

"Because I paint for the joy it brings me, period."

She gave him a penetrating look. "In other words, it's too personal, too revealing."

Though he quickly turned away, Kathleen saw the startled look in his eyes and knew she'd hit on the truth. Ben put too much of himself into his paintings, he exposed raw emotions he didn't want anyone else to guess at.

"Bottom line, it's not for sale," he said gruffly. "And your time has just run out. I can live without the scones. Take the rest and go."

Kathleen cast a longing look in the direction of the paintings she had yet to glimpse, but she recognized a brick wall when she ran into it. Maybe Destiny had been right, after all, and she should have waited longer before coming back out here. Ben's defenses were solid and impenetrable at the moment.

"Okay then," she said, resigned. "I'll go, but I'll

leave the scones." She walked around until she could look him directly in the eyes. "And I'll be back to claim that half hour tour you promised me."

"It was ten minutes, but don't bother. You'll be wasting your time," he said again.

"My choice," she said pleasantly. "And fair warning, you have no idea how persuasive I can be when I put my mind to it. This morning was just a little warm-up."

Her gaze clashed with his and it gave her some satisfaction that he was the first to look away.

"I think maybe I'm getting the picture," he muttered.

Kathleen had heard him perfectly clearly, but she feigned otherwise. "What was that?"

"Not a thing, Ms. Dugan. I didn't say a thing."

"It's Kathleen," she reminded him.

This time he caught her gaze and held it. "It's Kathleen if this thing between us is personal," he told her. "As long as you think it's business, it's Ms. Dugan."

There was another hint of challenge in his low voice. Since she knew he wasn't looking for a relationship any more than she was, it had to be deliberate. A scare tactic, basically. Just like that kiss on Thanksgiving.

She kept her own gaze steady and unblinking. "Then by all means, let's make it Kathleen," she taunted, throwing down her own gauntlet.

Surprise lit his eyes. "Obviously you've forgotten about that kiss we shared or you wouldn't be quite so quick to tempt me."

Kathleen trembled. Her blood turned hot. That kiss hadn't been out of her mind for more than a minute at a time for the past couple of nights. What the hell had she been thinking by throwing out a dare of her own?

She should be concentrating on getting those pictures of his, not on reminding him of the chemistry between them.

"You don't scare me," she said with sheer bravado.

"I should."

"Why is that?"

"Because even though I'm sadly out of practice, when I want something—*someone*—I usually get exactly what I go after," he told her, his gaze steady and unflinching.

He made it sound like fact, not arrogance, which should have terrified her, but instead merely made her knees weak.

"You still don't scare me," she repeated, half expecting—half hoping—for a wicked, dangerous kiss that would immediately prove her wrong.

As if he'd guessed what was in her head, he backed away a step and shoved his hands in his pockets. "Stay away, Kathleen."

"I can't do that."

"Please."

She should do as he asked. There was no question about that. It would be smart. It would be safe. If it weren't for the art, maybe she could.

If it weren't for the man with the torment burning in his eyes, maybe she would.

As it was, there wasn't a chance in hell she'd do the smart, safe thing.

Chapter Five

"It's Sunday. Where on earth have you been? Not at that little shop of yours, I hope," Prudence Dugan said the minute Kathleen picked up her phone.

It was typical of her mother that she could manage to inject so much criticism, petulance and disdain into so few words. Kathleen wasn't in the mood to be drawn into an argument. All she really wanted to do was take a long, hot bath and think about the quicksand she was playing in with Ben Carlton.

"Did you call for any particular reason, Mother?"

"Well, that's a fine greeting," her mother huffed, oblivious to the fact that her own greeting had been less than cheerful. "When I didn't hear a word from you on Thanksgiving, I was worried."

Kathleen bit back the impatient retort that was on the tip of her tongue. She knew perfectly well this wasn't about any sudden burst of maternal concern. If it had been, her mother would have called on Friday or even Saturday.

No, the truth was that Prudence was incapable of thinking of anyone other than herself. She always had been. No matter how bad things had gotten with Kathleen's father or the succession of stepfathers that had followed, Kathleen had always been told not to rock the boat. Silence was as ingrained in her as were proper table manners. Her mother had never seemed to notice the high price Kathleen had paid for living up to her mother's expectations.

"Did you have a nice Thanksgiving, Mother?" she asked, because it was obviously what her mother expected.

"It would have been lovely if I hadn't had to spend the entire meal making excuses for you."

"You didn't need to make excuses for me. I'm perfectly capable of making my own."

"But that's the point," Prudence said irritably. "You weren't here, were you? Your grandfather was not pleased about that."

The only person in Kathleen's life who was stiffer and more unyielding than her mother was Dexter Dugan, patriarch of the Dugan clan. Yet somehow he'd managed to turn a blind eye to his daughter's foibles. He'd even encouraged Prudence and Kathleen to take back the prestigious Dugan name, no matter how many men had followed in Kathleen's father's footsteps. It was that blend of love and restraint that had confused her early on.

Once, Kathleen had tried to tell him about what was going on at home. She'd run to him crying, choking out the horror of watching her father hit her mother, but before the first words had left her mouth, her grand-

father had shushed her and said she was never to speak
of such things again. He'd told her she was far too
young to understand what went on between adults.

"More important, what happens inside this family is
never to be shared with outsiders," he told her sharply.
"Whatever you see or hear is not to be repeated."

The comment had only confused her. He was family,
not an outsider. She'd only been able to conclude that
there was to be no help from him for the violence at
home.

Despite her grandfather's admonishment, though, her
father had suddenly left a few days later. Kathleen had
wanted desperately to believe that her grandfather had
relented and dealt with the situation, but she'd never
quite been sure, especially when the pattern between
her mother and father had been repeated over and over
with other men. Kathleen never spoke of it again, but
the men always left eventually, usually after some particularly nasty scene, so perhaps her mother was the
one who eventually stood up for herself.

Only as an adult had Kathleen recognized that her
mother would always be a victim, that she saw herself
that way and sought out men who would see that nothing changed in that self-perception. Perhaps it was the
only way Prudence could justify turning to her parents
for the financial stability that her marriages never provided.

Whatever the reason, the cycle had been devastating
for Kathleen, giving her a jaundiced view of relationships. Her grandfather's seemingly accepting attitude
had reinforced that view. When her own marriage had
crashed against the same rocks, she'd put an immediate
end to it and vowed never to take another chance. Obviously, Dugan women were prone to making lousy,

untrustworthy choices when it came to men. She, at least, was determined not to be a victim.

"I spoke to Grandfather and Grandmother myself Thanksgiving morning," Kathleen told her mother now. "If he was hassling you about my absence, I'm sorry. I thought I'd taken care of that."

Her mother sniffed. "Yes, well, you know how he can be."

"Yes, I do," Kathleen said dryly. They were two of a kind, grand masters of employing guilt as a weapon.

"What did you do on the holiday?" Prudence asked, now that she'd been somewhat mollified. "You didn't work, I hope."

"No. I was invited to have dinner with friends."

"Anyone I might know?"

"I doubt it. Destiny Carlton invited me. She's been a good friend to me and to my gallery."

"Carlton? Carlton?" Her mother repeated the name as if she were scrolling through a mental Rolodex. "Is she part of the family that owns Carlton Industries?"

"Yes, as a matter of fact. Her nephew Richard is the CEO. I'm surprised you've heard of the company."

"Your grandfather has some dealings with them," her mother said, proving that she wasn't entirely oblivious to the family's business holdings even though she'd never worked a day in her life. "Richard would be quite a catch. He's about your age, isn't he?"

"He's a bit older, but he's also happily married and expecting his first child," Kathleen replied with a hint of amusement. "I think you can forget about that one, Mother."

"Isn't there another son?" Prudence asked hopefully. "He owns some sports franchise, a football team or something like that, perhaps."

"That's Mack. Also married."

"Oh." Her mother was clearly disappointed. "Why would Destiny Carlton invite you over if there are no available men in the family?"

Kathleen wasn't surprised her mother didn't know about Ben. Not only did he stay out of the public eye, but he was an artist, a career not worthy of note in her mother's book. That was one reason she dismissed Kathleen's gallery as little more than a ridiculous hobby. If she'd seen the profits, she might have taken a different attitude, but it was doubtful.

"I'm fairly certain Destiny invited me because she thought I'd enjoy spending the day with her family," Kathleen responded, deciding not to mention Ben.

"And spending the day with strangers is preferable to being at home with your own family, I suppose," her mother said, the petulance back in her voice.

Kathleen lost patience. "Mother, that was not the issue. I stayed here because I wanted to work Friday and Saturday. I'd already made that decision and spoken to you by the time Destiny said anything at all about joining them. When she found out I had no plans, she included me in hers. I think it was very generous of her."

"Of course, your *work* was what actually kept you away," her mother said scathingly, making it sound like a dirty word. "How could I have forgotten about that?"

Kathleen desperately wanted to tell her mother that perhaps if she'd had work she loved, she might not have fallen into so many awful relationships, but again she bit her tongue. Getting into an argument wouldn't serve any purpose. They'd been over the same ground too many times to count, and it never changed anything.

"Mother, why don't you come down to visit and see the gallery for yourself?" she asked, knowing even as she made the invitation that she was wasting her breath. Her mother hadn't made the trip even once since Kathleen had opened the doors. Seeing her daughter happy and successful didn't fit with her own view of a woman's world. Kathleen had finally come to accept that, too, but she kept trying just the same. Maybe if her mother met someone like Destiny, it would enlighten her, as well. Heaven knew, Kathleen's grandmother with her passive nature hadn't been an especially good role model.

"Perhaps one of these days I'll surprise you," her mother said.

There was an oddly wistful note in her voice that Kathleen had never heard before. She took heart. "I hope you will," she said quietly. "I really mean that, Mother."

"I know you do," her mother said, sounding even sadder. "I am glad you had a nice holiday, Kathleen. I really am."

"I wish yours had been happier," she told her mother.

"My life is what it is. Take care, dear. I'll speak to you soon."

She was gone before Kathleen could even say goodbye. Slowly she hung up the phone and felt the salty sting of tears in her eyes, not for herself, but for the woman whose life had been such a bitter disappointment. Kathleen wanted to shout at her that it wasn't too late, but who was she to say that? Maybe for her mother who'd allowed herself to be defeated at every turn, it was impossible to imagine that there was any hope to be had, much less reach out for it.

"Let that be a lesson to you," Kathleen muttered to herself, immediately thinking of Ben.

That was the difference between herself and her mother, she told herself staunchly. She wasn't going to let any man defeat her. She'd get those paintings of his and maybe even a few more of those amazing kisses. She just had to be careful she didn't lose her heart along the way.

Ben gave up any attempt at painting after Kathleen left on Sunday. If his feeble attempts on Saturday had been a disaster, anything he tried after seeing her again was bound to be worse. The fact that she was affecting his work irritated the daylights out of him, but he was a realist. When the muse was in turmoil, he might as well get away from the farm.

Going to see his family was completely out of the question. His unexpected arrival on any of their door-steps would be welcomed, but it would also stir up a hornet's nest of questions he didn't want to answer. Mack was out of town with the team, anyway, and Richard was probably driving Melanie mad with his doting. As for Destiny, her home was absolutely the last place he could turn up.

Usually he would have been content with his own company, maybe a good book, a warm fire and some music, but he knew instinctively that none of that would soothe him today.

Maybe he'd go for a drive, stop in one of the res-taurants in his old neighborhood and have a good meal. If that put him in proximity to Kathleen's art gallery and gave him a chance to peek in the windows, well, that was nothing more than coincidence. Happenstance. Accidental.

Sure, and pigs flew, he thought darkly.

Still, once he was on the road, he headed unerringly toward Alexandria, cursing all the way at the traffic that didn't even take a rest on Sundays anymore. What the hell was wrong with all these people, anyway? Surely they couldn't all be suffering from the same sort of malaise that had gotten him out of the house. Wasn't anybody content with their lives, anymore? Did everyone have to go shopping? He directed the last at the lineup of cars backed up in the turn lane to a mall.

By comparison, Old Town Alexandria was relatively quiet and peaceful. There were still cobblestone sidewalks here and there and an abundance of charm. The big chain stores hadn't made many inroads here. He parked off King Street and got out to walk. If he stayed away from the street where the family town house was, there was little chance he'd run into his aunt.

Destiny was probably sitting in front of a fire with her feet tucked under her, a glass of wine at her side and some sort of needlework in hand. She'd recently taken up—and quit—crocheting and knitting. He suspected her attempts at cross-stitching wouldn't last, either. Once she'd tried quilting and given up on that, he figured she might be ready to do some serious painting again. It was obvious to him that these other creative outlets were no match for the talent God had given her.

Ben turned a corner on a street near the Potomac River and stopped short. There it was right in front of him, Kathleen's gallery. The bold, modern paintings in the window weren't to his taste, but he could appreciate the technique and the use of color. He wondered what had drawn Kathleen to them. Was it the art or the artist?

A black-and-white photo of the man had been blown up, along with a brief biography, and placed on an easel between the two paintings. The man wasn't handsome in the conventional sense. His expression was too fierce, his eyes too close-set. Shifty looking, Ben concluded. He scowled at the portrait, feeling a startling streak of jealousy slice through him.

Maybe if it hadn't been for that, he would have ignored the light that was on in the back of the shop. Maybe he would have done the smart thing and crept away before getting caught lurking around outside Kathleen's gallery like some lovesick kid.

Instead, he walked over to the door, tried it, then pounded on the door frame hard enough to rattle the glass panels.

When Kathleen emerged from the back, she looked as if she were mad enough to spit. Ben didn't care. He wasn't particularly happy himself.

"What are you doing here?" she demanded as she jerked open the door. "I'm closed."

"I thought you were anxious for me to see the place," he said, shoving his hands in his pockets and avoiding her gaze. The impulse to drag her into his arms was almost impossible to resist. He wanted to feel her mouth under his again, wanted to taste her. Instead, he resorted to temper. "I can see that I came at a bad time, though. Forget it."

He turned to go, only to hear her mutter an oath he wouldn't have expected to cross such perfect lips. Oddly, it made him smile.

"Don't go," she said eventually. "You just caught me in a particularly foul mood. I wouldn't even be here, except I was afraid if I stayed at home I'd start breaking things.''

He turned back slowly. ''Who put you in such a temper?'' he asked curiously. ''Or was it left over from our encounter this morning?''

''You merely exasperated me. My mother's the only person who can infuriate me.''

''Ah, I see,'' Ben said, though he didn't. His own family relationships were complex, but rarely drove him to the kind of rage Kathleen had obviously been feeling before his arrival. He met her gaze. ''Want to get out of here before you start slicing up the paintings?''

She gave him a hard look. ''I thought you came to see the paintings.''

''So did I, but apparently I came to see you,'' he admitted candidly. ''Have you had dinner?''

''No. I figured food and all that acid churning in my stomach would be a bad combination.''

''As a rule, you'd probably be right, but I think we can deal with that.''

She regarded him curiously. ''How?''

''We'll take a long walk and release all those happy endorphins. By the time we eat, you'll be in a much more pleasant frame of mind.''

''Unless you exasperate me,'' she suggested, but there was a faint hint of amusement in her eyes.

''I'll try not to do that,'' he assured her seriously.

''Then dinner sounds good. I'll turn off the lights and get my coat. I'll just be a minute.'' She hesitated, her gaze on him. ''Unless you really do want to look around.''

''Another time,'' Ben told her.

''Promise?''

He smiled and tucked a finger under her chin, rubbed his thumb across the soft skin. "Promise."

The word was out, the commitment made before he could remind himself that he never made promises, never committed to anything.

Ah, well, it was only a visit to an art gallery, he told himself. Where was the harm in committing to that?

He gazed into Kathleen's violet eyes and felt himself falling head-over-teakettle as Destiny might say. The shock of it left him thoroughly unsettled. If he'd been a lesser man, he'd have taken off the instant Kathleen went to get her coat, running like the emotional coward he was.

Instead he stayed firmly in place, telling himself there was no danger here unless he allowed it. No danger at all.

It was the first lie he'd told himself in years.

"Okay," Kathleen said as she sat across from Ben in a dark, candlelit restaurant that boasted some of the best seafood in town. "If we're going to get through dinner without arguing, here's what's off-limits—art, Destiny and my mother."

Ben lifted his beer in a toast. "Sounds perfectly reasonable to me." He gave her a disarming grin. "Think you can stick to it?"

"Me?" she scoffed. "You'll probably be the first to break the rules."

"Believe me, there was not a topic on your list that I'm interested in pursuing," he assured her. "If you want to talk about your favorite scone recipes, it's okay with me."

Kathleen grinned despite herself. "You want me to share my recipes with you?"

"Not share them," he said, giving her a look that made her toes curl. "I was thinking we could go to your place later and you could demonstrate."

"You got all the scones you're getting from me this morning," she assured him.

"Too bad. I'm really partial to the old-fashioned kind with currants. A dozen of those and I might let you have your way with me."

Now, there was an image meant to rattle her. She gave him a hard look meant to bring him back into line, then spoiled it by asking, "Are we talking sex or are we talking about me getting to poke around in your studio to my heart's content? No restrictions. No time limits."

"Which will be the best way to get you into the kitchen?"

"The studio, of course."

"Because?"

"Do you even have to ask? All that art just begging for an expert to appraise it."

He chuckled. "I win."

She stared at him blankly. "Win what?"

"You were the first one to break the rules and bring up art," he said.

She studied him with a narrowed gaze. "Then that entire discussion was some sort of game to get me to trip myself up?"

"Maybe."

"You're a very devious man."

"I come by it naturally."

"Destiny, I presume," she said, then groaned as she saw the trap. "Got me again."

He laughed. "Shall we move on?"

"To?"

He held her gaze and waited.

"I am not bringing up my mother, dammit!"

"Too late," he said, clearly delighted with himself. "And since you brought her up, tell me why she had you so upset that you had to leave home to save the crockery."

"The story is far too long and boring," she insisted, then smiled brightly. "And here's our food. Isn't that perfect timing?"

"Only if you think my memory is so short that I'll forget about this by dessert," he said mildly.

"I'm certainly counting on it," she told him.

For several minutes silence fell as they ate. Usually Kathleen was comfortable with silence. She rarely felt a need to fill it with inane chatter, but being with Ben was different. Maybe it was the fear that if she didn't initiate some innocuous topic, he would go right back to all the subjects that made her uncomfortable or caused conflict between them. She'd had all the conflict she could handle for one day. A quiet evening of pleasant conversation was what she wanted now. Ben was not the man she would have chosen for that, but he was here and, truthfully, they weren't doing so badly so far.

She glanced across the table and noted that Ben didn't seem to share the same fear that the silence would be filled with some disquieting topic. He seemed perfectly content to eat the excellent rockfish.

"Ben, what were you really doing in town this afternoon?" she asked eventually.

He looked vaguely startled by the question. "I told you. I came to see you."

"But you didn't know I'd be at the gallery," she said.

"No. And if I'm being perfectly honest, a part of me hoped that you wouldn't be."

"Why?"

He met her gaze. "Because seeing you only complicates things."

"How?"

"There's something between us, some powerful pull. That kiss the other night proved that." He paused and waited, apparently for some acknowledgment.

Hiding her surprise that he was willing to acknowledge that, Kathleen nodded.

"So we're agreed on that much," he said. "But unless I'm misreading the situation, you're not much happier about that than I am."

"Not much," she conceded.

"And you want something from me that I'm not prepared to give," he added.

"Your paintings."

"Yes. So, where does that leave us?"

She sighed at the complexity of the situation. He'd pegged it, all right. Then she brightened. "That doesn't mean we can't have a friendly meal together from time to time, does it? This is going pretty well so far."

He grinned. "So far," he said agreeably. "But what happens when I take you home and want to go inside and make love to you?"

Kathleen had just taken a sip of her tea and nearly choked on it. She stared at him. "Are you serious?"

"Very serious," he claimed, and there was nothing in his somber expression to suggest he was merely taunting her.

"Do you always want to sleep with someone you barely know?" she asked shakily.

"Never, as a matter of fact."

The fact that she was an exception rattled her even more than his initial declaration. But could she believe him? She didn't know him well enough to say if he was capable of a convenient lie or not. And Tim had been a smooth talker, too. Maybe it was some secondary gene in certain artists or maybe even in men in general. She reminded herself yet again that she needed to beware of anything that crossed Ben's lips, any admission that seemed to come too easily.

"I don't think it's going to be an issue," she said firmly, proud of the fact that she kept her voice perfectly steady. "Because the answer will be no."

"Because you don't want to?" he asked, his gaze searching hers. "Or because you do?"

"Doesn't really matter, does it? No is still no."

His lips quirked. "Unless it's maybe."

She frowned at that. "It most definitely isn't maybe."

He nodded slowly. "Okay then, friendly dinners are out because they could only lead to trouble. Any other ideas?"

Oddly, Kathleen desperately wanted to find a compromise. She was surprised by just how much she wanted to go on seeing Ben, whether he ever let her near his art or not. Not that she intended to give up on that, either.

"I'll give it some thought," she said eventually. "As soon as I come up with something, I'll let you know."

He gave her one of his most devastating smiles. "I'll look forward to that."

Still a little shaky from the impact of that smile, she studied him curiously. "Aren't you scared that your aunt will get wind of this and gloat or, worse yet, take it as a sign that her meddling is working and try a whole new plot?''

"Oh, I think we can count on Destiny getting mixed up in this again, no matter what we do," he said, sounding resigned. "Unfortunately, she doesn't give up easily."

He glanced up just then and groaned.

"What?" Kathleen asked, then guessed, "She's here, isn't she?"

"Just walked in," Ben confirmed. "I imagine we can thank the maître d' for that. I swear the man is on her payroll. He probably called her the instant we came through the door."

"Took her a while to get here, if he did."

"She probably hoped to catch us in a compromising position," Ben said, then forced a smile as he stood up. "Destiny." He gave her a kiss.

Kathleen gave her a weak smile. "Nice to see you, Destiny."

Destiny beamed at them. "Please, don't let me interrupt. I just came in to pick up a dinner to take back to the house. I didn't feel much like cooking tonight."

"Why don't you have them serve it here?" Kathleen said. "You can join us."

Even as she spoke, Ben was saying, "Don't let us hold you up. Your food will get cold."

Destiny gave him a scolding look, then smiled happily at Kathleen. "I'd love to join you, if you're sure you don't mind."

Kathleen shot a fierce look at Ben. "Please stay."

Ben sighed heavily and relented. "Have a seat," he said pulling out a chair for his aunt.

"Thank you, darling. I must say I'm surprised to see the two of you here together."

"Surprised?" Ben asked skeptically. "I imagine you already knew we were here before you ever walked through the door. In fact, my guess is that it's what got you over here with that flimsy excuse about ordering takeout."

Destiny's gaze narrowed. "Are you suggesting I'm lying?"

"Just a little fib," he said. "You're not all that great at it, you know. You should give it up."

Destiny turned to Kathleen. "See what I have to put up with. I get no respect from this man."

"Oh, you get plenty of respect," Ben countered. "I'm just on to you."

Destiny sat back contentedly. "If you know why I'm here, that'll save me the trouble of asking all those pesky questions. Just tell me how you two wound up here."

"It was an accident," Ben claimed at once. "We bumped into each other."

"Alexandria is a long way from Middleburg. How did you just happen to be on the streets around here?" Destiny asked. "Were you coming to see me?"

"No," Ben said at once.

Destiny chuckled. "I see. Then it was the thought of seafood that drew you?"

"Something like that," Ben said.

Destiny regarded him smugly. "Something like that, indeed," she said, a note of satisfaction in her voice.

Kathleen stole a look at Ben. He did not look happy. In fact, judging from his expression, she figured their gooses were pretty much cooked. Destiny would never give up now.

Chapter Six

Ben spent two days kicking himself for choosing to take Kathleen to that particular restaurant for dinner. He knew perfectly well that Destiny had sources there. That was where Richard had met Melanie, and his aunt had had every detail of that meeting before they'd finished their first cups of coffee. Ben knew because she'd gloated about it.

Since he should have guessed the risks, did that mean some part of him had wanted to be caught? Was he hoping in some totally perverse way that Destiny would keep meddling until both he and Kathleen were firmly on the hook?

Surely not, especially after just a couple of brief encounters. He might be in lust with Kathleen, but it certainly didn't go beyond that, and beyond that is just where Destiny wanted him to go. He didn't believe for one single second that this was about art, not from his aunt's perspective, anyway.

But any relationship was doomed. He and Kathleen had discussed the situation and viewed it through clear eyes. It simply wasn't meant to be. Period.

That didn't mean he was having much success in ignoring the attraction. Goodness knows he was tempted to drag her into his arms about every ten seconds, but that was another thing they'd agreed on. Sex was a bad idea.

Not that they'd hold out forever, he concluded honestly, especially if they kept on seeing each other on one pretext or another. Proximity was about as dangerous for the two of them as holding a match near the wick on a stick of dynamite and simply hoping there wouldn't be an explosion.

He was still pondering the entire situation over his morning coffee when he looked up and spotted Richard coming up the front steps. First Mack, now Richard. His brothers were apparently determined to get an unprecedented amount of enjoyment out of watching him squirm.

Richard rang the bell, then used his key and came on in. No one in the whole damn family ever considered that he might be busy or might not want to see them, Ben thought gloomily. Maybe Middleburg hadn't been quite far enough to move when he'd wanted solitude. Ohio might have been better. Or maybe Montana.

"You in here?" Richard called out.

"If I weren't, would you go away?" Ben replied, not even trying to hide his sarcasm.

Richard strode into the dining room, picked up the

pot of coffee and poured himself a cup without bothering to respond.

"I'll take your silence as a no," Ben said. "If you're here to make something out of the fact that I had dinner with Kathleen, don't bother. I'm in no mood to discuss it."

Richard regarded him with seemingly genuine surprise. "You had dinner with Kathleen? When was that? You certainly didn't waste any time, did you? I thought you were made of tougher stuff than that."

"Very funny," Ben said, then frowned at his brother. "You mean Destiny didn't tell you? I thought she'd announce it to the wire services."

"Nope, and apparently she didn't see fit to tip off her favorite gossip columnist, either," Richard said with an exaggerated shudder. "Be grateful for small favors."

"I'm not feeling especially grateful," Ben told his big brother. "Okay then, let's change the subject. Why are you out here on a weekday morning, if not to gloat?"

"I needed a sounding board," Richard said.

His tone was so serious, his expression so gloomy, that Ben stared at him in shock.

"Is Melanie okay?" he asked at once. "There's nothing wrong with the baby, is there?"

"Aside from being annoyed with me for hovering, Melanie's perfectly fine. So is the baby," Richard said. "This is about business."

"And you came to me?" Ben asked, astonished. "Why not Mack? Or Destiny?"

"I didn't go to Mack because he's out of town," he admitted with typical candor. "And I didn't want to discuss this with Destiny, because the last time brought up this particular subject, she got really weird on me.''

''Then I was third choice? That's a relief,'' Ben said. ''I thought the business had to be close to collapse if you were desperate enough to seek advice from me.''

''Actually, in this instance, you really were first choice. You know Destiny better than Mack or I do.''

Ben groaned at the frequently-made claim. ''That's ridiculous and you know it.''

''Come on, Ben. It's no secret that the two of you are tighter than the rest of us. Maybe it's because you were the youngest when she came to live with us, so she was even more like a mother to you. Or maybe it's the art thing, but you're her favorite. I figure she's bound to share things with you that she doesn't confide in Mack or me.''

''You've said something like that before, and I still say you're crazy,'' Ben said. ''Destiny doesn't have favorites. Sure, we have a bond because of art, but that's it. She loves all of us.''

''I know she loves us. That's not the point,'' Richard said impatiently. ''Look, can we talk about this or not?''

Ben sat back. ''Fine. Talk, but I have to tell you that Destiny does not sit around sharing confidences with me, either. She's meddling in *my* life these days. She's not letting me poke around in hers.''

''That doesn't mean she hasn't let something slip from time to time,'' Richard insisted. ''Here's the deal. I've got a huge problem with the European division. We've nearly lost out on a couple of big deals over there because of some minor player who jumps into the mix and drives up the price. So far we've only lost one acquisition, but that's one too many. And I don't like the fact that it's always this same guy whose name keeps popping up. It's like he's carrying out his own personal vendetta against Carlton Industries. This company of his is not a major player, but he's smart enough to know precisely what to do to make a muddle of our negotiations.''

Despite his total lack of interest in the family business, Ben hadn't been able to avoid absorbing some information over the years. Richard introduced the topic at almost every family gathering. Because of that, so far he was following Richard, but he didn't see the connection to their aunt.

''What does any of that have to do with Destiny?'' he asked.

''I'm not a hundred percent certain, but I think this was a man she was involved with years ago. It's the only explanation I can come up with,'' Richard told him.

''Have you asked her?''

''Of course. When I brought up his name, she turned pale and flatly refused to tell me anything. She said I was in charge of Carlton Industries and I should deal with it.''

The whole scenario seemed a little too far-fetched to Ben. Destiny with some long-lost secret love who'd been pining for years and was now making a move on Carlton Industries in retaliation for some slight? He'd always thought the business world was a whole lot more logical and, well, businesslike than that.

''What makes you think she knows him, much less was involved with him?'' he asked Richard. ''Maybe she simply doesn't want to get drawn into company politics.''

''I had someone in the division over there do some

quiet checking. I wanted to see if this man and Destiny could have crossed paths. The guy is British, but he lived in France for several years. In fact, he lived in the very town where Destiny lived at the same time she was there. That can't be pure coincidence. I even sent my guy over to France to poke around, but people wouldn't tell him a blessed thing. He said those who remembered her got very protective when he mentioned Destiny's name.''

Ben had always known that Destiny had hidden things from them. Because of the vibrant, extraordinary woman she was, he'd also supposed that there had been a man in her life back then. Only recently had she alluded to such a thing, though. Even so, she hadn't acknowledged a broken heart and she certainly had never mentioned a name.

"I don't know, Richard," Ben said skeptically. "I suppose you could be right. It makes sense that there was someone in her life back then, but why would he be driven to make a play at this late date for companies Carlton Industries wants to acquire?"

"Beats me," Richard said candidly. "But I have this gut feeling there's a connection."

"Is he a real threat to the company?"

"More an annoyance," Richard admitted. "But I don't like anything I can't explain."

"Then you need to ask Destiny again."

"I thought maybe you could," Richard suggested, then grinned. "Since you're bound to be seeing more of her these days than I am, what with the whole Kathleen thing going on."

"Ha-ha," Ben retorted, unamused.

Richard's expression sobered at once. "Will you talk to her?"

"You really are worried, aren't you?" Ben asked.

"It's gnawing at me, yes. And there's a deal coming up soon that could be really important to our future growth in Europe. I don't want to have this particular gnat in the mix."

Ben nodded slowly. "Okay then, I'll do what I can, but you know how prickly Destiny is about the past. She's never wanted us to get the idea that she gave up anything important to come and take care of us. If she blew off your questions, she's just as likely to blow off mine."

"I think we're past the time when she needs to worry about us feeling insecure about her intentions toward us," Richard said. "We all know she loves us and that she has no regrets about the choice she made. I just need to know if she walked out on a love affair that could be coming back to haunt us."

"I'll see what I can find out. What's this man's name?"

"William Harcourt."

Ben pulled an ever-present pen out of his pocket and jotted the name down on his hand, since he didn't have paper handy and didn't trust his memory to even recall the conversation once he'd spent a few hours in his studio. Richard watched him, looking amused.

"Try not to wash up before you call Destiny," he advised.

Ben grinned. "Waterproof ink," he noted, waving the pen. "I learned that lesson a long time ago. I figure even with a few long, cold showers, I've got till the end of the week to remember to chase down Destiny and ask her about this."

"Don't wait that long, okay?"

Something in his brother's tone alerted him that this

mess was even more serious than Richard had admitted. Ben nodded.

"I'll get back to you tonight. Will that do?"

"Morning's soon enough," Richard assured him. "Tonight I have to wallpaper the nursery to keep Melanie from trying to do it herself."

Ben chuckled. "I'm sure she'll appreciate your consideration."

"Actually she won't," Richard conceded with a shrug. "She'll sit there and grumble and tell me I'm doing it all wrong."

"Then let her do it," Ben advised.

"Let her climb a ladder in her condition?" Richard asked with a look of genuine horror. "I don't think so. I can take three or four nonstop hours of grumbling."

"Do you even know how to hang wallpaper?" Ben asked curiously.

"No, but how hard can it be?"

Ben smothered a laugh. "I'll be by tonight."

"I told you morning's soon enough."

"Maybe for the report you want," Ben agreed. "I'm coming by for the entertainment."

She had no business going out to the farm, Kathleen told herself even as she turned onto the country road that led to Ben's. Destiny's arrival at the restaurant the other night had been fair warning that the meddling and matchmaking were far from over.

But she'd awakened this morning thinking about Ben—about his *art,* she corrected, determined to stay focused—and had decided that the only way she'd ever get what she wanted was to keep up the pressure. He'd had two days off now. As distracted as an artist could get, he could easily have forgotten all about her by now.

Before leaving the house, she'd taken an extra hour to bake some of the bear claws she made for the occasional morning receptions she held for the media to meet artists before their shows opened. She told herself she'd baked them because she'd had a sudden craving for one herself, but the truth was it was another bribe. If the man had a sweet tooth, she was not above exploiting it.

Just as she reached the end of Ben's driveway, she saw a car turning onto the main highway and recognized Richard behind the wheel. She waved at him as he passed and got a friendly wave and a smug grin in return.

Then she turned into the long drive leading up to the secluded house. Not that she was any expert on recluses, but it seemed to her that Ben's reputation for craving solitude was slightly exaggerated. In the few days she'd known him, he'd had plenty of company right here at the farm and he'd come into town to seek her out. That didn't sound like any recluse she'd ever heard about.

Still, there was no question that his expression was forbidding when he walked out of the house and spotted her just as she was pulling to a stop beside his studio.

"This place is turning into Grand Central Station," he complained.

Kathleen gave him a cheery smile. "I was just thinking the same thing. I saw your brother leaving."

Ben's scowl deepened. "Great. Just great. That will hit the family grapevine as soon as he can hit speed-dial on his cell phone."

"Still running scared of Destiny?"

"Aren't you?"

"Not so much. Besides, I'm here on business, not for pleasure."

"A distinction I'm sure Richard will make when he reports your arrival before eight in the morning."

She refused to be daunted. "At least he didn't catch me going in the other direction," she said. "Just imagine what he could have made of that."

Ben sighed, then glimpsed the bag in her hand. His expression brightened marginally. "Have you been baking again?"

"Bear claws," she told him. "I took a chance you'd like them."

"Real ones?" he asked incredulously. "With almond paste and flaky pastry? Fresh from the oven?"

She grinned at his undisguised enthusiasm. "As authentic as any bakery's."

He snatched the bag from her hand and peered inside, then drew in a deep, appreciative breath. "Oh, my God." He peered at her curiously. "Why aren't you married?"

"I was. He didn't seem to care that much for my baking."

"Fool."

Kathleen laughed. "He was, but not because he didn't like my pastry." It was the first time she'd ever been able to laugh at anything related to her marriage. She met Ben's gaze. "Since you're obviously awed and impressed, are these going to get me into your studio?"

His expression turned thoughtful as he took his first bite. "Fantastic," he murmured, still not answering her question.

He took another bite, then sighed with seeming rapture. "Incredible, but no."

Kathleen was tempted to snatch away the rest of the pastries. Instead, she settled for giving him a severe look. "May I ask why?"

He grinned. "You've made a slight miscalculation. Don't worry about it. People are always doing that where I'm concerned. They think I know very little about business, because I'm the artistic Carlton, but I did pick up a thing or two."

"So?"

"I've obviously got something you want, something you want desperately enough to ply me with baked goods. Why would I cave in too quickly, when holding out will get me more?"

Despite her frustration, Kathleen couldn't help chuckling. "You're impossible."

"So I've been told." He gave her a considering look. "But just so your trip won't be a total waste, how about going over to Richard and Melanie's with me tonight?"

Kathleen was startled by the invitation. "For?" she asked cautiously.

"We get to watch Richard try to hang wallpaper, while Melanie criticizes him."

Kathleen laughed. "Oh, hon, I think you're the one who's miscalculated. We set foot in there tonight and Richard won't be hanging that wallpaper alone. You'll be right in there with him, while Melanie and I sip tea in the kitchen."

"Want to bet?"

"Sure," she said at once, always eager to take advantage of an opportunity to best someone who'd just tricked her. "If it turns out the way I predict, you show me at least one more painting. If you win, I bring you the pastry of your choice next time I come.''

He considered the offer, then nodded. "Deal. Oh, and just so you know, we have to take a little side trip past Destiny's on the way.''

"As in drive past and don't stop?'' she asked hopefully.

"Nope,'' he said, sounding oddly happy. "We're dropping in to do a little snooping. I think it might require a woman's touch. What time does the shop close?''

"Five-thirty tonight.''

"Good. I'll pick you up at six.'' He looked her over. "You might want to wear something you don't care too much about.''

"Oh?''

"If I wind up papering those walls, sweetheart, you won't be sipping tea. You'll be right there next to me.''

If he had a hundred years, Ben was pretty confident he wouldn't be able to explain what had made him ask Kathleen to join him in going to see Destiny. Oh, sure, maybe he'd had some vague notion that Destiny would be more inclined to open up to another woman, but it wasn't as if Kathleen were a trusted confidante. Melanie or Beth might have been better suited to the task.

No, he'd acted on impulse, something he never did, not since he'd been involved with Graciela, who'd taken impulsive behavior to an art form. Now he was usually thorough and methodical about just about everything, measuring words and actions, because he couldn't forget the last time he'd made an impulsive decision, demanded that Graciela leave his home immediately, and she had died because of it.

But despite his misgivings about the invitation to Kathleen for tonight, he hadn't called and canceled. It was yet another instance of making a commitment and then being too proud, if not too honorable or too stubborn, to break it. Kathleen already thought he was cowardly when it came to his art. He couldn't give her another reason to believe that he was scared of her or his feelings for her.

He considered seeing Destiny first, then picking up Kathleen, but figured that would raise a whole lot of questions that he wouldn't want to answer, as well. Instead, he drove through the horrendous Washington rush hour traffic to the address Kathleen had given him. He was on her doorstep precisely at six. He reassured himself that it was absolutely not because he was anxious to see her again. He knew artists had a reputation for being forgetful, but punctuality was one of those lessons that had been ingrained in him by his parents even before Destiny had come along to reiterate it.

When Kathleen opened the door, his mouth gaped. He couldn't help it. She'd taken his advice to wear old, comfortable clothes to heart, but few women could turn that particular sort of getup into a fashion statement. Kathleen did. The faded, low-slung hip-hugger jeans encased her slender legs like a glove and reminded him all too vividly just how long those exquisite legs were. She was wearing a bulky knit sweater that looked warm enough, except for the full two inches of bare skin it left exposed at her waist.

"Um," he began, then swallowed hard. He cleared his throat and tried again. "Aren't you going to be cold?"

She grinned. "I was thinking of wearing a coat over this."

He nodded, still trying to get the blood that had rushed to other parts of his anatomy to flow back to his brain. "I meant indoors."

Her grin spread. "Your aunt doesn't have heat?"

Ben sighed and gave up. He wasn't going to get her into something that covered that enticing skin without point-blank asking her to change, and he would not do that. She'd only demand to know why, just to hear him admit that he could hardly keep his hands or his eyes off her. He'd simply have to suffer and keep a tight rein on his hormones.

"Let's get going, then."

Kathleen gave him a knowing smirk. "I'll get my coat," she said cheerfully.

On the drive to Destiny's, Ben finally managed to untangle his tongue long enough to explain their mission to get at the truth about Destiny and this William Harcourt who was interfering in Carlton Industries business.

"What makes you think I can get her to say anything, when Richard couldn't?"

"You're a woman. Maybe she'll confide in you, woman-to-woman."

"With you sitting there?"

"I'll make some excuse and hide out for a little bit," he said, no doubt sounding a little too eager.

Kathleen looked at him with amusement. "That will certainly make her less suspicious."

He had a hunch she was right. "Do you have a better suggestion?"

"Ask her directly. Even if she doesn't answer, you should be able to read her expression. And *I'll* be the one to make myself scarce while you do it. Women are always having to run to the powder room. She won't think a thing about it.''

"I suppose," he said gloomily. He was no good at this kind of stuff. Subterfuge and subtlety weren't in his nature, but Richard had already warned him that the direct approach hadn't gotten him a thing.

"Trust me, Ben. It's the only way," Kathleen insisted. "A woman like your aunt appreciates someone who's straightforward. Trying to slip something past her won't work. Or if by chance it does, she'll be furious with you for having tricked her into saying something she didn't intend to reveal. That's the last thing you want."

"Okay, okay," he grumbled. "I know you're right. I just hate doing what I'm always accusing her of doing, meddling in something that's none of my business."

"Tell her that, too," Kathleen suggested. "She'll identify with your position. Heck, maybe it will even give her a nudge to back off with her own meddling."

"I think we can eliminate that possibility. I'm not in the miracle business," Ben responded.

He pulled up in front of the town house where he'd grown up. In some ways it still felt more like home than the farm, but at the moment he was dreading going inside. He glanced at Kathleen.

"I guess it's showtime," he said unenthusiastically.

"Don't sound like you expect to be shot on sight," she said, regarding him with obvious amusement. "This is Destiny. The mere fact that I'm with you ought to buy you a certain amount of good will."

It ought to, Ben agreed. But he had a hunch that Destiny was going to be more furious than smug tonight. He also had a gut feeling that he and Kathleen were going to be back out on the front steps in record time. In fact, given what Richard had told him earlier, there was a distinct possibility that Destiny might kick them straight to the curb.

...

Chapter Seven

Destiny's initial delight at finding Ben and Kathleen
on her doorstep was pretty much doomed to fade
quickly, quite likely because her nephew had absolutely no notion how to finesse such a touchy conversation. Kathleen barely contained a sigh when Ben declined a drink, declined to take off his coat. It was
pretty much apparent that he was on a mission and he
was impatient to get it over with. Kathleen spotted the
immediate suspicion in Destiny's eyes at his curt man-
ner.

"Actually we're on our way to Richard's," he told
Destiny the instant they'd stepped inside. He showed
absolutely no inclination to set one foot any farther into
the house.

Destiny looked a bit taken aback, but quickly rallied.
"Really? For dinner? And you invited Kathleen to join
you. How lovely."

"We're probably going to order pizza," Ben told her, oblivious to the hopeful note in Destiny's voice. "Richard's wallpapering the nursery. And we're planning to watch."

Destiny's deep-throated chuckle cut through the tension. She seemed to relax a bit. "Yes, I can see how that would be immensely entertaining. Perhaps I'll come along."

"Sure," Ben said. "But I need to talk to you about something first." He glanced pointedly in Kathleen's direction.

"May I use the powder room, Destiny?" she asked dutifully.

Destiny clearly wasn't fooled for a second by the abrupt pretext. She gave Ben a piercing look. "What is this about?" When Kathleen started to leave, Destiny arrowed a look in her direction. "Stay right here, Kathleen."

"But—" Kathleen protested, only to be cut off.

"I would appreciate it if you would stay," Destiny repeated, then frowned at Ben. "Does this have anything at all to do with your brother or Carlton Industries?"

Ben stared at her in obvious shock. "How do you know that?"

"Oh, please, do you think I don't know what goes on over there?" Destiny scoffed. "I have an office right down the hall from your brother's. It might be mainly for window dressing, since I'm family and I am a member of the board, but I've been known to spend time there. I'm privy to what's going on in the company. I even have a secretary, as you very well know. And people actually stop in to chat from time to time.

There's very little that goes on around there that I don't know about.''

Kathleen bit back a smile as Ben sighed, and asked, ''More of your inside sources, I presume.''

''Of course,'' she said without apology. ''I know how invaluable contacts can be. It's how the business world works. And despite my refusal to take my proper place at Carlton Industries, it was impossible to grow up around your grandfather and father without learning a thing or two about how important it is to keep one ear to the ground at all times. It avoids a lot of nasty surprises.''

''Did your insider tell you what Richard is upset about?'' Ben asked.

''The European division,'' she said at once, proving that she didn't spend all of her time in that office sipping tea and gossiping with the friendly staff. ''It hasn't been performing as well as he'd hoped and he thinks it's being victimized by the owner of a British company.''

''Exactly,'' Ben said. ''A man named William Harcourt.''

Kathleen kept her gaze locked on Destiny's face when the name was mentioned. Aside from the faint shadow that darkened her eyes, she betrayed nothing.

''Do you know him, Destiny?'' Ben asked point-blank.

For a moment Kathleen thought Destiny was going to evade Ben's question. Instead she drew herself up regally.

''I did at one time,'' she admitted. ''But I imagine your brother already knows that. He certainly paid enough to that private detective who was poking around over there.''

Ben regarded her with chagrin. "You found out about that, too?"

"Darling, I lived in that village in France for a number of years. Of course I have friends there who would let me know about a stranger who was asking too many questions. It wasn't all that difficult to find the payments to him on the Carlton Industries books."

Kathleen was impressed. "Nice work, Destiny."

Ben shot a daunting look at both of them. "Let's cut to the chase, then. How well do you know William Harcourt?" he asked bluntly.

"The answer to that depends on many factors," Destiny said evasively.

Ben gave her an impatient look. "It's not a difficult question, Destiny. Any answer at all will do, as long as it's truthful."

She frowned at his tone. "I don't see the need to discuss this with you."

"Then you'll just have to discuss it with Richard," he warned.

"Oh, for heaven's sakes, the two of you are acting as if there's some grand conspiracy. I haven't seen William or heard from him in years."

"Did you know him well?" Ben asked again, this time more gently, as if he'd finally caught on to just how touchy this subject was.

"I really don't think that matters," Destiny said stiffly.

"It does if you're the reason he's targeting Carlton Industries," Ben said.

"That's absurd," Destiny said flatly. "Tell your brother that whatever's going on has nothing to do with me. I'm certain of that. If he's found himself in a hostile business environment over there, he needs to fix the problem. Richard is the one in charge, after all. I'm sure William will be reasonable.''

''Why don't you tell Richard that yourself?'' Ben asked. ''You two can talk this out when we get to his house. Given your insights, maybe you can give Richard some advice on how to handle the man.''

Destiny shook her head, looking suddenly tired. ''I don't think I'll go after all. I've just remembered a prior engagement.''

''Destiny—''

Kathleen cut off Ben's protest, even as she gave Destiny's icy hand a squeeze. ''It's okay, Ben. We should be going.''

Ben looked as if he might argue, but Kathleen all but shoved him toward the front door. Only after he was outside did she claim to have forgotten her purse.

''Start the car. I'll be right with you,'' she told him.

He gave her a penetrating look. ''What are you up to?''

''I'm not up to anything,'' she insisted.

He studied her with obvious skepticism, then shrugged. ''Okay, whatever. I'll warm up the car.''

Kathleen hurried back inside and found Destiny still standing where they'd left her. ''Are you okay? Is there anything I can do for you?''

Destiny tried to smile, but failed. ''No, dear, there's nothing anyone can do.''

''This Mr. Harcourt really mattered to you, didn't he?''

Destiny's expression turned even sadder. ''He was the love of my life,'' she said simply, her voice catching.

''But none of your nephews knows that, do they?''

"No, I never saw the point in telling them. It ended when I came back to the States to care for them."

"Maybe it's time you explained all that."

Destiny shook her head. "I've never wanted them to think there was any sacrifice at all in my returning home to look out for them. It would only have upset them. Besides, it's in the past."

"It doesn't sound as if Mr. Harcourt agrees with you," Kathleen pointed out.

Destiny looked startled by that. "What on earth are you saying?"

"That Ben could be correct. You could be the reason Mr. Harcourt has become a thorn in Richard's side. Sooner or later you'll have to consider that and deal with it."

Destiny sighed heavily. "Perhaps you're right," she said slowly.

"And if I am?"

A glint of determination suddenly lit Destiny's eyes and she squared her shoulders, looking stronger than she had since the whole topic had come up. "Then I will deal with William," she said firmly.

Kathleen grinned at her fierce tone. "If you need any help, let me know."

"Thanks for helping me to clarify what I must do," Destiny said. "But if you wouldn't mind, please keep this conversation to yourself. Until I decide how I want to handle this, it's best that Ben and the others don't know about my intentions."

"They could help," Kathleen suggested, uncomfortable at being asked to keep Destiny's secret from Ben. He wasn't going to be happy if she left the house tonight without something to report.

Destiny laughed. "I love my nephews, Kathleen, but

in a situation like this, they won't help. They'll only pester me to death.''

"The way you meddle in their lives?"

"Exactly." Destiny gave her a wry look. "I did raise them, after all."

Ben was thoroughly frustrated. Kathleen had refused to reveal a single word about her conversation with Destiny.

"Confidential," she said when he asked.

"But I'm the one who wanted you to talk to her," he protested.

"And I told you to handle it yourself. Just look how well that turned out. She clammed up and refused to reveal a single thing about her knowledge of this Harcourt person."

"She admitted she knew him," Ben said defensively.

"Oh, please," she scoffed. "You knew that before you ever walked in there. So did Richard, I suspect. What you knew nothing about was the extent of the relationship and how it fits with what's going on now. You don't know any more about that than you did before you spoke to her."

He regarded her intently. "Do you?"

"Confidential," she said again.

"I'll bet Richard can pry it out of you," he said.

"Doubtful," she said.

"Or Melanie," he suggested.

She chuckled. "I don't think so. Whatever Destiny did—or didn't say—to me is not going to cross these lips. Give it up, Ben."

"I might reconsider letting you see a few paintings," he coaxed.

"We already have a bet going that I plan on winning. I'll see at least one of the paintings as soon as you wind up wallpapering that nursery right alongside Richard." She gave him a sideways look. "Unless you intend to renege on our deal."

"Not a chance."

She regarded him with a cheerful expression. "Any other offers you want to put on the table?"

"Not at the moment," he said, exasperated. "I'll get back to you."

"Yes, I imagine you will." Her smile expanded. "It's nice to know that I now have something *you* want. Sort of evens the playing field, doesn't it?"

"You're a sneaky woman. You know that, don't you?"

"Of course."

"It must be why Destiny has taken to you."

"That's one reason," Kathleen agreed. "The other has a lot to do with this impossible nephew she's trying to marry off."

Ben was surprised that she could joke about that. "I thought you found that idea as terrifying as I do."

"Maybe it's growing on me."

He stared at her in shock. "You have to be kidding me."

Kathleen laughed at the unmistakable panic he didn't bother trying to hide. She reached over and patted his white-knuckled grip on the steering wheel. "No need to panic. As flattering as it is to be considered a candidate to be your wife, I'm not interested."

There was no question that she meant exactly what she said. Ben should have been comforted by that, but for some reason he didn't understand, he felt as if someone had just doused him with cold water.

* * *

"Well, don't you two look cheery," Richard said as Ben and Kathleen arrived a few minutes later.

"You don't look so hot yourself," Ben retorted, shocked to see his usually impeccable brother covered with some sort of white paste. His hair was a mess and his expression was grim. "Things not going too well?"

"Don't start with me," Richard warned. "Otherwise you can take your sorry ass out of here right now." He turned to Kathleen. "No offense."

"None taken," she said, her lips twitching as she fought a grin.

"Fine," Ben said, holding up his hands in a gesture of surrender. "I'll keep my comments to myself. Where's Melanie?"

"Actually she's in the nursery with her feet propped up, a glass of milk beside her and a gloating expression on her face. She's having the time of her life," Richard grumbled.

"Why don't I order some pizza?" Ben suggested. "It looks to me like you could use a break and some food. It might improve your mood."

"A professional wallpaper hanger would improve my mood, but I suppose pizza will have to do," Richard said gloomily. "Better order two. Melanie's appetite is huge these days. And don't tell me she's eating for two. I think she's eating for a dozen future football players."

"When the baby comes and it's a delicate little girl, you're going to regret those words," Kathleen told him.

Richard merely shrugged. "So Melanie keeps telling me. I'd better get back in there before she climbs up on the ladder and tries to hang a strip of paper herself.

She does that every time my back is turned. I finally had to turn off my cell phone and stop taking calls from the office.''

"It's after seven. Why were you taking calls, anyway?'' Ben asked.

"This was earlier. I took the afternoon off,'' Richard explained. "I thought I could get this all done during Melanie's afternoon nap. Naturally she wasn't the least bit tired today. And then I ran into a little problem with the actual papering.''

"I could order the pizza,'' Kathleen offered generously. "Ben could help you.''

Ben scowled at her. "You don't win, if you're the one who plants the idea in his head.''

Richard stared at them, clearly confused. "You two have some sort of bet going?''

"It doesn't matter,'' Ben assured him. "I'll order the pizza and be right in. I can't wait to see what you've accomplished so far.''

Richard shot him a look filled with pure venom, then hightailed it back to the nursery.

"I love what imminent fatherhood is doing to my big brother,'' Ben said, watching him with amusement.

"I wouldn't do too much gloating, if I were you,'' Kathleen advised. "If Destiny has her way, you're heading down this same path.''

She set off after Richard, leaving him to contemplate a future that not only included a wife but babies. His heart did a little stutter-step, but the effect wasn't so bad. Once again, there was none of the expected panic at the idea.

Then he remembered what it was like to lose someone and his resolve to remain unattached kicked right back into high gear.

Forget the daydream about a house filled with rambunctious little ones. It wasn't going to happen. There would be no wife filling the kitchen with the aroma of pies and cakes and bear claws. No Kathleen, he thought a bit despondently.

Dammit, for a minute there, the idea had held an astonishing appeal. No doubt that had been his hormones trying to rationalize what *they* wanted.

He picked up the phone and called for pizza, one loaded with everything, the other plain. Melanie didn't need heartburn adding to her woes. She had enough to contend with just enduring her doting husband.

En route to the nursery, he stopped in the kitchen and picked up a few cans of soda, then went upstairs to find both women sitting side by side, feet propped up and instructions tripping off their tongues. He was amazed that Richard hadn't bolted by now. He pulled up his own chair and was about to sit down when Melanie scowled at him.

"I don't think so. Maybe you can line up the stupid stripes. Richard doesn't seem to have an eye for it," she said.

"Hey," Ben protested. "I'm just here as an artistic consultant."

"Not anymore," his sister-in-law informed him. "You're on the team."

"Why?"

"Because you're male and you're a Carlton. I want all of you to pay." She grinned at him. "And I want Kathleen to win that bet."

Ben frowned at her. "If I didn't love you so much, I would not let you badger me into doing this, you know."

Melanie beamed at him. "I know. Now, please, help before we run out of paper."

Ben took a look around the room to see what was left to be done. So far Richard had only managed to successfully hang a half-dozen strips, not even enough to finish one wall. A very large pile of soggy, tangled paper was testament to earlier failed attempts.

"Are you sure you're going to have enough, as it is?" he asked skeptically.

Melanie gave him a smug smile. "I bought extra, since Richard insisted he was going to do it."

Ben noticed that Kathleen was taking in the friendly byplay with an oddly wistful expression on her face. To his surprise, she struck him as someone who was used to being left out but who desperately wanted to be part of things.

"You know," he said mildly. "I hear that Kathleen is amazingly adept at hanging wallpaper."

Kathleen's gaze immediately clashed with his. "I never said any such thing."

Ben shrugged. "Pictures, wallpaper, how different can it be?"

She gave him a look brimming with indignation. "You can't be serious."

"You saying you can't do this?" he asked.

"Of course I can," Kathleen retorted. "But I never told you that and I most certainly never compared it to hanging pictures in my gallery."

He held out a roll of paper. "Care to show us how it's done?"

She gave him a suspicious look, but she accepted the paper and stood up. Winking at Melanie, she walked over, looked at the wall measurements Richard had jotted down on a board straddling two sawhorses, spread out the paper, cut it, smoothed on paste and had it on the wall in about five minutes flat. Richard stared at her in awe.

"My God," he murmured. "What are your rates?"

Kathleen chuckled. "No charge. Actually I did the bedrooms in my house one Saturday afternoon. It was fun."

"Fun," Richard repeated incredulously. He turned to Ben. "She thinks this is fun."

Ben kissed the tip of her nose. "I knew there was a reason I brought you along tonight."

"And here I thought it was because you couldn't resist my company," she said.

He shrugged. There was little point in denying it, not even with his brother and sister-in-law paying avid attention to the entire exchange. "That, too," he said. "Tell me what you need and I'll help. Richard, you and Melanie can go and wait for the pizza."

"I thought you were buying," Richard complained.

"Hey, you're getting two free workers, one of whom actually appears to know what she's doing," Ben retorted. "You can pay for the damn pizza."

"Seems fair to me," Melanie agreed, holding out her hand so her husband could help her out of her chair. "Come on, Richard, let's give these two some privacy."

"What do they need privacy for?" Richard asked. "They're supposed to be hanging wallpaper."

Melanie tugged him toward the door "Maybe your brother will get some other ideas," she told him. "This is a bedroom, after all."

"It's the baby's room," Richard protested indignantly, even as he followed his wife out the door.

Ben glanced at Kathleen and saw that her cheeks

were pink. "Don't pay any attention to the two of them, especially Melanie. She may not be too fond of her doting husband, but she's very big on romance these days. She's as bad as Destiny."

Kathleen's gaze caught his. "Actually I was sort of hoping she was right."

Ben stared at her, not entirely sure he was comprehending. This was one of those things he definitely didn't want to get wrong. "Oh?"

"I was hoping you might have an idea or two that required privacy."

"Such as?"

"I wouldn't mind so much if you kissed me," she told him, moving closer. "Being around those two has given me a couple of wild ideas of my own."

Ben tucked his hands under her elbows and held her in place, scant inches away, close enough that he could breathe in her vaguely exotic scent. "I thought we'd agreed—"

"Don't panic. This will pass," she reassured him. "But right this second, I really want you to kiss me as if you mean it."

"But—" he began, still trying to cling to a shred of sanity.

Before he could complete the thought, she was on tiptoe, her mouth on his. That pretty much shot their agreement to hell, he concluded, as his blood roared through his veins.

The kiss might have gone on forever, might have led to all sorts of things neither one of them had planned, if the sound of the doorbell hadn't finally penetrated the sensual haze enveloping them. He had a hunch Melanie had deliberately let the pizza delivery guy

keeping ringing that bell just to tip them off that it was
time to quit fooling around.

Or, come to think of it, she might have been slow
to answer because she and Richard were downstairs
doing the exact same thing, he decided, smiling.

"Pizza's here," Richard called up, sounding faintly
distracted.

Melanie gazed around, looking dazed. "We didn't
get the first sheet of wallpaper hung."

"Hey, let them hire somebody," Ben said unrepentantly. "My brother's rich enough."

"I wanted to help," she said, that odd wistful note
back in her voice.

He regarded her with surprise. "Why?"

When she didn't reply at once, he took a stab at it.
"Because it would make you feel like you're part of
the family?"

She nodded slowly. "Silly, isn't it? It's not as if
they're family."

"It's not silly at all," he said, wondering again about
the mother who could send her into a rage and the
marriage she refused to discuss. "We'll make this our
baby gift and come back and finish it."

Her eyes brightened. "Really?"

"Sure. Why not?" He winked at her. "As long as
me helping you doesn't mean you've won our bet."

She laughed. "No, I'll give you a pass this time. I
have a few other tricks up my sleeve, anyway."

Ben shook his head. "Why doesn't that surprise
me?"

Chapter Eight

Kathleen felt an unfamiliar sort of contentment stealing through her as she sat around the kitchen table with Ben, Richard and Melanie until nearly midnight. The pizza was long gone, every single slice of it. She had a nice burst of energy thanks to the caffeine in the diet sodas she'd consumed. And Melanie was making noises about wanting to make ice-cream sundaes, though so far she hadn't summoned the energy to move. It all felt comfortable and friendly, the way a family was supposed to be.

She'd had that same feeling earlier in the nursery, which was why she'd volunteered to help with the wallpaper. She'd had an uncontrollable need to be a part of the anticipation for this new baby. She'd seen all the questions in Ben's eyes when she'd said as much, but thankfully he'd simply agreed to work with her, rather than pestering her for answers. She wasn't sure she could have explained her reasons, anyway.

"I think we should be letting you get to bed," Ben told Melanie. "You have to be exhausted."

She gave him a disgusted look. "From doing what? Richard won't let me work more than a couple of hours at my PR business in the morning. You saw how he is about letting me do anything remotely physically demanding. I took a walk around the block today, and he almost had heart failure."

"The baby's due any second," Richard reminded her. "What if you'd gone into labor?"

"I had my cell phone in my pocket and, believe me, I *want* to go into labor. This baby can't get here soon enough for me. Otherwise I might be tempted to strangle my overly protective husband."

Richard regarded her with a wounded expression. "I just want you and the baby to be safe."

Melanie's expression softened. She reached for his hand. "I know," she soothed. "Which is the only reason I let you get away with this."

Kathleen bit back a sigh that would have been far too telling. She glanced at Ben instead. "If this baby's coming any day now, we'd better finish up that nursery. The gallery's closed tomorrow. I can come by. Can you?"

He nodded. "I'll be here."

Melanie stared at them. "You guys don't need to do that."

"We want to," Kathleen assured her. "It's our baby present."

"Oh, really?" Melanie said, looking a little too smug. "It's from the two of you? Together?"

"Yes, and don't get any wild ideas about it," Ben

warned her. "It just beats the hell out of shopping for itty-bitty booties and diapers."

Melanie grinned at him. "You're not fooling me, Benjamin. You're as sentimental as the rest of us. You want to know that when that baby gazes around the room, he or she will know that Uncle Ben, the world-famous artist, decorated it."

Ben rolled his eyes at the comment, but Kathleen thought she detected something else in his expression, maybe a hint of excitement. Not until they were finally in the car and on their way to her place did she call him on it, though.

"You had a brainstorm back there, didn't you?"

He regarded her innocently. "I have no idea what you're talking about."

"Oh, can the innocent act," she retorted. "What's your idea?"

"It occurred to me that since babies like things that stimulate them and that they spend a lot of time in their cribs on their backs, maybe this baby should have a mural on the ceiling."

Kathleen stared at him in delight. "Oh, Ben, that's a wonderful idea. And when he or she is all grown up, they can tell the world that the ceiling in their nursery was painted by a famous artist."

He frowned at that. "We're not talking Michelangelo and the Sistine Chapel."

"No, we're talking about Ben Carlton and the Carlton nursery being painted with love."

"Don't make too much of this," he said, clearly embarrassed.

"Of course not," she agreed dutifully. "But is there time before the baby comes?"

"You hang the paper tomorrow and let me worry about the ceiling."

"Fair enough," she said happily. "What time should we get started?"

"I'll pick you up at eight."

"But that means you'll be driving back into town in rush hour," she protested.

He gave her a long, steady look. "You have a better idea?"

She knew what he was asking, but she wasn't quite ready to say yes. Things between them were complicated enough without throwing sex into the equation. The occasional kiss was one thing, but anything more? Too dangerous.

The temptation was there, though. It was in the heat stealing through her, the quickening of her pulse. She forced herself to ignore all that.

"Absolutely," she said at once. "You could stay with Destiny."

To her surprise, he didn't immediately scoff at the idea. In fact, his expression turned thoughtful.

"I could at that. It would give me one more shot at getting her to open up to me, since you won't spill the beans about the conversation the two of you had."

"I should have known you'd only stay there if you had an ulterior motive," she said. "It's not enough just to be there because she could use the company."

"If there's one thing we Carltons all have in common, it's that we never miss a chance to seize an opportunity when it smacks us in the face," he said.

"Sure you do," she replied. "I've offered you an incredible opportunity, one many artists would kill for, and you're ignoring that."

"That's not an opportunity, sweetheart. It's a tangled

web I don't want to get drawn into, thank you very much.''

"Be careful what you say," she warned him. "One of these days I might decide to believe you, withdraw my offer, and then where will you be?"

"Left in peace on my secluded farm?" he suggested hopefully.

"That's not really what you want," she said confidently.

"Yes, it is," he said emphatically.

Kathleen studied his face intently, then shook her head. "No, you don't."

"You calling me a liar?" he asked with a hint of amusement in his voice.

"No, I'm saying you're a bit confused and misguided. It happens to people sometimes. They lose their way."

His gaze caught hers and held it. "Like you lost yours?"

She trembled under the intensity of his scrutiny. The question called for honesty, so she gave it to him. "Yes," she said softly. "Exactly like that."

"Something tells me that tonight you came close to finding it again," he said, his gaze still on her face. "You ran up against an old dream, didn't you?"

She thought of the contentment she'd felt earlier, the sense that she was finally part of a group of people she could like, maybe even love. She glanced at Ben, then amended that—people she could trust. Because, she suddenly realized, it wasn't the loving that was going to hold her back from finding happiness. It was the inability to trust.

She stole another glance in Ben's direction. Maybe, just maybe, she was about to turn a corner on that.

* * *

Destiny was still up when Ben got back to her place after dropping Kathleen off. He found her in the den with the lights low, a seemingly untouched glass of brandy beside her.

"You okay?" he asked, taking a seat on the sofa opposite her.

She blinked as if she'd been very far away and hadn't even heard him come in. "What are you doing back here?" she asked irritably. "If you came to pester me for more information, you're wasting your time."

"Actually I came looking for a place to spend the night. Kathleen and I are going to finish up the nursery for Richard and Melanie in the morning. We want to get an early start, so it made more sense to stay in town, if you don't mind."

Destiny's expression brightened, then, as if she feared that too much enthusiasm on her part might spook him, she said cautiously, "You two seem to be getting closer."

"She's a nice woman," he said just as cautiously. "Very thoughtful."

"Yes, I like that about her, too."

He gave his aunt a wry look. "She's also damned discreet, in case you were wondering. She didn't breathe a word of whatever you said to her."

"And I imagine that's driving you crazy," Destiny said grumpily. "Well, too bad."

"I'm not trying to pry. I'm really not," he told her. "It's just that if there could be a connection to what's happening at Carlton Industries, I think maybe Richard has a right to know. Not even *me*," he emphasized. "Richard."

"I'm giving that some consideration," she admitted

"And that's all I intend to say on the subject for now. You might as well drop it."

"Suits me," he said agreeably. "So, can I stay here tonight?"

She regarded him with an impatient look. "Since when do you have to ask? This is the home you grew up in. You'll always have a place here. You know that."

"I thought you might prefer to be alone."

"If I did, it's a big house. I could go to my room. As long as you keep all those pesky questions to yourself, I'll be glad of the company." Her expression brightened. "Tell me about the nursery. I haven't been by to see it yet."

Ben described the mess he and Kathleen had found on their arrival and their plans to finish it. When he described the mural he had in mind for the ceiling, Destiny's face lit up with the kind of animation he was used to seeing in her, the kind of animation that had been sadly missing earlier.

"That's absolutely perfect, but there's so little time," she fretted, then beamed at him. "I could help."

He stared at her in surprise. "You would do that?"

"Well, of course I would. It'll be fun. What time are we going over in the morning?"

"I'm picking Kathleen up at eight. Will that work for you?"

She hesitated as if mentally going over her schedule. "I had a seven-thirty breakfast meeting with a committee chairman, but I'll call her and cancel first thing in the morning. I'll make it work," she assured him. "This is far more important."

"Richard's not going to be one bit happier about you

being up on a ladder than he was about Melanie trying
it," Ben said.

Destiny waved off his concern. "What your brother
doesn't know won't hurt him. He'll be at work by the
time we get there, and we'll be finished long before he
comes home."

"Apparently he came home in the middle of the day
today," Ben told her.

Destiny stared at him in shock. "Richard left the
office early?"

"It's like some sort of cataclysmic event, isn't it?"
Ben said.

"Definitely," Destiny agreed, then grinned. "But I
can take care of that with a couple of calls first thing
tomorrow, too. He won't get out of the office till we
want him to."

"Have I told you how delightfully devious you
are?" Ben asked.

"Yes, but usually it's not with that note of approval
in your voice," she told him wryly.

"Well, I think you're wonderful. Now we both need
to get some sleep."

"You run along, darling. I'll be up shortly."

"Destiny—" he began worriedly.

"It's okay, really. I'm feeling much better. I just
want to jot down a few ideas before I lose them."

"Ideas for the nursery?"

"No, nosy. Ideas that are none of your business."

Ben sighed, but gave up. He pressed a kiss to her
cheek and noted that her color was much better now,
her eyes livelier than when he'd first come in. Whatever was troubling her, she was getting a grasp on it.
He didn't doubt for an instant that whatever she was
sorting through, she would triumph in the end.

* * *

The wallpapering was going a whole lot more smoothly than the painting, Kathleen thought as she took a break for a soft drink and stood back to admire what they'd accomplished so far.

The walls were almost finished, but Ben and Destiny were having some serious artistic differences over whether there should be any sort of ogre in the fairy-tale scenes they were depicting on the ceiling.

"I want this child looking up at happy things," Destiny said again, facing Ben with her hands on her slender, jeans-clad hips and a defiant expression on her face.

"But real life is not all happy," Ben argued. "And there are ogres in fairy tales."

"That is not something a brand-new baby needs to know," Destiny argued heatedly. "Good grief, Ben, we're not painting a morality play up there."

"And you're not going to be here to get the baby back to sleep when the nightmares start thanks to your ogre," Melanie chimed in.

Destiny nodded her agreement, her gaze clashing with Ben's. "Well?"

"Okay, okay, you win. No ogre. But do all the animals have to look happy?"

"Yes," Destiny and Melanie told him in a chorus.

Kathleen grinned at him. "I think you're overruled, pal. Give it up and get another cheery character in that corner. Peter Rabbit had a lot of pals for you to choose from. And I think this one ought to be a girl. Maybe Jemima Puddleduck," she suggested. "She's cute. That ceiling is surprisingly devoid of feminine characters. What kind of message will that send if Melanie has a girl?"

"It's not some damn treatise on society," Ben groused. "Where's the damn *Peter Rabbit* book?"

Melanie chuckled and grinned at Kathleen. "He seems a bit testy."

"I'm surrounded by women," he retorted. "Strong-minded, stubborn women. What the hell do you expect?"

"A better attitude and less cussing would be nice," Destiny chided.

"Maybe another blueberry tart would help," Kathleen said. "I think there's one left."

Ben's scowl faded at once. "Really?" he said so eagerly that all three women laughed.

Kathleen shook her head. "It's a good thing I woke up early and had time to bake this morning."

He dropped a kiss on her lips as he passed by. "A very good thing," he agreed. "Otherwise, I might have to lock all of you out of here and paint footballs and baseball bats on the ceiling just to keep my male identity intact."

"If it's a boy, you can do that when he's six," Melanie offered consolingly.

"Six?" Ben scoffed. "Four at the latest. Otherwise he'll be scarred for life by all these happy characters. A boy needs guy stuff." His expression suddenly turned nostalgic and he looked at Destiny. "You painted my walls with all sorts of sports stuff when you came to live with us, didn't you? I just remembered that."

"I thought the room needed a little personality," Destiny told him. "Richard was perfectly content with that sterile room of his, and Mack already had his walls covered with posters, but your room was a blank canvas just waiting for some attention." She grinned at him, then turned to Kathleen. "Not that it lasted long. Within a year or so, he painted over it and filled it with all sorts of jungle creatures. I had to take him to the zoo in Washington at least once a week to take snapshots, so he'd have the real animals for inspiration when he painted."

"They weren't half-bad, given they were done by a kid," Ben said thoughtfully.

Kathleen wished she'd had a chance to see his early work. She couldn't help wondering if the promise had been there even back then. "I suppose they're long since painted over."

Destiny gave her a smug look. "Not exactly."

Clearly startled, Ben stared at her. "What on earth do you mean? Those paintings are long gone. I slept in that room last night and the walls are plain white."

"*Those* walls are," Destiny agreed.

Ben's gaze narrowed. "Meaning?"

"Oh, stop scowling at me like that. It's nothing dire. Rather than painting, I had a contractor come in and replace the wallboard. The original panels are stored in the basement."

"You're kidding me," Ben said. "Why would you do something like that?"

"Because I've always known you'd be famous someday, and I know how early paintings can add to a gallery's retrospective of an artist's work," she said without apology.

"Could I see them?" Kathleen pleaded.

Destiny glanced at Ben. "It's up to you."

He feigned shock. "Really?"

"Don't be an idiot," Destiny scolded. "It is your work."

Ben faced Kathleen. "I'll make you a deal. When

we take Destiny home, I'll go down and have a look. If they're not too awful, you can see them.''

Kathleen was beginning to lose track of all the bets and deals they'd made, but this one was definitely too good to pass up.

"Deal," she said eagerly. "Who gets to decide if they're awful?"

"I do," he said at once.

"I want an independent appraisal," she countered. "Destiny, will you do it?"

"Happily," Destiny said at once. "Though I can already tell you the outcome. The paintings are quite wonderful. If they hadn't been, I would have destroyed them to protect his reputation."

"Oh, yes, you're definitely independent," Ben retorted. "I don't think so. If it were up to you, I might as well just let Kathleen head over there now."

Kathleen held out her hand. "That's okay by me. Let me borrow the key."

"You can wait a couple of hours," he told her, his gaze clashing with hers, then filling with sparks of genuine amusement.

"Besides," he added lightly. "The anticipation will be good for you."

Kathleen had a hunch he was no longer talking just about the wait to see those wall panels. The sexual tension simmering between them was its own sweet torment. She had a feeling once that was unleashed, neither of their lives would ever be the same.

Ben was still shocked that Destiny had gone to such lengths to save the murals he'd done years ago in his bedroom. He considered it a crazy, sentimental act, even if she thought she was merely showing amazing foresight. He couldn't help feeling a certain amount of pride and anticipation, though. It had been years since he'd even thought of those early paintings. Getting the chance to see them again was an unexpected treat.

Still, he hesitated at the top of the steps to the basement. Kathleen was right on his heels, since they'd all conceded that Destiny was going to overrule any objections he might formulate to letting Kathleen see the wall panels.

"If you're not going to walk down those stairs, get out of my way," she told him impatiently.

"Don't rush me."

"What are you afraid of?"

"I'm not afraid," he retorted sharply.

"Then why are we still up here?"

"Because there's this nagging art expert dogging every step I take. These paintings could be awful," he said. "I'm not sure I want to expose them to your critical eye."

"You agreed," she reminded him.

"In a moment of weakness."

Kathleen tucked a hand under his elbow and dragged him back into the kitchen. She gazed at him with disconcerting intensity.

"Are you really worried that I'll criticize them? Or are you more worried about your own reaction? Believe me, I know what it's like to realize that your own art doesn't measure up."

He regarded her with surprise. "You do?"

"Why do you think I'm running a gallery rather than painting myself? Once I realized that nothing I put on canvas would ever be good enough, it was either choose another field of work entirely or choose to live on the fringes of the one I loved."

Ben wasn't sure which part of that to tackle first. "Sweetheart, you're not on the fringes. You're right in the thick of things. Your gallery has quite a reputation for discovering new artists."

Astonishment lit her eyes. "How do you know that? Did Destiny tell you?"

He laughed. "I can use the Internet. I've poked around a bit to look at the articles that have been written about your shows."

"Why?"

"Call it curiosity."

"About me? Or about whether I could be trusted to adequately represent your work?"

"About you," he admitted. "The other is a non-issue."

"It won't be forever," she retorted, then tilted her head and studied him. "So, did you discover anything about me reading those articles?"

"That you have an excellent eye for talent, that you're a savvy businesswoman and that you're very mysterious about your personal life."

She laughed. "That's because I don't have one."

Ben wondered if that was the opening he'd been waiting for. He decided to seize it. "You did, though."

She frowned at him. "Nothing worth talking about," she said tightly. "Are we going downstairs or not?"

"In a minute," he said. "As soon as you tell me why you don't like to talk about your marriage."

"I don't talk about it because it's over and it no longer matters."

The words were smooth enough, but the turmoil in her eyes was unmistakable.

"You don't want it to matter," he corrected. "But it obviously shapes the way you live your life."

"Just the way your past shapes yours?" she replied heatedly.

"I'll admit that," he said at once. "Losing my parents and then Graciela had an impact on me, no question about it. I don't want to go through that kind of pain again, so I don't let anyone get too close." He looked deep into her eyes. "Until you. You're sneaking past all my defenses, Kathleen. I'm not sure yet what the hell to do about that."

She looked shaken by that, so he pressed on. "Now's the time to speak up, if you're going to keep the door locked tight against anything more happening between us. I don't intend to be hanging out here on this limb all alone."

"I don't know," she admitted shakily. "I don't know if I can open that door again or not."

"Because your ex-husband hurt you so badly?"

"He never hurt me," she said just a little too fiercely. "Not like that."

Ben stared at her, stunned. He doubted she realized that her reaction suggested exactly the opposite of her words.

"Kathleen?" he said gently, feeling an impotent rage stirring inside him. "Did he abuse you?"

Tears filled her eyes and spilled down her cheeks. "Not the way you mean," she said eventually. "He never hit me."

"But he did abuse you?"

"With words," she said as if that were somehow less demeaning, less hurtful. "He had this nasty temper and when it got out of hand, he could be cruel."

"Is he the one who told you your art was worthless?" Ben asked.

She hesitated for so long that Ben knew he was right.

The son of a bitch had destroyed her confidence in her own talent, probably because his own ego was incapable of handling the competition. Only an artist would know how easy it would be to shatter another artist's confidence, would know precisely how a cutting criticism could destroy any enjoyment.

"He did, didn't he? He's the one who told you that you weren't any good, and you gave up painting because of that."

"No," she said miserably. "I gave it up because I was no good."

He studied her with compassion. "Maybe instead of you pestering me to see my work, I should be insisting on seeing yours."

She laughed, the sound tinged with bitterness. "No chance of that. I destroyed it all."

"Oh, sweetheart, why would you do that?"

"I told you," she said impatiently. "I recognize talent when I see it. I had none."

"But you enjoyed painting?"

"Yes."

"Then isn't that alone reason enough to do it?" he asked. "Isn't the pleasure of putting paint on canvas all that really matters?"

"You would say that, wouldn't you?"

He laughed at her. "Okay, it's a convenient response from my point of view, but it's true. Not everything has to be about making money or doing shows or garnering critical acclaim."

"Easy for you to say. You're rich. You can afford to indulge in something that might not be profitable. I can't."

"And you don't regret for one single second that you no longer paint?" he challenged. "There's not a part of you that gets a little crazy at the sight of a blank canvas and a tube of paint? Some secret part of you that looks at another artist's canvas and thinks that you could have done it better?''

"It doesn't matter," she said, not denying that she had regrets.

"Of course it does."

She brushed impatiently at the tears on her cheeks. "How on earth did we get off on this tangent?" she demanded, standing up. "I want to see those panels downstairs and then I need to be going."

Ben knew that anything he said now would be a waste of breath, but his determination to give Kathleen back her love of painting grew. He would find some way to accomplish that, no matter what else happened—or didn't happen—between them.

Chapter Nine

The wall panels in the basement were remarkable. Kathleen stood staring at them, astonished by the brilliance of the colors and the extraordinary detail. As the painting in Ben's dining room had done, these drew the viewer right into the scene, an especially astonishing feat given that the artist was so young at the time he'd painted them.

Oh, sure, the work wasn't as expert as that which had come later, but the signs of promise were unmistakable. In the kind of retrospective Destiny had envisioned when she'd saved them, they would be a treasure.

"Tell me again," Kathleen said. "How old were you when you painted these?"

"Twelve, I guess," he said with an embarrassed shrug. "Maybe thirteen. I did them when it became evident that I wasn't going to be the athletic superstar that Mack was. That made all the sports equipment Destiny had painted on the walls seem somewhat misplaced. Besides I loved the zoo and all the animal shows on TV. I wanted nothing more than to go on a safari.''

"Have you ever gone?"

He nodded. ''Destiny took me when I got straight A's in eighth grade.''

"Was it everything you'd imagined?"

"Even better," he said at once. "But I like the tamer setting where I live now even more. One is exciting and vibrant, the colors vivid, but I like the pastel serenity of the world around me. It's more soothing to the soul. No fear of getting gobbled up by a lion where I live.''

Kathleen gazed into his eyes and detected the hint of humor. ''It shows in your work, you know. These are quite amazing, especially given the age you were when you painted them, but your more recent work has soul. There's an obvious connection between artist and subject.''

''You know that from seeing one painting?''

She laughed at his skepticism. ''I am an expert, remember?''

"How could I forget?"

He surveyed her intently, warming her. A part of her wanted desperately to respond to that heat, to the promise of the kind of intimacy she'd never really known, not even in her marriage, but fear held her back. Ben had already cut through so many of her defenses. She intended to cling ferociously to those that were left. She finally blinked and looked away from that penetrating gaze.

"I should go now," she said, unhappy with the way her voice shook when she said it.

"Seen what you came to see, so now you're ready to run?" he taunted. "Or are you running scared?"

"Doesn't matter," she insisted. "It's time to go."

For an instant she thought he might argue, but he finally nodded. "I'll take you, then."

Kathleen was silent on the brief trip home. She was grateful to Ben for not pushing. It had been an emotional day for her, not just with the probing questions about her marriage, but with the tantalizing intimacy she'd experienced decorating the nursery. She wanted to get home and sort through all of the emotions. She couldn't help wondering if that would help or hurt. Were there any that she could trust?

At her door, Ben gazed into her eyes. "It was a good day, wasn't it?"

Unable to deny it, she nodded. "A very good day."

"We'll have to do it again."

"You have more nurseries that need decorating?" she asked, deliberately flippant because the prospect held so much appeal.

He stroked her cheek, amusement twinkling in his eyes. "No, but I think we can find other things to do."

"I don't know. Maybe we should get this back on a more professional footing."

"Meaning you chase after my art and I keep saying no?"

She smiled sadly. "Something like that."

His fingers still warm against her face, he traced a line along her jaw. Her pulse jerked and raced at the tender touch. His gaze held hers.

"I think we're past that, don't you?" he asked.

"We can't be," she said emphatically.

He covered her mouth with his, ran his tongue along the seam of her lips. Her pulse scrambled, proving that she was a liar, or at the very least denying the truth. To her relief, though, there was no satisfaction in his expression when he pulled back, just acceptance, which was something she wished she could attain. It would be so much easier if she could go with the flow, if all that past history hadn't made her jumpy about all relationships, much less one with an artist who had his own demons to fight.

"Ben," she began, then fell silent, uncertain what she could say that wouldn't sound ridiculous. Denying the attraction certainly wouldn't be believable. They both knew it was there, simmering and on the way to a boil.

And if she were being totally honest, it was also inevitable that they would do something about it. The only real question was when...and maybe how much risk it would be and how much pride it would cost her.

"Never mind," he said, apparently reading her confusion. "Take your time. I'm not going anywhere. I can wait till you catch up to where I am."

"And if I don't?"

"You will," he said confidently.

"Arrogance is not an attractive trait."

"Don't all artists have to have a little arrogance just to survive?" he taunted.

"But you say you're not an artist," she reminded him, regaining her equilibrium. "And for the moment, I have no real proof to the contrary."

He laughed. "But you seem so certain, Ms. Expert."

She shrugged. "I've been known to be wrong."

"When?"

"That's not something I like to spread around." She

gave him a thoughtful look. "Perhaps if I were to see a few more paintings, I could be sure."

"Nice try," he told her, laughter dancing in his eyes. "You'll have to be a bit more persuasive than that, though. I still don't know what's in it for me."

Kathleen fell in with his lighthearted mood, because it got her out of the far more dangerous territory they'd been in only moments before. "I'll give that some thought," she promised. "Since money and fame don't seem to matter to you, I'm sure I can come up with something else."

"I can think of one thing," he said.

He made the claim in a suggestive way that threw them right back into the same dangerous fires she was so sure they'd just escaped.

"Something other than that," she said, ignoring the eager racing of her heart.

He laughed. "Too bad. If you come up with something—I doubt it could be better—keep me posted."

"You'll know the minute I do," she assured him, an idea already taking shape in her mind, something that would render him incapable of forgetting about her for a single second without putting her own flagging defenses to the test.

Already lost in her planning, she gave him a distracted kiss. "Good night, Ben."

Before he could recover from his apparent surprise, she stepped inside and shut the door in his face.

The doorbell rang almost immediately. Fighting a smile, she opened it.

"Forget anything?" he asked.

"I don't think so."

"Sure you did," he said, stepping into the house and dragging her into his arms.

He kissed her till her head spun, then walked back outside and closed the door behind him.

Kathleen stared at the door and touched a finger to her still-burning lips. There was no escaping the fact that this latest round had gone to him. She wasn't sure whether to start plotting a way to get even or to run for her life.

Ben was getting far too much enjoyment out of rattling Kathleen. He was forgetting all about protecting himself. He needed to lock himself in his studio and get back to work. It was the most effective way he knew to block out the world.

And up until a few days ago, it had been more than enough for him. He hadn't craved anyone's company, hadn't yearned for any woman's kisses. Maybe he could get that back again.

Not likely, he concluded a few hours later when Kathleen breezed in with a bag of freshly baked banana nut muffins and a large latte. She was like a little whirlwind that touched down, left a bit of collateral damage and was gone an instant later. He stared out the door of his studio after she'd gone, fighting the oddest sensation that he'd imagined the entire visit.

But the coffee and muffins were real enough. So was the edgy state of arousal in which he found himself.

"Well, hell," he muttered and tried to go back to work.

Inspiration eluded him. All he could think about was the faint scent of Kathleen that lingered in the air.

She did the same thing the next day, this time leaving him with an entire blueberry pie and a container of whipped cream. His vivid imagination came up with a lot of very provocative uses for that whipped cream that had nothing at all to do with the pie.

By the weekend he was the one who was rattled, which was exactly what she'd obviously intended. He was also vaguely bemused by the fact that not once had she lingered in his studio or attempted to sneak a peek at his paintings. She'd come and gone in a heartbeat. In fact, one day she'd paid her mysterious visit even before he got to the studio. He found raspberry tarts and another latte on the doorstep, as if to prove that she hadn't even attempted to take advantage of his absence to slip inside the unlocked studio for a look around.

Ben sat in front of his easel, munching on a tart and considered not the painting he was working on, but Kathleen and these little sneak attacks designed to get under his skin without putting her own very delectable skin at risk. He couldn't help wondering if the baked goods were meant as bribes or simply as taunting reminders of her. He suspected she intended the former, while the effect was most definitely the latter.

Since he wasn't accomplishing a blasted thing, he stalked back inside, picked up the phone and punched in a familiar number. Two could play at this game.

"Studio Supplies," Mitchell Gaylord said.

"Mitch, it's Ben Carlton."

"How are you? You can't possibly be out of supplies. I just sent a shipment out there a few weeks ago."

"This isn't for me," Ben said. "Here's what I need."

Ten minutes later he hung up and sat back, satisfied. "That ought to get her attention."

* * *

Kathleen was feeling very smug about her little forays to the country. Maybe it was ridiculous to drive all that way just to torment Ben with coffee and a few pastries, but she had a feeling it would pay off eventually. He'd feel so guilty—or get so annoyed—he'd have to let her poke around among his paintings just to get rid of her and restore his much-desired serenity.

She was in the back of her shop planning the Christmas decorations, which needed to be up by the first of the week, when the bell over the front door rang. She went out expecting to find some browser who'd come inside primarily to get out of the cold. She rarely got serious customers this early in the day.

Instead, she found a delivery man.

"You Kathleen Dugan?" he asked, looking from her to his clipboard and back again.

"Yes, but I'm not expecting anything."

"Hey, Christmas is coming. 'Tis the season of surprises." He handed her the clipboard. "Sign here and I'll be right back."

Kathleen signed the page and waited for his return, feeling an odd sense of anticipation, the kind she vaguely recalled feeling as a very small child at Christmas, before things with her mother and father had gone so terribly wrong.

When the deliveryman walked back inside, her mouth gaped. He was pushing a cart laden with what looked like an entire art store. There was an easel there, a stack of canvases, a huge wooden box that could only contain paints, a ceramic holder filled with brushes. Everything was premium quality, meant for the professional artist.

"This can't possibly be for me," she said, but she knew it was. She also knew who had sent it. This was

Ben's retaliation for her little hit-and-run visits to the farm.

The delivery man stood patiently waiting.

"What?" she asked, half-frozen by a mix of anticipation, annoyance and something she could only identify as fear.

"Do you want this in the middle of the floor or somewhere else?" he asked patiently.

In the basement, she thought, locked away where it couldn't torment her. Aloud, she said, "In the back room, I suppose. Just pile it up anywhere."

When he emerged a moment later, he had a card in his hand. "This came with it. Happy holidays, Ms. Dugan."

She accepted the card, then dropped it, her nerves jittery. She managed to get a tip for the man from the cash register, then continued to stare at the card long after he'd gone.

Just then the phone rang.

"Yes," she said, distracted.

"Is it there yet?" Ben asked bluntly.

"You!" she said, every one of her very raw emotions in her voice.

"I'll take that as a yes. Have you read the card?"

"No."

"Call me back when you have," he said, then hung up in her ear.

She stared at the phone, not sure whether she wanted to laugh or cry. Instead of doing either one, she dutifully opened the card.

"For every canvas you complete and show me, I'll show you one of mine," he'd written.

Hysterical laughter bubbled up in her throat. She

hadn't thought it possible, but Ben had managed to find the one thing on earth that could get her to back off.

When Ben still hadn't heard back from Kathleen by late afternoon, he heaved a resigned sigh, climbed into his car and faced the daunting rush-hour traffic to head to Alexandria. Apparently his gift hadn't gone over the way he'd anticipated.

Or maybe it had. He'd meant to shake her up, though, not infuriate her. Judging from her lack of response, he worried he'd done both.

He wasn't entirely sure what was driving him to head over there and find out. It could be intense curiosity, or maybe a death wish.

He found the gallery already closed by the time he arrived. The window shade in the door was drawn, but he could still see lights in the back of the shop, which suggested that Kathleen was still on the premises.

As he had once before, he banged on the door and kept right on banging until there was some sign of movement inside.

He heard the tap of her footsteps coming toward the door, saw her approaching shadow on the other side of the shade, but the door didn't immediately swing open.

"Go away," she said instead.

"Not a chance," he retorted, alarmed by the hint of tears he thought he heard in her voice. "Open up, Kathleen."

"No."

"Are you crying?"

"No," she said, despite the unmistakable sniff that gave away the blatant lie.

"Why?"

"I said I wasn't crying."

"And I don't believe you. Dammit, open this door, Kathleen."

"I don't want to see you."

"Because I sent you a few art supplies?" he asked skeptically.

"That's one reason."

"And the others? I assume there's a whole list."

"Yes," she said, then added more spiritedly, "And it's getting longer by the minute."

"I annoy you," he guessed.

"Yep."

"And I ripped the scab off an old wound."

She sighed at that. "Yes," she whispered.

"Sweetheart, please let me in. I want to see your face when I'm talking to you."

"I should let you," she muttered.

Ben laughed. "All puffy and red, is it?"

"Pretty much."

"You'll still be beautiful."

"It's too late for sweet-talk, Ben. I'm mad at you."

"I got that. I want you to tell me why."

"You said it yourself."

"But I want *you* to say it. I want you to scream and shout till you get all the insecurities that man filled your head with out of your system."

"It's not that simple," she said impatiently. "Tim said a lot of cruel, hurtful things to me while we were together, that's true. But what he said about my art wasn't one of them."

"Are you so sure?"

"Yes, dammit. Do you think I would have quit painting just because of what he said?"

"I don't know. Did you?"

"No. I quit because what I painted could never measure up to what I saw in my head," she said.

Ben could hear the misery in her voice and saw his mistake then. He'd assumed they were just alike, both being modest about their talents. He'd supposed that she was good but had been told otherwise, not that she had such a low opinion of her own work.

"Maybe—" he began, but she cut him off.

"There are no maybes," she said flatly. "Not about this."

He sighed. "I'm sorry I upset you. I thought I was helping."

"I know you did."

"Can I come in now?" he asked again, wanting to hold her, to offer some sort of comfort.

"I suppose you're not going to go away until you've patted me on the head," she said, sounding resigned.

"I was thinking of something a bit more demonstrative," he said, fighting the urge to chuckle. "A hug, maybe."

"I don't need a hug. I need you to drop this."

"Consider it dropped," he said at once. "I'll haul all that stuff right back out of here tonight and toss it in the nearest Dumpster, if it'll make you feel better."

A key rattled in the lock at last and the door swung open. She met his gaze. "It was a nice gesture, Ben, even if it was misguided."

"I'm sorry," he said, his heart twisting at the misery in her eyes. She'd been telling the truth. Her face showed evidence of a long crying jag, but he'd been right, too. She was still beautiful.

She forced a smile. "Maybe we should get out of here," she said before he could set foot inside. "Give me a second to turn off lights and I'll lock up."

Something in her voice alerted him that there was a reason she didn't want him coming in, which, of course, guaranteed that he followed her to the back.

There on an easel sat an unfinished painting...of him. He must have made a whisper of sound because she whirled around and her gaze flew to clash with his.

"I told you to wait," she said accusingly.

"I know."

"I didn't want you to see it."

"Because it was meant to be a surprise?"

"No, because it's awful."

He stared at her in shock. "Awful? How can you say such a thing? Kathleen, it's wonderful. You've got every detail just right."

"No, I don't," she insisted adamantly. "Maybe if I'd had a photo I could have gotten it right. This is awful. It looks nothing like you."

As if to prove her point, she picked up the brush with which she'd been working and started to take an angry swipe at the canvas. Ben caught her arm before she could do any damage.

"Don't you dare ruin it," he said heatedly.

"It's no good," she said again.

He held her, looking down into her tormented eyes. "I can see that you don't believe me," he told her quietly. "But let's get another opinion, one you will trust."

She searched his face as if desperately wanting to believe he wasn't lying to her, but not quite daring to hope. "Whose?"

"Destiny's," he suggested. "You trusted her to be unbiased about my work."

"Not at first," she said.

"But enough to believe her when she said those old wall panels were decent," he reminded her.

She sighed and he could feel her muscles relaxing.

"Okay," she said eventually. "But only when it's finished. Will you let me take a picture or two?"

He could understand why she wanted it to be the best it could possibly be, but he wasn't sure that waiting was wise. She could suffer another one of these attacks of inadequacy and ruin it.

"Will you promise me that you won't damage it?"

"Yes," she said, meeting his gaze evenly. "I promise."

"No matter how discouraged you get?"

"Yes," she repeated, this time with a trace of impatience.

"Okay, then. I'll bring you some snapshots of me. You have till Christmas. In fact, if you want to make Destiny extraordinarily happy, you could give it to her as a gift. I never would sit still for her to paint me."

But Kathleen was already shaking her head. "No, if it turns out that it's any good at all, I want to keep it."

"To prove that you are an artist, after all?" he asked.

"No," she said, her expression solemn. "Because it's of the man who cared enough to give me back my love of painting."

Chapter Ten

Standing in her office with paints scattered around, her own painting on an easel for the first time in years and Ben's assurances still ringing in her ears, Kathleen felt her heart fill with joy and something else she refused to identify because it felt too much like love.

She didn't want to love this man, didn't want to be swayed by tubes of oil paints and a few blank canvases, so she wouldn't be, she decided. It didn't have to matter that he'd gone to such extremes to give her back the joy of holding a brush in her hand. It didn't have to mean that on some level he understood her better than she understood herself.

In fact, in the morning when she saw her work again, she might very well decide once more to hate him for getting her hopes up.

She faced Ben and caught the surreptitious glances he was casting toward the painting.

"Admiring yourself?" she asked.

He gave her a wry look. "Hardly. I'm admiring your brush strokes. You have an interesting technique, not quite Impressionistic, but close."

She laughed at that. "I'm definitely no Renoir."

"Few artists are," he agreed. "But you're good, Kathleen. Damn good."

She drank in the compliment, even as she tried to deny its validity. "Come on, Ben. Don't go overboard. You've won. I'll finish the painting, but if you're expecting something on a par with the great masters when I'm done, you're doomed to disappointment."

"You could never disappoint me," he said with quiet certainty.

She started to offer another protest but the words died on her lips. How could she argue with such sincerity? Why would she even want to? Instead, she merely said, "Please, can't we change the subject?"

He seemed about to argue, but then he said, "Okay, I'll drop it for now. Get your coat. I'm taking you to dinner."

"Why don't I cook?" she said instead.

He regarded her with a hopeful expression. "Is your cooking anything at all like your baking?"

She laughed. "It's not half-bad. A lot depends on what's in the refrigerator. I just shopped this morning so I think I can do something decent tonight. How do you feel about grilled lamb chops, baby red bliss potatoes and steamed vegetables?"

He sighed with undisguised pleasure. "And for dessert?"

"I left you a half-dozen raspberry tarts this morning," she protested. "Isn't that enough sweets for one day?"

"No such thing," he insisted. "Besides, I only ate one. I'm saving the rest, along with the extra muffins and the remainder of the blueberry pie."

She chuckled. "Maybe you should go home for dessert."

He shook his head. "I'd rather watch you make something from scratch."

"So you can steal my secret for flaky dough?"

"No, because there is something incredibly sexy about a woman who's confident in the kitchen."

Kathleen laughed. "Good answer. I'm very confident when it comes to my chocolate mousse. How does that sound? Or would you prefer something more manly and substantial like a cake?"

"The mousse will definitely do," he said with enthusiasm. "Can I lick—" he gave her a look meant to curl her toes, then completed the thought "—the spoon?"

Kathleen's knees had turned rubbery somewhere in the middle of the sentence, but she kept herself steady with some effort. "You can lick any utensil you want to," she agreed. "And then you can wash the dishes." She gave him a warning look. "And I tend to be a very messy cook."

Ben laughed. "A small price to pay. Shall we walk to your place, or do you want to ride?"

"It's only a few blocks," she said. "Let's walk."

Though the night air was cold, the December sky was clear and signs of Christmas were everywhere. There was a tree lot on a corner and the fragrance of pine and spruce filled the air with an unmistakable holiday scent.

"Do you have your tree yet?" Ben asked as they drew closer to the small lot.

"No, I usually wait till the last second, because I have to get the store decorations done first. Sometimes the only festive touch at home is a small, artificial tree that's predecorated."

He looked aghast at that. "You can't be serious."

"Why on earth not?" she asked. "It hardly seems worth the effort just for me. I'm rarely at home during the holidays, and by Christmas Day I'm usually visiting my family."

He seemed surprised. "The mother who infuriates you?"

"And the stepfather of the moment, plus my grandparents," she told him. "I can take a day of all that, then I run back here as quickly as possible."

Ben's expression turned thoughtful and then he halted in front of the trees. "I think it's time that changed. Pick out a tree, the biggest one on the lot, the one you used to imagine when you were a little girl."

"I don't need a tree. Besides, I certainly can't fit a huge tree into my house," she protested, though she was just a little charmed by the idea of it.

"We'll make it fit," he said, clearly not intending to give up. "Come on now. Pick one. I'll put it up while you fix dinner. We can play Christmas carols and sing along."

The whole idea sounded temptingly domestic. In fact, it reminded Kathleen of all the dreams she'd once had for the perfect holiday season. Instead, most of her holidays had been spent avoiding arguments that quickly escalated into something nasty. She couldn't recall a single Christmas that bore any resemblance to those happy occasions she'd read about in storybooks.

Ben's desire to give her one more thing she'd always longed for cut through all of her practical objections and had her walking amid the fragrant trees without another hesitation.

She sniffed deeply as the vendor held up first one tree and then another for her inspection. Ben did all the practical things. He tested needles and checked the trunk to see if it was straight. Kathleen concentrated on finding a tree that filled her senses with the right scent, a tree that was perfectly shaped for hanging ornaments.

When she found it at last, she overcame all of Ben's objections about the curve in the trunk. "Who cares if it's a little crooked? We can use fishing line to make sure it doesn't topple over. This one smells like Christmas."

He regarded her with amusement. "Your heart is really set on this one because it smells right?"

"Absolutely," she said, drawing in another deep breath of the strong spruce aroma. Heavenly. If the tree didn't have a decoration or light on it, she could be satisfied with that scent alone filling her house.

"I guess this is it, then," Ben told the vendor.

The man winked at her. "Don't let him put you off, miss. It's a beauty. Would you like me to bring it around to your house when I close up?"

"No," Ben said. "We can manage."

Kathleen gave him a skeptical look but took him at his word. He hoisted the tree up as if it weighed no more than a feather and despite its awkward size, carried it along easily for the remaining two blocks to her house.

Once inside, she helped him find a spot for it in the living room. "There," she said, standing back to admire the tree leaning against the wall. "That will be perfect, don't you think so?"

When she glanced at Ben, he was looking not at the tree, but at her.

"Perfect," he agreed softly.

"Ben?" she whispered, her voice shaky. It was the second time tonight he'd looked at her like that, spoken with that barely banked heat in his voice, the undisguised longing written all over his face.

The moment went on for what seemed an eternity, filled with yearning, but eventually he shook himself as if coming out of a trance.

"No distractions," he muttered, as if to remind himself. "You tell me where your stand, decorations and lights are, and I'll get those started while you fix dinner."

It took Kathleen a moment longer to come back to earth and drag her thoughts away from the desire that had simmered between them only seconds before. "The attic," she said in a choked voice. "Everything's in the attic."

Ben's gaze clung to hers a minute longer, but then he looked away. "Just point me in the right direction. I'll find my way," he said as if he feared being alone with her an instant longer.

Kathleen sent him on his way and only then did she realize she'd been all but holding her breath. She released it in a long sigh, then headed for the kitchen…and comparative safety.

Of course, she wouldn't be entirely safe until he was out of the house, but the prospect of letting him go filled her with a surprising sense of dismay. The man was getting under her skin, knocking down defenses as emphatically and thoroughly as a wrecking ball, no question about it. If he kept making these sweet gestures, guessing her innermost thoughts and doing his utmost to give her her dreams, she would be lost.

When Ben came down from the attic, Christmas carols were playing and some incredible aromas were drifting from the kitchen. The whole atmosphere felt so cozy, so astonishingly right, that warning bells went off in his head. In response, he set down the boxes of decorations and tried to remember the holidays he had spent with Graciela.

They'd been nothing like this. Graciela hadn't been a sentimental woman. She was more than content to call a decorator who would spend a couple of days and a fair amount of Ben's money to turn the house into a showcase. What appealed to her was the subsequent entertaining, assembling the right guests, doling out gifts that were more expensive than thoughtful, and drinking. Ben couldn't remember even one holiday occasion when Graciela hadn't had a glass of wine or champagne in hand from start to finish.

He tried to recall a single instance when her eyes had sparkled with childlike excitement as Kathleen's had on that tree lot. He couldn't think of one.

Once the memory of Kathleen's delight stole into his head, he realized what it had reminded him of…holidays years ago when first his parents and then Destiny had worked to assure that there was something magical about the season. He'd lost that sense of magic, that undercurrent of anticipation somewhere along the way, but he was getting it back tonight.

By the time Kathleen announced that dinner was ready, he was feeling nostalgic, despite his overall lack of progress getting the lights untangled to put on the tree. He grinned as he recalled how many times his father and later Destiny had complained about the same thing. Richard had been the one with the patience to unravel them and get them hung properly, while the rest of them had drunk hot chocolate and eaten the cookies that Destiny had decorated with an artistic flair so perfect they could have been on the cover of a magazine.

"How's it going in here?" Kathleen asked, then burst out laughing when she saw the tangled mass of lights. "Uh-oh. I guess I should have been more careful when I took them down."

He gave her a wry look. "You think?"

"I'll help you with them after dinner," she promised. "Did you plug them in to make sure they still work at least?"

"Who could find the plugs? I've never seen such a mess."

"Hey, you asked for this job," she reminded him. "I didn't ask you to get involved."

"True enough, but if that dinner tastes even half as good as it smells, I'll forgive you for every tangled strand of lights I'm expected to deal with."

"The lamb chops might be a bit overdone," she apologized when they were seated at her dining room table. "And I'm pretty sure I didn't steam the vegetables quite long enough."

He regarded her with curiosity, wondering at the sudden lack of self-confidence. "Is this something else your ex-husband criticized? Your cooking?"

She seemed startled by the question. "Yes. But why would you think that?"

"Because neither of us has even picked up a fork, and you're already offering excuses."

She sat back in her chair and stared at him. "Oh,

my God, you're right. I do that all the time. I'd never even noticed it before.'' Her expression turned thoughtful. ''I suppose it's something I picked up from my mother. She was always trying to forestall a fight. If she said everything was lousy first, it stole the ammunition from my father or my stepfathers. Now that I think about it, my grandmother did the same thing. There's one heck of a family tradition to pass along.''

Ben heard the pain behind that sad description of what her life had been like, a succession of excuses from two women who'd apparently lived their lives in fear. Rather than being a positive role model, first Kathleen's mother and then her grandmother had apparently set her up to expect very little from men other than criticism. It was little wonder that Kathleen had chosen a man who would fit into that male-as-a-superior-being mold. The fact that she'd dumped him rather quickly was the miracle.

''I'm sorry,'' he told her quietly.

She shrugged, looking vaguely embarrassed at having revealed so much. ''It's over.''

''No, it's not,'' he pointed out. ''You're still apologizing unnecessarily.''

She forced a smile. ''You haven't tasted your dinner yet. Maybe the apology was called for.''

His heart ached at her attempt to make a joke of something that had shaped her life. ''Even if it tastes like burnt sawdust, it wouldn't give me the right to demean you,'' he said fiercely. ''You made the effort to make a nice meal. That's the only thing that counts.''

She stared at him, her eyes filled with wonder. ''You really mean that, don't you?''

Wishing there weren't a whole expanse of table between them so he could reach for her hand, he nodded. "Every word," he said gently.

Then he picked up his fork and took his first bite of the perfectly grilled, perfectly seasoned lamb and sighed with genuine pleasure. "I should be grateful for that bad example your mother set for you," he told her. "Something tells me it's the reason you learned to cook like a gourmet chef."

The delight that filled her eyes was like the sun breaking through after a storm. It filled him with a matching joy…along with the desire to strangle a few more people on her behalf. But maybe he didn't need to do that. Maybe all he needed to do was to teach her that she was worthy of being treated well. Then if he left—no, when he left—she would be ready for and open to the man who could make all her dreams come true.

Kathleen lay awake most of the night thinking about the evening she'd just spent with Ben. It might well have been the most perfect evening of her entire life.

It wasn't just about the Christmas tree that they'd managed to finish decorating after two in the morning. Nor was it about the laughter they'd shared or the gentle teasing. While all of that had been special, it had paled compared to the gift he'd given her—the reminder that she deserved to be treated well. It was something she'd always known intellectually, something she'd been smart enough to see when she'd ended her marriage, but experiencing it again and again with every word Ben uttered, with every deed he did finally made the lesson sink in.

It was funny how she'd always insisted on respect professionally, knew that she commanded it even as a

rank amateur in an elite circle of very discerning gallery owners, but she'd never expected or demanded it
as a woman. Ben was right. It was what she'd learned
at her mother's knee and it was past time she put it
behind her.

Oddly, she thought she'd done that simply by having
the strength to end her marriage, but that hadn't gone
far enough. The fear of repeating the same mistake had
kept her from moving on, from allowing another man
the chance to get close. How ironic that the one who'd
breached her reserve was a man who had scars of his
own from the past. She wondered if he knew how
deeply they continued to affect his own choices.

Since she'd sent Ben home the night before with
leftover mousse, she'd decided against taking a run out
to the farm this morning. That gave her a few extra
minutes to linger over coffee and the rare treat of one
of the leftover banana nut muffins she'd made earlier
in the week for Ben.

She was still savoring the last bite when the doorbell
rang. Glancing at her watch, she was surprised to see
that it was barely seven-thirty. Who on earth dropped
in at that hour?

She opened the front door to find Destiny standing
there, looking as if she'd just stepped from the pages
of a fashion magazine. Kathleen immediately felt
frumpy. She hadn't even run a brush through her hair
yet this morning.

"Sorry to pop in so early, but I was sure you'd be
up," Destiny said, breezing past her without waiting
for an invitation.

"Barely up," Kathleen muttered. "Would you like
coffee and maybe a banana nut muffin?"

Destiny beamed. "Ah, yes, I've heard about those

muffins. I'd love one. You've definitely found the way to my nephew's heart."

Kathleen paused as she poured the coffee. "I beg your pardon."

"You're getting to him," Destiny explained patiently. "Ben is a sucker for sweets. I told you that. You're handling him exactly right. I'm not sure it's a tactic that would have worked on any of my other nephews, though I did pack Melanie off to see Richard once with a picnic basket filled with his favorite foods and wine. That turned out well enough."

The last was said with a note of smug satisfaction in her voice.

Kathleen set the coffee in front of Destiny, then brought in a muffin from the kitchen. The extra minute gave her time to try to figure out what she wanted to say to dispel Destiny's notion that she was waging any sort of campaign for Ben's heart or that she was willing to be drawn into Destiny's scheme.

When she was seated at the table again, she met Destiny's gaze. "You do know that the only thing I'm after where Ben is concerned is his art, don't you?"

Destiny regarded her serenely. "I'm sure you want to believe that."

"Because it's the truth," Kathleen said, feeling a little bubble of hysteria rising in her throat thanks to the confident note in Destiny's voice.

"Darling, it was after two in the morning when Ben came in last night."

"He stayed with you?"

"Of course he did. Did you think he would drive all the way back out to the farm at that hour?"

"I honestly never gave it a thought," Kathleen responded. If she had, she would have sent him packing a lot earlier just to avoid this exact misconception on his aunt's part.

"Yes, I imagine there was very little thinking going on at that hour," Destiny said happily.

Kathleen choked on her coffee. "Destiny!" she protested. "It's not like that with Ben and me."

Okay, so she was ignoring all the kissing that had gone on from time to time between them, but very little of that had occurred in the wee hours of the night before. A safe good-night peck on the cheek was the closest they'd come.

Destiny frowned. "It's not?" she asked, her disappointment plain. "The two of you aren't getting closer?"

"Of course we are. We're friends," Kathleen said, almost as unhappy with the label as Destiny obviously was.

Destiny sighed. "Friends," she echoed. "Yes, well, I suppose that's a good start. I can see, though, that I'll have to do a little more work on my end."

"No," Kathleen said fiercely. "You've done enough. Let it be, Destiny, please."

Ben's aunt looked taken aback by her vehemence. "Why are you so opposed to anything coming of this relationship with my nephew?"

Kathleen was having a hard time remembering the answer to that herself. It had started because she'd been afraid to trust another man. It had been magnified by the fact that Ben had a reputation as a moody, reclusive artist.

But the truth was that he was nothing like what she'd been led to believe, in fact quite the opposite. He was so far removed from the kind of man her ex-husband had been that the only thing the two had in common was their gender.

She faced Destiny and tried not to let her bewilderment show. It would be just what the sneaky woman needed to inspire her to get on with her campaign.

"It's not that I'm opposed to anything happening with Ben," she said candidly. "But the two of us are adults. We don't need someone running interference for us. You've done your part. Now leave it be. If anything's meant to come of this, it will happen."

"Even if I can see that you're both too stubborn to admit what's right under your noses?"

"Even then," Kathleen told her.

Destiny nodded slowly. "Okay, then, I can do that."

Her easy agreement made Kathleen instantly suspicious. "Really?"

"For now," Destiny told her cheerfully. "I suppose I should go along to my meeting. Thanks for the coffee and the muffin. Our little visit has been very enlightening."

Enlightening? Kathleen thought as she watched Destiny depart at the same brisk pace with which she'd entered. In what way had their exchange been enlightening? Destiny had said it in a way that suggested she'd read some undercurrent of which Kathleen was completely unaware.

She shivered in the morning chill and then made herself shut the door. If Ben left her feeling edgy and discombobulated, his aunt had the capacity to strike terror in her. Because it seemed that Destiny could see into the future…and saw a very different picture from the one Kathleen envisioned.

Kathleen was dreaming of a wildly successful showing of Ben Carlton paintings in her gallery, while Destiny was clearly picturing the two of them living happily ever after. Kathleen didn't even want to contemplate that image, because it was quickly becoming far too tempting to resist.

Chapter Eleven

With Destiny's visit still fresh in her mind, Kathleen made a decision that she needed to seal this deal with Ben to show his paintings. The sooner that was done, the sooner she'd be able to get him—and his clever, matchmaking aunt—right back out of her life. Of course, solitude no longer held the appeal it once had, but she'd get used to it again.

She was sitting at her desk trying very hard not to look at her half-finished portrait of Ben, when the bell on the outer door rang. Heading into the gallery, she plastered a welcoming smile on her face, a smile that faltered when she found not the expected customer but her mother.

Shocked, it took her a moment to compose herself before she finally spoke, drawing her mother's attention away from the most dramatic of Boris's paintings.

"Mother, this is a surprise. What on earth are you

doing here?'' she asked, trying to inject a welcoming note into her voice when all she really felt was dismay. She'd expected that if her mother ever did show up in Alexandria, it certainly wouldn't be without warning.

''I decided to take you up on your invitation to visit.'' Prudence tilted her head toward the large painting. ''I can't say that I like it, but it's quite impressive, isn't it?''

''The critic from the Washington paper called it a masterpiece,'' Kathleen said. She still had the uneasy sense that her mother was merely making small talk, that at any second the other shoe would drop and land squarely on Kathleen's head.

''I know,'' Prudence replied. ''I read his review.''

That was the second shock of the morning. ''You did?''

Her mother gave her an impatient look. ''Well, of course, I did. Your grandfather finds every mention of your gallery on the Internet and prints the articles out for me.''

''He does?''

Her mother's impatience turned to what seemed like genuine surprise. ''What did you think, darling, that we didn't care about you?''

''As a matter of fact, yes,'' Kathleen said. ''I thought you all thoroughly disapproved of what I was doing.''

Her mother gave her a sad look. ''Yes, I can see why it must have seemed that way, since none of us have come down here. I'm sorry, Kathleen. It was selfish of us. We wanted you back home, and we all thought this would pass, that it was nothing more than a little hobby.''

Kathleen felt the familiar stirring of her temper at

the casual dismissal of her career. "It's not," she said tightly.

"Yes, I can see that now. The gallery is as lovely as any I've ever seen, and you've made quite a success of it. You obviously inherited your grandfather's business genes."

Kathleen had never expected her mother to make such an admission. The morning was just full of surprises, she thought.

"I have to wonder, though," her mother began.

Ah, Kathleen thought, here it comes. She should have known that the high praise couldn't possibly last. She leveled a look into her mother's eyes, anticipating the blow that was about to fall.

"Yes?" she said, her tension unmistakable.

"What about your own art, Kathleen? Have you let that simply fall by the wayside?"

"My art?" she echoed weakly. Where on earth had that come from? If everyone back home had thought the gallery was little more than a hobby, they'd clearly considered her painting to be nothing more than an appropriate feminine pastime. Not one of her paintings had hung on the walls at home, except in her own room. She'd taken those with her when she'd married, but had soon relegated them to the basement when Tim had been so cruelly critical. Most had gone to the dump even before the marriage ended. She couldn't bear to look at them.

She met her mother's gaze. "Why on earth would you ask about my art? You always dismissed it, just as you have the gallery."

"I most certainly did not," her mother replied with more heat than Kathleen had heard in her voice in years. "I always thought you were quite talented."

"If you did, you certainly never said it," Kathleen pointed out. "Not once, Mother."

Her mother appeared genuinely shaken by the accusation. "I didn't?"

"Never."

"I suppose I didn't want to get your hopes up," her mother said, her expression contrite. "It's a very difficult field in which to succeed. I should know."

Shock, which had been coming in waves since her mother walked into the gallery, washed over Kathleen again. "What on earth are you saying?"

"You never saw anything I painted, did you?" her mother asked.

"No," Kathleen said, reeling from this latest bombshell. "In fact, I had no idea you'd ever held a paintbrush."

"Actually I took lessons from a rather famous artist in Providence for years," her mother said as if it were of little consequence.

"You did?" Kathleen asked weakly. "When?"

"Before you were born. In fact, once I married, I never painted again. Your father thought it was a waste of time and money." She gave Kathleen another of those looks filled with sorrow. "I'd like to think that you inherited your talent from me, though. It broke my heart when you gave it up because of that awful husband of yours. I hated seeing you make the same mistake I had."

Kathleen suddenly felt faint. Too many surprises were being thrown at her at once. "I think I need to sit down," she said. "Come on into my office."

Her mother followed her, then stopped in the doorway. Kathleen heard her soft gasp, and turned. Prudence was staring at the portrait.

"You did that, didn't you?" her mother asked, her eyes ablaze with excitement.

Kathleen nodded. "It's far from finished," she said, unable to keep a defensive note from her voice.

"But it's going to be magnificent." When Prudence turned back to Kathleen, her eyes were filled with tears. "I am so proud of you. You've done what I was never able to do. You've taken your life back, after all."

Puzzled, Kathleen stared at her mother. "I don't understand."

"I think you do. You're a survivor, Kathleen. I haven't been."

"Of course you are," Kathleen replied heatedly. "You're *here,* despite everything that happened to you. You don't have to be a victim ever again. And if painting really did mean so much to you, then do it. I'll buy you everything you need myself. I'll pass on the gift that was given to me."

Her mother gave her a quizzical look. "Oh?"

For the first time in her life, Kathleen felt this amazing sense of connection to her mother. She went to stand beside her and put an arm around her waist. "Ben bought paints for me—just yesterday, in fact. He's the one who gave me the confidence to try again. That portrait is the first thing I've painted in years."

"Tell me about this Ben," her mother said. "Is he someone very special?"

"Yes," Kathleen said simply.

Her mother gazed knowingly into her eyes. "He's the man in the portrait, isn't he?"

"Yes."

"And you love him." It wasn't a question at all, but a clear statement of fact.

"No," Kathleen said at once, then sighed. "Maybe."

Her mother tapped the canvas with a perfectly manicured nail. "The truth is right here, darling."

Kathleen studied the painting and tried to guess what her mother had seen. Even in the portrait's unfinished state, Ben appeared strong. Kindness shone in his eyes. Had it been painted with a sentimental brush? Most likely.

"I don't want to love him," Kathleen admitted at last.

"Why not?"

"Because he's an artist," she explained.

To her surprise, her mother laughed. "Not all artists are as unpredictable and awful as Tim was, you know. There are bad apples in every barrel. Goodness knows, I've found more than my share in a great many walks of life, but you can't taint a whole profession because of it."

For the first time, Kathleen understood the optimism that underscored her mother's repeated attempts to find the perfect match. "I just realized something, Mother."

"What's that?"

"You're the one who's the real survivor. You've made some fairly awful choices—"

"An understatement," her mother confirmed.

"But you haven't closed your heart," Kathleen explained. "I did."

Her mother gave her a squeeze. "Then it's time you took another chance on living. I'd like to meet this young man of yours. He has a kind face."

Kathleen smiled. "He does, doesn't he? And the best part of all is that he has a kind soul."

And maybe, just maybe she could be brave enough

to put that kindness to the test and give him a chance…if he wanted one. Now there, she thought, was the sixty-four-thousand-dollar question.

"Stay here for a few days, Mother. Meet Ben," she pleaded.

"Not this time," Prudence said. "But I will come again soon."

"Promise?"

"Absolutely. The ice is broken now. It won't be so difficult next time. Perhaps your grandparents will come, too."

"I'd like you to meet Ben's aunt, too. She's a remarkable woman, and she's an artist, as well. I think the two of you would hit it off." She imagined the two women sitting in the sunshine on the coast of France, easels in front of them. She could see the image quite vividly. It made her smile.

Her mother gave her a fierce hug. For the first time in years and years, Kathleen felt that she had a real mother again. Not that there weren't likely to be bumps in the road. They were both, after all, strong-willed people in their own very different ways. But today had given them a fresh start, and Ben, even though he hadn't been here, had played an amazing part in that. It was just one more thing she owed him for.

Ben was feeling fairly cranky, and he wasn't entirely certain why. Okay, that was a lie. He knew precisely why he'd been growing increasingly irritable over the past week. He was growling at everyone who dared to call or come by. Even the usually unflappable Mack had commented on his foul temper and taken a wild stab at the reason for it.

"Something tells me you haven't seen Kathleen

lately," Mack had observed in midconversation. "Do yourself a favor and go see her or call her. Do something. Otherwise the rest of us are going to have to start wearing protective gear when we come around."

This last was a reference to the mug Ben had tossed across his studio at Mack's untimely interruption of his work. Not that his work was going all that well, but he was sick of people turning up without so much as a phone call to warn him. Not that Mack had ever called ahead. He just brought food to pacify his beast of a younger brother.

"My mood has nothing to do with Kathleen," Ben had all but shouted.

"If you say so," Mack responded mildly.

"I say so."

Mack had wandered around the studio, careful to keep a safe distance away from Ben, then asked casually, "Have you slept with her yet?"

Ben's gaze shot to his brother. If Mack had been closer, he'd have slammed him in the jaw for asking something like that. Fortunately for both of them, there was enough distance between them that it didn't seem worth the effort. Besides, Mack still had a few quick moves left over from his football days. Ben probably wouldn't have caught him squarely on the jaw, anyway.

He scowled at Mack instead. "Do you think I'd tell you if I had?"

Mack, damn him, had grinned. "You haven't, then. I figured as much. You need to make your move, pal. I think you can chalk this black mood of yours up to suppressed hormones."

"I think I can chalk it up to an interfering brother

who doesn't know when to mind his own damn business.''

Mack had shrugged. ''That, too.'' He'd headed for the door, then. ''Think about it, bro. If the woman's tying you up in knots like this, it's time to do something about it. Stop sitting on the fence. Get her into your bed or out of your life.''

Ever since Mack had walked out, Ben had thought of very little else. It was true. He wanted to make love to Kathleen, had wanted to for a long time now. Hell, he'd even started to miss her popping up out here, pestering him, bringing along those delectable baked goods of hers.

And despite all of her declarations reminding him to keep things professional, he was all but certain she was going just about as crazy as he was.

He'd eaten every last muffin, every scone, the rest of the blueberry pie and all those raspberry tarts, all the while mentally grumbling that if she kept it up, he was going to gain twenty pounds before Christmas.

And yet, when no further pastries had appeared, he'd felt oddly bereft. The running he'd been doing to burn off calories suddenly had to burn off the restless frustration that plagued him.

Mack was right. He needed to do something and he needed to do it now.

As if Kathleen were once more attuned to his thoughts, he heard her car tearing up the driveway, taking it at a reckless speed that only she dared. He'd mentioned that more than once, his heart in his throat, but she'd remained oblivious to his entreaties. Because he hadn't wanted to get into why her driving terrified him, he let it pass each time. Today she seemed to be in a particular hurry.

Ben stood up, but hesitated rather than going outside to wait for her. When she skidded to a stop mere inches from the side of the barn, he bit back another lecture and counted to ten instead, waiting for his thumping heartbeat to slow down to normal before going to greet her.

She bounded out of the car with long-legged strides, then tossed a bag in his direction. One whiff and her driving no longer mattered. He'd reminded her of a particular fondness for blueberries over dinner the other night, and he knew exactly what he'd find in the bag...homemade blueberry muffins this time.

She handed him a cup of his favorite latte as well, acting for all the world as if it had been only yesterday when they'd last parted. He wasn't sure whether to be charmed or annoyed by that.

"I can't stay but a minute, but something amazing happened earlier this morning and I couldn't wait to come out to tell you about it."

"You could have called."

"Not about this. And since I was coming, I stopped long enough to bake the muffins so I wouldn't arrive empty-handed. I wanted to get them out here while they're still warm from the oven."

"And that's why you drove like a bat out of hell?" he asked testily.

"No, I drove that way because I enjoy it," she replied, undaunted by his disapproval.

"If you slowed down, you might enjoy the landscape."

"I do enjoy it."

"How? It must pass in a blur."

She gave him an innocent smile. "All I have to do

is think about that painting in your dining room and it all comes back to me.''

Ben shook his head at the sneaky way she'd brought the conversation right back to the same old point. "We've been over this more than once. Flattery, muffins and latte are not going to get you inside the studio, sweetheart.''

"What will?'' she asked curiously. "Is there some trick I'm missing?''

"Just one. A sincere promise to forget about trying to talk me into selling what's in there.''

She shrugged. "Sorry, no can do.''

"Since you knew that would be the outcome even before you asked that question, let's not belabor it. Why don't you tell me about this amazing thing that happened this morning.''

"My mother came to my gallery.''

He regarded her intently, looking for evidence of the simmering outrage that usually followed any contact with her mother. He saw none. In fact, her eyes were shining. "I take it that it went well.''

"Better than that,'' she said excitedly. "I think we're finally starting to communicate. For the first time in years, I can actually see a woman I could like, not just the mother I'm supposed to love.''

"What brought on this astonishing turnaround?''

"Believe it or not, your portrait had a lot to do with it.'' She told him about their conversation, about her discovery that her mother had once painted, too. "And I never knew. Isn't that amazing?''

"Amazing,'' he agreed, enjoying the fire in her eyes and wishing somehow that he'd been the one to put it there.

"Well, that's all I came to tell you,'' she said.

"Since you still won't let me into the studio, I guess I'll be off now. One victory is probably the best I can hope for in a single day."

"Aren't you getting tired of driving all this way just to have me rebuff you?" he asked curiously.

"Not really," she said, then added with a wink, "Catching a glimpse of all that scenery is worth it."

Ben shook his head. "I have no idea what to make of you."

"I'm a pretty straightforward woman. When I see something I want, I go after it."

Ben noted the accompanying gleam in her eye. It made him wonder once again if what she wanted was still his art...or him. There was one way to find out, a way he'd been avoiding for some time now, because he was terrified to go down that particular path again. Each time he had before had left him rattled and uneasy. He struggled with himself once more, told himself it would be foolish to tempt fate by taking his brother's advice and plunging into a relationship that was bound to butt headlong into the brick wall around his heart.

But when he couldn't stand it one second longer, he kissed her, a hard, demanding kiss that drove his senses crazy and made his heart pound.

Big mistake. No, *huge* mistake. If she'd been in his head all morning long, now she was in his blood. He couldn't seem to get enough of her.

When he finally released her, she stared at him, clearly dazed.

"What? Why?" She shook her head, then asked more steadily. "What was that for?"

"It was a long time coming," he said, then raked his hand through his hair.

"You've kissed me before," she reminded him.

"I remember."

"But not quite like that," she admitted. "As if you wanted more."

Because he couldn't deny it, he said only, "I think you should probably go now."

"Oh, no, you don't. You don't kiss me like that and then dismiss me as if nothing important happened," she retorted.

He heard the exasperation in her voice and smiled. "Do you want to talk it to death?"

"Yes," she said stubbornly. "That's exactly what I want."

To shut her up, he kissed her again. This time when he released her, she didn't ask a single thing. Instead, she whirled around and headed for her car.

"Leaving?" he inquired.

She scowled at him. "Yes, I am."

Ben thought he was home free, until she faced him.

"Come and see my gallery tonight. I mean really look at it," she said in a tone that was less invitation than command. "You promised you would weeks ago and you've barely glanced around when you've been by there."

It was true. He hadn't wanted to look around. If he had, he might have been tempted to give her her way, to let her show his work.

"I'll fix you dinner after," she coaxed.

Ben regarded her doubtfully. "And spend the rest of the evening giving me your best sales pitch, I imagine. Or do you have more Christmas lights that need untangling?"

"Quite a few at the shop, as a matter of fact, but we'll save those for another day. I've finished the decorating for this year, anyway. No, tonight will be all about you and me.'' She grinned and held her fingers less than an inch apart. ''And maybe just a tiny bit about your art.''

Ben gazed into her eyes. If he was going to get dragged deeper and deeper into this web she was spinning around him, then he had a far more intriguing way they could spend the evening, one that was every bit as long overdue as those heated kisses they'd just shared.

With Mack's advice still ringing in his ears, he moved closer, then lifted his hand and swept a finger along her cheek. He felt the skin heat, felt her tremble. ''Make love with me, instead,'' he suggested, gazing into her eyes. ''Then we'll have something much more interesting to discuss.''

Color climbed into her cheeks, but her steady gaze never wavered. Then she politely held out her hand as if they were closing some very proper business arrangement.

''Deal,'' she said, taking him by surprise.

Ben closed his hand around hers and felt the shock of the contact slam through him. Making love with this woman was going to be an extraordinary, life-altering experience. He should have been terrified by that knowledge, but he wasn't. The desire that had been simmering ever since he'd kissed her the very first time reached a boil.

''You're sure? You're not going to lure me into town, then change your mind?''

She regarded him indignantly. ''Dugans never back out on a business contract.''

''I'm not sure that business describes what we're talking about,'' Ben said wryly.

"It may not be directly business-related," she agreed. "But a verbal contract is binding where I come from. I don't take them lightly, no matter the context."

"Well then, I guess we have ourselves an iron-clad contract, Kathleen."

Eyes flashing, she met his gaze. "Assuming you Carltons have the same kind of integrity as the Dugans."

Ben laughed. "Oh, sweetheart, I think in this instance you can most definitely count on me living up to my word. I've been waiting a very long time to complete this particular transaction."

Chapter Twelve

Kathleen was more jittery than she had been on her first date way back in junior high school. She told herself it was the prospect of making love with Ben that had her so jumpy, but the truth was, she was almost as anxious about his opinion of the gallery. She harbored this faint hope that if he really, truly looked around he'd have confidence that she could showcase his work in a professional way that would guarantee he'd be treated seriously and respectfully by the art world.

She spent the entire afternoon polishing and dusting, adjusting the lighting on Boris's paintings, rearranging the tastefully elegant Christmas decorations she'd completed only the day before.

When the doorbell jangled just before three, she nearly jumped out of her skin, but it was Melanie who came in, not Ben. She immediately noticed Kathleen's undisguised disappointment.

"Expecting someone else?" Melanie asked, then grinned.

"Not really," Kathleen said, struggling for nonchalance. Ben wasn't due for a few more hours, actually.

"Oh? I heard my brother-in-law might be dropping by."

Filled with dismay, Kathleen stared at her. "How on earth did you hear that? We just set it up a couple of hours ago."

"Carlton grapevine," Melanie said succinctly. "Ben mentioned something to Destiny about coming into town. Then he happened to speak to Mack, who already knew and guessed that he was coming in to see you. Ben didn't deny it. Then it was just a hop, skip and a jump till the news was spread far and wide. If I could get the word out on my public relations clients half as efficiently, I'd be a Fortune 500 company by now."

"How can you even joke about it?" Kathleen asked. "Isn't it disconcerting to have the entire family know what's happening practically before you do?"

"At times," Melanie admitted. "But I've kept an occasional secret. That's been all the more enjoyable because everyone is so shocked when they finally find out. No one knew about this baby, for instance. Not until Richard and I agreed it was time to let them in on it." She shrugged. "Of course, Destiny guessed, but kept it to herself for once. She probably knows down to the second when it will be born. She seems to be intuitive when it comes to that sort of thing, or maybe God is one of those infamous inside sources of hers."

Kathleen laughed. "Speaking of that, does Richard know you're roaming around loose with the baby due any second?"

Melanie rolled her eyes. "No. I made my escape from the office while he was tied up on a conference call." She gave Kathleen a sly look. "I thought you might want some advice on what to wear tonight."

"Excuse me?"

"For the big date."

Kathleen looked down at her long skirt and colorful tunic. "I never thought about changing," she said. "Is this all wrong?"

Melanie gave her a thoughtful once-over. "Not for selling paintings, but it could use a little work when it comes to seduction."

Heat flooded Kathleen's cheeks. "I never said... Surely Ben didn't say..."

"No one had to say a word. It's pretty obvious to anyone who's watched this dance the two of you have been doing." Melanie chuckled. "Don't be embarrassed. Just be glad I talked Destiny into letting me be the one to come over here. She's very busy gloating this afternoon. I suspect it would have gotten on your nerves."

Kathleen groaned. This just got worse and worse. As if she weren't nervous enough, now she knew that Ben's entire family was waiting with bated breath to see how things progressed between them tonight.

"Now, here's the plan," Melanie announced in a take-charge way that proved why she'd been able to cope quite successfully with the strong-willed Carltons. "I will stay here and take care of business, while you run home to change. I won't let anyone steal the paintings or mess up anything. Just get back here so I can get home before Richard figures out I've disappeared. I usually go home about this time and supposedly nap for an hour. He doesn't call, because he doesn't wan to wake me." She shrugged. "I let him think that, so I can get a few errands done before he gets all crazy."

"Twenty minutes," Kathleen promised. She'd grabbed her coat and was halfway out the door, when she was struck by panic. "Melanie, what on earth can I wear in here that's also suitable for seduction?"

"In your case, something that shows a little cleavage and a lot of leg," Melanie advised.

Kathleen laughed, her panic easing. "I think I've got just the dress."

"Good. Can I stick around and watch Ben try to get his tongue untangled?"

"Not a chance," she said with heartfelt emphasis. "Even if you could elude your husband for that long, which is highly doubtful, I think it's best if the Carlton grapevine doesn't get wind of the details on this one."

Ben stood on the sidewalk outside of Kathleen's gallery, unable to propel himself inside. This was it. The moment of truth. He was going in there not just to let her try to woo him into making some sort of deal for his art, but to do his own share of wooing. What the hell was he thinking? There were so many potential complications, he ought to have his head examined for even being here.

But once Mack had planted the idea in his head—okay, it had already been there, his brother had merely brought it into the open—it had been impossible to ignore. There hadn't been a chance in hell that he would stay away.

He was still staring in the window, brooding, when the door opened and Kathleen stepped outside.

"You're going to freeze if you don't get in here," she told him, amusement tugging at her lips. "Surely you can't be scared of stepping into a tiny little art gallery. It's not some house of horrors.''

He had been only moderately scared until he'd caught a glimpse of her. Then his mouth went dry and he knew the meaning of genuine terror. She was wearing a little black dress, the kind that was supposed to be suitable for any occasion. Somehow, though, on Kathleen that basic black dress took style into a whole other realm. It was barely more than a slip, actually, with tiny straps, a draped bodice that clung to her breasts, and hardly enough material to skim the tops of her knees. She had incredible knees and very long legs, slender and shapely.

Looking at her set his body on fire. He was definitely in no danger of freezing.

She, however, was shivering.

''You're the one who needs to go inside,'' he said, putting a firm hand in the middle of her back, then snatching it away when a current of electricity jolted through him. Touching her was not a good idea, he reminded himself. Not just yet. Not if he was expected to tour this gallery, make coherent comments, and register suitable approval.

In her strappy little black heels, Kathleen was almost as tall as he was, her gaze even with his. Her huge violet eyes were fringed with lashes that seemed darker and longer than he'd remembered. He lost himself for a minute or two in her eyes, then dragged his attention away again to firmly shut the door behind them.

Her gaze still locked with his, Kathleen stepped around him, threw the lock and drew the shade. Ben' heart started to thunder in his chest.

''Um, Kathleen, what are you up to?''

''Just locking up,'' she said, her expression innocen

"So we won't be interrupted." She smiled brightly. "What would you like to see first?"

You, he thought a little wildly. All of you.

"In here," she added, as if she'd read his mind. Her eyes were dancing with amusement. "What would you like to see in the gallery?"

He tried valiantly to unscramble his thoughts and focus. "You're the tour guide," he said.

"Then we'll start with Boris's work," she said and slipped into a professional persona as she described the first painting they came to.

When Ben said nothing, she frowned at him. "You're not looking at the painting," she scolded.

He gave it a dutiful glance and concluded as he had the first time he'd seen it, that it was expert, compelling but not to his taste. "I'd rather look at you," he told her honestly.

She swallowed hard. "We're wasting our time here, aren't we?"

Ben noted that her disappointment didn't seem nearly as great as the thread of anticipation in her voice. "Sorry, but I'd have to say yes. I can't concentrate with you looking the way you do."

She regarded him curiously. "How do I look?"

"Incredible. Sexy. Alluring. Tempting."

She laughed. "You don't have to go on. I get the idea."

He searched her face. "Do you?"

The laughter died. "Oh, yes," she said huskily.

"Then we can postpone this tour?" he asked hopefully.

She nodded without the faintest flicker of regret in her eyes.

"I'll get your coat."

"I can get it," she protested.

"No, I need a minute. Otherwise we might not even make it out of here."

She sighed. "I knew there was a reason I should have put a sofa in my office."

He grinned at her. "Maybe I'll order one, something that opens up with a queen-size mattress."

"Maybe you should wait until you see how tonight goes," she said, a surprising hint of worry in her eyes.

"There's no question in my mind about how tonight is going to go," he told her. "None."

"How can you be so sure?"

Ben heard the insecurity in her voice and knew yet another moment of impotent rage at the man who'd destroyed her self-confidence in yet another area. He had a pretty good picture of her ex-husband by now, a man who took his own weaknesses and lack of success out on the woman he'd married, cruelly filling her with self-doubt, because he couldn't measure up. He'd cut her to ribbons as an artist, as a chef and, maybe worst of all, as a woman.

Ben crossed the gallery in a few strides and took her in his arms and kissed her thoroughly, determined to make up for the cruelty of another man. He could practically feel the heat shimmering through her. He pressed her hand to his chest, where he knew she'd feel his heart pounding.

"That's how," he told her gently, gazing into eyes that had turned smoky with pleasure. "It's not just the dress that's sexy, Kathleen. It's you, every inch of you. We're going to make magic tonight."

He said it with complete confidence and saw eventually that she believed him. She should. She'd definitely cast a spell over him, one that had vanished all the heartache from his past. For the first time since Graciela's death, he was daring to think about the future.

And about love.

Even though they walked at a very brisk pace, Kathleen didn't think they were ever going to get to her house. Her whole body was virtually humming with anticipation, the sort of anticipation she'd never expected to experience again. Not even the icy December wind could chill the heat set off just by Ben's gloved hand wrapped around her own. If he'd suggested slipping into an alley along the way, she might very well have agreed without a single reservation.

Neither of them said much. It was as if words might break the spell that held them in its grip. She certainly didn't want it broken. It had been much too long since she'd believed she had the power to make a man want her with the desperation and hunger she'd seen in Ben's eyes, that she'd felt when his lips were on hers.

As edgy as she was already, it wasn't going to take much—a clever stroke, an intimate caress—to set off an explosion that would rock her. As impatient as she was for that to happen, she wanted to savor every second, wanted this delicious buildup to go on and on and on.

Despite the simmering passion, there was also a niggling doubt. Ben had guessed it earlier and tried to put it to rest, but it wouldn't go away. It was too entrenched. She didn't believe for a moment that Ben wouldn't satisfy her, but she was terrified of not satisfying him. He'd tried to reassure her that that wasn't possible, but she knew it could happen.

How many times had the heat built between herself

and Tim, only to have her husband roll away from her, cursing about her ineptitude, blaming her for all the failures in their lovemaking? Of all the things Tim had done to demean her, that had been the worst. He'd struck at the core of her, all but said she wasn't woman enough for him or for any man. And she'd believed him because she had absolutely no basis for comparison. Tim had been her first and only lover.

And her last. She'd never let another relationship get this far, had rarely been on anything more than the most casual dates. Ben had lured her out of her comfort zone, perhaps because he'd barely even tried. Tonight had slipped up on her, catching her by surprise. She'd been so intent on one goal—getting those paintings— that she'd barely even realized what was right under her nose, an attraction that wouldn't be denied.

Given all that, it was amazing that she was here at all, walking hand in hand with a man who'd come to mean so much to her, risking a failure that could rip them apart before they'd even begun.

She stumbled. Ben steadied her, then gazed into her eyes.

"You okay?" he asked, his brow creased with worry.

"Fine."

"About everything?"

She kept her gaze steady, took heart from the concern and love shining in his eyes. "About everything," she replied at last.

And she was. It was going to be okay, because this was Ben, not Tim. Tim was over. She'd been brave enough to make sure of that, even if she hadn't been strong enough to move on before now. But maybe that was the way it had been meant to be, not moving on until the timing and the man were absolutely right.

When they got to her house, she fumbled with the key until Ben took it from her shaking hand and turned it in the lock, then stepped aside to let her enter.

She was reaching for the light when he stilled her hand and solemnly shook his head.

"There's moonlight coming through the windows. I want to see you first in moonlight."

Her knees very nearly buckled at that. "Upstairs," she said unsteadily. "There's a skylight in my room." It was a gift she'd given to herself, a way to see the stars at night, the ideal light for painting in the daytime, though until very recently she'd never thought it would serve that function again.

"Perfect," Ben said.

She led the way up the carpeted stairs, then turned into her room which was, indeed, bathed in silvery moonlight. It was better than candlelight, she decided as she turned to face him.

"Now what?" she asked, her voice still shaky.

He grinned, taking the edge off her jitters. "Are you expecting me to give you five seconds to strip and meet me in the bed?" he asked.

She smiled a little less nervously. "Given the way we rushed over here, it did occur to me."

"No way, sweetheart. We're going to take this nice and slow." He grinned slowly. "You can lose the coat and gloves, though."

Kathleen shed them where she stood, letting the coat slide to the floor before kicking it aside. She tossed the gloves in the general direction of a chair. Ben's coat and gloves landed on top of them.

"Do you want a glass of wine or something?" she asked.

"You're intoxicating enough for me. What about you? Will it help you to relax?" he asked, stepping behind her to knead her tensed shoulders. "Your muscles are tighter than a drum, Kathleen."

The warmth of his touch began to ease through her, releasing the tension. "I think you're more effective than any wine could be," she said.

"Good to know."

Kathleen could almost hear the smile in his voice. "It wasn't just idle flattery, Benjamin. You really are making this easy."

"Easy?" His hands stilled. "Are you really afraid, Kathleen?"

"A little nervous," she admitted, because there seemed no point in denying it. She wanted there to be honesty between them, not the lies and evasions that she'd attempted to keep her marriage bearable.

His massage resumed, even gentler now. "Sweetheart, there's no need to be scared of anything, least of all making love. We don't have anywhere to go. There's no rush, no timetable. Nothing is going to happen until you're ready. You're with me now. There's no one else in the room. No ghosts, okay?"

His patience almost made her weep. What had she ever done to deserve a man like this? Was Ben God's reward for what she'd endured during the few brief months of her marriage? If so, she would spend the rest of her life on her knees thanking Him for His gift.

"Would you kiss me?" she pleaded, needing the fire of his mouth on hers, his tongue tangling with hers. That would chase away the last of her fears. She knew it would.

He turned her in his arms and took a long time simply gazing into her eyes before slowly covering her mouth with his own. It was a sweet, gentle kiss for about a heartbeat. Then the familiar hunger and need kicked in and Kathleen's fears fled, just as she'd predicted. Instead, all she felt was the rising urgency, the powerful pull to have Ben's hands all over her, teasing and tormenting until she was writhing beneath him.

Now she was the impatient one, fumbling with the buttons on his shirt, tugging at the buckle on his belt, reaching for taut, hot skin that felt totally masculine, totally alive beneath her fingers. The textures, the masculine scent inflamed her. She had something to prove...to him, to herself.

"I guess slow and easy is out of the question," Ben commented, laughing.

"Yes," she said, skimming her hand over his abdomen, reaching lower until she felt the hard, reassuring thrust of his arousal against her palm.

It wasn't a lack in her—had *never* been—she exulted, when she felt that solid evidence of her power to stir a man. She was enough woman for any man, for *this* man. It was a heady, exhilarating discovery. The last of the tormenting doubts from her marriage vanished. If nothing more came of this night, she could be grateful for that.

But there was more. Ben wasn't satisfied to let her do all of the exploration. His restless hands stroked and teased, first through the silky fabric of her dress, then against bare skin until her whole body was humming again, her flesh so sensitive that the slightest touch could make her soar.

When her knees went weak, he scooped her up and placed her in the center of the bed, where she was bathed in moonlight. The look of awe and wonder in his eyes was something she knew she would cherish for years to come.

"Do you have any idea what your body does to a man?" he asked. "Those beautiful breasts, those slender hips, those long, long legs? You're incredible. I don't think I'll ever get enough of you."

His words filled her heart, but it was the reverent way he touched her that made her fall in love with him yet again. That touch chased away already fading memories of the past and gave her the future.

"Come to me," she said, unafraid.

He knelt over her, his gaze warm, his smile gentle, and waited, giving her time, she knew, time to accept his body, time to yearn for him.

"Really," she said softly. "Come to me."

He kissed her then, stroked her everywhere, and when the fire was at its peak, when her blood was thrumming through her veins, he entered her with a sure, deep thrust that stole her breath.

Again he waited, patient as ever, and only when her hips moved restlessly did he begin to move inside her, leading her to the top of an incredible precipice, then waiting for her yet again.

And then, when her heart was pounding, her pulse racing and her whole body aching with the sweet torment of it, he carried her over the edge into magic, just as he'd promised he would.

Chapter Thirteen

Ben lay in bed, Kathleen cradled in his arms, sunlight now spilling over them from that amazing skylight in her bedroom ceiling. He was filled with an astonishing range of sensations that he'd never expected to experience.

Desire, of course. He hadn't stopped wanting her for a single second all night long. No matter how many times they'd made love—and he'd lost count of that— he'd wanted more. He wished he could attribute that to the long, dry spell in his love life, but that wasn't it and he knew it. It was all about Kathleen and what she did to scramble his senses.

Then there was the raging possessiveness she inspired. He wanted her to be his and his alone, even though he knew that he was incapable of making the same level of commitment. Sooner or later he was going to have to face facts—he couldn't have one without the other.

And then there was the flood of protectiveness that nearly overwhelmed him. He would die before he let anyone hurt her ever again.

And finally fear, because despite all the rest, he wasn't sure he was brave enough to risk his heart, to chance another loss. Kathleen deserved nothing less than a man who could share himself completely and without reservations, and he could lose her because he couldn't give her what she needed.

Mack had been wrong. Getting her into bed wasn't enough. Not by a long shot.

She stirred against him and that alone was enough to make him forget the fear for now. There would be time enough to worry about that when he was back out at the farm, alone, his equilibrium restored.

"Hey, sleepyhead, wake up," he murmured against her ear.

"Mmmm?"

"It's morning."

She moaned and snuggled more tightly against him. That was no way to get them both up and out of this bed, Ben concluded. Most of the ideas raging around in his head, in fact, involved this bed and a long, leisurely day spent right here. That was probably not a good idea. If he stayed now, he might never want to leave. History told him that as soon as he wanted anything that much, wanted *anyone* that much, he was doomed to lose them.

He forced himself to ease away from Kathleen and sit on the side of the bed, ignoring her little whimper of protest. It was harder to ignore the sneaky hand that reached unerringly for a part of him that had no thought processes at all, only feeling. He'd spent the whole night listening to that part of his anatomy. It was time for his brain to kick back into gear.

"Oh, no, you don't, you wicked, wicked woman," he said lightly, ignoring the temptation. "It's a workday."

"Doesn't have to be," she mumbled sleepily.

"You'd leave the gallery closed and spend the whole day right here?" he asked skeptically. She'd always struck him as a businesswoman, first and foremost. She'd never abandon potential customers to seek her own pleasure.

She rolled over and blinked at him. "In a heartbeat, as long as you'll stay with me," she said without hesitation, proving him wrong.

Now that raised an interesting quandary, Ben decided. It left him with a dangerous choice. He opted for emotional safety, as always. "Wish I could, but I can't."

"I don't see why. After all, you keep telling me you're not a professional artist, so it can't be that you have to rush back to your studio to complete a painting."

"No, it's not that," he agreed, almost regretting that he couldn't claim that as an easy excuse, one she would readily understand. "But if I don't show my face around Destiny's this morning, she's liable to come over here pounding on the door to see for herself what we've been up to."

"Your own fault. She could only do that because you blabbed that we had a date," Kathleen reminded him. "Why you let her in on that little tidbit is beyond me."

"I didn't," he said. "I merely told her I was coming

into town. Then Mack called and asked me point-blank if I was seeing you. I made the mistake of admitting that we had a date. Foolishly, I thought he'd keep it to himself.''

"And now it's costing you," she concluded, sliding from the opposite side of the bed wrapped in a sheet. She frowned at the clock. "Serves you right that there's not even time for me to bake you some muffins, if I'm expected to open the gallery right on time."

He laughed. "I think I've proved that I'm interested in more than your baking. You can stop plying me with pastry now."

She gave him an oddly sad look. "I like baking for you. You're a very appreciative recipient."

"Then by all means keep it up," he told her, not even trying to hide his enthusiasm for the prospect of more delectable goodies appearing on his doorstep. "But just for today, I'll be in charge of breakfast. I think I saw eggs in the refrigerator when I was in there looking for a snack for us in the middle of the night. I'll have something ready by the time you come downstairs."

She stared at him in shock. "You cook?"

"Adequately. I didn't survive this long by waiting around for somebody to do it for me. Don't expect much, though. Richard's the real chef in the family."

"Really?" she said, apparently finding that fascinating. "And Mack?"

"He can order takeout with the best of them," Ben said, smiling. "It's a good thing this family owns restaurants. He has every one of them on speed dial."

Kathleen chuckled. "Poor Beth."

"Oh, I think she figures she got a good deal. Mack has other attributes, to say the least. Besides, as much

as Beth's at the hospital and as unpredictable as her
hours can be, takeout suits their life-style and Mack's
version is definitely top-of-the-line. There are no fast-
food hamburgers on his menu.''

His gaze drifted to the curve of Kathleen's bare back
and his body stirred again. Once more he ignored the
temptation to drag that sheet off her and haul her right
back into this warm, comfortable bed.

"Scoot," he said instead, reaching for his pants.
''You're giving me ideas, standing there looking all
rumpled and sexy.''

"What ideas?" she taunted.

Rather than tell her what she expected to hear, he
said, "I'd like to paint you looking exactly like that."

His response surprised them both, but he realized it
was true. He'd never painted people, but he wanted to
paint Kathleen. He wondered what that said about how
she'd managed to sneak into his heart.

Usually he stuck to nature, because of its beauty, but
also because it was safe. To paint a portrait and do it
well, he'd always known he'd have to get inside the
person's head, to understand their soul. He'd never
wanted to risk it before, not even with Graciela. Maybe
on some level he'd understood even then that if he dug
too deep beneath Graciela's polished surface, he
wouldn't like what he found.

But with Kathleen, he already knew he'd find a gentle, caring soul. He shook off the implications of that
and grinned at her. "Now that's a painting I could see
hanging in your gallery," he teased to lighten the
mood.

"Not in my lifetime," she retorted and scampered
quickly into the bathroom and firmly shut the door behind her as if that would end the threat.

"I remember what you looked like," he called after her. In fact, he suspected that her image was burned in his head forever.

Downstairs, he pushed that image aside and immersed himself in the comforting domestic tasks required to get breakfast on the table. Scrambled eggs, toast, jam, orange juice and coffee. Lots and lots of coffee. He was going to need it to face Destiny and what was bound to be a litany of intrusive questions. He could sneak back out to the farm without answering a one of them, but experience had taught him it was always better to do a preemptive strike.

When Kathleen finally breezed into the kitchen, she was wearing slim black pants and an exotic-looking tunic that shimmered with silver threads. It made him think of the night sky and moonlight, which of course made his pulse scramble all over again.

"What's your day like?" he asked.

"In retail you never know," she told him. "But this time of year, it's usually busy, especially around lunchtime." She gave him a sly look. "And this morning I have a tour to give."

"Oh?"

She nodded. "It's a very personal and private tour before the gallery officially opens. It was scheduled for last night, but somehow the tourist and I got side-tracked."

"You want to do that this morning?" he asked, surprised. He wasn't entirely sure why he found the prospect so daunting. Maybe it was because he was rapidly reaching a point where there was very little he could deny her.

"You're here, aren't you?" she said briskly. "And

your car is still by the gallery. I can't think of a single reason not to pick up where we left off, can you?''

There was no refuting her logic. "You think you're clever, don't you? What makes you think it won't lead us right back here all over again?''

A slow grin spread across her face. "I could live with that outcome. How about you?''

"It is an intriguing prospect," he agreed, enjoying the flash of confidence in her eyes. He'd given her that. "But a risky one. You said yourself that it's a busy time of year. Do you want to lose business by sneaking off for some hanky-panky?''

"Oh, I think you could make it worthwhile.''

"I would do my best," he agreed. "Okay then, you can show me the gallery before I head over to Destiny's, but we really do need to make it quick or she'll be joining us.''

"I'll talk fast," she promised. "Try to keep up.''

Ben laughed at her obvious desire to avoid an encounter with his aunt. To be truthful, he wasn't much looking forward to it, either. Destiny was never at her most attractive when she was gloating.

An hour later Kathleen had shown Ben every nook and cranny of the gallery. He had to admit that what she'd accomplished in just a few years was quite impressive. The displays were carefully thought out, the lighting impeccable. Everything had been done with simplicity, style and elegance. The scrapbook she'd kept from past showings, the collection of glowing reviews proved that she had a discerning eye for talent.

"You've done an incredible job here," he told her honestly. "You should be very proud.''

"I am," she said, regarding him thoughtfully. "Is it

impressive enough to convince you to let me show your work?''

He frowned at the question, even though he'd expected it. "It was never about your professional skill," he reminded her. "It's about me. I'm not interested in showing my paintings, much less selling them."

"Ben, that doesn't make any sense," she said impatiently. "You have talent. Why not share it with the world? If you don't want to sell it, fine, but at least give other people the joy of looking at it."

He knew it didn't make sense, not from her perspective anyway, but it did to him. His paintings were intensely personal and private, not in the subject matter, but in the way he poured his heart and soul into each and every one. He didn't want anyone, let alone strangers, getting a glimpse of the world as he saw it. He feared it would tell them too much about him. It would take something that gave him joy and open it to criticism that might rob him of the serenity that painting gave him. The world was neat and orderly on the canvases he painted, and he desperately needed to keep it that way.

That was another reason why there were never people in his paintings. People were never neat and orderly. Emotions were never tidy and predictable. And he'd been shattered too many times by life's unpredictability.

"Let me ask you something," he began, hoping to make her see his point. "There was a time when you loved painting, right? When it brought something beautiful and joyful into your life?"

She nodded slowly, and he could see by the quick flash of understanding in her eyes that she already knew where he was going with this.

"And when Tim criticized, when he told you that you weren't good enough, what happened?" Before she could answer, he told her, "All the joy went out of it, correct? He robbed you of something that really mattered to you."

"Yes, but—"

"Don't tell me it's different, Kathleen, because it's not. Art meant as much to you as it does to me. So you, of all people, should understand why I don't want to risk losing that. I can't do it, not even for you. If I cared about fame, if I needed the money, maybe I'd feel differently, but I don't."

"Oh, Ben," she whispered, tears in her eyes. "It wouldn't be like that."

"Why? Can you guarantee that some critic won't rip my work to shreds? Why expose myself to that when I don't need to?"

"Then this is just because you're afraid of a little criticism?" she demanded incredulously. "That's absurd. Why would you let the opinions of people who supposedly don't even matter to you affect whether or not you continue to paint? They're not important. Tim's cruelty mattered because *he* mattered."

"You're right," he agreed. "The critics aren't important. That doesn't mean their words don't have power. I don't want to lose the joy I find right now when I sit in front of a blank canvas and envision a painting, beginning with that very first brush stroke, the first hint of a crystal-blue sky, the line of a tree. That feeling is something I can count on now. It's the only thing I can count on."

"You could count on me," she said quietly.

A part of him desperately wanted to believe that, wanted to have faith that nothing would ever take her away, but experience had taught him otherwise. People he loved went away, no matter what promises they made.

He stroked a finger down her cheek, felt the dampness of tears. "I wish I could," he said with real regret. "If ever I was going to count on another person, I'd want it to be you."

"Then do it. Take a leap of faith. Forget about the paintings. I would love to show them, and I think the show would be wildly successful, but it doesn't matter. Just believe in me. Believe in what we found last night. It was real, Ben. You can't deny that."

He smiled sadly, regretting that the subject had shifted so quickly from his work to the two of them. While one topic only exasperated him, the other terrified him.

"No, I can't deny that it was real," he agreed. "I just can't count on it lasting."

And before she could utter another word, before she could try to persuade him to stay, he turned and left the gallery.

Outside he hesitated, then dared to look back. Kathleen was standing where he'd left her, her expression shattered. He realized then that being left wasn't the only thing that could break a person's heart. Leaving was tearing his to pieces.

When Ben left the gallery, he didn't go to Destiny's. Instead, filled with anger and regret and anguish, he drove back to the farm and went straight into his studio seeking that solace he'd tried to explain to Kathleen.

Filled with an almost frenetic energy, he pulled out a canvas, daubed paints on his palette and went to work.

He began, as he often did, with a wash of blue. As the color of sky filled the canvas, his tension began to ease. He was able to convince himself that nothing had changed, that his world was still orderly. He sat back, filled with relief, and sighed deeply.

He took the time to brew himself a pot of coffee, then went back to the canvas, but this time the first stroke of the brush betrayed him. It wasn't the familiar, sweeping line of a majestic oak at all, but the curve of a woman's body. Kathleen's body. There was no mistaking it. Why would this come to him now with no photo to work from, no live Kathleen there to guide him?

He threw down his brush, tossed his palette across the room and began to pace, muttering to himself as if that alone would get her out of his head. When he was certain he was back in control, he went back to the easel.

Impatiently he tried to change the form, to add a texture that spoke of something solid and unyielding. Instead, the image softened and blurred, the very picture of welcoming arms and tender flesh.

Another tantrum, another attempt, another failure to regain control.

Defeated, he gave himself up to the inspiration, then, letting the image flow from the brushes as if they had a mind of their own. His usual palette of greens and browns and grays gave way to the inky blackness of night and the shimmering pastels of a woman in moonlight.

Her body took shape before him, as intimately familiar as the skies he usually painted. Without a picture, without her, it was her face that gave him the most trouble, especially the eyes. He cursed himself time and

again for not getting them right, then sat back for a
moment in dismay.

He knew in his gut why they wouldn't come to him.
It was because he couldn't bear to look into those eyes
and see the pain he'd put there. And that's what he
would have to paint if he completed this now. It was
the truth, the reality, and that's what he always insisted
on when he painted, absolute clarity.

Exhausted, he finally put aside the brushes and paints
and methodically cleaned up the studio, which seemed
to be in more disarray than usual thanks to his impatient pacing and frequent rages of temper.

He went into the house, grabbed a sandwich, then
fell into bed and spent a restless night tortured by
dreams of Kathleen and his determination to throw
away what they were on the brink of having.

He was back in his studio at the crack of dawn,
armed with renewed determination, a strong pot of coffee and some toaster pastry that didn't hold a candle
to anything Kathleen had ever baked for him. Rather
than satisfying him, that paltry pastry only exacerbated
his irritation.

He wasn't all that surprised when Destiny came
wandering in around eight. To his shock, though, she
didn't immediately pester him with questions. She
merely came to stand beside him, her gaze locked on
the canvas.

"She's very lovely," she said at last.

"No denying it," he said tightly, knowing she was
talking about the woman, not the painting.

"Why not just admit that you love her?"

"Because I don't," he lied.

Destiny gave him a chiding, disbelieving look. "Oh,
please," she admonished. "You need a real woman in

your life, Ben, not a portrait, however magnificent it might turn out to be.''

"Stay out of this," he told her flatly.

"Too late. I'm in the thick of it. I brought her into your life and now you're both hurting because of it.''

"I forgive you," he said. "Eventually Kathleen will, too. Now go away."

She smiled at that. "Forgiveness doesn't come that easily to you," she chided. "Besides, there's nothing to forgive, is there? Kathleen is the perfect woman for you."

"It doesn't matter."

"It's the only thing that matters," she said fiercely.

He gave Destiny a hard look. "I thought you dragged her out here because of my art. Wasn't she merely supposed to convince me that I had talent?''

"I think we both know better than that."

"Well, whatever your intentions, it was a mistake."

"You keep telling yourself that. Maybe you'll wind up believing it. Of course, you'll also be old and alone and bitter.''

"Not so alone," he muttered, not liking the picture she painted. "I'll have you."

"Not forever, darling," she reminded him matter-of-factly. "And your brothers have their own lives now, their own families. You'll always be a part of those lives, of course, but you need to be—you deserve to be—the center of someone's universe. Even more important, you need to make someone the center of yours.''

"Why?" he asked, not even beginning to understand. Loneliness had become a way of life long ago. Even when his whole family had been around, he'd felt alone.

"Because, in the end, love is the only thing any of us has that truly matters."

"You've been courted. You've been admired by many a man, but you've chosen to live without the love of a man all these years," he reminded her.

"And that was probably a costly mistake, not just for me, but for all of you," she admitted. She gave him a surprisingly defiant look. "Moreover, it's one I intend to correct before too long."

Ben seized on the implication. "What on earth does that mean?" he demanded, not entirely sure he liked the sound of it and not just because he hated having his own world turned upside down, which any change in Destiny's life was bound to do.

"Nothing for you to fret about," she reassured him. "I won't do anything until I know you're settled and happy."

He scowled at her. "Isn't that blackmail? If I decide to maintain the status quo, you're stuck here, so therefore I have some obligation to what? Get married?"

She beamed at him. "That would do nicely. Let me know when you and Kathleen have set a date."

"Hold it," he protested when she started toward the door. "No date. No wedding. I am not letting you blackmail me into making a decision I'm not ready to make, will probably never be ready to make."

"Oh, for goodness' sakes, Benjamin, now you're just being stubborn," she declared, facing him with an exasperated expression. "It's the worst of the Carlton traits. Everyone has always said you were the most like me, but I see absolutely no evidence of that right now. Whatever the choices I made, at heart I'm a romantic. I believe in happily ever after. I certainly thought I taught you more about grabbing on to life with both hands.''

"You tried,'' he admitted grudgingly.

"Then why are you here when there's a woman in Alexandria who's brokenhearted because she thinks she pushed you too hard? She's terrified you'll think she only slept with you to get her hands on your paintings.''

The thought had never crossed his mind, at least not until this moment. Now he had to wonder. As soon as he did, he dismissed the idea. There wasn't a shred of duplicity in Kathleen. He wished he could say the same about his sneaky aunt.

"Nice try,'' he congratulated her. "For a minute there you had me going.''

"I have no idea what you're talking about. I was with Kathleen yesterday after you'd gone. She's beside herself. If you don't believe me, call Melanie or Beth. We were all there.''

The thought of that made his skin crawl. "What the hell was going on, some sort of Carlton hen party?'' He shuddered. "Just thinking about all four of you gathered around discussing me and Kathleen is enough to twist my stomach into knots.''

"It should,'' Destiny said without a trace of sympathy. "You're not very popular with the females of the family right now.''

"What did I do?'' he asked, bewildered. "I was honest with her. I've been honest with Kathleen from the beginning. She knew what she was getting into when we were together the other night.''

"Did she really? You slept with her and then you walked out on her,'' Destiny accused. "Do you think she was expecting that?''

"In a very condensed version, that much is true," he acknowledged. "But a lot went on in between." He raked a hand through his hair as he realized that he wasn't going to win, no matter how he tried to explain away that scene in the gallery. "What do you want from me? What does Kathleen want from me? Besides my paintings, of course."

"Oh, forget the stupid paintings," Destiny said. "I want you to tell that woman you love her before it's too late."

He stared at her bleakly, filled with dismay that this woman who understood him so well could ask the impossible of him.

When he said nothing, she walked over to his painting. "Look at this," she commanded. When she was apparently satisfied that his gaze was on the canvas, she asked, "What do you see?"

"Kathleen," he said. "And I've never painted a portrait before. Is that your point?"

"No, darling," she said more gently. "I want you to open your eyes and really look at what's on this canvas. It's not just a very nice likeness of Kathleen."

He tore his gaze from the painting and stared at her, not comprehending.

"It's a portrait of love in all its radiance," she told him quietly. "Any man who could paint this is capable of great passion."

After she'd gone, Ben sat and stared at the painting. He could see the passion she was talking about. In fact, passion was something he certainly understood, but love? Only four little letters, but they added up to something that scared the living daylights out of him. He didn't think there were enough weeks in a lifetime or enough reassurances to help him move past that terror.

Chapter Fourteen

Kathleen still couldn't get over the way the Carlton women had rallied around her two days ago. Within moments of Destiny's arrival at the gallery and her discovery that Ben had walked out on Kathleen that morning, she sent out an alert to the others. Minutes later Melanie and Beth had burst into the gallery like the calvary arriving. Melanie had brought a huge bag of junk food, and Beth had brought nonalcoholic drinks for Melanie and champagne for the rest of them. These women clearly knew how to prepare for a crisis.

Satisfied with the reinforcements, Destiny had locked the gallery door and they'd all proceeded to get thoroughly intoxicated on potato chips, cheesecake, ice cream and old-fashioned gossip.

Ben had not fared well, despite Kathleen's half-hearted attempts to defend him or at the very least to make them see his point of view. She'd been amazed to find them all on her side.

"Take him out and shoot him," Melanie had suggested with real enthusiasm. "Maybe that would get his attention."

"Aren't you being just the teensiest bit bloodthirsty?" Kathleen had asked weakly. "That can't possibly be good for the baby."

"Boy or girl, this baby needs to know that there's right and wrong in the world when it comes to the way men treat women," Melanie insisted. "Besides, this baby is now officially overdue and getting on my nerves. I want the man responsible for this pregnancy—no, I want *all* men, especially Carlton men— to pay."

"Don't get too carried away and do anything you'll regret. You'll stop blaming Richard once you hold the baby," Beth assured her. She turned to Kathleen and added, "As for Ben, shooting's too good for him. Tie him up and torture him. You have no idea how often I was tempted to do that to Mack, when he was being pigheaded."

"But you didn't," Kathleen reminded her, then hesitated. "Did you?"

"No," Beth said with apparent regret.

"That's because the person you really wanted to torture was Destiny," Melanie said, then gave their aunt-in-law an apologetic look. "No offense."

Destiny laughed. "None taken. But since we're obviously not going to convince Kathleen to shoot or torture Ben, perhaps we should try to focus on some more practical solutions to this dilemma. How can we get through to him? Goodness knows, I've tried. If it hadn't been for Graciela, I doubt he'd be making this so difficult, but her death destroyed whatever progress he'd made in terms of having faith that people he cared about would stick around. He seems to have forgotten all about what brought on their fight that awful night."

Kathleen took all of this in. She'd known that the woman Ben had loved had died, but she hadn't realized there had been any sort of fight.

"Why were they fighting?" she asked.

The three women exchanged a look.

"He never told you?" Destiny asked.

"Not really. I just knew that he felt horribly guilty," she said.

"Oh, please," Destiny said. "Of course it was tragic, but Ben has absolutely nothing to feel guilty about. Not only was she far too drunk to get behind the wheel that night, but they fought in the first place because he'd caught her cheating on him. It wasn't the first time, either, just the first time he'd seen it with his own eyes."

"Oh, my," Kathleen whispered. It was even worse than she'd thought. Ben had suffered not only a loss, but a betrayal. It was little wonder he didn't trust anyone.

They'd all fallen silent then, Beth munching thoughtfully on chips while Melanie ate the last of the chocolate fudge ice cream from the half-gallon container. Kathleen picked disconsolately at her third slice of cheesecake. She was pretty sure if she finished it, she'd throw up, but she couldn't seem to stop eating.

"I don't think there's anything any of us can do," Kathleen ventured after a while. "Ben has to figure out for himself that I would never betray him. He has to want this relationship enough to get past his fear of loss. He has to see that either way he's going to lose and at least if we've tried, he'll have had something good for a while.''

''Good?'' Beth asked in a mildly scolding tone. ''*Extraordinary*. He'll have had something extraordinary. Don't lose sight of that, Kathleen. This isn't just some happy little diversion. It's the real deal.''

It was still hard for Kathleen to see herself in that kind of glowing light. She'd felt that way in Ben's arms. She'd had a hint of it when he'd praised her painting, when he'd gone into raptures over her cooking. But those feelings of self-worth were new and fragile. It would be far too easy to retreat into the more familiar self-doubt.

''Thank you for reminding me of that,'' she told Beth. ''You have no idea how hard it is for me to remember that, especially this morning, but it's coming back to me. I owe Ben and all of you for that.''

Beth gave her a curious look. ''Is there a story there?''

''Yes,'' she admitted. ''But it's not worth repeating ever again. I am finally going to put it where it belongs, in the past.''

''Good for you!'' Melanie cheered.

''Does Ben know?'' Destiny asked, a frown knitting her brow.

''Yes.''

''And he still walked out of here and left you feeling abandoned?'' she said indignantly. ''What is wrong with that man? Obviously I need to have another talk with him. In fact, right now I'd like to shake my nephew till something stirs in that thick head of his.''

''Don't,'' Kathleen pleaded, but her request fell on deaf ears. She'd seen the determined glint in Destiny's eyes and known Ben was in for a blistering lecture

She tried to work up a little sympathy for him, but in the end she'd concluded he was only getting what he deserved. She had a few choice words she'd like to say to him herself. Too bad they hadn't come to her before he'd slunk out of the gallery.

Now, though, with the hours crawling by and no word from Destiny or Ben, she had to wonder if Destiny had failed to get through to him, if it wasn't over, after all, simply because Ben had decreed that it was. They said you couldn't make a person fall in love with you, but she didn't believe that was Ben's problem. He *had* fallen in love with her. He was even willing to admit it. He just wasn't willing to act on it, not in the happily-ever-after way she'd begun to long for. And in the end what difference did the admission make, if it wasn't going to go anywhere?

She sighed and tried to concentrate on tallying up the day's sales, but the numbers kept blurring through her tears. She needed to get out of the gallery. She needed to walk or maybe run.

She needed a drive in the country.

She sighed again. That was the last thing she dared to do. Going to Ben's—going anywhere near Ben's—was beyond self-destructive. It was stupid, foolish, pitiful. The list of adjectives went on and on.

None of them seemed to prevent her from getting into her car and driving out to Middleburg, but when she reached the entrance to the farm, her pride finally kicked in. She drove on past, then turned around, muttering another litany of derogatory adjectives about herself as she drove. She hadn't done anything this adolescent and absurd since high school.

Thoroughly irritated with her cowardice and immaurity, she made herself turn in the gate and drive up to the house, determined to see Ben and clear the air. But when she got there, the studio and house were both dark as pitch, and Ben's car was nowhere in sight.

Obviously, he wasn't sitting around alone, moping about their relationship. Why should she? She should go back to town, open the gallery and take advantage of the last-minute Christmas shoppers roaming the streets.

In the end, though, she simply went home, too emotionally exhausted to cope with anything more than a hot bath and warm milk and her own lonely bed. With any luck Ben, who'd managed to torment her all day long, would stay the hell out of her dreams.

After forcing himself to go into Middleburg to grab a beer and some dinner after Destiny's visit, Ben spent another tortured night dreaming of Kathleen and an endless stream of paintings that began as landscapes and turned into portraits, always of the same woman. By morning he was irritable and in no mood for the 7:00 a.m. phone call from his brother.

"You'd better read the paper," Mack announced without preamble.

"Why?"

"Destiny and Pete Forsythe have struck again."

"What the hell are you talking about?" he mumbled, still half-asleep, but coming awake fast.

"Get your paper, then call me back if you need to rant for a while. I've been through this, so you'll get plenty of sympathy from me. Richard, too. This is vintage Destiny. It's our aunt at her sneakiest."

Ben dragged on a pair of faded jeans and raced downstairs, cursing a blue streak the whole way. He had a pretty good idea what to expect when he turned to Forsythe's column. After all, the gossip columnist was Destiny's messenger of choice when all her other tactics had failed. Letting the entire Metropolitan Washington region in on whichever Carlton romance wasn't moving along to suit her was supposed to motivate all the parties. It was the kind of convoluted logic he'd never understood, but he couldn't deny it had probably pushed things along for Richard and Mack, despite the havoc the column had wreaked at the time.

He opened the paper with some trepidation. There it was, summed up right in the headline: Art Dealer Courts Reclusive Carlton Heir.

"But is Alexandria art expert Kathleen Dugan, known for finding undiscovered talent, looking for something other than paintings to hang on the walls of her prestigious gallery?" Forsythe asked. "Word has it that she's after something bigger this time. Marriage, perhaps?"

Ben groaned.

"That's what insiders are telling us," Forsythe continued, "but artist Ben Carlton, who rarely leaves his Middleburg farm, may be a reluctant participant in any wedding plans. Then, again, when it comes to the wealthy Carlton men, love does have a way of sneaking up on them when they least expect it. Stay tuned here for the latest word on when this last remaining Carlton bachelor bites the marital dust."

Ben uttered a curse and threw the paper aside. "It's not going to work, Destiny. Not this time. You've overplayed your hand."

He picked up the phone, not to call Mack, but Destiny, then slowly hung up again before the call could go through. What was the point? This was what she did. She meddled. She did it because she loved them.

Misguided as she might be, he could hardly rip her to shreds for acting on her convictions.

Unfortunately, he was at a loss when it came to figuring out a way to counteract that piece of trash that Forsythe had written based on his latest hot tip from Destiny. Truthfully, it didn't matter to him all that much. He didn't see enough people on a daily basis to worry about embarrassment or awkward explanations.

Kathleen, however, was right smack in the public eye all the time. He could just imagine the curiosity seekers this would send flooding into her gallery. Maybe she'd be grateful for the influx of business, but he doubted it.

He should call her, apologize for his aunt dragging her into the middle of this public spectacle, but he couldn't see the point to that, either. The one thing Kathleen really wanted to hear from him he couldn't say.

Of course, there was one thing he could do that would at least give people pause, if not make that article seem like a total lie. But did he have the courage to do it?

He spent the entire morning waging war with himself, but by noon he'd made a decision. He began crating up all the pictures in his studio. It took until midnight to get them boxed to his satisfaction. He'd gone about the task blindly, refusing to pause and look at his work for fear he'd change his mind. He owed this to Kathleen, this and more. Maybe if he gave her the showing she'd been working so hard to get, it would prove to the world that whatever was between them was all about his art.

Besides, with Christmas only two days away, it was

the only gift he could come up with that he knew she truly wanted…and that he was capable of giving.

Christmas Eve day dawned bright and clear, but Kathleen thought she smelled a hint of snow in the air. The prospect of a white Christmas normally would have made her heart sing, but today all she could think about was what a nuisance it would be when it came time to drive to Providence, where her mother and grandparents were expecting her in time for midnight services at the church that the Dugans had attended for generations.

There still hadn't been another peep from Ben. She'd thought for sure he would call when that ridiculous item had appeared in the morning paper the day before. He had to be as outraged as she was to see their private relationship played out for the entire world to speculate about over their morning coffee. Maybe he'd been too humiliated or, given the way he hid out at that farm of his and kept the world at arm's distance, perhaps he hadn't even seen it.

Despite her indignation when she'd first seen Pete Forsythe's column, Kathleen had clipped it from the paper. Maybe it would serve as a reminder that she was still capable of misreading people. She took it out of her desk drawer now and read it yet again, shaking her head anew at the idea that anyone might actually care what was going on in her love life.

For all of its juicy, speculative tone, the column had gotten one thing right. She had started out wanting to represent Ben's art and now she simply wanted him. Fortunately, neither Pete Forsythe nor his inside source—Destiny, she imagined—had any idea just how badly she wanted Ben. No, she corrected, Destiny did know, which made what she'd done unforgivable.

The truth was that Kathleen craved Ben's touch, yearned for the times when he studied her with his penetrating, artist's eye as if he were imagining her naked, in his studio…in his bed.

Despite their superficial differences—his privileged background, her childhood struggles and disastrous marriage, his need for privacy, hers for a constant, if somewhat impersonal, social whirl—Kathleen had the feeling that at their core they were very much alike. They were both searching for something that had been missing from their lives. She recognized that about herself, recognized that she'd found it in Ben. He hadn't yet had that epiphany. It was possible, she was forced to admit, that he never would.

She'd discovered in that one glorious night they'd shared that he was a generous, attentive lover, a kind and gentle man, but he withheld a part of himself. She knew why that was. It couldn't be any more plain, in fact. The strong, self-assured man she knew was, at heart, a kid terrified of losing someone important again, a kid who'd grown into a man who'd lost the woman he loved, as well. Three devastating, impossible-to-forget losses. Add in Graciela's betrayal and it is was plain why he found it easier to keep her at a distance than to risk being shattered if she left or tragedy struck.

To a degree he even kept the family he adored at arm's length, always preparing himself to cope in case something terrible happened and they disappeared from his life.

Unfortunately, Kathleen had absolutely no idea how to prove that she was in his life to stay, that her initial desire to represent his art had evolved into a passion for him, a passion that wasn't going to die. It would take time and persistence to make him believe that. She had persistence to spare, but time was the one thing he obviously didn't intend to give her, to give them. And how much good would it really do, anyway? His family had had a lifetime to convince him and it hadn't been enough. Not to heal the pain caused by those who had gone.

Fortunately, on this last shopping day before Christmas, there wasn't a single moment to dwell on any of this. From the moment she opened the shop's door, she was deluged with customers, many of them no doubt drawn in by curiosity because of that stupid gossip column. Still, she was grateful, because it kept her busy, kept her from having to think.

By midafternoon she'd written up dozens of very nice sales and cleaned out a wealth of inventory. She was about to eat the chicken salad sandwich she'd brought from home when a delivery truck pulled up in front of the gallery, double parking on the busy street.

"What on earth?" she murmured when she recognized the same driver who'd brought her the art supplies. Could this possibly be another gift from Ben? Maybe a peace offering? How typical that he was having someone else deliver it, someone else face her.

She opened the door as the driver loaded his cart with what looked to be packing crates, the kind used for paintings. As the stack grew, her heart began to pound with an unmistakable mix of anticipation and dread.

"Merry Christmas, ma'am," the driver said cheerfully as he guided the precariously balanced stack into the gallery's warmth. "It's a cold one out there. I'm thinking we'll have snow on the ground by morning."

"Seems that way to me, too," Kathleen said, eyeing the bounty warily. "Is this from Mr. Carlton?"

"Yes, ma'am. Picked it up from him first thing this morning. He was real anxious for you to get it, but traffic's a bear out there, so it took me a while to get over here." He eyed the stack with a frown. "You need me to help you open these?"

"No, thanks. I'm used to opening crates like this," she said, offering him a large tip. "Merry Christmas."

Once he had gone, she stood and stared at the over-whelming number of paintings Ben had sent. The temptation to rip into them and get her first glimpse of the art he'd been denying her was overwhelming, but she resisted.

So, she thought, running her fingers over one of the crates, this was it. He'd thrown down the gauntlet. She was filled with a sudden, gut-deep fear that this was either a test or, far worse, a farewell gift. Whichever he'd meant it to be, she knew she couldn't accept. If she did, it would destroy all hope. It would be the end of the most important thing that had ever happened to her, perhaps to either of them.

She looked at her copy of the receipt the driver had given her and immediately called the delivery service. "Do you have the ability to get in touch with one of your drivers?" she asked.

"Yes, ma'am, but most of them are coming in for the day. It's Christmas Eve and they're getting off early."

She explained who she was. "Your driver just left here not five minutes ago. I need him to come back. I know it's an inconvenience, but please tell him I'll make it worth his while. It's very important."

Apparently the dispatcher caught the urgency in her

voice, because he said, "Sit tight, ma'am. I'll do what
I can."

Ten minutes later the truck pulled up outside and the
driver came in.

"Is there something wrong, Ms. Dugan? Was there
a problem with the shipment?"

"Yes, you could say that," she said. "I need you to
take all of this back to Mr. Carlton, please."

"Now?" he asked incredulously, then took a good,
long look at her face and nodded slowly. "No problem.
I'll be happy to do it."

She dragged out her checkbook. "Name your
price."

He shook his head. "It's on me, ma'am. Headquarters is out that way, anyway." He grinned at her. "Besides, I read that stuff that was in the paper about the
two of you. I figured this might have something to do
with that. I want to see the look on Mr. Carlton's face
when all of this lands right back on his doorstep."

Filled with a sudden burst of expectancy, Kathleen
found herself returning his smile. "Yes. I'm rather anxious to see that myself. In fact, I'll be right behind
you."

Ben Carlton was not going to toss potentially
thousands of dollars in paintings at her and convince
her she'd won. Until they were together—truly, happily-ever-after together—neither one of them would
have won a blasted thing.

Chapter Fifteen

Mack and Richard converged on the farm twenty minutes after Ben had sent the shipment of paintings off to Kathleen.

"Why didn't you ever call me back yesterday?" Mack demanded.

"We'd have been here sooner, but I didn't want to leave Melanie alone at the house," Richard said. "Beth's there now, watching her like a hawk, I hope. Melanie keeps trying to slip out to finish her Christmas shopping. I swear that baby is going to be born in an aisle at some boutique."

Ben chuckled. "Bro, I think you're fighting a losing battle. If Melanie wants to shop, you should know by now that you're not going to stop her."

Richard raked a hand through his hair, then stopped himself. "Yeah, I'm beginning to get that," he admitted with evident frustration. "I swear to God, though, I'm going to be bald by the time this kid gets here."

"It's not going to be much longer," Mack soothed. "Beth predicts a Christmas baby."

Richard's eyes immediately filled with panic. "Christmas is tomorrow. That means Melanie could be going into labor right now. First babies always take a long time, right?"

Mack looked at Ben and rolled his eyes. "Do you have your cell phone?"

"Of course," Richard snapped impatiently.

"It's on?"

"Yes."

"Then stop worrying," Mack advised. "We're here to solve Ben's problems, not to watch you panic over contractions that haven't even started."

"Just wait," Richard said grimly. "One of these days the two of you are going to be in my place, and I'm not giving you one single shred of sympathy."

"I will never be in your place," Ben said wearily, then almost immediately regretted it because both of his brothers turned their full attention on him. He should have been grateful for the temporary distraction from their obvious mission and kept his mouth shut.

"Do you want to be where I am?" Richard asked. "Remember, I was where you are for a very long time, but I've got to tell you that nothing compares to where I am now." He shrugged. "Okay, maybe not right this minute, but generally speaking being married to Melanie is the smartest thing I've ever done."

"Same here," Mack said. "Beth is incredible. Destiny's got her faults, but when it comes to picking the right women for us, she nailed it for Richard and for me. Do you really think she made a mistake in your case?''

Ben thought about it, really thought about it, for the first time. Truthfully, he knew that Destiny hadn't made a mistake. And if he were being totally honest, he realized that the prospect of having a family wasn't half as scary as it had once been.

"No, there's no mistake," he admitted.

"Then what are you going to do about it?" Mack asked. "You're not going to accomplish what you want sitting around out here. The woman I presume you want to have a family with is probably packing her bags for Providence right about now."

"Providence?" Ben echoed. "Why?"

"Destiny says Kathleen is going to spend the holidays with her family," Richard told him. "She's worried she might decide not to come back."

Ben couldn't imagine such a thing. Kathleen would never close the gallery she loved and move back home. "That's just Destiny trying to get me all worked up," he said confidently.

"You willing to take a chance that she's wrong?" Richard asked, just as his cell phone rang. He jumped as if he'd been shocked, fumbled to get it out of his pocket, then dropped it.

"Good grief, man, she'll have the baby before you get yourself together," Mack told him with a shake of his head. He picked up the phone and handed it to Richard.

"Yes? Are you okay?" Richard demanded when he finally answered the phone.

The color immediately washed out of his face. "I'm on my way," he said, turning the phone off and jamming it back into his pocket. "The baby…" He dragged his hand through his hair again. "My God, the baby's coming. I have to get home. We have a plan. How are we going to follow the plan if I'm not even there?"

"Beth is there," Mack reminded him. "She's a doctor."

"But the plan," Richard protested. "It was all written out so we wouldn't forget anything."

"Melanie knows this plan, right?"

"Sure, but—"

Ben stared at the sight of his cool, unflappable brother basically falling apart in front of him. Mack immediately took charge.

"Forget the damn plan," Mack said. "Let's just go." He steered Richard toward the car.

"I'll follow you," Ben said.

Mack nodded toward the driveway and the plume of dust that was being kicked up. "You might want to reconsider that, pal. Looks to me like company's coming."

"Company?" Ben echoed blankly, then saw a familiar delivery truck and right on its tail an even more familiar car being driven by a sexy, speed-crazed maniac. His heart leaped into his throat, but this time the reaction had less to do with fear than it did with pure, unadulterated delight.

Maybe he hadn't ended this thing with Kathleen, after all. And given the mushy way he was feeling about babies and family right now, it was a damn good thing.

Even as Mack tore away from the house, Ben watched with bated breath as the delivery truck pulled up next to the studio. Kathleen's sporty little car

screeched to a halt right beside it. She bounded out of
the car with eyes blazing and headed straight for him.

"What is *that* all about?" she demanded, gesturing
toward the van. The driver was standing beside it, grinning broadly and taking in every word they exchanged.

Ben stared helplessly toward the driver, who merely
shrugged. "I'm on her clock now," he told Ben. "She
wants these back here, I'll put 'em back in the studio."

"Go ahead," Ben said, defeated.

Struggling to figure out what the devil had gone so
wildly wrong, Ben turned back to Kathleen. "I thought
you wanted to do a showing. Isn't that what the last
past few months have been about?"

She hauled off and slugged him. "You are such an
idiot," she said, then stomped past him and went inside
to watch as the driver unloaded the last of the paintings.

Ben followed, rubbing his stinging jaw. As soon as
they were alone, he asked, "Did I get it wrong? You
don't want to do a show?"

"Of course I do, but not like this. Not if it's some
sort of weird trade-off for sex," she said furiously.
"Or, just as bad, a way to buy yourself a little peace
of mind and get me out of your life, now that you've
satisfied that itch I stirred in you."

To his shame, he could see exactly how she could
leap to such a tawdry conclusion. He'd never told her
how he felt, never admitted that he'd come to trust
her…that he loved her. How could he, when he was
terrified by the admission?

He could see from the flash of fury in her eyes that
if he didn't find the words, he was going to lose her.
Besides, what difference did the words make, really?
The feeling was there, in his heart, every time he
looked at her. It was too late to stop that. There was

no way to take it back, to protect himself. He'd only deluded himself into thinking that sending those paintings would put an end to things.

He remembered the very recent conversation with his brothers and forced himself to keep his eye on the only goal that really mattered. Then he drew in a deep breath and looked into her eyes.

"What if they were a wedding gift, from me to you?" he asked, watching closely for her reaction.

She blinked rapidly. "What?"

He grinned at her confusion, at the hint of hope that burned in her eyes. "I'm trying to propose here and making a mess of it. I should have asked Destiny to write a proper speech for me."

"I think Destiny's been involved a little too much in this already," she responded. She stepped close, rested a gentle hand against his still-burning cheek. Her eyes were soft and misty. "You're doing fine on your own. A few little words, Ben. That's all I need to hear."

"The pictures are yours?"

She frowned at his teasing. "Not even close."

"I trust you with my art, with my life."

She nodded. "Better."

He took a deep breath. "I love you, Kathleen. I want to marry you, raise a family with you, wake up with you every morning till we're both old and gray."

"Bingo." She stood on tiptoe and kissed him. "Was that so hard?"

"Yes," he told her honestly. "It scares the hell out of me."

"It'll get easier," she promised. "You're going to have a lifetime to practice."

A lifetime. The word echoed in his head and he

waited for the panic to follow. Instead he was filled with incomparable joy. He'd finally gotten it right. About damn time. He wouldn't mind staying right here and sealing this deal with something far more intimate than a kiss, but there was someplace the two of them needed to be.

"Much as I'd like to hang around here and keep on practicing, there's a little matter of a baby who's about to arrive," he told her. "If this baby is anything like its daddy, it's bound to be impatient, now that it's decided the time is right."

She stared at him in shock. "Melanie and Richard's baby?"

He nodded.

"*That's* why he and Mack went tearing out of here just as I arrived! I thought they just didn't want to stick around for the inevitable fireworks," she said, then scowled at him. "Why didn't you say something sooner? You need to be at the hospital."

"I've barely gotten a word in edgewise since you got here," he reminded her. "Well, except for the proposal. I did fit that in. Anyway, we need to be there. You're going to be part of this family now."

A slow smile spread across her face. "How soon?"

He chuckled. "Are you in a hurry for some reason?"

"I want to be your wife when I open this show in my gallery." At his shocked look, she added, "You don't get to take them back now, buster. You gave them to me as a wedding present, and I don't want any other woman thinking she can poach on the sexiest artist in the United States."

"And you want to do this show when?" he asked, amused by her eagerness.

"January," she said at once. "February at the latest."

He laughed at that. "Destiny's counting on a June wedding."

"Well, she's just going to have to be disappointed," Kathleen said adamantly. "She's gotten her way with everything else. We're picking the wedding date."

"Seems fair enough to me. You can talk about it at the hospital."

"Let's go," she said eagerly, heading for her car.

"Kathleen!"

She turned back. "What?"

He gestured toward her car. "Not a chance in hell. We'll take mine."

She laughed. "Mine's closer."

"Then I'll drive."

"What's wrong with my driving?" she asked, even as she docilely went around to the passenger side of the car.

"Too fast and too dangerous," he said succinctly. He decided it was time to lay his greatest fear on the table, the one he couldn't shake because he was reminded of it every single time he saw her behind the wheel. "It reminds me of the way Graciela drove."

Her mouth dropped open and tears immediately filled her eyes. "Oh, Ben, why didn't you say something? I thought you were just being a macho jerk."

He shrugged. "Maybe a little of that, too," he admitted. "Think you can slow down, just enough so I don't go crazy worrying every time you're on the road?"

She reached for his hand. "I'll never go above the speed limit again," she promised.

"That's something, I suppose."

"You wouldn't want me to poke along, would you?"

"It would make my day, actually."

"Then I'll drive like some little old lady heading for church on Sunday," she promised. "You're not going to lose me in an accident, Ben. Not if I can help it."

"I wish it were possible to be sure of that," he told her. "But I know it's not. I just know I don't want to lose you by pretending that I don't love you."

She touched his cheek. "Then isn't it a good thing you've admitted it at last? We've got that all cleared up."

"Yes," he said quietly. "It's a very good thing."

The best, in fact.

At the hospital they found Destiny, Mack and Beth gathered in the waiting room. There was no sign of Richard.

"Did he faint?" Ben asked.

"No, he's in the delivery room," Mack said. "Pity the poor doctor with Richard looking over his shoulder. I'm sure he had a plan for just how this delivery is supposed to go, too."

Kathleen and Beth exchanged a look and chuckled.

"Fortunately, Dr. Kelly has dealt with a great many expectant fathers before," Beth said confidently. "I think he can keep Richard in line."

"Ha!" Mack said. "Richard is used to running a multinational corporation. Organizing a delivery room to suit him will be a piece of cake."

"Not after the first time Melanie screams her head off," Beth predicted.

Mack paled at that. "There's going to be screaming?"

"Plenty, I imagine," Beth confirmed.

He scowled at her. "We are adopting all of our kids."

Beth gave him a long, lingering look, then said quietly, "Too late for that."

Mack simply stared at her. "A baby," he said eventually. "We're going to have a baby?"

"In about eight months," Beth said, grinning.

Mack sank onto a chair as Kathleen and Destiny rushed over to hug Beth. Ben went to sit beside his obviously shaken brother.

"You okay?" Ben asked.

Mack nodded slowly. "I didn't know about the screaming."

"Can't be much worse than some football player who's just gotten his collar bone dislocated." He gave Mack a pointed look. "Or his knee shattered."

"I didn't scream," Mack said defensively. "Either time."

"Tell that to someone who couldn't hear you from twenty rows up on the fifty-yard line," Ben said. "Women have been doing this since time began. They're tough. Tougher than we are, in fact."

Mack glanced over in the direction of his wife and smiled slowly. "Yeah, they are, aren't they?" He turned back to Ben. "So what about you and Kathleen? Did you work things out?"

"We're getting married," Ben admitted.

"Well, hallelujah!"

His exuberant shout brought the three women across the room.

"More good news?" Beth asked, her gaze on Ben.

He glanced at Kathleen. "Looks like we're all going steal the new baby's thunder."

"I seriously doubt Richard or Melanie will even notice," Beth told him. "Come on, spill it."

"I asked Kathleen to marry me," he said, reaching for her hand. "And she's said yes."

Destiny began to cry. "Now that is worth celebrating. Oh, darling, I am so happy for you. For both of you." She sighed. "A June wedding will be perfect."

"Not June," Kathleen told her without apology. "January."

Destiny's mouth gaped. "This January? As in next month?"

"That's what she said," Ben confirmed. "Before my show opens at her gallery."

Destiny sank onto the chair next to Mack and reached for his hand. "Well, this really is moving along quickly."

Ben caught an odd note in her voice. "Too quickly?" he asked worriedly.

"Oh no, darling. Getting you happily settled could never come too quickly."

"Then why did you say that?" he asked.

"Never mind," she said briskly and turned her attention to Kathleen. "We have a lot to do. I think we should get your mother down here right away, don't you?"

Kathleen paled. "Oh, my God. I forgot all about going to Providence." She glanced at her watch. "They're going to be expecting me any minute now."

"Call them," Destiny advised. "Tell them about the baby and the engagement and invite them all to come here tomorrow. I can't imagine a better way to celebrate Christmas. We have so much happy news."

"You know, you could be right," Kathleen said. "Maybe this will be enough to get them all to final come down here. I'll go outside and call right now on my cell phone.''

Ben followed her. ''You sure you want to drop this bombshell on them like this?'' he asked. ''We could go up there tomorrow. Maybe they should at least meet me before we spring the rest of the family on them.''

''No,'' she said decisively. ''I like the idea of all of us being together here on Christmas. Maybe they'll see what a real family holiday can be like.''

''Whatever you want,'' he said. ''Want me to wait for you inside?''

She reached for his hand. ''No, stay with me,'' she pleaded as the call went through. ''Hello, Mother.''

Ben couldn't hear exactly what her mother said, but it was communicated in an aggrieved tone he couldn't mistake. He watched Kathleen intently, but her expression never wavered.

''Mother, if you'll just listen for a minute, I can explain. I got engaged tonight, to Ben Carlton, the artist I told you about, the man in my painting.''

Her expression softened at whatever her mother said then. ''Yes, it is wonderful news. And there's more. His brother's wife is in the hospital right now having a baby, and we want to stay for that, but Destiny's invited all of you for Christmas dinner tomorrow. Will you come? Please.''

Relief spread over her face. ''I'll call grandfather with the directions, then. Thank you, Mother. I love you and Merry Christmas.''

She turned off the cell phone and stood staring at it, ears shimmering in her eyes.

''I gather she said yes,'' Ben said.

Kathleen nodded. ''She says she can't wait to meet ll of you.'' She grinned. ''She also said she knew it was inevitable from the minute she saw the portrait of you."

"Really? Wonder what she'll say when she sees the one I've painted of you," he said, glad that he'd hidden it away before sending the shipment to her gallery.

Kathleen's mouth gaped. "You painted a portrait of me?"

"In the moonlight," he confirmed.

"Oh, sweet heaven," she murmured, her cheeks turning pink. "Do I have any clothes on?"

"Enough," he told her, laughing. "Too many to suit me, though, but I wanted our kids to be able to look at this and see you the way I see you."

"I want to see it," she said at once.

"You will," he promised. "But right now we'd better get back inside and see what kind of progress that baby is making."

It was one minute after midnight when Amelia Destiny Carlton arrived, the Christmas baby that Beth had predicted. Destiny's eyes shone with tears when she heard the baby's name.

"You didn't have to do that," she whispered, clutching Richard's hand.

"We wanted to," Melanie said. "If it weren't for you, none of this would ever have happened."

"Amen to that," Mack agreed, his gaze on Beth.

She smiled and tucked her hand into his. "I predict a lot of little Destinys in this family before too long."

"I am not naming any boy of mine Destiny," Mack grumbled.

"And if it's another girl?" Ben asked him.

"That's different," Mack said, giving their aunt hug.

Ben gazed at the tiny, perfect little girl in Richard

arms. He glanced back at Kathleen. "I wonder if I can get that portrait finished in time for the show?"

They all stared at him.

"You're painting portraits now?" Melanie asked.

"And showing your work?" Richard echoed.

Ben laughed at their shocked expressions. "Oh, yeah, that's right, you were out of the room when I mentioned that I'm also getting married."

"Oh, sweetie, that's wonderful," Melanie said and began to cry. She swiped at her eyes. "Don't mind me. Hormones."

"Hormones nothing," Richard scoffed. "You're just sentimental."

"I notice you've got tears in your eyes, too, bro," Mack commented.

Richard shrugged. "What the hell! I'd say the Carlton men have come a long way, wouldn't you?"

"A very long way," Melanie and Beth agreed.

Destiny gazed at each of them in turn, then clucked her tongue. "Don't encourage them too much, ladies. There's always room for a little improvement."

Ben picked his aunt up and twirled her around until she told him he was making her dizzy.

"Not until you promise to stop meddling," he said. "Your work here is done, Destiny."

She gave him a long look that was tinged with just a hint of sorrow. "Yes, it is, isn't it?"

"Oh, no, it's not," Melanie piped up.

"Absolutely not," Kathleen and Beth agreed. "There's a whole new generation to worry about now."

To Ben's relief, Destiny's expression brightened. "My goodness, I can't leave this precious baby and all the ones to come to the likes of you, can I?"

"Hey!" Richard protested. "I don't think we turned out too badly."

"Neither do I," Mack said.

Ben looked at his brothers and the women in their lives, then turned to Kathleen. "What about you? Do you think I've turned out all right?"

She moved into his arms and pressed a kiss to his cheek, then whispered in his ear, "I wouldn't want the others to hear this, but I think you turned out best of all."

"You're biased."

She laughed. "Hey, I'm only following Destiny's lead. Everybody knows you're her favorite."

"I heard that," Richard grumbled.

"Me, too," Mack protested.

"Oh, stop squabbling," Destiny said. "I don't have favorites."

"Of course not," Ben agreed at once, then leaned down. "But if you did, I'd be the one, right?"

"Isn't knowing that you're Kathleen's favorite enough?" Destiny scolded.

Ben met Kathleen's gaze over Destiny's head. "More than enough," he agreed at once. It was something he would never allow himself to forget.

Epilogue

For a wedding that had been pulled together in less than a month, Kathleen thought it was pretty spectacular. Her mother and Destiny had used every contact, called in every favor and invited a cast of hundreds to witness the occasion. She didn't think it could have come together any more beautifully if they'd had an entire year to plan it.

Kathleen stood at the back of the church in a sleek, strapless satin gown from a well-known designer whom Destiny knew personally. She was holding a simple bouquet of lily of the valley and white velvet ribbons that her mother had created. Her grandfather, looking incredibly distinguished in his tuxedo, stood at her side.

"Are you happy, angel? Truly happy?" he asked.

"You can't begin to imagine how happy," she assured him. "I've gotten it exactly right this time."

"I hope so. Ben seems like a fine young man and

it's plain that he adores you. I don't suppose you'd reconsider and settle in Providence?''

She squeezed his hand. ''No, but it means the world to me that you'd want us to.''

He nodded, his expression sad. ''I wish I'd done better by you and your mother.''

''That's in the past, Grandfather, and it has nothing to do with me wanting to stay here. My life is here now.''

He patted her hand. ''No need to explain. Now it seems to me that I hear music. Are you ready?''

''I've been waiting my whole life for this,'' she said as they took their places at the back of the church and waited for Melanie and Beth to reach the front.

''Let's do it,'' she said eagerly as the organ music swelled.

Then she had eyes only for Ben, who was standing in front of the altar, Mack and Richard beside him. Destiny was in the front pew, tears streaming down her face as she watched Kathleen come down the aisle.

When Kathleen reached Ben's aunt, she impulsively leaned down and kissed her cheek, then crossed the aisle and kissed her mother. ''Thank you both,'' she murmured before stepping into place beside Ben.

Ben solemnly shook her grandfather's hand, then reached over to clasp hers. His grip was solid and com- forting, the grip of a man who finally knew his heart and was ready to reach out to grab the future.

''I love you,'' he mouthed silently as the minister began the ceremony.

Kathleen beamed at him. Once he'd started saying the words, it seemed he hadn't been able to say them often enough, which suited her just fine. If they lived to be a hundred, she would never tire of hearing them

* * *

"Okay, Destiny, the wedding's over," Richard said not five minutes after the ceremony, even though the photographer was impatiently waiting for them to gather for pictures. "You said you'd tell me your idea about dealing with William Harcourt once Ben and Kathleen were married."

Destiny gave him a look that would have daunted most men, but Richard was a Carlton. He simply stared right back at her and waited.

"Oh, for goodness' sakes," she snapped finally. "You're not going to let this alone, so I might as well tell you." She turned to Ben and Kathleen. "Sorry, dears, but if I don't get this over with, he'll spoil your reception by dogging my every footstep."

"Please, Destiny, go ahead," Kathleen told her. She was actually anxious to hear this scheme herself. It was bound to be a doozy.

Destiny looked each of her nephews in the eye, then said with quiet determination. "I intend to take over the European division of Carlton Industries," she said. "I will deal with William. In fact, I predict it will be some time before he knows what's hit him."

With that, she turned and walked away, back straight, shoulders squared, looking for all the world as if she were heading into battle.

Kathleen was the first to break the silence. She began to chuckle.

"What's so blasted funny?" Ben demanded.

"I agree," Richard said, his expression grim. "I don't find this the least bit amusing."

"Oh, chill, big brother," Mack said. "I think Kathleen's right. This is perfect retribution."

"On who? Us?" Ben asked irritably.

"No. On William. If you think it was fun watching the three of you squirm while she was matchmaking," Kathleen responded, "something tells me this is going to be a whole lot more entertaining."

"Absolutely," Beth agreed.

"Oh, yes," Melanie added happily.

Ben turned a sour look on all the women. "Good God, they're all ganging up on us now. I knew there was a downside to adding all these women to the family. We're outnumbered now."

Kathleen laughed at his dismay. "And don't you forget it," she said cheerfully. "But we do love you."

"Most of the time," Melanie added.

Beth gazed pointedly at Mack. "When you're not trying to control things."

He held up his hand. "Hey, have this baby on your own. I won't hover."

"That'll be the day," Beth said. "Now come on. We have pictures to be taken and a reception to get to before the guests eat all the food."

Melanie grinned at her. "Appetite growing, Beth?"

"By leaps and bounds. If this keeps up, I'll be waddling around the hospital by my fifth month."

"I told you I could give you an exercise regimen," Mack said.

Ben and Richard immediately hooted. "Oh, brother, please tell me you didn't say that," Richard said.

"What's wrong?" Mack asked. "I'm trying to be helpful."

"Keep it up and you'll be a dead man," Beth warned.

Kathleen turned to Ben. "I hope you're taking all this in," she told him. "That way when I'm pregnant you'll have all the dos and don'ts down pat."

"I already have a plan," he assured her. "I'm moving out of the country."

She pulled his face down and kissed him hard. "Not a chance. You're never leaving my side, so get that idea right out of your head."

"Like I said, I'll stay and keep my mouth shut."

"There you go," she said happily.

If he'd learned that lesson already, they were destined for a very joyous marriage.

* * * * *

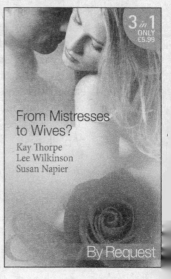

0910/05b

...Make sure you don't miss out on these fabulous stories!

3 in 1 ONLY £5.99

The Tycoon's Desire

Anna DePalo
Arlene James
Chantelle Shaw

By Request

Montana Passions

Christine Rimmer
Allison Leigh
Pamela Toth

By Request

featuring

UNDER THE
TYCOON'S PROTECTION
by Anna DePalo

TYCOON MEETS TEXAN!
by Arlene James

THE GREEK TYCOON'S
VIRGIN MISTRESS
by Chantelle Shaw

featuring

STRANDED WITH
THE GROOM
by Christine Rimmer

ALL HE EVER WANTED
by Allison Leigh

PRESCRIPTION: LOVE
by Pamela Toth

On sale from 1st October 2010

*Available at WHSmith, Tesco, ASDA, Eason
and all good bookshops*

www.millsandboon.co.uk

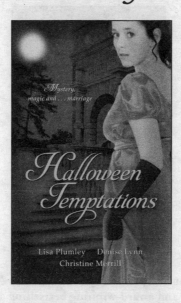

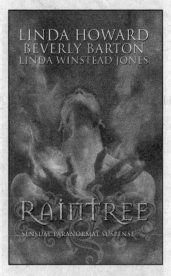

THE *Balfour* LEGACY

Eight Sisters, Eight Scandals

VOLUME 5 – OCTOBER 2010
Zoe's Lesson
by Kate Hewitt

VOLUME 6 – NOVEMBER 2010
Annie's Secret
by Carole Mortimer

VOLUME 7 – DECEMBER 2010
Bella's Disgrace
by Sarah Morgan

VOLUME 8 – JANUARY 2011
Olivia's Awakening
by Margaret Way

8 VOLUMES IN ALL TO COLLECT!

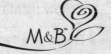